A RED SUN ALSO RISES
is dedicated to
Lynne Blackburn and Ian Bailey

— A WORD — FROM THE AUTHOR

Those of you familiar with my "Burton & Swinburne" tales might also be aware that I live in Valencia on the east coast of Spain. Among my friends, I count a few members of the yachting community, an international crowd that comes and goes on a seasonal basis. In July 2011, one of them—Raymond Villeneuve—gave me the journal that became the basis for A RED SUN ALSO RISES.

Villeneuve had just returned from a diving expedition to the west of the Azores, where he'd been part of a team exploring the wreck of *The Hermes*, a small steamer that sank in 1947. We met for a beer in one of Valencia's seafront bars, and after we'd exchanged the usual pleasantries, he said, "In one of your novels, you make a passing reference to the island of Koluwai in the South Pacific. Why that particular place?"

"In remembrance of my Great Uncle James Leigh," I replied. "He was a missionary back in the 1920s. He's thought to have died there."

"Of what?"

I shrugged. "The records don't say. I suppose that's why he fascinates me. There's a mystery surrounding him."

My friend nodded thoughtfully, then abruptly changed the subject. "This ship I've been exploring—not much is known about it. *The Hermes* was privately owned by a Captain Franklin Powell and seems to have made regular runs between Gibraltar and the Caribbean. It went down a couple of years after the end of the Second World War. There were no traces of cargo aboard the vessel, but we found a watertight safe, which had kept its contents well preserved, though they didn't amount to much."

He placed a small package in front of me—something wrapped in waxed paper with an elastic band around it.

A
RED SUN
ALSO RISES

MARK HODDER

DEL REY

1 3 5 7 9 10 8 6 4 2

First published in the US in 2012 by Pyr,
an imprint of Prometheus Books
First published in the UK in 2013 by Del Rey, an imprint of Ebury Publishing
A Random House Group Company

This edition published in 2014

Copyright © 2012 by Mark Hodder

Mark Hodder has asserted his right to be identified as the author of this
Work in accordance with the Copyright, Designs and Patents Act 1988

The Random House Group Limited Reg. No. 954009

Addresses for companies within the Random House Group can be found at:
www.randomhouse.co.uk

A CIP catalogue record for this book is available from the British Library

The Random House Group Limited supports The Forest Stewardship
Council® (FSC®), the leading international forest-certification organisation.
Our books carrying the FSC label are printed on FSC® certified paper.
FSC is the only forest-certification scheme supported by the leading
environmental organisations, including Greenpeace.

Our paper procurement policy can be found at
www.randomhouse.co.uk/environment

Printed and bound in Great Britain by Clays Ltd, St Ives PLC

ISBN 9780091950644

To buy books by your favourite authors and register for offers visit:
www.randomhouse.co.uk

"There were documents, a small bag of coins, and this. Take a look."

My curiosity piqued, I pulled off the band, opened the paper, and found a leather-bound notebook inside. Its delicate, browned, and slightly crumbling pages were filled with almost illegible handwriting.

"As you can see, it's written in English," Villeneuve said. "I've read a little of it, and it seems to be your sort of thing. I thought you might like to have it. It also mentions Koluwai, and a missionary who went there."

He had little else to say regarding the book—the handwriting was so bad he'd given up reading it—so I thanked him, took it home, and over the next few days struggled to decipher it.

What you hold is adapted from that journal. Adapted, because the man who wrote it, Aiden Fleischer, possessed an exceedingly archaic and long-winded style, entirely unsuitable for a modern audience. My revisions involved editing and untangling the grammar, updating and standardising the spelling, and excising a lot of fairly dull material—extensive notes on flora and fauna, and so forth. I did, however, remain faithful to the author's rather eccentric capitalisation of certain nouns.

I undertook a small amount of research with regard to the names and places mentioned in the account and can confirm that the parish records in the little town of Theaston Vale, in Hampshire, England, show that a man named Gregory James Mortimer Fleischer was the Anglican priest there from June 1868 to September 1883. He had a son, Aiden Mortimer Fleischer, born 22nd November 1863, who took his vows in 1882 and replaced his father as parish priest the following year, resigning the post in 1887.

Aiden Fleischer next shows up in the archives of the London Missionary Society, where he trained during 1888—the year of the infamous Ripper killings—before being posted to Papua New Guinea. He was twenty-five years old when he left Britain. I've discovered no further traces of him.

The once-famous Hufferton Hall, mentioned early on in the journal, is now gone and all but forgotten. The last of the Huffertons,

Sir Rupert, was murdered there in 1923, after which a succession of occupants came and went before the manor fell into disuse. It stood empty throughout the 1950s, was inhabited by squatters in the 1960s, and fell victim to an arsonist in 1972. I've not been able to find any evidence of the Stark family who, according to Fleischer, once worked there.

Mark Hodder
Valencia, Spain
August 2012

CHAPTER I

CLARISSA and ALICE

I didn't intend to drop the crystal there. Even in my own time, it was a busy shipping lane. Now aeroplanes cross the area as well. Two days ago, a United States Navy training flight, comprised of five TBM Avenger torpedo bombers and fourteen men, entered the region and has been neither seen nor heard from since. I don't doubt that Flight 19, as it was designated, has gone through the rupture.

I can go home at last. My hand will be restored to me.

The crystal, though, is beyond retrieval. I can only hope that Artellokas, if he still lives, will find a different solution—a way to close the portal before it swallows even more unwitting travellers.

And what of Clarissa? Oh, sweet Heaven, let her still be there.

Wait. My apologies. This is not the way to start. My emotions are spilling onto pages meant only for the cold facts of the matter. I shall begin again. I must complete this account before *The Hermes* reaches Bermuda. When we dock at Hamilton, I'll entrust it to Captain Powell, who, upon his return to England, will post it to my old vicarage in Theaston Vale. Whoever occupies the position I once held might know what to do with it. I, meanwhile, will steer a motorboat south-westward to a point some two hundred miles north of the Bahamas, there to vanish from this world forever.

A confession: I'm not Peter Edwards. That name belongs to a young Australian soldier, born on the 18th of May 1920, who was shot through the head on the 23rd of July 1942, during the Battle of Port Moresby.

My real name is Aiden Mortimer Fleischer. I am British, but my rather too Germanic surname would have been viewed with suspicion during the war, which is why I appropriated Edwards' identity. I'm not proud that I did so, but the poor lad had no further use for it and I was in desperate straits. He bore some small resemblance to me and his date of birth was useful, for while I appear to be in my mid-twenties, I was, in fact, born on the 22nd of November 1863. By that measure, I am an old man.

Indeed, my youth feels a long way off. It belongs to far gentler times. The world is not what it used to be. Nor am I.

So, to my history.

My father was an Anglican clergyman. He became my sole parent when puerperal fever took my mother within days of my birth. I was an only child, and as I grew up, I felt her absence keenly. Father, by contrast, survived her loss with his character intact, remaining a kind, content, stable, and outwardly happy man. His faith gave him comfort, and I envied him. I suppose it was inevitable, then, that I spent my early years as he'd spent his, following a meek and scholarly path into the priesthood. I was eighteen when I took my vows. Barely a man! That was in January of 1882. Just a few months later, dear old dad suffered a brain embolism and dropped dead. The Church appointed me as his successor and I took over his role as vicar in my home town, the aforementioned Theaston Vale, in Hampshire.

For the churchgoers, it should have been a smooth transition from one Reverend Fleischer to the next.

It wasn't.

My predecessor had been a dynamic sermoniser. He was compassionate, engaging, funny, and popular. I was none of those things. I may have been doing the work of Our Lord, but it was immediately apparent that I wasn't very good at it. Crippled by nerves, I stuttered through each Sunday service while my flock first snored, then strayed.

Nevertheless, I was well-meaning—or so I told myself—and every word of comfort I uttered from the pulpit and, occasionally, in the bedrooms of the sick and the dying, was spoken, if not with true feeling, then at least with due care and attention. I knew the Bible from front to back. I always had an appropriate line of scripture at the ready and I never misquoted.

I was erudite.

They told me I was pedantic.

I was dutiful.

They said I was remote.

I was attentive.

They called me a cold fish.

As my daily failures accrued, I began to realise the truth of Jonathan Swift's dictum: "*We have just enough religion to make us hate, but not enough to make us love one another.*"

I admit it. Sometimes I grew close to hating my parishioners! I hated that the men avoided me and appeared to regard me as some other gender—not female but definitely not properly male—as though my education and intellectual demeanour had rendered me an incomprehensible hermaphrodite. I hated that the women regaled me with interminable and pointless gossip, which sounded to me spiteful and uncharitable, but which, to them, was obviously as vital as the oxygen they breathed.

Three years of this passed, and an ever-intensifying resentment seethed in the darker recesses of my mind, for I felt helpless to change, and I was constantly and crushingly lonely.

I despised being a priest.

But what else could I be?

○

The first of many alterations in my circumstances knocked at the vicarage door late one morning in August of 1885. It arrived in the form of the most disreputable-looking woman I'd ever seen. It pains me to describe her as she was then, but I must, for it was her deformities that initially bound us together.

She was, at most, five-foot-two, obviously a vagabond, hunch-backed, with crooked legs and swarthy sun-browned skin. Her jet-black hair—with streaks of white growing from the temples—was swept back from a deep widow's peak and fell in waves to her twisted shoulder blades. The dress and jacket she wore might have been fashioned from old potato sacks. However, by far the most remarkable thing about her was that the upper part of her face was concealed behind tight-fitting black-lensed leather-bound goggles.

"Forgive my imposition," she said, and her voice was sweet and mellifluous, surprising me with its cultivated tone. "I've fallen upon hard times, Reverend, and I am starving. If you have anything about the place that needs doing, perhaps you would be kind enough to allow me to work in return for a morsel? I can put my hand to any task you care to name, including labour you would normally assign to a man."

Her grotesque appearance unnerved me, but I managed to stammer, "Quite, quite," and blinked at my reflection in the shiny glass of her eyewear. "I have some shirts that require darning. Can you—um—but no, probably that wouldn't—I'm sorry—"

She smiled and tapped the side of her goggles with a finger. "I'm not blind. I can do needlework. I suffer a condition of the eyes that allows me to see with perfect clarity in darkness but which causes me great pain in daylight or in the presence of gas lamps. I would be entirely incapacitated without these glasses."

"Ah. Good!" I said, before hastily correcting myself. "Er, that you're not blind, I mean! Is it—is it a congenital condition?"

"Quite so, Reverend. I was born with it." She made a gesture that indicated her entire body. "As for the rest, a childhood accident is to blame—a chance occurrence, or perhaps it was the will of God, or maybe I was responsible for some misdeed in a past life and am now suffering a natural retribution. I suppose I must have done something very bad to have been thus punished!"

Startled by this statement, I replied, "You refer to the Buddhist belief in reincarnation, and in reaping what you sow over the course of multiple lifetimes?"

She nodded. "They call it *karma*. But I was merely being facetious. I don't really believe in it—I'm a strictly practical sort. Supernatural and theological explanations for the world and our existence in it interest me only in so far as they might give hints of forgotten scientific knowledge. I mean no offence."

"None taken! I'm not so dyed in the wool that I would deny a person the right to question the veracity or usefulness of the Christian faith—or any other creed, for that matter. I was simply taken aback that you know of Buddhist beliefs, that is all."

"Because I appear a down-and-out, and you therefore presumed me ill-informed about such matters?"

I hesitated, feeling rather disoriented by the strange conversation that had come out of nowhere to interrupt my morning studies. "Forgive my forthrightness," I said, "but yes, you do have the air of a beggar about you, and I've never heard a man or woman of that unfortunate class speak as you do."

"Class! It is not a class, sir! It is misfortune and adverse circumstances that cause a person to fall to this state, not inherited qualities of character!"

I shifted from one foot to the other, a vicar made awkward and embarrassed by a vagrant, and stuttered, "Of c-course. Forgive me. It was a bad choice of—of—of words. I meant nothing by it. I appear to have jumped to conclusions about you on sight and now find that all of them are wrong. You are obviously not at all what I took you to be. May I—may I ask your name?"

"I am Clarissa Stark."

"Would you care to come in, Miss Stark? I'm moved to hear your story, and I have a thick vegetable soup on the stove. It won't take long to heat up. We'll forego the needlework. The people of this town are used to seeing me in frayed shirts. They'd be confused if I presented them with otherwise."

"Thank you, Reverend—?"

"Fleischer."

I ushered her through to my small kitchen and she sat at the table while I put a flame under the soup and set some water to boil. Later, if I could do so without sounding impolite, I'd offer her the opportunity to wash.

"Are you from the North, Miss Stark? I hear the vaguest trace of a Scottish burr in your voice."

"Have you heard of Hufferton Hall?"

"The one near Edinburgh? Of course. It once housed a famous Museum of Mechanical Marvels."

"I was born there."

I turned and looked at her, my eyebrows raised. She smiled and shook her shaggy head. "No, no, I'm not one of the eccentric Huffertons. My mother was their cook, my father their groundsman." She saw my expression and went on, "Ah! You're surprised a child of servants is educated. The explanation is connected with the sorry state of my back and legs. When I was five years old, Lord Hufferton's eldest son, Rupert, who was then in his thirteenth year, took his father's autocarriage without permission and—"

"Autocarriage? What's that?" I interjected.

"A conveyance that moves without need of a horse."

I considered her reply while I ladled soup into bowls, set one before her, and put bread and a glass of water beside it.

"You mean like Étienne Lenoir's *Hippomobile*?"

I remember that Miss Stark directed her face at me, and her eye lenses reflected the light from the kitchen window. I can still see every detail of that scene, as if it was preserved in amber. I don't know why I recall it with such clarity. Maybe because it was the first moment she considered me with obvious respect.

"I'm astounded!" she exclaimed. "You've heard of Étienne Lenoir?"

I sat down opposite her and broke my bread. "I'm a reader, Miss Stark, and not merely in theology. I'm interested in where the human race is going, both spiritually and materially. I keep up with the latest inventions."

She took a spoonful of soup, and it suddenly became apparent just how hungry she was, for our conversation was temporarily halted as she applied herself to the meal with an enthusiasm that was sad to witness.

I had led a very sheltered life in Theaston Vale. The only cities I'd ever visited were Southampton and Winchester. I'd yet to experience the teeming masses of London's poor and had never seen starvation before. It shocked and humbled me.

Silently, I served the young woman a second bowl, cut her another chunk of bread, then crossed to a cupboard and took from it a bottle of red wine. After pouring her a generous glass, I finished my own meal before transferring the now boiled water from the stovetop to a tin bathtub in the scullery. I refilled the pan and set it back on the flame, then, without a word, left the kitchen and went to the church storeroom. There were bundles of clothes in it, all clean, all contributed by the charitable. I took up as many as I could carry and transported them back to the scullery.

"That was delicious," Miss Stark said as I rejoined her. "Thank you very much. It's been longer than I care to remember since my appetite was properly assuaged."

I didn't know how to offer her the opportunity to wash without sounding indelicate, so I opted for blatancy and hurriedly said, "When a couple more pans have boiled, you'll be able to—to—to bathe. I've placed clean clothing beside the tub. Please take whatever you need."

I felt my face glowing red.

"You are very kind," she responded softly.

I topped up her glass and decided also to indulge. As I sat back down, she took a sip and muttered, "Bordeaux. From the Pomerol vineyards, I should say."

"Great heavens!" I blurted.

She chuckled. "It's not a claret I'd expect to find in the vicarage of a sleepy little Hampshire town. Are you a connoisseur?"

"It's a hobby of mine," I admitted. "How is it that you possess a knowledge of wines?"

"Reverend Fleischer, I'm happy to tell you my story in its entirety, and you must reveal to me how you know of the inventor Étienne Lenoir, but would you mind if we wait until after I've bathed? It is surely bad enough that I've intruded upon your day, but to do so with the odour of the road upon me, and to then remain and enjoy your hospitality without first correcting the problem, would be nothing short of uncivilised."

I acceded her point, and an hour later we reconvened in my sitting room, which, as she observed, more resembled an overstocked and chaotic library.

Much to my surprise and confusion, Miss Stark not only appeared considerably younger—perhaps a couple of years my junior—now the grime was scrubbed from her, but had also dressed herself as a man, in trousers and white shirt, waistcoat and a light jacket. I'd heard of "bloomerism," of course—it was much discussed in newspaper articles about female suffrage—but I'd never witnessed it "in the flesh," so to speak.

"The bloomerists wear trousers as a protest against the inconveniences of women's attire," my guest explained as she painfully manoeuvred her twisted form into an armchair by the fireplace. "For if a lady fails to hold up her skirts while out walking, the hems are soon soaked in all manner of foul substances. Yet they are made from such heavy linen that, after hoisting them up for half an hour, one's wrist cramps and aches abominably. But this is beside the point. I'm no bloomerist. I chose this attire simply because it better suits the life I have been forced to lead."

I also sat. "Let us begin again, Miss Stark. You were telling me about it—your life—and that you came by your education in relation to a thing called an autocarriage."

"Yes, a conveyance invented by the late Lord Hufferton—Sir Philip—and, as you correctly supposed, similar to Étienne Lenoir's *Hippomobile*."

"Powered by a combustion engine, then?"

"No. The Lenoir engine consumes fuel inefficiently, is exceedingly noisy, and is forever overheating and seizing up. Sir Philip employed a steam engine instead. Have you heard of Thomas Rickett?"

"I'm afraid not."

"Of Buckingham. He invented a steam plough some twenty years ago, which inspired the Marquess of Stafford to commission a steam carriage from him. The machine Rickett constructed was a three-wheeler, with a rear-mounted coal-fired boiler and a two-cylinder engine. Power was transmitted via a chain connected to the right-hand rear wheel. Sir Philip employed a very similar design, but introduced into it a horizontal double-acting steam-powered beam engine, gave the vehicle four wheels, and connected the chain to the middle of the rear axle. The front seat could hold three passengers, the one in the middle steering with a tiller, accelerating by means of a regulator lever, and braking via a foot pedal."

"Fascinating! My goodness, Miss Stark, you appear to have a firm grasp of mechanical design, though I suppose that's to be expected of anyone brought up in Hufferton's orbit. But, I say, while I knew he collected such wonders for his museum, I had no idea he'd designed one himself. So this is the carriage his son took?"

I'd supplied my guest with a fresh glass of wine. She imbibed a little, nodded, and said, "Rupert was a dreadfully disobedient child, forever getting into trouble. In 1870, he was thirteen and I was five. My parents and I lived in a tiny cottage on the estate. I used to stay with my mother in the manor's kitchen until it was too dark for my father to be working outside. He'd then come to fetch me home. One evening, as he and I were crossing the grounds, the autocarriage came careening toward us, out of control, with Rupert at the tiller. It hit us square on, killing my father outright and breaking my back and legs."

I pondered this disaster for a few moments, then murmured,
"'When he shall die,
Take him and cut him out in little stars,
And he will make the face of heav'n so fine
That all the world will be in love with night
And pay no worship to the garish sun.'"

After a further pause, Miss Stark said, "I loved my father dearly. That is a very appropriate quote."

"It's from Shakespeare's *Romeo and Juliet*."

"I know. And I'm much impressed that you chose to reflect upon my loss rather than the calamity of my injuries. You accurately detected how I was most wounded that horrible day. Such power of insight must make you a very good priest, though I'm intrigued that you chose to recite Shakespeare rather than the Bible."

I shifted uneasily in my chair. "As a matter of fact, I don't think

I'm a very good priest at all. When I quote from the Bible, I rarely feel that it's truly coming from my heart. But let's not talk about me. Please continue with your story; I'm thoroughly captivated by it."

She looked into the fireplace, and the light of the flames momentarily turned her eye lenses a glaring red.

"Lord Hufferton commissioned Edinburgh's famous surgeon, Joseph Lister, to attend to me and ensure my survival. My convalescence was long and agonising, and despite that my internal injuries healed and my bones knitted together, over the ensuing years, as I grew, my body warped out of shape, causing me incessant pain. Six months after my father's passing, my mother died—I think of a broken heart—and Sir Philip made himself my legal guardian. He transferred his affections to me, leaving Rupert, with whom he'd always had a difficult relationship, out in the cold. Tutors were hired, my education began, and I immediately found that the process of acquiring knowledge distracted from my pain. I was thus extremely attentive and diligent in my studies, and made rapid progress in a great many subjects. Most of all—due, no doubt, to the environment in which I lived—I developed a love for engineering. Sir Philip was very supportive of this, despite my gender. He allowed me free use of his extensive library, and of the museum and workshops, and took care to involve me in every one of his projects. We constructed traction engines together. We invented a steam-powered cable car system. We drew up blueprints for armoured war machines that could travel over the land or through the air—machines so huge they will never be built. We even perfected the autocarriage by returning to, and improving upon, Thomas Rickett's original three-wheeled design."

"Lord Hufferton was obviously a very good man," I observed.

"Yes, he was. His generosity extended to my social education as well. He allowed me to attend his famous annual *bals masqués*, and told the guests that treating me with respect was a condition of their attendance. Inevitably, there were examples of the vacuous variety of young aristocrat at the soirées, and when one such suggested that I should have costumed myself as Quasimodo from Victor Hugo's

Hunchback of Notre-Dame, Sir Philip flew into an uncharacteristic rage and threw the fellow out by the seat of his pants. That, however, was an exception. The majority of guests were very generous to me. Can you imagine it? Me, sitting discussing philosophy and politics and science with men whose faces were hidden behind Viennese masks? Men who were the luminaries of High Society? They were the people who've shaped this land and its culture, and I, a mere slip of a girl, spent many an engaging evening in their company. I learned a great deal from them—predominantly, how to think."

"And from the vacuous ones, how not to," I ventured.

"Precisely. I don't mean to suggest that it was exclusively cerebral, though. The balls were marvellous fun, and Sir Philip always laid on a variety of entertainments, such as singers and acrobats and magicians. Such wonders! They were the happiest days of my life, Reverend."

"What an extraordinary young woman you are, Miss Stark! I feel positively embarrassed that I offered you shirts to darn!"

She tut-tutted. "I can sew and look after a home just as well as the next woman. We made an agreement, Reverend Fleischer. You fed me. I will mend your clothes. I insist upon it."

"It really isn't necessary, but thank you. How came you, then, to such dire straits?"

"It's very simple. Two years ago, Sir Philip suffered a seizure and died. Rupert became the new Lord Hufferton, inherited the estate, closed the museum, and threw me out onto the streets."

"What? How could he do such a thing when it was he who caused your injuries? Has he no conscience?"

"What little guilt he may have harboured quickly turned to hatred. Perhaps he felt that he lost his father to me. Certainly, he always treated me with disdain and constantly mocked my appearance. Once, he encountered me in the grounds and snatched the goggles from my face, leaving me blinded and agonised by the sunlight."

I shook my head despairingly. "'The Lord is known by his justice; the wicked are ensnared by the work of their hands.'"

"From Psalm Nine, if I remember rightly," she responded. "But judging by your earlier statement, should I take it that the sentiment comes not from your heart but from your head?"

"My intellect tells me it's appropriate to suggest that Our Lord will cause your tormentor to learn the error of his ways, but, frankly, my heart doubts the truth of it."

"Rupert is rich, influential, and living a very comfortable life, despite his bad reputation," she responded. "While I've spent two years as a vagabond, spurned and isolated everywhere I go because of my appearance. It is, indeed, difficult to see any justice in it, or to have faith that justice will eventually come, whether by the hand of God or through the mechanism of *karma*."

I was moved by a sudden impulse. "Perhaps I can do a small thing to at least weigh the balance a little more in your favour. I need a sexton—someone to maintain the church, which is old and in disrepair, and the cemetery, which is overgrown. I would benefit from a housekeeper, too, just to keep the place tidy and free of dust, for I'm useless at such things. Would you be willing to fulfil such a role? There's an outbuilding that could be converted into modest living quarters if you're disposed to tackle it, and the Church would provide a small stipend for your services."

She said nothing, then leaned forward, and a quiet sob escaped her. It was an entirely unexpected response, and I felt horribly awkward that I'd been the cause of it, but I fully realised in that instant how dreadful the past two years had been for her, and was struck by a powerful sense of kinship. In truth, she and I couldn't be more different, for she seemed a thoroughly *authentic* character—if you understand my meaning—for whom the world denied a place, while I, by contrast, felt rather a fake, though my position was secure. Nevertheless, a bond had formed.

"You have my sincere gratitude," she whispered.

In this manner, my long association with the remarkably practical, resourceful, and inventive Clarissa Stark began. Many weeks passed before I could even begin to accurately gauge the extent of her abilities, but I can tell you now that she excels in engineering and chemistry, knows a great deal about medicine, is an artisan of unparalleled talent in metals and wood, and performs miracles as a cook, gardener, housekeeper, and bookkeeper. Much to my delight, I also discovered that she is well read in Latin, French, Spanish, Portuguese, and Dutch. For a man who studies in many languages, what could be more welcome than a companion with whom to discuss the merits of José de Cadalso y Vázquez, or the Comtesse de La Fayette, or João de Barros, or, of course, our own William Shakespeare?

Occasionally, we even debated the Good Book.

In intellect, we tended to come at things from opposing directions. I was always looking for evidence of God's plan in man's many innovations and accomplishments, whereas Miss Stark sought only to thoroughly understand and improve upon them, without reference to any possible divine influence. Her technical knowledge appeared inexhaustible. By contrast, I soon began to comprehend that my grasp of "things eternal" lacked equivalent depth, making of whatever wisdom I possessed a fairly useless commodity. Miss Stark one day advised that I could best address this problem by travelling.

"It is not healthy that your engagement with the world is conducted through books alone. If you believe in the divine, then you must seek to witness it in action."

I considered this an unrealistic proposition. "Do you not think it more efficient to learn from what other men have written? Surely it would take me a lifetime to gain through direct means even a scrap of the knowledge that I can read on a single page."

"But it is *experience* that promotes insight and personal growth, Reverend. You must grasp life by the scruff of the neck and struggle with the challenges it presents, otherwise how can you progress as a human being? And if you do not progress as a human being, how can you contribute to the furtherance of our species, whether our advancement follows a divine design or not?"

I shrugged this off, little suspecting that my naivety was about to propel the two of us along a path that would involve the dramatic furtherance not of mankind, but of a completely different order of being.

Our opinions were also divided on the subject of evil. Miss Stark insisted that Rupert Hufferton was wicked by nature, but when she revealed to me that his mother had died during his birth, I was quick to observe that, just as I'd been mistaken in suggesting the poor were a "class" rather than the product of unfortunate circumstances, so she might be wrong in her assessment of her former tormentor.

"Evil must be caused," I insisted. "Is it not obvious that Sir Philip was prejudiced against his son as a consequence of his wife's death? Rupert was a badly behaved child—and is now a dissolute adult—because he felt unloved, and perhaps even guilty. His misbehaviour was a cry for help."

"Tosh and piffle!" Miss Stark exclaimed. "The same misfortune was visited upon your family, yet your father doted on you, and you are kind and generous. Why different results from an almost identical circumstance?"

"The source must be farther back," I responded. "Sir Philip's reaction was shaped, perhaps, by some ill that was done to him by his own parents."

My companion snorted dismissively and said, "Back and back and back until, no doubt, you arrive at Cain! But why stop there? Cain's murder of Abel was prompted by a jealous rage, and that a response to God's cruel preference for a blood sacrifice over a gift of fruit and grain. Must we then consider God as the source of evil?"

"God is the epitome of good!" I objected.

"So your argument falls down. Cause and effect are an insufficient explanation."

"Do you have an alternative?"

She shrugged. "Maybe there's no origin, and no point to evil at all. Perhaps it's simply a component of some personalities, in the same way that gregariousness is, or shyness, or boldness, or timidity, or any other characteristic."

In 1887, two years after Clarissa Stark joined me in Theaston Vale, the Tanner family arrived in the town, having moved from Southampton, and in them I saw demonstrated a wickedness that appeared to support my sexton's assertion, for there was neither rhyme nor reason to it. The Tanners were simply bad.

They were a large clan, headed by a brute of a man named Oliver who came to set up shop as the town's new blacksmith. On their first Sunday in the parish, they attended my morning service, descending upon the church in an unseemly manner, with much shouting and boisterousness. Despite it being an early hour of Our Lord's day, the head of the family was obviously drunk and slurred his words as he introduced his pinch-faced wife, his three burly and sneering sons, and his two daughters, the youngest of whom was a mousy, runny-nosed girl of about ten years.

The other was Alice.

Alice—who promised Heaven and sent me to Hell.

She was curly-haired, tall, and shapely, with dark direct eyes that glittered and flashed like those of an angry cat. Her beauty was mesmeric—and she used it with ruthless efficiency. When she stepped forward that morning, I, who had no defence, was conquered in an instant. I stammered like a fool and turned red as a beetroot. She giggled, fluttered her lashes, smiled coquettishly, and entered the church. Her father slapped my shoulder and emitted a bellow of laughter before following her in.

The service that day was the worst of my life. Again and again, my gaze found its way to where Alice sat watching me with her lips curved into a slight smile, and each time I lost my train of thought and stumbled dreadfully in my speech. Meanwhile, the three Tanner boys disregarded me and talked to one another loudly throughout my liturgy, while their father sprawled with his head back and snored with the volume of a passing locomotive.

The crudeness of her family notwithstanding, over the course of the next few weeks, I found myself thinking obsessively about the girl and the way she'd looked at me—with a challenge and an invitation—and when I discovered that her father had purchased a small allotment on the outskirts of town, and that she worked there each afternoon, I began to take daily postprandial strolls so I might walk by it and stop to exchange a few words with her. She was always polite but distant, regarding me with pursed lips and hooded eyes, as if she knew something about me of which I was not myself aware. Our conversations were short and restricted to meaningless observations about the weather or the progress of her vegetables. What few attempts I made at greater depth were met with a giggle and a dismissive wave of the hand. It was obvious she was sorely lacking in education, but like an idiot, and contrary to all the signs, I interpreted this as a sort of purity, seeing in her a wholesome naturalness through which the divine spirit might be expressed in an unadulterated manner.

In my regular evening debates with Clarissa Stark, I again and again tried to legitimise my infatuation by dwelling on theories of female beauty, oblivious to the fact that this may have been a painful subject for my disfigured friend. I proposed, as the ancient Greeks had done, that perfection of physical form was somehow an expression of well-balanced internal virtues, and it was to these that I was drawn in Alice.

"Then I am obviously entirely without virtue," Miss Stark observed.

"Heavens above! I didn't mean to imply that!" I objected. "Your physique was damaged by your terrible accident, so it cannot be judged on such a basis!"

"Regardless, I think any such evaluation is flawed at the outset," she replied. "And the girl's beauty makes her all the more dangerous."

"Miss Tanner isn't dangerous!"

"Your inexperience blinds you." She ran a finger over her goggles. "What a shame these only filter light. I wish you could look through them and see what I see in the girl."

"Which is what?"

"Rupert Hufferton."

"Pah! Back to your conception of causeless evil!"

My friend shook her head and limped out of the room, quietly saying over her shoulder, "If God is good and no one is evil by nature, then you, as a priest, have just one option remaining."

"And what is that?"

"Give the Devil his due, Reverend. Give the Devil his due."

In hindsight, I can acknowledge that I probably knew all along that Miss Stark was correct in her assessment of Alice Tanner. I was aware there was something rotten inside the girl and was cognisant that I was on a course for disaster—yet I couldn't pull myself back from the brink. In truth, the unfamiliar and irresistible force of bodily desire propelled me, and I was helpless to resist it. So I took my daily walks, exchanged pleasantries with the girl, and every day fell deeper under her spell.

I don't want to dwell on this for too long. The memory is embarrassing.

The trap was sprung on the first Monday of June in '87. I was next to the allotment, at the side of the road, making small talk across the fence, when a heavy hand slapped down on my shoulder and yanked me around. Oliver Tanner stood there, his eyes blazing, his breath stinking of whisky, and his mouth twisted into an ugly smirk.

"Here now, what are you up to, my lad?" he demanded.

"I'm just—I'm just—"

"Is he bothering you, Alice?"

"Yes, Dad. He bothers me every day."

I looked at her in astonishment. "Alice! What do you mean?"

Tanner shook me hard and growled, "Shut up, you! I'll hear my daughter!"

"He's always a-comin' here," the girl said, and looked at me with scorn in her eyes. "Always pushin' 'imself at me with 'is foolish sweet talk an' flattery. I'm sick of it!"

My heart hammered violently. "What? But—no— this isn't true! Alice, why—?"

"Has he ever laid hands on you, girl?" Tanner snapped.

She looked down and quietly replied, "He tried. I 'ad to run away."

It was a scandalous lie, and it was spoken with ease.

Tanner gripped me by the collar and practically lifted me off my feet. He thrust his face into mine.

"You'd do that? You'd touch my daughter with your filthy damned hands?"

"I didn't! I never—I never—"

He shook me again and my teeth rattled. I wasn't scared—I was too dumbfounded. My brain had frozen with the shock of it. I simply couldn't comprehend what was happening.

"Stop yammering and explain yourself, or by God, I'll knock you into Kingdom Come!"

Alice laughed. "He'd like that! He's a vicar, ain't he? Don't do 'im any favours!"

Tanner snorted and grinned. "She don't come free, my lad. If it's a taste of Alice you're after, you'll have to ruddy well pay for it!"

"P-pay?"

"Aye, pay. There ain't nothing for nothing in this life, and that includes the liberty you've already taken! How much does he owe us, Daughter?"

"I'd say fifty nicker, Dad."

"But—what?" I spluttered. "This is outrageous! Fifty pounds? That's a fortune! What for? I haven't done—"

Again, I was shaken.

"You're calling my girl a liar, are you?" Tanner roared. "You want me to tell the whole bloody town what you've been up to?"

"No! I only—I mean—I love her!"

"What?"

"I love her, Mr. Tanner. I haven't—I wouldn't do anything to harm her!"

The blacksmith released me and stepped back. He put his hands on his hips, doubled over, and roared with laughter. "Hah! What do you think of that, Alice? The scoundrel loves you!"

The girl walked a short distance away, clambered over a stile, returned to us, and looked me in the eyes. She said, in a tone of such cruelty that I felt claws of ice digging into my chest, "You love me, Reverend Fleischer? You think I might find 'appiness with a dusty old bookworm—a tall, thin dullard? Look at you! A bundle o' bloomin' sticks bound together in last century's togs! Pah! I'd rather be alone for the rest o' me life than be bonded to such a wretched scarecrow!"

With dreadful relish, she cleared her throat, spat onto my boots, and added, "I don't even consider you a man."

"Fifty pounds, lad!" Tanner added. "You'll pay fifty pounds, and if I don't receive the money by Friday, the town'll know you for the degenerate you are!"

CHAPTER 2
WHITECHAPEL
AND KOLUWAI

"**I**'m ruined! If I don't pay the money, the Tanners will destroy my good name!"

We were in my sitting room, Clarissa Stark in an armchair by the fireplace, while I anxiously paced up and down.

"Inform the police," my friend advised. "You've been a respected member of this community your entire life. Your word will be believed over that of these newcomers."

"Maybe so, but they'll still be here to spread their vicious lies. They'll still disrupt my Sunday services. I'll still—I'll still have to look upon Alice!"

Overcome by the awfulness of my position, I suddenly ran from the room and up to my bedchamber, where I threw myself down and wept, piteous fool that I was.

I didn't emerge for two days. Miss Stark left trays of food outside the door, but I had no appetite, and by the time I descended the stairs on Thursday morning, I felt physically and emotionally hollow, and thoroughly exhausted.

I also felt determined.

As I entered the kitchen, where my sexton was preparing breakfast, I announced, "There is only one solution."

She turned and presented me with the black circles of her goggles. "And what is that?"

"I shall pay Mr. Tanner his fifty pounds, then I shall leave Theaston Vale."

"To go where?"

"To study at the Anglican Missionary College in London, and, after that, wherever they send me."

"As a missionary?"

"Yes."

"Reverend, forgive me, but don't you think it a little extreme to—"

I held up my hand to stop her. "My mind is made up, Miss Stark. You were right. I've hidden behind books for too long. I have no experience of life. I didn't recognise evil even when it looked me straight in the eye. I cannot believe this crisis has come into my life without there being some purpose to it. That purpose is clear—to do the greatest good, I must know its opposite. And in order to do that, I must start to live."

She was silent for a moment, then limped over to me, held me by the elbows, looked up into my face, and said, "'Cast all your anxiety on Him, because He cares for you. Discipline yourself, keep alert. Like a roaring lion, your adversary, the Devil, prowls around, looking for someone to devour. Resist him, steadfast in your faith. And, after you have suffered for a little while, the God of all grace, who has called you to His eternal glory in Christ, will Himself restore, support, strengthen, and establish you.'"

I felt the muscles of my jaw flex. "For a non-believer, you quote the Book with more conviction than I can ever muster. But you chose a passage that suggests my problems have only just begun."

"The attainment of wisdom inevitably involves a prolonged struggle with adversity," she replied. "Much more so if the wisdom you seek is an understanding of evil. But the Tanners have set the course, so let us sail it, weather the storms, and see where it takes us."

"Us?"

"You are my friend—my sole friend. In the time since I was ejected from Hufferton Hall, you've been the only person who's judged me by who I am rather than by what I look like. You've been generous, attentive, and agreeable. In short, you are a good man, and, though you doubt it, you're a good priest, too—but rather a naive one. It is my duty and my desire to accompany you, and to see that you come to no harm."

I was incapable of immediate response, but that evening, I said to her, "We've been meticulous in our observation of social proprieties, but under the circumstances, it feels ridiculous to continue with such formality between us. I'd much prefer it if you would call me Aiden, and allow me to address you as Clarissa."

She smiled. "Already, the crisis prompts progress."

The following day, I visited the blacksmith's, and, standing beside a blazing furnace, handed over the money.

"This'll do for a start," Oliver Tanner said with a contemptuous smirk.

"You have my forgiveness, Mr. Tanner," I replied. "And I thank you."

"Eh?"

"I believe you are—albeit unknowingly—doing the Lord's work. You have sacrificed yourself that I may live."

"What are you gibbering about? I've sacrificed naught!"

"Your immortal soul, sir."

"Superstitious claptrap!" He held up the pound notes I'd given him. "This is what's real, and it can't be spent in no bloomin' afterlife!"

I stared into the furnace. "In that, we are agreed. When payment is demanded of you, those notes will be worthless."

"The only payment you need worry about, lad, is the one you'll hand over after I've spent this lot. My silence don't come cheap! Now get out of here! But don't think this business is finished, 'cos it ain't—not by a long shot!"

Tanner was wrong. His bribery of me ended there and then— Clarissa and I never saw him, his family, or Theaston Vale ever again. A few days later, we left town and travelled by train to the capital.

London. 1888. God in Heaven. What a place.

It was a city divided. Its opulence was incomparable, its sophistication astonishing, its indulgences entrancing, its poverty terrifying, its ruthlessness overwhelming, its vileness unremitting.

The capital's split personality was perfectly embodied in a sensational novella published two years before my arrival, entitled *The Strange Case of Dr. Jekyll and Mr. Hyde*, by a Scottish author, Robert Louis Stevenson. It told of a rather immoral man who, by means of a chemical formula, embodied his weakness of character in an alter ego, which then rampaged about the city.

The tale unnerved me, for Alice Tanner's wickedness had given such strength to the aspect of my character which, in Theaston Vale, had felt frustrated, isolated, trapped, and inadequate—adding to it a ferocious resentment against the woman who'd spurned and humiliated me—that I could almost believe it might overtake me.

"It's an inner darkness," I told Clarissa, "and it won't be quelled. I hate it!"

"It's just a phase," she advised. "Most young men go through it, especially after their first rejection. It'll wear off."

She was wrong. London made it worse.

We had enrolled in the Missionary Society upon our arrival in the city, and for a year I'd been taught how to disseminate my religion to those who worshipped at pagan altars. My companion also received instruction as my sexton, and as a part of our training we were assigned three days a week to a workhouse in Whitechapel.

Despite being within reasonable walking distance of the glamorous West End, the district in which we now found ourselves might have been a different world altogether. Overcrowded, filthy, noisy, stinking, and vicious, it was a place where emotions were stripped to their most wretched essence. Need was surpassed by desperation. Hopelessness was eclipsed by utter despair. Love was obliterated by lust. Conditions there had pushed its inhabitants to the brink of animalism, making the men loutish beyond belief, but reducing the women in particular to such a state of bestial savagery that no social propriety or boundary survived in them. I could not walk down a street without being mocked, pawed at, and propositioned by these dreadful creatures. They uttered every blasphemy, put every perversion up for sale.

Whitechapel was a nightmare made real, and every day that I endured it saw an increase in my loathing of the place and its despicable inhabitants.

On the penultimate day of August, I was sent to a lodging house on Thrawl Street, where I was supposed to offer comfort to the fallen women who crowded into its small, damp, mildewed rooms. I arrived there at seven o'clock in the evening and spent the next few hours being regaled with appalling tales of destitution, vice, and violence, all the while trying to remain impassive while seething with detestation.

It was well past midnight by the time I left that awful house and made my way back toward the rooms the Missionary Society had assigned to me. I was tormented and confused, and, inevitably in the warrens of Whitechapel, my preoccupied state caused me to quickly lose my bearings.

Splashing through sewage and bound by the slumping walls of half-derelict and overcrowded tenements, I wandered from alleyway to alleyway, and the voices that jeered and threatened and wheedled suggestively from all around me seemed to close in, until I felt I was drowning in them.

I trudged on, closing my ears to the catcalls, averting my gaze from the ragged clothes and pockmarked faces, from the rotting teeth and alcohol-reddened eyes, from the taunting expressions and obscene gestures.

I wanted to be somewhere else.

No, it was more than that.

I wanted to be *someone* else, someone immune to all this hatred and revulsion.

My jaw ached, the pressure burning outward from my clenched teeth.

My hands were fisted, fingernails digging into the palms.

I felt rage.

Rage at this world.

Rage at Alice Tanner.

Rage at being Aiden Fleischer.

It filled me and overflowed from me. I saw red. Nothing but red.

My foot bumped against something and I staggered, tried to regain balance, slipped on wetness, and fell to my hands and knees. A growl of impatience escaped me, followed by a horribly primeval and panicked whine that I only vaguely recognised as my own voice.

My fingers had sunk into the slime, refuse, and excreta of an unpaved East End alleyway—and into the rivulets of flowing blood that cut through it.

Suddenly, I was gasping for air. The world snapped back into focus. I pushed myself to my knees. A woman was lying beside me, wreathed in shadows. I'd tripped over her extended leg. Now I couldn't tear my eyes away from her. She was sprawled on her back, the excruciated grin on her face echoed by two long lacerations in her throat, so deep they'd almost severed her head from her neck. Her skirt had been pushed up to her shoulders, exposing her abdomen. It was deeply slashed and torn wide open. Her internal organs glistened wetly.

My whine increased in volume, became a shriek, and I ran.

I don't properly recall what happened next. Somehow I arrived at my lodgings. I think I disturbed Clarissa. I washed my hands over and over, took off my bloodied suit and threw it into the fireplace, then blacked out.

It was noon when I regained consciousness. I opened my eyes and looked into the expressionless circles of my sexton's goggles. She was sitting at my bedside.

"You woke the household at five in the morning, Aiden. You were incoherent. Then you fell asleep as if drugged. What happened? There was blood on you."

"I can't remember!" I answered, truthfully. "I got lost, Clarissa. I was walking and—and—and that's all! I don't know where the blood came from! I don't know how I found my way back here!"

Throughout the afternoon and evening, I struggled to recall what had occurred, but my memory didn't return until the following day—and then only partially—when the discovery of the corpse was reported in the newspapers. According to the *Daily News*, the woman I'd fallen over was a drunkard and prostitute named Polly Nichols who often stayed at the boarding house on Thrawl Street where I'd been the night of her murder. A cart driver had discovered her body in the alley—Buck's Row.

"But I think I found it first," I told my companion, "and was so shocked that cowardice took over and I ran away."

"Don't judge yourself so harshly," she advised. "You reacted instinctively, that's all, and I'm glad you did."

"Glad? Why?"

"Because according to the coroner, the victim wasn't long dead when she was discovered, which means you were mere moments away from interrupting the killer at work. He may have been in the alley when you entered it. It's possible that, by taking to your heels, you escaped being murdered yourself."

I swayed and put a hand to my forehead. "God in Heaven, can it get any worse than this? The sooner the Society sends us overseas, the better!"

Days of darkness and death followed.

A week after Polly Nichols was killed, a woman named Annie Chapman was found dead, with almost identical wounds.

My state of mind deteriorated. I was engulfed by a black mood. My thought processes became lethargic and fragmentary. I undertook my duties, was out night after night, but returned with little memory of where I'd been or what I'd done. I'd disengaged from reality.

On the 30th of September, two more women—Elizabeth Stride and Catherine Eddowes—were slaughtered, and journalists gave the killer a name: "Jack the Ripper."

"What drives him to commit such atrocities?" I enquired of Clarissa.

"Must there be something aside from pure evil?" she asked in response. "Would you explain away this man's crimes as symptoms of a deprived childhood? Do you believe that Jack is crying out for love and forgiveness?"

"No," I replied. "Nothing could possibly justify his barbarity.

You were right all along—absolute evil exists, and its embodiment is stalking the streets of Whitechapel."

A fifth killing occurred on the 9th of November, this one so ferocious that the victim, Mary Kelly, was literally gutted and her organs arranged about the room in which the murder took place. It was reported the following day. Clarissa read the details to me from the *London Evening News*, and while she did so, I opened a letter from the Missionary Society.

"This maniac will be caught soon," she said. "He obviously can't control himself. Someone is bound to notice him behaving abnormally."

"Praise the Lord!" I exclaimed.

"I'd wait until he's dangling in a noose before you do that."

"No! This!" I waved the letter. "We've been given our marching orders. The Society is sending us to Papua New Guinea—we're to depart next week!"

Clarissa put the newspaper aside. "Good! Good! I'll tell you something, Aiden: you're not the same man upon whose door I knocked when I was at my lowest ebb. That Tanner girl and the horrors of London and the Ripper have demolished you. You needn't tell me how traumatic it's been; I've seen it in your face and manner. But this—" She pointed at the letter in my hand. "This marks the commencement of your rehabilitation. Soon you'll see that the malevolence you've experienced and witnessed is not endemic. The world is a wonderful place. It will rebuild you, and you'll be a better person for it."

"Perhaps so," I mumbled.

I was eager to be off but felt little enthusiasm for the task that now lay before us. My missionary training had been desultory and inadequate. It was obvious that a prospective evangelist required little more than a thorough grasp of the Bible, a modicum of zeal, and the ability to endure the worst possible conditions. The first, I had. Zeal, I feigned. Endurance, well, where could be worse than Whitechapel?

It was a question I asked again five days later when the Society provided me with a Webley-Pryse revolver. Holding the thing gingerly, I showed it to Clarissa. "They told me the life of a missionary is sometimes perilous."

"It's an undeveloped land, Aiden. They are right. Who knows what we might encounter?"

So it was that I abandoned London, leaving it in the demonic grip of Jack the Ripper, and sailed away, a faithless priest with a faithful hunchbacked woman at his side.

Three different ships took us in a roundabout manner to Australia. The initial ten days at sea saw me confined to my cabin, my skin a bilious shade of green and my stomach squirming in my throat. Thankfully, I then gained my sea legs and, for the remainder of the voyage, the fresh winds and far horizons did much to dispel the miasmatic dread that had enshrouded me since August. By the time we reached Sydney—a little over two months later—my face and forearms were a deep brown and my blond hair had been bleached almost white. This weathering hardly made me a "man of the world," though. On the morning we sailed into the harbour, when I examined my visage in a shaving mirror, I saw the same gaunt features and the same guileless pale blue eyes—the same dolt that Alice Tanner had so callously mocked. Yet I also noticed something different. The veneer of intellectualism that had for so long disguised my emptiness was gone. There was a new sort of honesty in my eyes, and it was terrible, for it made a blatant display of my deficiencies. I couldn't hide. I was exposed for all to see.

After a week's layover in Sydney, Clarissa and I sailed in a clipper to the Melanesian Islands and landed at Port Moresby. It was our intention to establish a Christian mission in one of the more remote regions of Papua New Guinea, as instructed by the Society, but within days of our arrival the German authorities disallowed the project. We twiddled our thumbs well into the new year while awaiting fresh instructions from London. They finally arrived in the second week of February, and directed us to instead establish a station on Koluwai, a humid hump that bulges out of the sea a thousand miles or so to the south-east of the principal island. Scarcely two hundred square miles in area, swathed in dripping jungle, and prone to particularly vicious seasonal storms, we found that it boasted one coastal town—Kutumakau—and a great many tiny villages, which, with an insane disregard for lightning strikes, were built in the treetops.

"It hardly seems worth the effort," I commented as we unloaded our baggage and trunks from the little steamer that had transported us there, "but the Church insists that God's work be done, even in far-flung corners such as this. What will the islanders make of us, Clarissa?"

"We shall be a novelty, at least," she responded.

In that, she was correct, for most of the Koluwaians had never seen a European before, despite the proximity of German colonies—an indication, perhaps, of just how small and remote their island was. They were untouched by civilisation and had, in fact, barely emerged from the Stone Age. Their diet consisted of fruit, tubers, nuts, fish, monkeys, and wild pigs, the land animals being hunted with barbed spears. The people eschewed ornamentation and wore only loincloths, with no necklaces, rings, or beads of any sort. They did, however, practise tattooism, and from head to foot were covered with swirling patterns of deep red and pale yellow dots. In stature they were a small but plump people, averaging about five-foot-four, with coffee-coloured skin, long black hair, and unfathomable brown eyes. Their jaws and cheekbones were prominent, as is common in primitive races, and their teeth large. Most of the men filed their incisors to points, and I was disturbed to learn that this was in connection with an aspect of their diet that, for them, possessed spiritual significance.

The Koluwaians were cannibals.

They were also slavers, making frequent raids on neighbouring islands and returning with young men and women who'd be spirited away into the jungle to who knows what fate—a cooking pot, I feared.

During the first few days after our arrival, we lived in a couple of semi-derelict shacks on the outskirts of Kutumakau—the town was little more than a sprawl of similarly dilapidated huts—and close to the edge of the steaming jungle. I found it almost impossible to sleep there, not only due to the oppressive humidity, the cacophonous night storms, the mosquitoes and invasive vermin, and the ceaseless din of chirruping tree frogs, but also because, from the moment I set foot on the island, I was subject to terrifying nightmares. These always began with a heightened awareness of my own pulse. Gradually, my heartbeat would increase in volume until it pounded in my ears, then I'd envision the blood coursing through my arteries and would sink into it until I seemed to exist at a microscopic level, with red cells roaring around me. From this crimson tide, Alice Tanner emerged, shamelessly naked, floating, smiling cruelly, her eyes filled with scorn.

In every nightmare, the same conversation occurred.

"Miss Tanner! You have to go! Please, hurry!"

"But I want to look at you, Mr. Skin-and-Bones."

"He's coming!"

"Mr. Books-and-Bible."

"Can't you feel him, Alice? Can't you sense him in my veins? He's approaching! He's close! Get away from here! Run! Run!"

"Mr. Thoughts-and-Theories."

"Oh, sweet Heaven, Jack is coming! He's coming for you!"

Something loomed behind her. A blade slid out of her belly and sawed up through her sternum.

An alleyway.

Alice, on her back, her eyes glassy, her throat slit twice through, her stomach ripped wide open.

The knife—in my hand.

Night after night, I'd jerk awake with a cry of horror, to find the atmosphere throbbing with the thunder of drums.

o

"I don't understand it," I said to Clarissa one morning. "It sounds like every village is drumming from midnight onward."

"There might be a purely practical explanation," she replied. "Maybe it's to keep nocturnal predators away."

Two weeks after our arrival, a wizened and uncommonly tall and thin islander named Iriputiz came to visit us. He was a grotesque individual whose dark skin was covered with scars, as if he'd suffered severe burns; whose long face radiated a malign intelligence; and whose eyes were forever restless, never settling on anything for more than a few seconds.

He was Koluwai's witch doctor.

We introduced ourselves and invited him in.

Speaking in German, which he'd apparently learned during visits to neighbouring, more developed islands, he said, "It is the time of storms on Koluwai."

His voice creaked like old wood.

"And very odd they are, too," I responded, speaking the same language and waving him to a chair. "All flashes and bangs but no rain. How long does the season last?"

"We do not measure time as you do, but I have knowledge of your calendar. By that, they come maybe every fifteen months and last for three. They grow stranger and stranger, and, after the strangest of them all, finish quite suddenly. We are now a month into the season. You are a priest, yes?"

"Yes."

"You have whisky?"

"No, but I have wine."

"Give me some."

Clarissa fetched a bottle and poured him a glass. He emptied it in a single swallow.

"More, and more again," he said.

Glancing at me, my sexton gave him a refill.

He swigged it back, held his vessel out for another, swallowed that, too, then dragged his skinny wrist across his lips. "You will both go from here today. You are not good for Koluwai. We will let you stay only if you speak like us."

"You mean we can remain if we learn the Koluwaian language?"

"Yes. Only if you do that."

"Then we will learn."

"You have more wine?"

"Yes."

"Then I will teach."

This sounded like a reasonable proposition, so we conceded, and from that day forward, Iriputiz visited us each evening and proved himself a very capable, if drunken, tutor.

The tongue of Koluwai is, I suspect, entirely unique. It doesn't at all resemble the languages of the other Melanesian Islands and probably exists nowhere else on Earth, but it is not complex. Consisting mostly of pops, snaps and clicks, buzzes, and long drawn-out vowels, its vocabulary is extensive but its grammar almost childish, requiring only that a noun be stated twice to indicate the plural, and having just three verb tenses. However, in common with many undeveloped idioms, nuances of meaning are primarily indicated through context and tone. Accompanying gestures are also far more extravagant and important than in English; so much so that many things are communicated solely with waved hands, nods of the head, and, especially, flicks and waggles of the fingers.

Clarissa and I were already fluent in a number of languages so we made rapid progress in our lessons, the main challenge being phonetics we weren't used to and which felt to us ill-designed for the human vocal apparatus. Many *ptahs* and *zz*'s and back-of-the-mouth "y" and "g" consonants were demanded, while vowels tended toward lengthy *oohs* and *aahs*. The "throat click" was particularly difficult. In isolation it presented no problem, but when it occurred in the middle of a word, it was hard to produce without pausing before and afterwards.

Nevertheless, it was only a few weeks before we were able to converse with the islanders, though when we did so, their reaction appeared somewhat strange to me, for no matter what the subject, our words would elicit first a nod of satisfaction, then, when we moved away, a whispered discussion, as if our progress was being assessed with reference to an agenda of which we weren't aware.

It was exceedingly odd.

We made fast progress in creating a home for ourselves and soon moved out of the shacks, thanks to Clarissa's remarkable skills. She positively blossomed on the island. With fairly inadequate assistance from twelve Koluwaians and despite her physical deformities, she constructed with astonishing rapidity an eight-roomed cabin, complete with a veranda, a library, a workshop, and a chemical laboratory. She then started to erect a church. These buildings, which comprised our missionary station, were located on a jungle-free hill overlooking the sea, half a mile to the south of Kutumakau.

I had never seen anyone work with such industry and unflagging energy.

"How do you do it in this tyrannical heat?" I asked one evening. "I can barely lift a finger, yet you race around carrying planks, sawing them up, knocking them together, building, building, building! You must have the endurance and strength of an ox!"

"The more engaged I am with a task, the less I feel the pain of my twisted bones," she answered.

"Do you really suffer so, Clarissa?"

"I barely remember the days when I didn't."

"I'm sorry. I wish I could help."

"You brought me here, Aiden. This is a place where everything needs doing. There's no time for me to stop and acknowledge that I hurt. That is a splendid gift!"

While my companion worked, I set about spreading the word of Our Lord with, I must confess, very little energy and an almost complete absence of true conviction. Just as I had resented my parishioners in Theaston Vale, so I now felt the same negative emotions toward my new flock. In retrospect, I can see the real reason for my discontent: I was professing a faith I didn't possess. It was all artifice—something learned by rote and presented as a spiritual truth. It was in my brain but had never touched my heart. It wasn't the parishioners or the islanders I begrudged—it was Aiden Fleischer, for I knew him a fraud.

My lackadaisical approach didn't really matter. My subjects had not one whit of interest in Christianity. Heaven, to them, was the bountiful sea, and the very idea of a single supreme deity they considered a flagrant absurdity. They had no need of my religion—they had their own, if "religion" is an appropriate word for the detestable practices and idolatry in which they indulged. Cannibalism was the least of it.

My awareness of the obscenities perpetrated deep in the jungle grew slowly. The drums were the first indication, for it occurred to me that, despite Clarissa's suggestion, there were no predators on Koluwai big enough to harm a man. Then I started to notice that most of the islanders bore scars between the swirling patterns of their tattoos, and on many occasions I observed that some of the scars were very fresh. Next, I became conscious that—from an age any civilised person would consider still a part of childhood—the female Koluwaians were almost permanently pregnant, but while there were many, many children on the island, the population wasn't expanding. In investigating this, I soon discovered that the town and all the villages were subject to mysterious disappearances. People simply vanished, and the islanders absolutely refused to talk about it, other than to acknowledge that it happened.

"Surely they don't eat them all?" I said to Clarissa.

My companion, who was at that time preoccupied with fitting pews inside the church, replied distractedly, "When this place is finished and the natives can gather in it and listen to you, and when I begin to practise medicine, we'll be better able to foster their trust. Perhaps then they'll be more willing to explain the way of things in this part of the world."

I looked around at the inside of the marvellous little church. "Assuming we can persuade them to come here at all."

It wasn't long before my suspicion that the islanders were engaging in blasphemous rites became inextricably bound to the phenomenal storms. These queer cloudless and rainless atmospheric disturbances crackled over the island with an almost clockwork regularity. Each night, when the first snap of electrical energy sounded, the men took up their spears and disappeared into the thick foliage—a fact that piqued my curiosity to such an extent that, one morning, I armed myself with my revolver, found the place where they'd pushed into the jungle, and followed their faint trail. It was a long and uncomfortable hike—the dawn's dew quickly made my clothes sodden and thorns nicked at the skin of my hands and face—but I pushed on, determined to solve the mystery of their nightly excursions.

The path led to a small glade at the summit of a steep hill. It was crowded with white flowers whose cloying scent made the atmosphere so thick and sickly that my senses began to swim. I held my wet shirtsleeve over my nose and mouth, stepped forward, and noticed that something was lying in the middle of the space, its inky-blue form half-concealed by the blooms. Hesitantly, I approached it, an inexplicable chill crawling up my spine.

It was a corpse—eviscerated, beheaded, slashed, torn, and rendered impossible to identify. However, as I gazed at it, spellbound, one horrifying fact gradually overcame me. Though vaguely humanoid, the thing was neither man nor woman. It wasn't any beast that I recognised. I didn't know what manner of being it was.

Staggering back, I tripped over the dried husk of a severed limb and saw that there were many more of the dead things strewn around the clearing.

I shrieked, dropped my pistol, turned, and ran. By the time I reached the cabin, I'd half-convinced myself that the pungent aroma of the flowers had caused me to hallucinate.

I made no mention of my excursion to Clarissa. I feared she might already regard me as prone to mental instability.

Perhaps I was.

My nightmares grew worse.

By the middle of the year, the missionary station was completed. Even in a comfortable climate this would have been considered fast work, but under the burning Melanesian sun it was incredible, and I stood in awe of Clarissa's practical skills, endurance, and knowledge.

"I shall send a man to deliver a message to all the villages," I told her, "to inform them that we shall hold our first service this coming Sunday. Perhaps curiosity will drive a few to attend, but even if just one person comes, it will be a start."

In the event, that's exactly what I got—a congregation of one.

Iriputiz.

So I gave my first and only sermon on the island to its witch doctor, employing as much Koluwaian as I could muster but resorting frequently to German. I explained what the Bible is, and how, through its guidance, a man might live according to God's will and thus gain eternal peace in the Kingdom of Heaven. I then asked Iriputiz to follow me in the recitation of the Lord's Prayer.

"And this will make your god come to us?" he asked.

"God is already present," I answered.

"I do not see him."

"He is in all that you see. He is in the air we breathe, the light that shines upon us, in the chirp of insects and the splash of the waves. God is everywhere and everything, for the world is His creation."

"I do not believe you. Take me to this place you call Heaven. I want to see it."

"The gates of Heaven open only to those who have professed faith in Our Lord, and in his son, Jesus Christ."

Iriputiz gave a snort of disdain. "This is all a story," he said, and stamped out of the church.

"I don't think I'm cut out for this," I confessed to Clarissa. "These people need something more tangible than words. It'll take fire and brimstone before they believe."

"Give it time, Aiden. I've noticed much disrepair in Kutumakau and the villages. I shall embark on a mission of restoration, and I have it in mind to create some sort of metal pylon at the top of the highest hill to draw the lightning away from the tree houses. Once these people gain material benefits from our presence, perhaps they'll be more willing to listen."

I nodded my approval but felt useless. It also occurred to me that, despite the frequency and ferocity of the electrical storms, Clarissa and I hadn't once witnessed or heard of an actual lightning strike.

Moving into our new station appeared to cure me of my nocturnal terrors—I credited the light sea breeze I allowed to blow through my room for this—but on the night of the sermon, I suffered a bad dream of a different sort, one so vivid that it might have been real.

I'd retired at about eleven o'clock and, after an hour of restlessness, had fallen into a fitful and incomplete sleep—that state of suspension where one is aware that the body is slack and snores are being produced, but still feels rather too conscious for it to qualify as proper rest.

I was aware of the salt air whispering through my window. I was aware of the perpetual trilling of the frogs. I was aware that drums were rumbling in the jungled hills.

And I was aware that my bedchamber door slowly creaked open.

A cloud of steam billowed into the room, and with it Iriputiz, who appeared to be floating a few inches above the floor. He slid to my bedside and looked down at me.

"I will send you into the final storm, Reverend Fleischer, there to meet the god I serve—a *real* god! He has a task for you."

He reached out and grasped my forearm, sinking his long, pointed fingernails into my flesh.

With a cry of pain, I jerked awake, sat up, and swatted a large spider from my wrist. It had bitten me, leaving two little puncture marks. I jumped to the floor and chased the pest into a corner of the room where I flattened it with a slipper. I returned to my bed and lay down. I was trembling and a fiery sensation was creeping up my arm. Moments later, everything skewed sideways and I knew no more.

°

A monotonous chanting and distant rumble of thunder summoned me to consciousness. I was on my back, with the stars overhead, and I was moving. It took me a moment to realise that I was being borne along on a stretcher and there were islanders crowding to either side of it. Clarissa's face hove into view and the light of burning brands reflected in her goggle lenses.

"Are you lucid, Aiden?"

"Of course. What's happening?" My voice sounded dry and husky.

"Lie still. You're seriously ill with fever."

"But I was just sleeping."

"No. You've been ranting and raving for more than a week."

A week! I could barely credit this, for I had no sense that time had passed.

"Iriputiz says you're suffering from something called *kichyo-machyoma*—a sickness of the spirit. The islanders are immune to it but we aren't. I've been through our entire pharmaceutical supplies trying to find something to treat it, but nothing has worked. The witch doctor assures me he can cure you with local herbs, so we're taking you to the place in the hills where they grow. Apparently, they are only effective in the few minutes after they are picked."

"No," I croaked. "I'll be all right. Don't take me into the hills. There are—there are *things* there."

"I'm scared you're dying, Aiden. I don't know what else to do. What things?"

"Things. They aren't human. I saw one. The villagers had killed it. It was—it was a demon!" I struggled to sit up, caught a glimpse of a long procession trailing behind us, then fell back, utterly lacking in strength. The jungle canopy closed overhead as we pushed into the vegetation.

"You aren't thinking straight," Clarissa said. "Don't worry—I'll see that no harm comes to you. If we have to endure a heathen ritual in order to restore your health, then what's the harm?"

My vision slipped in and out of focus. The stars, flickering through the branches, went from pinpricks to blurred lozenges and back again. The jungle's shadows enveloped me and I tumbled into oblivion.

The next thing I knew, there was a loud crackle of lightning and I was looking up at Iriputiz.

"Open your mouth," he said.

I wanted to ask what he was doing, but the moment I tried to speak, he forced something between my lips and pushed it to the back of my throat with his filthy thumb. I started to choke and felt a ferocious burning expand out from my gullet and into my skull. My heels, which, I dimly realised, were tightly tied together, drummed against the stone surface on which I lay. My wrists pulled at bindings. I bucked and writhed, unable to catch a breath. Then, just as I thought my heart might burst, the old man leaned forward and thumped my chest. I coughed vegetable matter into my mouth and spat it out.

As I sucked shudderingly at the humid air, my mind instantly cleared and I felt a fresh strength pouring into my limbs. I lifted my head and saw that I was stretched out on an altar in the centre of a clearing, around which a crowd of natives had gathered. Male and female, they were unashamedly naked, holding aloft burning brands, chanting their slow and repetitive dirge.

Clarissa was standing nearby. An engorged full moon hung overhead. The sky was cloudless but jagged lines of electrical energy were snapping back and forth across it.

"Get me out of here!" I pleaded hoarsely. "This is the Devil's work!"

"Iriputiz is saving your life, Aiden!" Clarissa responded.

"Then why am I bound?"

The witch doctor interrupted. "The fever will return, Reverend Fleischer. These bonds are to keep you still while I do my work."

I looked at my sexton and urged, "Please! Don't let him touch me again."

She hesitated and bit her lower lip irresolutely, then limped forward. An islander rushed up behind her and swung a knob-stick into the side of her head. Her goggles went spinning away as she flopped unconscious to the ground.

I groaned, fought, but failed to rise. Iriputiz came to my assistance. He put his arm under my shoulders and hoisted me into a sitting position.

"Your church," he said, pointing to my left.

I looked and saw that a gap in the trees gave an unrestricted view down a long slope to where Kutumakau town slumped. A little beyond its shacks, the church that Clarissa had built stood whitely in the moonlight.

It burst into flames.

"Such a place does not belong here," Iriputiz hissed. "In the morning, its ashes will be thrown into the sea. Your imaginary god is not for us. Our gods are real, and it is time for you to serve one."

He pushed me back down, drew a knife from his loincloth, and sliced at my clothes, tearing them from me. Then he applied the blade to my skin and began to cut me all over—small incisions, about an inch long and a quarter of an inch deep. He made hundreds of them, and into each he inserted a small seed that burned like acid. I screamed. I begged. I prayed for succour. It didn't come.

Multiple bolts of lightning hissed and fizzled deafeningly overhead.

The islanders' chanting changed its tone and tempo. It gained a menacing quality, and even through my terrible agony, I could feel an air of expectancy creeping over the jungle clearing.

A woman stepped forward and began a writhing, sensuous, then progressively frantic dance, keeping rhythm with the rolling intonation. At first shockingly unrestrained and animalistic, her movements became increasingly monstrous as her joints, with nasty groans and snaps, started to bend in unnatural directions. She scratched viciously at her own flesh, causing blood to stream over her glistening tattooed skin.

Iriputiz held out a bowl to her. From it, she plucked large thorns, which, one by one, she pushed into her legs, arms, torso, and face. Around each, the flesh swelled rapidly. I watched, horrified, as her skin stretched, split, and spurted blood. Finally, accompanied by an appalling scream, she practically flew apart, showering the gathering with gore.

Her shredded corpse dropped to the ground and lay twitching.

There was a momentary pause, then drums suddenly boomed from beyond the trees, adding their din to the clamouring storm, which was now directly above the clearing and appeared to be descending toward it.

The witch doctor smeared foul-smelling grease over my skin then rubbed a gritty glasslike powder into it, covering my entire body. A prickling sensation needled into every inch of me, as if I'd become filled with a strong static charge.

"It is ground crystal," he said. "It will ensure that the gods take you."

He applied his blade to his own palms, threw the weapon aside, held his hands poised above my face, and began to sing.

His blood dripped into my eyes and onto my lips. Each time I opened my mouth to scream, some of it dropped onto my tongue and oozed to the back of my throat.

God! Please! I don't want to die! I don't want to die!

My church, and the last remnants of my faith, burned.

The air above turned into a writhing ball of energy. It flashed and shimmered, boiled, flattened into a disk, and opened in the middle. Warm air, tangy with the scent of lemons, gusted against my face, then suddenly reversed direction and howled as it was sucked upward. I felt a tremendous force pulling at me.

Clarissa Stark tottered to her feet and screamed my name. She staggered over with her eyes clamped shut and tears streaming from them, and threw herself on top of me.

Iriputiz bellowed, "No! Not you, woman!"

I felt myself rising, carrying Clarissa with me.

My senses left me.

°

CHAPTER 3

YATSILL AND
YARKEEN

❖

I look back upon the man I was prior to that ritual on Koluwai and I see a pathetic individual. I see a man who professed faith when he felt secure but who had none when he felt threatened.

True faith is steadfast. When mine was tested, it failed instantly and completely.

The Tanner family, the women of Whitechapel, the abominable crimes of Jack the Ripper, and the ghastly ordeal I suffered on the island, these things convinced me that God is a figment of the human imagination, for surely if He existed, He would not allow such iniquities to be visited upon one of His advocates.

So I was born again, a non-believer.

I was born again, under the palest of yellow skies and with a citrus fragrance in my nostrils.

I was born again, and I was lying on my back on the ground.

A voice said, in Koluwaian, "By the Saviour! Look at this one!"

Panicking, petrified, I turned over and scrambled away on my hands and knees. Then I stopped and sucked desperately at the air, my eyes fixed on the grass between my hands. It possessed a peculiar bluish-green hue and its blades were tubular with minuscule white flowers at their tips. I began to tremble all over. A mewl of mortal terror escaped me as my body was consumed by the unendurable agony of the witch doctor's torture, except—

Except it wasn't.

The pain was but a memory.

A second voice exclaimed, "Suns! What is it? Look at its colour!"

The first voice: "An aberration?"

"By virtue of there only being two of them, yes, of course. When before have so few been delivered to us?"

"Is the other awake?"

"It is moving."

I fell onto my side, drew my knees up to my chest, and hugged them. In a quavering whisper, I recited, "Our Father, who art in heaven, hallowed be thy—be thy—"

I swallowed and felt my lips drawing back against my teeth.

The words had emerged as empty sounds. Meaningless. There was no comfort in them. They didn't alter the fact that it was no longer a stifling tropical night but a bright and fresh day, or that the air smelled not of the jungle but of lemons, or that when I turned my head and blinkingly looked upward, I saw, directly above me through the branches of a pink tree, four small moons in a cloudless cadmium sky—three of dusty red and the fourth, the smallest of the spheres, purple with a dark blemish in its centre.

Four moons.

I broke into hysterical laughter, uncurled, clambered to my feet, and looked around. Pastel colours slid past my eyes. Nonsensical shapes. A bizarre forest. Long shadows.

Plum-coloured fruits, shaped like pears but the size of a man, hung from gargantuan trees. The nearest to me emitted an incomprehensible mumble.

I flinched away from it, turned, and saw Koluwaians standing around me. Koluwaians and . . . *other things*. One of the latter was bending over the prone form of Clarissa Stark. It said, "This one appears to be damaged."

My laughter rose in pitch and became a long, despairing wail. I toppled to one side and hit the ground in a dead faint.

o o

I was aboard a ship, on a voyage to the other side of the world. I was on a stretcher being carried up into the jungled hills of Koluwai. I was being shaken back to consciousness by a hand on my shoulder. I yelled and pushed myself away from it, bumped into warm bodies, and lashed out with my fists and feet.

"Aiden, is that you?"

Clarissa Stark. *Clarissa Stark!*

I opened my eyes and looked down at myself. I was naked. The grease Iriputiz had smeared over me was dry and breaking off in large glittering flakes.

Then I looked up and saw figures. There were the—the *things* I had seen earlier, there were Koluwaians, and there was Clarissa.

She was still wearing the clothes I'd last seen her in—the trousers hanging over misshapen legs, the shirt pushed up by a humped and twisted spine. Her eyes were squeezed tightly shut, with tears streaming from them.

"Clarissa, where are we? Where are we?"

"I don't have my goggles, Aiden. I'm blind. Were we rescued?"

"I don't—I don't think so."

Though I tried desperately to avoid looking at anything but her, I couldn't help myself, and glance by fearful glance I took in the immediate environment. We were sitting among a group of Koluwaians, five plump men and three fat women, in a forest clearing. The trees were the same as I'd glimpsed before—of phenomenal size, raised up on mangrove-like roots and heavy with enormous purple fruits from which faint sounds issued. The air was filled with the muted whispering and mumbling, which reminded me of the noise one hears in a theatre during the brief seconds between the lights going down and the curtain going up.

Six creatures were busy around the edges of the glade. They were pushing sharp hollow sticks, similar to bamboo, into the fruits and collecting, in what appeared to be skin containers, the juice that ran out through them.

One of the things noticed that I'd regained my wits, stepped away from the trees, and approached us. It looked down at me. It was so dreadful in aspect that it was all I could do to suppress a scream.

In terms of species, it resembled an amalgam of mollusc and crustacean, with a carapace of slate grey. Its body was reminiscent of a mussel shell, standing on end with the seam at the front. From the base of this, four crab-like legs extended, while the top of the torso curled outward in a frilled and complex manner to form wide armoured shoulders. The arms—which like the legs reminded me of the limbs of a crab or lobster—had two elbows and ended in three extremely long fingers and a thumb, all of which moved without cease. A fluted shell—shaped like a hood—protected the head. A revolting "face" bulged out of it. This was the only visibly soft and fleshy part of the creature. It had the appearance of a snail or a slug, in that the skin was grey and wet-looking, with no bones beneath it to give a defined shape. It was, in fact, almost entirely mouth—the long opening dividing it vertically—with outer lips fringed with small red feelers, like a sea anemone, and a further set of flexible inner lips which slid over a hard beak, just visible at the back of the orifice. There were four eyes, two to either side of the mouth, the upper pair being the largest. They were like black beads, circular and carrying no expression. A small bump was located above each upper eye, like nascent horns.

The creature was about seven feet tall and wore nothing but a leather harness, which held five long wooden barbed spears against its back.

"I am Yazziz Yozkulu," it said, in Koluwaian. "You have been delivered, as these others once were—" It wiggled its fingers at the islanders. "This place is the Forest of Indistinct Murmurings. Your appearance is very curious. Are you damaged?"

I couldn't answer. With each word that emerged from the creature's horrible maw, I seemed to recede from the world, until I felt that, rather than participating in it, I was merely looking on as a spectator.

"We are not injured," Clarissa said. "Forest, you say? Where is it located?"

"It is where it is. Where else could it be?"

Another of the loathsome things scuttled over. It bore a jagged gouge running down the left side of its body—an old wound.

Yazziz Yozkulu turned to it. "Have we gathered enough Dar'sayn, Tsillanda Ma'ara?"

"We have. I will be glad to depart. I find the forest repellent."

"As do I. I always feel a sense of trespass when we come here.

However, the Saviour demands it, and the Ptoollan trees have served us well, so I suppose the diversion was worth the effort. Look at these misshapen things, though!" The creature gestured at Clarissa and me. "I don't know what to make of them!"

"I think we have encountered a potential dissonance, my Yazziz."

"Perhaps so. You have greater sensitivity to such matters than I. Should we withdraw from the Ritual of Immersion?"

"If you will it."

"Do you advise it?"

"No. I recommend we proceed as normal. These new ones are curious but the dissonance I sense is fledgling. Let us take them with us. When we return to Yatsillat, we can present them to our fellow Wise Ones."

"Very well. Saviour's Eyes, but they are peculiarities, though!"

The Yazziz—it appeared to be a title rather than a name—lifted the hollow rod it held and very gently prodded Clarissa with the blunt end. "The other ones will feed you if you require it."

"The other ones?" my friend asked.

One of the Koluwaian women leaned forward and touched my companion's shoulder. "Us. Do not be concerned. We are children of the Saviour, and the gods are kind."

"That is true," Yazziz Yozkulu said, then addressed the woman. "Take your people back to the Ptall'kor. We will join you presently." The beast scurried away with the one called Tsillanda Ma'ara following behind.

A shrill giggle escaped me, and I heard a sharp edge of madness in it.

Clarissa reached out, groped for my hand, and held it tightly. "Aiden, what's wrong? I don't know where we are, but at least we're not with Iriputiz, and the people seem well disposed toward us."

"People!" I screeched. "They're not people, Clarissa! They are— they are—*monsters*! And this place—it's a nightmare! A nightmare!"

The islander who'd spoken before said, "My name is Kata. This is Ptallaya. Those with us are the Wise Ones. Come. I will lead you to the Ptall'kor."

She stood, as did the other islanders. I helped Clarissa to her feet and we followed the group through the trees.

"How far are we from Koluwai?" Clarissa asked.

"As far as can be," Kata responded. "Ptallaya is where the gods dwell."

A few moments later we came to the edge of the forest, and here I was confronted by yet another paralysing sight. It was a living thing, floating in the air, but whether animal or vegetable I couldn't say. In shape, it was similar to a mermaid's purse—the egg case of a shark or skate, dried examples of which I'd seen in bric-a-brac shops—but a powdery brown, and massive, at least a hundred feet long and thirty wide. Seaweed-like ribbons rose high into the sky from its corners, buoyed up by gas-filled sacs, and from the thing's underside a great many tendrils dangled to the ground, about twenty feet below. Each of these had finger-like appendages at its end, which gripped the grass, appearing to hold the thing down.

"It is a Ptall'kor," Kata explained. She emitted a trilling whistle and the thing responded by sinking down. There were Koluwaians and more of the mollusc creatures sitting on its back.

Following the islanders, I guided Clarissa up onto it and we settled on its chitinous hide. My companion let go of my hand and pressed her palms against her eyes. "It won't do. It won't do at all. I need my goggles. You must detail everything, Aiden. I must know our circumstance. Tell me! What is around us?"

Feeling drunk and remote, I started to speak mechanically, my emotions disengaged. I described the weird forest and its mumbling fruits, the Ptall'kor, and the landscape beyond the trees.

"The sky is pale yellow, Clarissa. There are four moons overhead and two small suns close together and very low, just above the horizon, which, incidentally, is too far away."

"Atmospheric illusions?"

"I don't think so."

"What else?"

I looked down at my limbs and, at last, emotions registered— embarrassment and humiliation! I was naked! Completely naked!

But my exposure also revealed that my body was covered from head to toe in small, thin white scars—Iriputiz and his knife, but healed already? How could that be possible?

"Reverend Fleischer!" my companion barked.

"I—I can't. It's too—too—"

She gripped my arm, almost viciously. "Be my eyes!"

Her voice was sharp and assertive, but I suddenly became aware that she was trembling, too.

I gave a deep, shuddering sigh. "The forest is at the mouth of a valley, which opens onto a wide savannah. I see a narrow river winding through it. There are mountains on one side of the valley and low hills on the other. All the colours are of a soft hue. There are exotic plants and giant trees, and herds of—of—I don't know what they are."

"Antelope, like in Africa?"

"No—similar, but not antelope. And a lot of flying things. They don't look like birds. More like sea life, but floating in the air with—um—buoyancy sacs, I suppose. Here come the—the—" My voice failed me as the "Wise Ones" scuttled into view and clambered aboard the Ptall'kor. They placed bulging and sloshing skins into a pile and the one called Yazziz Yozkulu announced, "Only two new ones delivered to us—and strange ones at that—but at least we have plenty of Dar'sayn and can now leave this accursed place. On with our journey, and Saviour protect us!"

Our "vehicle" rose into the air and pulled itself past one of the colossal trees. At my companion's request, I described it in greater detail: the raised roots, so tall a man could easily walk among them; the trunk, silvery grey, at least thirty feet wide but proportionately short; and the feathery fern-like leaves that arched outward from its top. They were of a soft pinkish hue and comprised of ever-thinning filaments that became so slight as to be almost invisible, causing the edges of the fronds to melt into the air. This was common to much of the flora that I subsequently observed—the thinning of foliage to the point where it became a nimbus around its parent plant. Together with the dominant pastel shades, it gave the landscape such a lack of definition that it might have been a dream.

Perhaps it was!

Wake up, Fleischer! Wake up!

"I'm so drowsy," I mumbled as the Ptall'kor glided out over the grassy plain.

"Probably shock," Clarissa said. "I daresay I'd be the same if I could see. Apart from that, how are you—your health, I mean?"

"I feel heavy and lethargic but—but I'm all right."

"No traces of fever?"

"No! Apart from this dragging weight and tiredness, I feel physically fine."

"Perhaps gravity is a little more powerful here, and that's why you feel so sluggish. But the *kichyomachyoma* is cured?"

"I'd forgotten about that! Yes, it appears to be. Gravity? What do you mean?"

"Isn't it obvious, Aiden? This isn't Earth."

"I have to sleep now."

I lay down, closed my eyes, and shut it all out.

∞

When I awoke, Kata, the Koluwaian woman, pushed an object into my hand and said, "Eat."

The thing, which was the size of a grapefruit, looked like a perfectly spherical nut with a single groove running around its circumference. It was green, and firm to the touch. Following Kata's lead, I bit into it. It had the texture of an apple but tasted like a cross between a melon and pear. It was delicious.

"For how long did I sleep?"

Clarissa answered. "It's hard to say, but I'd estimate three or four hours. What time of day is it?"

I looked at the twin suns. They hadn't moved at all. Our shadows were still long.

Kata said, "We are early in the sight of the Saviour."

I examined her more closely. She was a short, fat woman of

indeterminate age with a very broad and flat forehead, a crooked nose, and a protuberant jaw.

"Kata has been telling me about Ptallaya," Clarissa said. I saw that she now had a cloth wound about her head, like a blindfold, to protect her eyes. "The things you called monsters are Yatsill. They are divided into the Wise Ones and the Shunned."

Kata gestured toward the front of the Ptall'kor, where the six creatures who'd been in the forest with us stood. "The Wise Ones," she said, and then pointed to the rear where nine more squatted, "Those are children. We are taking them to Immersion, where some will be made Wise and others Shunned. All the newly born Yatsill make this journey when the Eyes of the Saviour open. The rest are on other Ptall'kors, which are far ahead of us. We will be last to Immersion, for we travelled first to the forest to collect Dar'sayn."

I didn't comprehend any of this.

I took another bite of the fruit and chewed it, the sweet juice quenching my thirst. We were drifting past a slow-moving river. I watched as little cone-shaped animals with long spidery legs and flat circular feet scampered across its surface. They looked comical. They looked like nothing on Earth.

The rising suns were directly ahead of us, in what I instinctively considered to be the East, even though the points of a compass may have been meaningless on this world. There were low hills to either side of us. At our rear, at the edge of the now distant Forest of Indistinct Murmurings, a range of jagged mountains rose up and stretched away "southward."

Kata saw me looking at them and said, "They are the Mountains That Gaze Upon Phenadoor." She passed a strip of material to me. I put the fruit aside, stood up, and wound the cloth around my hips. My goodness, what comfort I gained from that simple rag! Adam's fig leaf!

"What is Phenadoor?" I asked.

"It is the sea. Phenadoor: the Place of No Sorrow or Pain, of Indescribable Joy, of Eternal Bliss. The Shunned enter it when it is time to die. It is their recompense."

"For what?"

"For not being Wise."

"And the ones who *are* Wise?"

"They are denied Phenadoor."

"Why?"

"Because the Saviour is not the only god."

"I don't understand."

Kata shrugged.

I examined the so-called "children." They looked identical to the other Yatsill except they lacked the little bumps above their upper eyes, were not armed with spears, and were very quiet, squatting motionlessly but for the constant movement of their fingers.

Clarissa asked, "So it's decided at Immersion which of the creatures will enter Phenadoor and which won't? Where does this ritual occur?"

"In the Shrouded Mountains. The children will go into a pool there. It is tradition."

As the seemingly interminable journey went on, I continued to describe the scenery to my friend. Gradually, I began to feel a little more in the "here and now."

"It's actually quite beautiful," I said. "Can you imagine, Clarissa, the subject matters of Hieronymus Bosch but painted, instead, by J. M. Turner?"

"Frankly, no. And I would hardly classify Bosch as beautiful," she responded.

"True, but there is so much to take in, and all of it so queer, that the effect is the same. I feel overwhelmed and mesmerised by it; my eyes can barely make sense of it; yet, undeniably, there is an allure in its softness and luminosity."

"Unfortunately, I can neither corroborate nor refute your impressions, Aiden. But I'm pleased to hear you sounding more yourself."

"You're right! A little sleep has done me a world of good!"

"An interesting choice of words," she responded.

I glanced at the group of Yatsill standing at the "prow" of our bizarre vessel. "Then we really are on another planet?"

"Can you doubt it?"

I watched a creature float through the air nearby. It was a hollow, transparent ball, about twelve feet across with a hole on opposite sides. The opening at the rear expanded, moved forward, enveloped the creature, then, having moved to the front, shrank, while the opening that was now at the back started the process all over again. The thing thus moved along by turning itself inside out.

"No," I said. "I don't doubt it at all. But how are we here?"

"A more pertinent question might be *why*."

"You think there's a reason?"

"If Iriputiz wanted to get rid of us, he could have killed us with impunity. Instead, he caused us to be transported to this place."

"Or—or—" I struggled with the idea that had just occurred to me.

"What?"

"Or he *did* kill us, Clarissa. He killed us, and we are in Heaven—or Hell."

"As a priest, surely you'd recognise which?"

"The landscape might be Paradise, but its inhabitants—" My voice trailed away.

Clarissa massaged the calf muscle of her right leg. "Why would Heaven have a heavier gravity? Why would the atmosphere of Hell have a citrus tang? If this is the afterlife, why do my legs still pain me? No, Aiden, this is undoubtedly a world of the flesh rather than of the spirit, and I suppose the reason for us being here will emerge in due course."

o o

In Earthly terms, day after day must have passed as the Ptall'kor pulled itself over the rolling grasslands, but on Ptallaya the twin suns barely moved at all. I ate, I slept, I examined the extraordinary flora and fauna, I even became bored, and still the journey went on.

Eventually, when I shaded my eyes and peered ahead, I saw, rising from the horizon, a wall of white vapour bubbling high into the air.

The Ptall'kor, making straight for it, entered a valley and pulled itself alongside a wide river, gliding over an ever-thickening forest of purple-leafed trees, transferring its gripping fingers from the grassy ground to the upper canopy and disturbing flocks of weird flying—or floating—creatures as it passed. It was becoming plainly apparent to me that many of this world's animals were tremendously buoyant, and used their long tendril-like limbs not to take to the air, but to hold themselves down. A large number of smaller animals, dislodged by the groping hands of the Ptall'kor, slipped out of the foliage behind us and shot upward before jerking to a halt at the end of silken threads, which they'd obviously attached to twigs and branches. Looking back the way we'd come, I could see hundreds of them, like oddly shaped balloons marking our passage, slowly drawing their bodies back down into the leaves.

"Soon we will stop so the Wise Ones can hunt Yarkeen," Kata told us. "After we have eaten, we'll travel through the Valley of Reflections to the Shrouded Mountains and the Cavern of Immersion."

"What is Yarkeen?" I asked.

"That is."

I followed her pointing finger and saw, between us and the wall of steam, a huge balloon-like gas sac floating high in the air. It was semi-transparent—which is why I hadn't noticed it before—and resembled an upside-down teardrop in shape. From its base, a long cord descended and, about thirty feet above the ground, flared outward like the mouth of a trumpet, forming into a broad disc, which—as became evident when we drew closer to it—was at least a mile in diameter. Multiple translucent tentacles extended from the edges of this and were probing about in the foliage below.

"How can something that size be hunted?" I exclaimed.

"What, Aiden? What is it?" Clarissa interjected.

I told her about the creature. She banged the palms of her hands against her blindfold in frustration.

"Hunting a Yarkeen is dangerous," Kata said. "When the Eyes of the Saviour are upon it, it will not purposely attack, but if it realises that it's in danger, it will defend itself, and it is very powerful."

"But why bother hunting it?" I asked. "It's gigantic! We couldn't possibly eat it all, and I see plenty of smaller creatures all around us, not to mention fruit-heavy trees and bushes filled with berries."

The Koluwaian nodded. "Only a small part of the Yarkeen is edible but traditions must be followed."

I don't know how long it took us to reach the massive creature. Time was stuck. Perhaps I slept again, I'm not certain.

Awareness returned to me when we drew close to the beast. Its vast disc lay off to our right, above low, forested hills. I saw that, high above, around the thing's buoyancy sac, a cloud of smaller things were flying. They were at such an altitude that I couldn't make out any details, but I guessed the individual creatures to be about the size of a man. They swooped and turned about each other the way starlings do, forming complex patterns of light and shade, somehow—almost inconceivably—avoiding collisions.

"They are Zull," Kata told me. "Usually there are more of them. They come to the Shrouded Mountains to die. Look." She pointed at the ground and I saw there the hollowed and desiccated remains of something that had once been rather humanoid in shape, though multi-limbed. It was lying beside a stream, partially obscured by a dried flap of skin. Tiny maggoty things were crawling from the carcass and disappearing into the fast-flowing water.

The corpse, I realised, belonged to the same order of being as the one I'd discovered in the glade on Koluwai.

"Are Zull dangerous?"

"No. They won't approach us."

By means that escaped me, the Yatsill caused the Ptall'kor to pull itself down to ground level, where it settled in a grassy clearing. They then took up their spears, and Yazziz Yozkulu stepped over to us. "You will remain here with the young ones. We will return with Yarkeen meat for you."

"We shall keep them safe," Kata answered. "May the Saviour grant you success in the hunt."

The Yazziz nodded and rejoined the other five adult Yatsill. They jumped from the side of the Ptall'kor and moved away toward the hills, where one of the Yarkeen tentacles was pulling leaves from the treetops. It reminded me of an elephant's trunk, but with teeth in the opening at its end.

I was surprised by the speed at which the Yatsill moved. With their four oddly jointed legs, they looked somewhat ungainly and walked jerkily, yet progressed rapidly across the sward.

Once they reached the treeline, Yazziz Yozkulu threw one of his spears up at the long appendage. He missed it. One of the other Yatsill made the attempt and also failed. However, a third spear hit its mark, and the Yatsill immediately huddled together and started moving in a manner which caused me to realise that, although I couldn't see it, a thin cord must have been attached to the end of the spear.

With much straining and shouts of encouragement, the creatures hauled on the line and pulled the Yarkeen's limb out of the foliage and down to the ground. The tentacle looked strong enough to send them all flying, yet put up no resistance whatever.

I'd been reporting the action to Clarissa, but now paused and turned to Kata to ask, "Why does it not struggle?"

"Because it doesn't know anything is wrong yet. The Yarkeen is very slow and stupid. If the hunters work fast enough, they will be able to kill it before it's even aware of the danger."

The Yatsill grabbed at the limb and pushed spears through it and deep into the earth, pinning it down.

Looking up at the disc, I could see that it was now leaning toward the hunters and watery ripples were playing across its surface. It seemed impossible that something so colossal could be pegged down with what, to it, must be nothing more than splinters, but it was fast becoming clear to me that the Yarkeen possessed even less substance than a jellyfish.

After ensuring the spears were all secured, the hunters left the edge of the clearing and disappeared among the trees. Nothing more happened for some considerable time, until one of the Koluwaian men cried out, "There! They have another!"

I saw that, farther around the circumference of the Yarkeen, a second limb was being drawn taut, causing the edge of the disc to dip so far down that it brushed the foliage.

Some moments later, I spotted the six hunters swarming into the upper canopy. The Yatsill do not by any means appear arboreal—far from it, in fact—yet they sped through the branches with all the ease and confidence of monkeys. Upon reaching the edge of the Yarkeen's disc, they hauled themselves up onto it and ran toward its centre. It sank and wobbled beneath their weight until they reached the slope where the flesh of the vast creature rose into the central cord.

The Yarkeen finally began to react. The tentacles around its edge flailed about in a distressed manner. The two that were pinned down tore themselves loose.

"They must work quickly now," Kata commented.

"What are they doing?" I asked.

"They are using their fingers to cut through the cord."

I looked at the young Yatsill and noted that the inside edges of their long, restless fingers were sharp and serrated.

"There!" Kata announced.

I turned back in time to see the Yarkeen collapsing downward onto the forest like a silken shroud, while the gas sac, high above it, shot up and rapidly vanished from sight. The Zull that had been circling it wheeled away and disappeared toward the cloud-obscured mountains.

The Yatsill dropped with the disc, but the fall was slow—it floated down rather than plummeted—and as it descended, its tendrils retracted into it, and the entire expanse of flesh withered and shrank before disappearing into the trees.

"They will now cut out the edible organ," the islander said. She rubbed her stomach and smiled. "Excellent! Yarkeen tastes good!"

A short time passed, then the Yatsill returned and clambered aboard the Ptall'kor. Yazziz Yozkulu was holding a long strip of rubbery flesh: a honeycombed diaphanous glob from which a clear jelly oozed.

While the Ptall'kor got moving again, the Yazziz crouched and, with keen-edged fingers, cut the meat into thick slices. These were then distributed among the children, the Koluwaians, and the Wise Ones.

I held the dripping slab that had been handed to me and looked at it doubtfully. Clarissa raised her piece to her nose. "It smells like lavender flowers." She tested it with her tongue. "Mmm! It's sweet! Taste it, Aiden!"

"I'm not sure—" I began, but stopped when my friend took a bite, chewed, swallowed, and sighed with satisfaction.

"It's very good!" she exclaimed. "Aren't you hungry?"

I couldn't deny it. I took a cautious bite. Clarissa was right—it tasted delicious.

o o

The Ptall'kor dragged itself over the forest, following the course of the river. The purple-leafed trees were gradually supplanted by a taller but more widely spaced variety of plant, the base of which resembled a perfectly spherical cactus, about fifteen feet in diameter, out of the top of which grew a thin and high-reaching trunk that divided at its top into horizontal branches. These divided again and again, thinning until the tips were almost invisible. The lower portions of the plant were the colour of suede leather; the upper parts a creamy white.

Gripping at the thick central branches, our vehicle slid over them and entered a second valley, through which the river flowed more rapidly. Its banks were thick with big white flowers that sent clouds of yellow pollen into the air, making the atmosphere misty.

Something was happening to the Yatsill. They'd started to twitch in a peculiar manner. I mentioned this to Kata, and she told me, "The reflections surround them. We will see them soon, too. It normally takes a bit longer for us. The meat is more difficult for us to digest."

Clarissa asked, "What do you mean?"

"Our sight must adjust. The future is—"

Kata suddenly stopped talking and her face went slack. Her

shoulders jerked. I looked at the other islanders and saw they all bore the same blank expression and were making inexplicable movements.

"Clarissa," I said. "I think we've been drugged."

Her reply, whatever it was, sounded like the deep chime of a bell. Its tone soaked into my skin and took the weight out of me. My will to move became entirely insignificant. The atmosphere wafted straight through my body and I saw, all around, intersecting planes and angles, as if the pollen was settling against invisible surfaces. The rays of the suns filled my eyes with gold, and the ringing in my ears merged with the light as my senses blended together. Suddenly I could see the lemony tang of the air; feel the lingering flavour of the Yarkeen meat like petals brushing my skin; smell the sunshine; taste the colours.

Parts of the air became reflective, as if shattered fragments of a giant mirror were floating around me. I saw myself in them, a tall, skinny man with untidy blond hair and pale blue eyes, stumbling along in a fogbound alley. Its surface was cobbled, but with seashells rather than pebbles, and the tenement buildings to either side of it were eccentrically designed and leaned inward in an exaggerated manner.

The atmosphere darkened, the yellow becoming the deepest of reds.

I was in fog. Very dense. I was lost in it. I began to feel afraid.

The soft glow of two gas lamps—or twin suns?—shone through the pall and illuminated the legs of a Yatsill. The creature was on the ground, lying face up. It had been wearing women's clothing, but these garments were now rent and tangled, ripped away from the body, the front of which had been shattered. I felt, heard, smelled the crushed splinters of its carapace, the ripped innards that had been torn from it, the red blood that puddled outwards, oozing along the channels between the inset shells of the road.

A large broken section of the thing's torso swam into sharp focus. It bore a long mark on it—the furrow of an old wound. The corpse was that of Tsillanda Ma'ara.

I looked down and saw that my hands were wrapped around the

grip of a long sword. Its guard was fashioned with ornately carved and curved quillons, and its pommel was large, heavy, and studded.

Blood dripped from the blade.

Darkness pressed against me.

The weapon. Tsillanda Ma'ara. The blood.

"I can't be!" I moaned. "I can't be!"

°°

CHAPTER 4
IMMERSION AND TRANSFORMATION

I lay still, with my eyes shut. The citrus air whispered past my ears. The yodel of an animal echoed from the far distance.

Kata's voice: "Sometimes it is this way. The Valley of Reflections can be difficult."

Clarissa: "You should have warned us. Had I known the meat would affect us in this manner, I would have refused it."

"But it is tradition. The valley cannot be traversed without first tasting Yarkeen."

My mouth felt dry and there was an unpleasant sensation in my stomach, as if I'd swallowed a ball of tobacco. I opened my eyes. "Clarissa."

"Aiden! Are you all right?"

I sat up, blinked, and saw that the Ptall'kor was gliding through an area of rocks and bubbling springs and waterfalls. The air was filled with pollen and steam. My skin was wet with perspiration.

"No, I'm not. Do you remember Jekyll and Hyde?"

"Yes, of course I do."

"There is a darkness in me, Clarissa. I'm afraid it can rise to the surface and take over, just as Hyde did with Jekyll. I think it has a name."

"A name? What are you talking about?"

"It is called Jack the Ripper."

"Aiden, surely you don't mean to suggest that you're the Whitechapel killer?"

"A part of me is. I'm insane. I can't control myself." I indicated the landscape. "And I've been sent to Hell."

"You've been hallucinating."

"I gutted Tsillanda Ma'ara with a sword."

"You did no such thing. Look around you. Are the Yatsill still with us?"

"Yes."

"Is the one called Tsillanda Ma'ara among them?"

"Yes."

"Then obviously you didn't kill it."

"The experience was real."

Kata said, "Not *was*, but *will be*. The valley shows the future, not the past."

"Then it is the same. I saw the dead creature. It had been slaughtered in the same fashion as the Ripper's victims and I was standing over the corpse with a long blade in my hand. The meaning of the vision is obvious—I was responsible for the murders in London and I will be responsible for more."

Clarissa reached out and gently touched me. "Do you actually remember killing any of the women in Whitechapel?"

"No, I black out when Jack possesses me."

"You're talking absolute rot. You're leaping to conclusions with no proper evidence to support them. It's a hysterical reaction. A hallucination is a hallucination and nothing more. The fact that you stumbled upon the corpse of Polly Nichols that night is explanation enough for your vision. Anyone who suffered such a shock would have difficulty in processing the experience. Their memory would return to it again and again."

"Where was I when the other atrocities occurred?" I asked.

"Out performing your duties."

"Alone?"

"Yes, but the fact that I can't vouch for your whereabouts on those nights doesn't make you a maniacal killer. I have absolute faith in your sanity and goodness."

I sat silently digesting this, then asked, "And you? You ate the meat, too. Did you experience a vision?"

"I saw myself driving an autocarriage through a London street. My passenger was wearing a Viennese mask. That's all I remember."

I accepted a skin of water from Kata and slaked my thirst.

"We are close to the Cavern of Immersion," the Koluwaian informed us.

Passing the skin back to her, I examined my hands, expecting to see blood on them. There was none.

Something occurred to me.

"Clarissa, if our visions were of the future, then we will be returning to our own world, for we both saw ourselves in London."

My friend shrugged. "If that's true, then Tsillanda Ma'ara will also be transported to Earth. Do you really believe a creature such as that would be left alone long enough for you to murder it? Of course not! As I said, just a hallucination."

The sound of falling, dripping, and trickling water, which was all around us, took on a hollow quality and the mist suddenly darkened.

"We are entering the cavern," Kata stated.

I peered through the vapour and gathering gloom and saw mighty stalagmites rising up to barely discernible points high overhead. Pools were dotted about. Some of them bubbled and steamed.

The Ptall'kor sank to the ground. Tsillanda Ma'ara crossed to us. "Please escort the children to the pool. We will protect you."

The Wise Ones disembarked and stood with their spears poised. One of them had a long length of rope coiled around its left shoulder.

"Protect us?" I asked Kata. "From what?"

The islander and her fellows began to guide the children off the Ptall'kor.

"We are sheltered from the Eyes of the Saviour here," she replied. "There are Amu'utu."

"What are they?"

"Dangerous."

I helped Clarissa down and we waited while the islanders pushed the children into a tight group then herded them forward along a trail of worn stone. I followed behind, with my companion holding on to my arm. The Wise Ones walked to either side of the path.

"Kata, you keep mentioning the Saviour," I said. "Do you mean God?"

"A god, yes. The Saviour watches over the Yatsill and protects them. The Saviour is good."

As we penetrated deeper into the cavern, the light slowly faded and hundreds of small, glowing indigo-coloured beetles swarmed around our feet, darting in and out, narrowly avoiding being trodden on, as if playing a game of "dare." At first, I took each step awkwardly as I attempted to avoid them, but then I noticed that Clarissa—who, unable to see the insects, was moving more naturally—hadn't crushed a single one, so I relaxed a little, allowed the insects to look after their own welfare, and turned my attention to our surroundings.

The walls and roof of the vault were closing in around us. The space was pierced through by a great many stalagmites and stalactites, and was increasingly illuminated by the little beetles, which streamed across the rock in incandescent rivulets, shining through the roiling mist, replacing the watery yellow light of the exterior landscape with an intensely shimmering blue.

"Might you risk removing your blindfold, Clarissa?" I asked.

She shook her head. "I sense enough through my eyelids to know we're surrounded by a peculiar radiance, and a gentle one, but it remains too much for me."

The path inclined downward.

We trekked along it for maybe half an hour before a gurgling moan echoed from somewhere ahead of us.

My hair stood on end.

"What was that?" Clarissa whispered.

"Amu'utu," one of the Koluwaians answered.

I glanced at Yazziz Yozkulu. All the Wise Ones had crouched down and were now absolutely motionless, with their spears at the ready.

Kata and the other islanders held the children back. The Yatsill youngsters stood quietly. Even their fingers stopped wiggling.

A Koluwaian man hissed at me, "Don't move!"

I felt Clarissa's fingers tighten on my arm.

A few yards in front of us, the path curved out of sight, disappearing behind an outcropping of rock. From around that bend, another awful moan now sounded, along with a scraping and the rattle of falling stones. There was something dreadfully uncanny about the noises. I trembled uncontrollably and would have taken to my heels were it not for Clarissa's firm grip.

A huger spidery leg came into view, but, bizarrely, it angled up to the cavern roof rather than down to the floor. It was a bluish-white, with long thorns projecting downward from its leading edge. I tried to back away but Kata whispered, "No! It will sense you!"

I froze—with terror, I admit—for the creature was coming into full view now.

The wormy blue-coloured body of the Amu'utu was around fifteen feet high and shaped somewhat like an upside-down cone. Three multi-jointed legs extended from the upper, thicker part of it and disappeared into the mist and shadows above us, where their ends clung to the ceiling by means that were hidden from view. As it moved, small fragments of rock dropped from above it. The thinner end of the creature, which hung six feet above the ground, flowered outward into a complex arrangement of snappers, teeth, jaws, and hook-like appendages. Its skin was semi-transparent and fluttering organs could be glimpsed pulsating within it, as could the blood, which radiated a milky blue as it throbbed through arteries and veins.

The monster swung slowly and deliberately toward our group then stopped. Pinkish light suddenly flowed in waves across its skin and I had the distinct impression that it was extending its senses into the cavern, groping around with them, seeking movement, seeking food—seeking us!

The Yatsill and Koluwaians remained motionless, as did my companion and I.

A tremendously long spiny tongue slid out of the Amu'utu's twitching maw, its end slithering to the ground where it began to feel about, like a blind serpent.

All of a sudden, without any indication they were about to do so, the Wise Ones scattered, each of them scurrying in a different direction.

The Amu'utu let loose a tremendous whistle, sounding exactly like a locomotive venting steam. The tongue whipped up, shot out, coiled around one of the Yatsill, and started to drag it toward the flexing jaws. Its prey—it was the individual with the rope around its shoulder—kicked and struggled and cried out, "My name is Tokula Pathamay, and I die untaken!"

"Untaken!" Yazziz Yozkulu shouted. "The Saviour has favoured you! You will be delivered to Phenadoor!"

The Wise Ones rushed in, jabbing their spears into the giant beast, aiming for the visible organs. Blood spurted and the Amu'utu shook and shuddered. A second tongue flopped out of its maw and wrapped around Tokula Pathamay's four legs, yanking the Yatsill up into the jaws, which, with a horrendous crunch, closed over the victim's head. I choked back a cry of horror and was almost pulled off my feet by Clarissa, who hissed, "Tell me, Aiden! Tell me what's happening!"

The Amu'utu's colour darkened to a sickly green and its whistle changed into a weird clanging. It dropped the shattered remains of the Yatsill and slumped closer to the ground. One of its three legs lost its grip on the cavern roof and folded as it descended. Then the whole thing suddenly fell and hit the floor with a squishy impact. Yazziz Yozkulu led the Wise Ones as they charged at the stricken monster and plunged their weapons deep into its body.

"An animal attacked us," I whispered. "A demonic thing. The Yatsill are killing it but they've lost one of their number."

A final chime escaped the Amu'utu. It gave a twitch and died.

Lifting dripping spears above their heads, the Yatsill chorused: "Tokula Pathamay! Tokula Pathamay! Killed unseen but untaken! Untaken! Untaken! Tokula Pathamay shall be given unto Phenadoor!"

I turned to Kata. "What do they mean?"

"The Saviour did not witness Tokula Pathamay perish," she answered. "Even so, it is better for a Wise One to die thus than the other way. The remains will be carried with us to Yatsillat and there deposited in Phenadoor. It is a rare honour for a Wise One."

"Other way?" Clarissa asked.

"Yes. Tokula Pathamay will never be other than Tokula Pathamay."

With that incomprehensible reply, Kata turned away, and she and her people repositioned themselves around the children.

The Wise Ones spread out, and after retrieving the rope from their fallen comrade, left the corpse behind and led us farther into the cave.

For what felt like hours, we descended along the path, our party illuminated from all directions by the millions upon millions of tiny beetles, so bright now that the mist itself glowed blue as it thickened around us. The sound of bubbling water increased, echoing from the walls and ceiling.

"I can't keep this up for much longer," my companion said quietly.

"Are your legs paining you, Clarissa?"

"Dreadfully."

Kata, overhearing this, pointed ahead. "The place of Immersion."

I guided Clarissa to a rock, and as she sat on it, told her, "The path has ended at the edge of a pool. Steam is rising from it and I cannot see the far bank."

Tsillanda Ma'ara approached, the ends of its four legs click-clacking over the rock. "You are strange," it said, "and this is a sensitive time, therefore I shall assign to you no duty other than to keep watch and alert us should another Amu'utu draw near."

I nodded.

The Yatsill reached over its shoulder and pulled a spear from its harness. "Take this."

"I'm sorry," I said. "I have no experience with weapons."

The creature's black, expressionless eyes glittered. It pointed a finger. "This is the sharp end. Stick it into any Amu'utu that comes close enough." And with that, Tsillanda Ma'ara pushed the spear into my hands, snapped its fingers together in what I took to be a sign of dismissal, turned its back, and stalked away.

"Was that humour?" Clarissa asked.

"I haven't the foggiest notion."

I watched and kept up a running commentary as Kata and the other islanders shepherded the children to the edge of the pool. Yazziz Yozkulu stepped forward with the long rope in its hand, tied the end around one of the juveniles, and said, "It is your time of Immersion. You will emerge from the waters Wise or Shunned."

The child turned its head and looked at the Yazziz, and though in size and form they were a match, with nothing but minor details to distinguish them from one another, there was something in the youngster's countenance that I was surprised to find myself interpreting as a sort of bemused innocence.

Could it be that I was starting to recognise expression in the ghastly features of the Yatsill? It seemed impossible, for they were entirely inhuman, yet, indisputably, something about the child struck me as immature and ingenuous.

Yazziz Yozkulu pushed it into the steaming water and it sank like a stone.

Perhaps two minutes passed, then the Yatsill hauled on the rope and pulled the youngster out of the pool. It stood meekly while he announced, "You are Shunned. Do not feel sad. You are favoured with a place in Phenadoor."

The process was repeated with a second child, then a third. They both joined the Shunned, though why Yazziz Yozkulu made this decision eluded me, for they both left the water exactly as they'd been upon entering it.

However, when the fourth child was dragged from the pool, it emerged limp and unconscious.

"Tsillanda Ma'ara, this one has been made Wise."

Tsillanda Ma'ara answered, "Denied a place in Phenadoor. Now a vehicle for the Saviour. Responsible for the protection of all. It is a sacrifice. It is an honour." The Yatsill signalled to Kata. The Koluwaian and three of her fellows stepped over to the stricken child, gently lifted it, and carried it away.

The ritual continued until every child had been in the water. Of

the nine, six were declared Shunned. Three were pulled out unconscious and Wise.

"As ever, fewer and fewer each cycle," Yazziz Yozkulu muttered. "I
pray those who travelled ahead of us have met with greater success."

"I feel it is unlikely," Tsillanda Ma'ara responded. "However, we
cannot know what the Saviour intends, and can but trust that there
is purpose behind our dwindling numbers."

A stone rattled behind me. I turned. The fat body of an Amu'utu
descended out of the mist, its intricate jaws flexing and quivering.
I gave a shout of fright, stepped backwards, tripped over the end of
my spear, and went sprawling onto my back.

Before I even realised what was happening, my right ankle was
clamped tightly in a coiled tongue and I was being dragged yelling
and screaming across the ground.

The Yatsill came racing over and Tsillanda Ma'ara shouted,
"Declare yourself! Do not die with your name unspoken!"

"I don't want to die at all!" I screeched. "Help me! Help me!"

The Amu'utu emitted a high-pitched whistle as thrown spears
pierced its flesh. I felt stones grinding against my back, spines
digging into my ankle, a wooden shaft in my hand. The spear! I was
still holding it!

With sheer terror powering my inadequate muscles, I forced
myself into a sitting position and jabbed the spear into the horrible
appendage that gripped my leg. The cavern suddenly whirled around
me as I was flung into the air. My back impacted against something
soft, my head against something hard, and I blacked out.

I think I was oblivious for mere moments. When my senses came
fluttering back, I sat up and saw the Amu'utu on the ground with
the Yatsill gathered around it, stabbing it over and over.

The islanders were guarding the children, with the exception of
Kata, who was standing at the edge of the pool, gazing into it.

I looked around.

"Kata! Kata! Where is Clarissa?"

The Koluwaian pointed down.

"You knocked her in."

I leaped to my feet. "What? She's in the water? Get her out!"

"It is forbidden to all but Yatsill."

Without thinking, I took three steps and dove into the pool. In the split second before I hit the water, it occurred to me that I would boil to death, for it was bubbling and producing thick clouds of steam. However, it was not heat that assaulted me but freezing cold, though in the first instant it was impossible to distinguish between either extreme.

I didn't stop to wonder why hot clouds were billowing up from icy water, but, fighting to overcome the shock to my system, I rose to the surface, sucked in a deep breath, then forced myself under, kicked hard, and peered around through slitted eyes. Blue light glimmered faintly in the upper reaches of the pool but it quickly became dark as I pushed downward. Tiny creatures wriggled against my skin. I groped around until my lungs were close to bursting, then propelled myself up, took another breath, and dived again.

Three times I went down and failed to locate my friend. On the fourth, I was so filled with despair, so afraid of being left alone in this world of grotesqueries and primitives, that I half-decided to stay under and let myself drown.

The fingers of my right hand encountered flesh, slid across an elbow, and closed tightly over a forearm. Mentally, I praised the God I no longer believed in and dragged Clarissa Stark to the surface, hauled her out of the pool, and collapsed beside her.

Kata leaned over me. As if from a great distance, she said, "She is alive, but you have committed a sacrilegious act. Perhaps the Yatsill will banish you to the Shelf Lands."

I didn't respond, but lay gasping, clinging on to consciousness. I'd passed out too many times since my arrival on Ptallaya. It had been a welcome release, but not one I'd allow myself while my friend was in danger.

I got to my knees and bent over her prone form. I called her name and shook her gently but she didn't stir. Closer examination revealed a long swelling above her eyebrows. Perhaps she'd knocked her head while falling. She was breathing steadily, though, so the injury probably wasn't serious.

Kata touched my shoulder. "We must leave the cavern now. I will help you with her."

I nodded miserably. We lifted Clarissa between us and bore her rather awkwardly along the path. The Yatsill trekked ahead, with the Koluwaians following behind, bearing the three senseless youngsters.

The party retraced its steps without incident, stopping only to pick up the body of Tokula Pathamay. The return journey felt interminable, and I could have wept with relief when I finally saw the Ptall'kor and, moments later, we climbed aboard it.

Yazziz Yozkulu approached and said, "Lay your friend beside the newly Wise. We will look after her. Do not be concerned. They will all recover."

"I'll stay with her."

"It is not necessary."

"I insist."

"As you wish."

The Ptall'kor moved out of the mouth of the cavern and back along the Valley of Reflections. This time there were no hallucinations during our passage through it, and the only vision of the future I saw was the dreadful possibility that I might find myself on this strange world without Clarissa.

I placed a hand on her arm, gazed down at her blindfold, and whispered, "Please, wake up. Please! I cannot stand to be alone."

o o

We were crossing a landscape of flowery hills and fat, sparsely distributed trees. The suns were behind us, still low. Overhead, long ribbony things were corkscrewing through the air, flying northward.

I didn't know how much time had passed. I'd been in a virtual stupor since Clarissa's accident—overcome by exhaustion but too concerned to sleep.

She was still unconscious.

The Wise Ones—Yazziz Yozkulu, Tsillanda Ma'ara, and the others—had been oddly quiet since we'd emerged from the valley. They appeared to be in some sort of deep contemplation—or, like me, in a trance—and were squatting motionlessly with their heads cocked at a curious angle, as if listening to something.

Fatigue finally won out. I flopped down, closed my eyes, and dropped into a dreamless void.

When I awoke, it was to find Yazziz Yozkulu squatting over me.

"How are you feeling, old thing? Sound as a bell, I hope! I say! What *is* a bell, anyway?"

He asked the question in clear, well-enunciated English.

"Par—pardon?"

"Ah! Somewhat befuddled, hey? Not surprising! You've been snoring away for an eternity. An *eternity*, I say! What! What!"

"I—how—um—you're speaking English!"

"Quite so! Quite so! And what a versatile lingo it is, too! Bally marvellous! Harrumph!"

I sat up, gaping at him.

The Yatsill waggled its long fingers. "Humph! Humph! Having adopted it, I feel it only right and proper that I should also assume a suitable moniker. *Yazziz* somewhat equates to *chief*, though I think I prefer *colonel*, but *Yozkulu* has no equivalent. Humph! What's your opinion of *Momentous Spearjab*?"

"Mom—Mom—what?"

"As a name, old boy. As a name."

"It's—it's—unusual."

"Ah! Splendid! Ha ha! Then it's settled! How do you jolly well do? I'm Colonel Momentous Spearjab."

The creature extended its hand. Hesitatingly, I took it and shook it, conscious of the sharp-edged digits pressing against my palm.

"I'm—I'm Aiden Fleischer." I looked down at Clarissa. "She hasn't awoken?"

"Ah, the redoubtable Miss Stark! Let us summon Mademoiselle Crockery Clattersmash. She's rather a medical expert, don't you know!"

The colonel waved at the Yatsill I'd known as Tsillanda Ma'ara, who was standing at the stern of the vessel. "Yoo-hoo! Mademoiselle! Would you join us, please?"

Colonel, Mademoiselle—the titles suggested genders, though I had made the assumption, perhaps unduly, that the Yatsill were hermaphroditic.

Tsillanda Ma'ara—now Crockery Clattersmash—scuttled over and greeted me in English. "Hello, Mr. Fleischer. Your friend is comatose but no need to fret—it's a normal reaction. She'll awaken before we reach Yatsillat."

"A normal reaction to what?"

"Why, to being made an Aristocrat—what we used to call a Wise One. You're very lucky she was or we'd have to banish you for your transgression. As it is, we suspect you were following the will of the Saviour when you entered the pool."

Clarissa muttered something unintelligible, shifted slightly, and groaned. I clearly heard the bones of her legs creak.

"I don't understand. Made an Aristocrat?"

Colonel Spearjab gave my back a rather too hearty slap. "Ha ha!" he exclaimed. "My good man, you'll be waiting on her hand and foot from now on! Hand and bally foot, I say!"

"But what has happened to her? For that matter, what's happened to you? You sound like an entirely different—er—person."

"Growth! Betterment! It comes to those the Saviour looks kindly upon! Indeed it does!" He threw his head back and took a deep breath. "Smell that fresh air! Sublime! Simply sublime! Harrumph! What!"

Mademoiselle Clattersmash wriggled her fingers. "Miss Stark will recover in due course. Don't worry yourself. Look." She reached down and pulled at the top of Clarissa's blindfold, gently yanking it until the eyebrows were exposed. The wide bump that had marked my friend's forehead before was gone, replaced by two small lumps, one above each brow, exactly like the nascent horns displayed by the Wise Ones, or "Aristocrats" as they now called themselves. I glanced at the three inert children and saw that they, too, had somehow acquired the protrusions.

I shook my head. "I'm sorry, but I'm still at a complete loss."

"Of course you are," Mademoiselle Clattersmash responded. "How could you not be? You haven't the wherewithal, I'm afraid. But there's no shame in being a Servant, Mr. Fleischer."

"A servant? What makes you think I'm a servant? I'm a priest! My title is *Reverend*, not *Mr.*!"

The Yatsill made a rapid clacking noise that sounded like a close approximation of laughter.

"Really! My dear sir! *I'm* the priest! Now don't you go getting ideas above your station! It's unseemly! Very bad form! Oh, dear me, yes!"

"If you would simply explain—"

Colonel Spearjab interrupted. "Humph! Mademoiselle, you were obviously quite right in your assertion that these two are a dissonance. Perhaps, then, we should postpone any conversation about the roles they will play in our society until we have arrived at Yatsillat. What! What! I'm certain the Circle of Elders—"

"The House of Lords," Mademoiselle Clattersmash corrected.

"Ah, yes. I do beg your pardon, the House of Lords—"

"And the Council of Magicians."

"Absolutely! Indubitably! Most certainly! Ha ha! I am certain that both august bodies will be eager to interview our new friends, so let us leave the questions and decisions until then, hey, what? Our responsibility, for now, should be nothing more than to get back home as rapidly as possible."

Mademoiselle Clattersmash nodded. "Very well. I acquiesce." She turned to me. "You'll not object to nursing Miss Stark, *Mr.* Fleischer?"

"Of course not!"

"Marvellous!" Colonel Spearjab enthused. He clapped his hands together. "Let us enjoy the journey, then! Smell that air! As fresh as a daisy! As a *daisy*, I say!" He looked down at me. "Incidentally, what in blue blazes *is* a daisy?"

o o

I was confused. The Yatsill were speaking English and I had no idea how or why.

The Aristocrats had taken on outlandish names: Colonel Momentous Spearjab; Mademoiselle Crockery Clattersmash; Sir Gracious Whipstripes; The Right Honourable Stirpot Quickly; and Lady Falldown Bruisebad. The Shunned—who were now, extraordinarily, referred to as "the Working Class"—went by the less extravagant appellations of Timothy Almost, Nicely Lookout, Sally Furniture, Dentworth Frosty, Jane Cough-Cough, and Harry Flopsoon.

It was madness. Total madness.

And the journey went on and on. The Ptall'kor clutched at grass and pulled itself over savannah, clutched at reeds and pulled itself along river courses, clutched at rocks and pulled itself across hillsides, clutched at trees and pulled itself over forests.

Mile after mile.

The three unconscious children regained their senses and I immediately realised they'd been transformed. Now, rather than sitting quietly like their "Working Class" fellows, they conversed in English with the other Aristocrats.

The Koluwaians retained the names they'd had before and still spoke their own language, to which the Yatsill switched when addressing them. The islanders were repeatedly referred to as "Servants," and I was counted among their number.

I was not inclined to ponder over these mysteries. I was too concerned for Clarissa, who remained unconscious and appeared to be in extreme pain. She writhed and jerked and moaned and whimpered constantly, and all the while her bones produced sickening creaks and crunches and crackles. Something was happening to her, that much was certain, but it took me a long time to recognise what.

Realisation, when it came, was akin to a revelation. I was witnessing a miracle. My friend was being *corrected*.

Her bones were straightening. Her surgical scars were fading. The white streaks in her hair were darkening. And it finally became apparent that she was growing taller.

I must have slept at least fifteen times, and if the period between each sleep was the length of an Earth day, then it took more than a fortnight to travel from the Shrouded Mountains to Yatsillat.

Clarissa Stark awoke on the equivalent, I estimated, of the twelfth day.

She sat up and stretched. Her limbs were long and, dare I say it, magnificent. Her shape had altered so much that her trousers now only reached her calves and her shirt had ripped. Her black hair cascaded down to the middle of her straight back. Her skin was deeply tanned but smooth and unmarked.

"I feel funny," she said.

I tried to speak but could only emit a croak.

"Good gracious, Aiden! Whatever is the matter with you? Have you caught a cold?"

"You—you—you look t-tremendous!" I stammered. "I mean—it's unbelievable!"

She frowned, then uttered a small cry and put a hand to her blindfold. "What are these things on my forehead?"

"You were knocked into the pool. I dragged you out. When you emerged, there were little bumps over your eyes, like the Aristocrats possess."

"Aristocrats?"

"The Wise Ones."

"But why do you call them aristocrats?"

Ignoring the question, I blurted, "Clarissa! You've been mended! Your legs and back are straight! You are beautiful! Utterly beautiful!"

She made a noise, almost a bleat, ran her hands over her legs, then reached over her shoulder and tried to touch her spine.

"Put your hand on my back!" she cried out. "Please! Do it! Do it!"

I placed my palm against the small of her back and slid it slowly up over her shirt, following her spine to the nape of her neck.

She collapsed forward, until her head was resting on her knees, and began to sob. I put my arms around her.

"How? How? How?" she whimpered.

"I can't explain it," I said. "Your eyes—are they repaired, too?"

"No—even the small amount of light that penetrates the blind-fold and my eyelids is uncomfortable."

"Don't worry about that, dear thing," came a voice. "We'll have you sorted out with a new pair of goggles in no time at all. Humph! What!"

I looked up and saw Colonel Spearjab standing over us.

"It's all change at Yatsillat!" he declared. "Look at that!" He pointed ahead, in the direction the Ptall'kor was travelling.

"Who is speaking, Aiden?" Clarissa asked.

"I say! Forgive me, Miss Stark!" Spearjab said. "Most rude! Most rude! I am Colonel Momentous Spearjab, formerly known as Yazziz Yozkulu. What! I'm very pleased to make your acquaintance!"

"Yazziz? That's you? Speaking English?"

"*Colonel*, my dear. *Colonel*. But yes, absolutely it's me, and I'm perfectly thrilled to see that you've made a full recovery. You appear to be as fit as the proverbial fiddle, whatever that may be. Ha ha! Harrumph!"

I tore my eyes away from the scene ahead of us and said, "Clarissa, there's a low mountain range on the horizon. I see excavations of some sort. What is it, Colonel?"

"We are once again approaching the jolly old Mountains That Gaze Upon Phenadoor, Mr. Fleischer," Spearjab answered enthusias-tically, "but the other end of the range, what! And those excavations are quarries. *Quarries*, I say! We're mining rocks and minerals, you see, to make bricks and iron and glass and whatnot. By the time we reach our destination, our artisans will have manufactured a pair of dark lenses for Miss Stark. Humph! Now, if you'll please excuse me, I must rally the troops, so to speak. I smell Quee-tan! Ah, yes! What! Ha ha! So we'll stop for a hunt soon. Have you ever tasted Quee-tan meat, Mr. Fleischer? Ah, no, probably not! The confounded beasts once infested all the trees in this region but have become extremely rare. Almost extinct. It's a crying shame, for they taste absolutely delicious! *Delicious*, I say! Oh well. What! What! Tally-ho!"

He scuttled away.

"You taught them our language?" Clarissa asked.

"No. I have no idea how they learned it. One minute they were all speaking Koluwaian; the next, English!"

"Puzzle after puzzle!" my friend exclaimed. "Help me up, would you?"

I stood, reached down, gripped her hands, and assisted her to her feet.

She cried out, "There's no pain! No pain at all! I feel—I feel *wonderful!*"

"And you look it. You're nearly as tall as I am!"

Her fingers clenched around mine, and in that pressure there was a wealth of inexpressible emotion.

We stood together and I resumed my descriptions of the passing landscape. The Ptall'kor was now sliding across fields of lilac-coloured heather toward a broad band of tangled jungle, beyond which I could see cultivated pastures laid out like a patchwork quilt, stretching all the way to the distant horizon.

Eventually, our conveyance came to rest at the edge of the trees. Colonel Spearjab disembarked with his fellows—including the three newly made Aristocrats, but excluding Clarissa, despite that she'd apparently joined their ranks—and they plunged into the undergrowth with spears poised.

While we awaited their return, I continued to examine the terrain, telling my companion about everything I saw. "There's something strange about the sky to the left of the mountain range," I noted. "It's darker. There's a sort of dirty smudge in the air."

"Perhaps it marks the position of Yatsillat," Clarissa responded. "If they're manufacturing glass and iron and so forth, they must have foundries and factories."

"I don't know whether I fear our destination or look forward to it," I replied. "This journey has been interminable but at least I've become somewhat accustomed to it. With travelling everything is transitory—whatever you can't accept is soon left behind. When we reach the city or town or whatever it is, then we have to face up to the challenge of living there, perhaps for a long time."

"Or permanently."

I didn't answer, not wanting to contemplate such a circumstance, though it also occurred to me that, in fact, I had nothing on Earth to go back to.

For some considerable time, Clarissa continued to ask questions about our environment, which I answered as best I could. Then she suddenly interrupted me with the exclamation, "Ah! They're returning already! The hunt was successful!"

I could see no sign of the warriors. "You can hear them?"

"No."

"Then how do you know?"

Clarissa furrowed her brow. "It's—I just—I *feel* them, Aiden."

Before I could probe this statement further, Spearjab's party reappeared, carrying between them an ovoid-shaped creature from which multiple flexible appendages extended. When they reached the side of the Ptall'kor, they squatted down and set to work ripping the thing's skin away from the white flesh beneath. They then slit it open and scooped out the guts. As I watched this, I felt cold fingers gripping my spine, for it was impossible not to think of the corpse of Polly Nichols with intestines exposed, which, of course, led me again to a contemplation of my hallucination and the monstrousness I suspected was lurking in the shadowy regions of my soul.

The Quee-tan was sliced up, and steaks, like dense crabmeat, were distributed.

With the exception of our meal in the Valley of Reflections, we had thus far subsisted only on berries, nuts, and fruits. The prospect of flesh, in light of my previous experience, was not one I welcomed. I turned to Kata and said, "I'm hungry but I cannot eat this if it will affect me like the Yarkeen."

"It won't," she answered. "This is not sacred. It will fill your belly but nothing more. Enjoy it—Quee'tan meat has become a very rare treat."

So, cautiously, I tucked into the raw flesh. It was delicious.

After we ate, the entire party slept, and it must have been for a considerable time, for when we were awoken, the slow-moving suns were noticeably higher in the sky.

It was the yodelling of animals that brought us to consciousness. A pack of around twenty glossy green creatures with ribbed exoskeletons, bulbous heads, and eight spidery limbs apiece were passing close by. They were leaping like gazelles, clicking the mandibles that extended from their pointed faces, and emitting wolfish yips, yaps, and yowls.

"They are Tiskeen," Mademoiselle Clattersmash told us. "They are harmless at the moment."

We embarked upon what proved to be the final leg of our long voyage.

As the Ptall'kor hauled itself over the jungle and across the cultivated fields, the uncertainty and fear I felt concerning our destination and eventual fate were kept at bay by my delight at witnessing Clarissa's transformation. Again and again, she stretched and danced and cavorted, sometimes coming perilously close to the edge of the living platform, and evidently causing much bemusement among the Aristocrats.

"I say! What in the name of the Saviour is she up to?" Colonel Spearjab asked me.

I regarded him, still astounded to hear the English language coming from his repulsive vertical mouth. "She's simply enjoying the sensation of healthy limbs," I said. "For most of her life she has been malformed and suffering pain."

"The sensation of healthy limbs," Spearjab echoed. He suddenly straightened his four legs, which caused him to almost double in height, and threw out his long arms, waggling his fingers. The outer lips of his mouth peeled open and the inner beak pushed outward.

"Gaaaah!" he cried out, then sank back down and said, "My goodness, that's very nice indeed! I shall recommend it to my colleagues. Hey? What? Harrumph!"

He scuttled away, leaving me to ponder the fact that I comprehended nothing—*nothing!*—of this world called Ptallaya and its demented inhabitants.

Throughout the remainder of the journey, Spearjab and the Aristocrats occasionally burst into spontaneous bouts of stretching and dancing, looking so utterly ludicrous that I couldn't help but laugh. Between that and Clarissa's obvious happiness, I might almost say that it was an enjoyable period, though whatever pleasure I felt most definitely was not shared by the Koluwaians. For some unaccountable reason, Kata and her group had become rather morose and silent, and, if anything, their mood blackened the nearer we got to Yatsillat.

I asked her what was wrong.

"It is all changing," she said. "The new ways are not our ways. The new language is not our language. We are afraid these things will be difficult to learn before we are released. How can we serve efficiently when we don't understand anything?"

"I'm the one who doesn't understand. Why are things changing, Kata?"

Her deep brown eyes slid away from me. I followed her gaze and saw she was looking at Clarissa.

"Because of her."

"Clarissa? What has Clarissa got to do with it? She knows no more of this world than I."

"It is not what she knows of this world. It is what this world knows of her."

I pressed her to explain this but she would say no more, lapsing into a sullen silence.

The countryside slipped past, field after field of grains and sweet-smelling herbs, and as we progressed, strange dwellings came into sight, clustered together and reminiscent of papery wasp nests but big enough to house many Yatsill. Kata explained that these were nurseries filled with the young, who grew to maturity with astonishing rapidity.

Yatsill farmers—dressed in frocks of coarse unpatterned linen—were busy tending to the crops. They paid us no attention as we glided past.

We made three short stops, during which Mademoiselle Clattersmash disembarked to collect herbs. Spearjab informed us that she used them to manufacture poultices for the treatment of wounds, and also to brew various concoctions that, when mixed with the Dar'sayn liquid we'd seen collected from the fruits in the Forest of Indistinct Murmurings, produced specific effects during meditations.

The farms were on a slight gradient, the land rising smoothly ahead of us, so the horizon appeared to be getting closer and closer as we drew nearer to the crest of the ridge lying across our path. We could now clearly see, on the other side of it, the tops of towers and chimneys, the latter sending plumes of smoke and steam into the air.

To our right, the slope steepened into much rougher terrain, which wrinkled upward in increasingly jagged waves until it became the range of quarry-scarred mountains. Three of the four moons dotted the heavens above the peaks, faint circles in the yellow sky.

"What! What!" Colonel Spearjab declared loudly. "Home sweet home! Hurrah!"

As he made this pronouncement, a breathtaking vista opened up before us, for the slope led not to the brow of a ridge but to the edge of the continent, and to the right and left the ground dropped away, a sheer cliff at least a mile high, with a sparkling emerald sea lapping at its distant base. Into this precipice a vast semicircular bay intruded, the land inside it descending to the sea in a series of nine colossal steps, and as I looked down upon them, I saw they were swarming with Yatsill. About a third of the terraces were heavily forested and the trees were filled with houses in the Koluwaian style, but it appeared that the forest was in the process of being cleared and a city the size of London built in its place. The size of *London*! It was simply staggering! The creatures, with the same wondrous efficiency of termites and ants, were constructing, at an apparently preternatural pace, what had taken centuries for my species to achieve—a vast, sophisticated city. And it was expanding before my eyes!

The topmost terrace was already entirely stripped of trees and looked to be a manufacturing district, for there were many large brick buildings and foundries with tall chimneystacks belching out the sooty clouds so symptomatic of industry.

The next level, which was half-complete, contained row after row of humble abodes, similar in size and arrangement—or so I later learned from Clarissa—to the "two-ups, two-downs" seen in England's northern cities, such as Manchester and Leeds.

Next came a terrace of spires and minarets, rising from what I took to be temples and administrative establishments, all constructed—or being constructed—from a white variety of stone much like marble.

The fourth, fifth, and sixth steps were being made into attractive residential districts, with many a square patch of greenery and long roads lined with shops.

The seventh level was partially landscaped and already resembled a dreamlike version of Regent's Park.

The eighth terrace, Colonel Spearjab revealed, was given over to barracks for the City Guard and workshops for artisans, while the ninth, and smallest, was an almost self-contained fishing village.

The most incredible aspect of the whole city, though, was the speed at which it was supplanting the forest. Every single part of it looked brand new, and every single one of its inhabitants appeared to be involved in its construction.

"Magnificent!" the colonel bellowed. "Welcome to Yatsillat! *Welcome*, I say! Ha ha!" He pointed at the sea. "And behold, Phenadoor!"

A number of very wide and steeply sloping avenues cut through the terraces all the way from the top of the city to the bottom. Our Ptall'kor passed into one that was lined with trees. It was paved with colourful cobbles, which, upon closer inspection, froze the blood in my veins, for they were hard shells rather than pebbles, meaning the murder I foresaw in my Yarkeen vision would transpire here, not in London. However, I was quickly—and thankfully—distracted from this disturbing thought by the crowds that gathered along the sides of the avenue to cheer our arrival. They were Yatsill but, unlike those we travelled with, they were clothed—and in such a bizarre manner that I repeatedly rubbed my eyes and pinched myself, half-convinced I was hallucinating again. Those creatures that stood in the front rows of onlookers wore four-legged trousers or billowing skirts. Their upper mussel-shell-shaped bodies were encased in colourful waistcoats over which long jackets were draped, some male in design, others female. Viennese masks covered their faces—all with four eye-holes, all resembling long-beaked birds or bejewelled human faces or Pierrots or Punchinello—while their heads were adorned with frilly bonnets or top hats, though in the latter case many among the crowd were throwing theirs into the air while yelling, "Hooray! Hooray! Three cheers for the new Aristocrats! Hup hup hurrah! Hup hup hurrah! Hup hup hurrah!"

The rearmost spectators were rather less extravagantly dressed, their "suits" being of a baggier cut, their heads adorned with cloth caps or drab bonnets, and their masks simplistic depictions of a human face.

The hullabaloo and dazzling sights so jumbled my senses that it was impossible for me to properly explain everything to poor Clarissa. Perhaps she understood this, for she stood at my side and gripped my hand tightly, as if to shackle me to the reality she represented—the reality of Earth and home—and prevent me from drifting off into realms of madness. Had she not done so, the sheer lunacy I was now witnessing might have pushed me over the brink.

"Hallo hallo!" Spearjab exclaimed. "There's trouble!"

He pointed to a small group of Yatsill who, unlike the majority, were unclothed. They were chanting, "Down with the dissonance! No to change! Back to the trees! No to change!"

"Backward thinkers!" he said dismissively. "Ignore the blighters. Only a bally fool stands in the way of progress. Hey? What? Harrumph! Now then, I propose a tour of the new city. But first we must stop at a tailor's. I feel positively naked! *Naked*, I say! It won't do at all!"

Mademoiselle Clattersmash placed a hand on his shoulder. "No, my dear. The matter of the dissonance must be addressed at once." She pointed at Clarissa and me. "We should deliver these two to the House of Lords immediately."

"Oh, very well, very well. Humph! Humph! Humph! But I insist that the acquisition of clothing must follow right afterwards! What!"

"I shan't argue," Clattersmash said. She raised her hands to her face and wriggled all her fingers excitedly. "I'm positively eager to pick out a dress!"

The Ptall'kor took us down to the third terrace, turned right onto a wide thoroughfare, and came to rest outside a monumental white edifice that reminded me a little of St. Paul's Cathedral.

Two figures were standing on the steps that led up to the building's ornate entrance. One, a Yatsill, was wearing top hat and tails, with a white shirt and perfectly enormous bow tie. While his trousers were black, as one would expect in such an outfit, the jacket and hat were pink. His mask resembled the face of a heron, with a long pointed beak.

The other was plainly a Koluwaian male, though, like the witch doctor Iriputiz, he was of a considerably taller and skinnier build than the average islander. He was wrapped from head to toe in purple robes, had a cloth of the same colour wound around his head, and wore a Pierrot mask over his face.

"Saviour favour you," the Yatsill said to Spearjab as we disembarked. "It's bloody good to see you again, Yazziz Yozkulu. Welcome to New Yatsillat!"

"Colonel Momentous Spearjab now, Prime Minister. Humph! And you, sir?"

"I have settled upon Lord Upright Brittleback."

Spearjab bowed. "Tip-top! Very nice! Very nice indeed! And *New* Yatsillat! How wonderfully appropriate! I sensed a great deal, of course, but not that particular morsel! Ha ha!" He waved a hand toward Clattersmash. "My Lord, you know Tsillanda Ma'ara, now Mademoiselle Crockery Clattersmash. Harrumph!"

"I do indeed."

Clattersmash held out a hand and the prime minister reached to shake it, hesitated, then took it by the fingertips and raised it to the end of his mask's beak, giving it a light peck. "You chose the female gender, then, Mademoiselle?"

"I did," she replied. "It occurred to me that those in the Council of Magicians would mostly select the male. I thought it might give me an advantage to go the other way."

"Shrewd, as always," Brittleback responded. He turned to Spearjab and flexed his fingers toward the purple-clad Koluwaian. "You know Mr. Sepik, of course."

"Harrumph! Back from one of your long meditations, hey, Mr. Sepik!"

The Koluwaian bowed and said, in a whispery voice, "I serve best when refreshed, Colonel. My occasional withdrawals are a spiritual necessity."

"Humph! If you say so, old thing! I can't quite see how not being present makes you a better Servant, but there you are! There you are! And you've learned this new-fangled lingo, too, hey? Jolly good show! Fast work! What! And the togs?"

Brittleback gestured toward the tall islander and said, "Mr. Sepik suggested that, in keeping with the changes to our society, his kind should be represented in Parliament, which I thought was a bloody good idea, so I made him my aide. I have acceded to his suggestion that all Servants who work with those of us in public office should be masked. A symbol of their authority over their fellows, so to speak."

"Splendid idea!"

"Now to business, old fruit," the prime minister said. "How many new Aristocrats do you have?"

"Only three Yatsill," the colonel replied.

Lord Brittleback shook his head. "By the depths of Phenadoor! I should rejoice at their arrival but I find myself bloody unsettled. The parties that preceded you did little better. I fear we're fast approaching a time when all will be Working Class and there'll be no one left to do the thinking. Mademoiselle Clattersmash, did you gain any insight while in the Valley of Reflections?"

"I'm afraid not, Prime Minister. We can but trust that this is the will of the Saviour."

"And what of the dissonance? From whence did it originate?"

Clattersmash turned and indicated that Clarissa and I should step forward. I led my companion to her side.

"Not from whence but from whom. These two were found in the normal manner, but as you can see, they themselves are far from normal."

"Saviour's Eyes! They don't look like the usual Servants! Were they the only ones?"

"That is correct, sir. Furthermore, this one—" she gestured toward Clarissa "—was made an Aristocrat."

I saw Mr. Sepik start slightly at this revelation.

"Ah!" Lord Brittleback exclaimed. "So the recent advances are explained! I shall present our guests to the House at once." He stepped forward and touched Clarissa on the shoulder. "I was given a rather baffling something-or-other by the leader of our Magicians. He saw you in a Dar'sayn vision and had the thing constructed. Not bloody sure what it is, but take it, please, with my compliments, and I hope it's of use!"

He fished inside his jacket, pulled something out, and pushed it into Clarissa's left hand.

"Clarissa!" I cried out. "It's a pair of goggles!"

"Thank God!" she whispered.

"What—?" Brittleback began.

"She is blind without them!" I said.

The Yatsill and Koluwaians watched as I reached up and began to untie my friend's blindfold. She held the goggles close over her eyes. I gave her a warning then pulled the material away, and she quickly pressed them into place and held them steady while I buckled the leather straps around her head.

"Done!" I announced. "Turn to face me, then open your eyes."

Clarissa spun until I saw myself reflected in the black glass lenses. The two little bumps on her forehead protruded above the eyewear. After a moment, she smiled widely, reached out, and grabbed me by the upper arms.

"Aiden! You have no idea how good it feels to see you again! Heavens above! What a beard you've grown!"

She looked down at herself, released me, and clapped her hands to her thighs. "Straight!" she almost wailed. "My legs! They really are straight!"

Spearjab said, "Though with insufficient knees and numbers, hey? What! Ha ha!"

Clarissa wheeled around and saw, for the first time, the quadrupedal mollusc-faced colonel.

She said, "Oh!" and, for the first time since I'd met her, she did something typical of her gender.

She fainted.

∘ ∘

CHAPTER 5
CITY AND HOME

Clarissa was unconscious for but a moment, then stood, leaned on me heavily, and said in a hoarse voice: "My goodness, Aiden!"

"Steady yourself," I said. "You'll get used to them, as I have."

Lord Brittleback asked, "Who leads the Servants in this group?"

Spearjab pointed. "That one. Humph! Her name is Kata."

"Much obliged, old fruit. Miss Kata! You'll find the foreman's office at the top of the main avenue. Will you take the Workers there, please? He'll give them their assignments."

Kata looked perplexed.

"Oops!" Brittleback exclaimed, realising he'd used English words to name things that had no meaning for the islanders—*foreman's office; avenue; assignments.* "Hum!" he muttered. "This is bloody awkward!"

Mr. Sepik stepped forward and said, "I'll deal with it, sir."

"Ah, good fellow!"

Sepik ordered the Koluwaians and the six young Yatsill to gather in a group. While they were doing so, I stepped over to him and said, "Mr. Sepik, my companion and I were transported here from Koluwai. Do you come from that island?"

"No. I am from a neighbouring island," he replied. "I was sailing to Koluwai to trade when a storm appeared over my boat. I was sucked into it and awoke here."

"How long ago was that?"

"I was just a boy."

He ushered the group away, back in the direction we'd come, and I returned to Clarissa's side.

The prime minister transferred his attention to the three new Aristocrats. "Hallo, chaps, what're your names?"

"Lord Prosper Possibly, Prime Minister," the first replied.

"Baroness Bellslant Jangle," said the second.

"Earl Nesting Beardgrow, sir," the third responded.

"Bloody excellent!" Brittleback exclaimed. "You go off with Colonel Spearjab and he'll sort out estates for you."

He received three nods of acquiescence.

Spearjab waved at me and said, "Cheery-bye, old thing!" then, "Toodle-pip, Miss Clarissa! Humph! Harrumph! What!" before leading his wards away.

The prime minister shouted after him, "Stop off at a tailor shop, Colonel! Have yourself and the nippers kitted out!"

He next addressed the remaining Aristocrats. "That goes for the rest of you, too. Clothes, please! Clothes! Can't have you running around with bare shell on display! By the Saviour's Eyes, it's positively indecent!" He gestured toward the Ptall'kor. "And take this bloody thing back to its pasture, would you?"

The Yatsill named Sir Gracious Whipstripes stepped forward and said, "I regret to inform you, sir, that Tokula Pathamay was killed by an Amu'utu. He declared his name. We brought his remains back with us."

"Blast it!" Brittleback exclaimed. "We can ill-afford the loss. Very well, make a detour, would you, and cast his remains into Phenadoor with all due ceremony. At least he's gained that which is denied the rest of us, Saviour be praised!"

Whipstripes nodded and, with his colleagues, reboarded the Ptall'kor.

As the living vessel departed, Mademoiselle Clattersmash said, "If there's nothing else, sir, I shall depart. I feel a wee bit out of sorts. Perhaps a Dar'sayn meditation will help. I shall go to the Temple of Magicians."

"Out of sorts, old fruit? Probably exhaustion. The journey to the Shrouded Mountains is a bloody demanding one. Off you pop, then, Mademoiselle."

She gave an awkward bob and went on her way. Lord Brittleback clapped his hands in satisfaction. He then spoke to Clarissa and me. "Well now! Your physical structure is a mite different from the other Servants'. Taller. Paler. Why is that?"

Clarissa found her voice and answered. "Because we aren't Koluwaians, sir. Our origins lie elsewhere."

"Humph! How odd! Well, let us not tarry here, hey? Parliament awaits! Don't be concerned—they'll ask you a lot of bloody questions, for certain, but I won't allow the session to trundle on forever. You'll be clothed, fed, watered, and housed in good measure. Come along! Come along! In we bloody well go!"

He ushered us up the steps. As I ascended, I again became aware of the heavier gravity. Clarissa felt it, too. "Phew!" she gasped as we reached the top. She stopped, turned, and surveyed the city that was fast growing around us. "I feel like I'm dreaming. It looks as if a crazed architect is recreating London."

"I can understand why Kata is feeling uneasy," I noted. "It must be very unsettling for someone who's only ever lived in the Koluwaian fashion."

"Chop-chop!" Brittleback cried out. "Follow me, please!"

We walked behind him, past a Yatsill in the uniform of a concierge—though with the addition of a brightly decorated hedgehog-faced mask—through tall doors and into a high vaulted hallway. Its floor was inset with a colourful mosaic of irregularly shaped ceramic tiles. Wooden scaffolding had been erected against its walls, and far overhead, platforms stretched from one side of the space to the other, close to the ceiling. A Yatsill was up there, painting a bewildering mural.

Oil lamps cast a complex web of shadows around us as we proceeded along the corridor. The click-clack of Lord Brittleback's feet echoed loudly, as did those of the various other Yatsill we saw hurrying back and forth between arched doorways that gave access to rooms to the right and left of us.

"There's so much to bloody organise!" the prime minister declared. "Social and economic policies, regulations and mandates, infrastructure and administration, industry and leisure, this and that, one thing and another, whatchamacallits and thingamajigs."

We stopped in front of another set of doors, lofty and narrow. Two Yatsill, dressed as Grenadier Guards and wearing duck masks, stood to either side of the portal. A great many muffled voices were audible from the chamber beyond.

"And this," Brittleback continued, "is where all the decisions are made." He reached up and grasped a handle. "Welcome to the House of Lords."

After pulling the door open, the prime minister ushered us through into an enormous circular room with a raised circular dais at its centre surrounded on all sides by benches, which were set progressively higher from front to back, the rearmost ones being far away and at a considerable altitude. High overhead, the domed ceiling was inset with large panels of stained glass. The light that shone through them illuminated the vast space with a soft haziness, through which dust motes drifted lazily. Everything looked and smelled brand new.

The seats were packed with top-hatted and bonneted Yatsill.

We walked through a narrow passage, between seats, from the door to the stage, and as we drew closer to the platform the words of the individual who stood in the centre of it emerged from the general cacophony.

". . . and, in conclusion, it must be evident to the right honourable ladies and gentlemen that these bladed weapons are far more suited to our needs than absurd and impractical projectile launchers. Those few who've urged the manufacturing of the latter are allowing themselves to be seduced by what *can* be done rather than by what *should* be done. I urge them to reconsider and to vote aye to this amendment, thus ensuring the City Guard is appropriately armed. What say you?"

The crowd roared, "Aye!"

A Yatsill seated behind a desk at the edge of the stage and dressed in red robes, a tricorn hat, and a very long curve-beaked bird mask, banged a gavel.

"The motion is passed!" he bellowed. "Thank you, Viscount Whoops Bumpknock. I now give the floor to Lord Upright Brittleback, the prime minister."

The crowd cheered as Brittleback escorted us up onto the dais.

"My Lords, ladies, and gentlemen," he announced, holding his arms outstretched. "None can deny that a dissonance has come among us. Indeed, one need only look at this magnificent chamber to see how significant its effects have been. I think it fair to say that we have all embraced this new permutation, and—"

"No!" someone shouted. "No, not all of us!"

The prime minister turned to the red-robed Yatsill and said, "Lord Speaker-Judge, I would—"

The gavel banged on the desk.

"I recognise the Right Honourable Yarvis Thayne," Speaker-Judge announced.

Ten benches back, the Yatsill who'd objected stood up. The creature, an unusually thickset specimen, wore neither clothes nor a mask. "Thank you, Lord Speaker-Judge," it said. "No, Prime Minister, not all of us have embraced the destruction of the old ways. Some of us ask why it is necessary. Some of us denounce the devastation of the forest and the replacement of perfectly serviceable tree houses with brick-built monstrosities."

"Monstrosities, Yarvis Thayne?" Brittleback cried out. "Monstrosities? I see nothing monstrous in progress!"

"Progress? What for? We have long enjoyed stability and tranquillity. Why change?"

"In order to become more than we bloody well are, old fruit! By the Suns, what will you object to next? Our language? Our ability to think? Would you have us revert to an animal state though we've been blessed by the Saviour with intelligence? It won't do! It won't do at all! We, the Aristocrats, have the ability to shape this world. Whatever we do must assuredly be as the Saviour intends. Would you have us remain immobile merely because the divine plan is obscure to us? No, sir! No! I say forward! Forward, not backward, nor static!"

Most of the gathered Yatsill loosed hurrahs of approval. Shaking his head disapprovingly, Yarvis Thayne sat back down.

The prime minister gestured for quiet, and when the crowd had settled continued, "I have at my side the origin of the dissonance,

Miss Clarissa Stark, and her companion, Mr. Aiden Fleischer. As you can see, they are, in form, rather peculiar."

"Thank you," Clarissa murmured.

"Indeed, they claim a different origin from that of the Servants."

"Different?" came a distant voice from the backbenches. "How is that possible?"

"That, sir, is the very question we shall seek to answer now." Brittleback turned to us. "I give you the floor, chaps. Would you explain?"

The crowd fell into an expectant silence.

I said, "Um."

Clarissa touched my arm and whispered, "May I, Aiden?"

I nodded. "Please."

My companion surveyed the gathered Yatsill. Raising her voice, she declared, "We are of the same species as the Servants but our origins lie far from their birthplace, which is called Koluwai. We are from Great Britain, on the other side of the planet Earth."

I saw masks turn as the Yatsill looked at one another.

"From the great where on the other side of the what?" Brittleback asked.

There then commenced one of the most frustrating debates imaginable. Again and again, Clarissa attempted to describe our world, but no matter what her choice of words, they were quite obviously lost on the Yatsill, who failed utterly to comprehend even the notion of continents, let alone the idea that Ptallaya was one planet among many.

Clarissa attempted to describe the differences between humans; tried to explain how racial characteristics, or culture, or both, separate the nations of Earth; tried to make it clear that Ptallaya and Earth were globes floating in a vast void; but, plainly, to the Yatsill it was incoherent nonsense.

Somehow, the conclusion was reached that the storm had behaved unusually and had damaged us.

Clarissa quietly spoke to me from the side of her mouth. "The more I talk, the less they understand."

Yarvis Thayne stood again and was announced by Lord Speaker-Judge.

"So we have welcomed these newcomers among us," Thayne said. He held out his arms and swept his long-fingered hands around. "And the repercussions are obvious. That we have allowed them to so completely sweep away our old traditions is, I maintain, regrettable and dangerous, for if the storm was abnormal, then might the dissonance not be abnormal, too? And if that is the case, then aren't all these changes also abnormal?"

The hall rumbled with hums and haws, some in agreement, most not.

"But I see my warnings will be disregarded," Thayne continued. "So I shall say nothing more on the subject at this moment, other than to table a request."

The prime minister asked, "And what might that be, sir?"

"I ask that these two be assigned to serve in my household."

A murmur of surprise rippled around the arena.

A short and bulky Yatsill in one of the front rows shouted, "Objection!" and stood. His mask resembled the face of a goat and had horns curling from its sides.

"Baron Hammer Thewflex," Speaker-Judge declared.

"I must correct the honourable gentleman," Thewflex shouted over the general hubbub. "Due to their form, as odd as it is, we keep referring to these newcomers as Servants." He pointed at Clarissa. "But I would remind you all that this one is an Aristocrat. Indeed! Indeed!"

More noise, and a voice called, "Aye! She must be given an estate of her own!"

"Yes," Thewflex agreed. "Despite that she is not Yatsill, she must have an estate. By the Saviour, anything but that would be perfectly rotten!"

"Absolutely!" Brittleback agreed.

Clarissa indicated to Lord Speaker-Judge that she wanted to address the Parliament.

"Miss Clarissa Stark!" he announced.

Clarissa cleared her throat. "If I understand it correctly," she said, "the Servants work in the houses of the Aristocrats."

Hundreds of masked heads nodded. Someone said, "Until they are released."

"In which case, if I am an Aristocrat, and, as such, am to be given an estate, I request that my companion, Mr. Aiden Fleischer, be assigned to serve me."

"I oppose that motion!" Yarvis Thayne shouted.

"I bloody well support it!" the prime minister countered.

"Indeed!" Baron Hammer Thewflex agreed. "Indeed! Indeed!"

Voices were raised. Cheers echoed.

Speaker-Judge banged his gavel until the assembly quietened.

"The motion is passed. A decision must also be made concerning the role Miss Stark will play in our society. The Council of Magicians will take up this matter. Baron Thewflex, will you escort Miss Clarissa and Mr. Fleischer to the Council at once, please?"

Thewflex gave a thumbs-up—such a mundane gesture struck me as incredible, coming as it did from such a bizarre-looking creature—and made his way to the edge of the platform and the narrow corridor that led out of the chamber. He waved for us to join him there.

"Toodle-pip, old things," the prime minister said to us. "When you've settled in, I'll drop by for a cup of tea."

"You have tea here?" I exclaimed.

"Of course, old fruit! Of course!"

Clarissa and I crossed the stage and followed Thewflex out of the building.

"So you've made me your skivvy?" I ruefully asked my companion.

"Whatever is necessary to keep us together, Aiden. Obviously I don't expect you to actually work in that capacity. I'm still your sexton."

"No, Clarissa. I relieve you of that duty. Here, we are equals. In fact, if anything, you are my superior, for you are certainly handling our peculiar circumstances far better than I."

We passed through the front doors and descended the steps to the road. To my utter astonishment, Thewflex raised a hand and yelled, "Cab!"

A two-wheeled vehicle came careening around a corner and drew to a halt in front of us. In design it was boxy and sloped from a wide base to a narrow and very high top upon which the driver was perched precariously. It was pulled by a cream-coloured beast, tubular in form, which ran along on multiple legs. The awful-looking monster had a thick knot of tails curling out from its rear—two of which were held by the driver like reins—while its pointed neckless front end was split by a massive mouth. There were at least twenty small eyes clustered irregularly above and below the long maw.

"What's that hideous thing called?" I asked Thewflex.

"A hansom cab," he answered, opening the vehicle's door. "Hop in."

"I meant the beast harnessed to it."

"Ah. It's a Kaljoor. Yes, indeed! Come along! All aboard!"

Rather clumsily, Thewflex hoisted himself into the cabin. I gave Clarissa a hand up and followed.

"Where to, guv'nor?" the driver called.

Thewflex leaned out of the window, looked up, and said, "The Temple of Magicians, and make it snappy!"

"Tell that to the Kaljoor, mate!" came the response.

Thewflex grunted, and as the hansom jerked into motion, he turned his goat mask toward Clarissa and said, "The Working Class have been singularly lippy of late. I can't abide their backchat. One might almost think they consider themselves our betters because they're assured a place in Phenadoor. I feel we Aristocrats are losing the respect that's our due. For crying out loud, the idiots would be nothing without us! Nothing!"

My friend frowned and was on the point of asking a question when Thewflex directed our attention to the scene outside.

"Look at that, Miss Stark! Marvellous efficiency! Busy days! Busy days! Indeed so!"

He was referring to a large tract of land that had been forested when we'd entered the House of Lords but which had, while we were inside, been cleared and was now swarming with a dense crowd of Yatsill. As we passed alongside it, we saw a seemingly endless line of Ptall'kors arriving, all laden with stone blocks, having their cargo unloaded, then departing. Roads and alleyways already criss-crossed the area, and in the squares between them, large edifices of a vaguely Georgian style were being erected with astonishing speed.

"Incredible!" I whispered.

A tall, thin tower caught my attention. It was similar to the minarets I'd seen illustrated in books about Damascus and other Arabian cities, and I realised it was but one of a great many that dotted every level of New Yatsillat.

"It's for the City Guard," the baron said in answer to my query.

"A watchtower? What are you watching for? Why does the city require guards?"

"The Saviour's Eyes are not always upon us," he responded.

Before I could pursue the subject further, the hansom rocked around a corner, veered across the road, and, though having travelled only a short distance, came to a jolting halt.

"Temple of Magicians!" the driver announced.

Thewflex pushed the door open and heaved himself out. We followed and saw we'd arrived at a colonnade-fronted structure.

"Gee-up!" the driver said. The hansom rattled away.

"You forgot to pay him," I noted.

"Pay?" Thewflex asked.

"Never mind. What do your Magicians do?"

"They have insight. Yes, indeed!"

"Into what?" Clarissa asked.

"I haven't a clue," Baron Thewflex replied. "I'm not a Magician."

We entered the building and were met by a Yatsill wearing a crow's-head mask and long yellow robes.

"Welcome, Baron Hammer Thewflex," he said, with a bow. "Welcome, Clarissa Stark. I am pleased to see that you've received your eye protection. Welcome, Aiden Fleischer. Baron, thank you, and you may go about your business now. Miss Stark, Mr. Fleischer, this way, please."

Thewflex nodded, saluted—the second Earthly gesture I'd seen him make—and departed.

We fell into step beside the Magician.

"I am Father Mordant Reverie," he declared.

"What a name!" I blurted. "But *Father*? Are you a priest?"

"Priest, Magician, sorcerer, call me what you will, young fellow. The title makes no difference to the function." The Yatsill regarded me curiously and emitted a small grunt. "Hmm! It's a shame you weren't also made an Aristocrat, Mr. Fleischer. As a mere Servant, your mind is closed to me, though your emotions play clearly across its surface. They are fascinatingly complex."

"Closed?"

"Obscured. Inaccessible. It doesn't shine with inventiveness like Miss Stark's."

"My apologies."

My sarcasm went unnoticed. "Accepted," Father Reverie replied. "What is this guilt you feel?"

"I'm sorry, Father, I don't know what you mean."

"You appear uncomfortable with yourself, as if you have done something wrong."

An image of Polly Nichols' corpse flashed into my mind's eye. I swallowed nervously.

"Well, it doesn't matter," the Yatsill said. "I'm sure you'll come to terms with the issue in due course. Now then, the Council awaits. Don't dawdle, please."

Like the House of Lords, the Temple of Magicians was new, clean, and still being decorated. Artisans were carving a frieze into the upper walls of the corridor we passed along, and a complex geometric pattern into the large door we came to at the end of it. Father Reverie dismissed the two Yatsill working on the latter. As the pair scuttled away, I realised that all the artisans, like the cab driver, wore flat caps, baggy suits, and plain masks. Obviously, it was the uniform of the Working Class.

Our guide conducted us through the portal into a big oblong cloister. We passed around the edge of this, through another set of doors, along a second corridor, and into a room that very much resembled the interior of a church. He escorted us to a bench beside a lectern and we sat facing a gathering of about a hundred Yatsill, nearly all in crow's-head masks and yellow robes, though I counted five who were unclothed.

Behind us, a stained-glass window depicted the two suns over a sparkling sea. The bright yellow light—which made the chamber far less gloomy than my little church back in Theaston Vale—shone through it and illuminated the billowing clouds of incense curling from a censer hanging above the congregation. I later learned that the scent, which was similar to cinnamon, was Dar'sayn, the liquid from the fruits of the Ptoollan trees. The Magicians employed it to deepen their meditations.

Father Reverie took up position behind the lectern and said, "Fellow Magicians, I present to you the dissonance, Miss Clarissa Stark, and her Servant, Mr. Aiden Fleischer."

"There it is again," I whispered to my companion. "No debate. I'm your lackey."

"What's important," she replied under her breath, "is that they keep referring to *me* as the dissonance, not to *us*. I think I'm starting to understand a little of what's happening, Aiden."

Before she could say anything more, Reverie asked her to explain how we arrived on Ptallaya and where we came from. Once more, Clarissa went through the story. This time, there were no questions. The gathered Magicians simply sat in silence.

"Mademoiselle Crockery Clattersmash," Reverie called. "Will you please recount the events of the Immersion and how Miss Stark came to be an Aristocrat?"

One of the crow-masked figures stood. Clattersmash had told Lord Brittleback that she was going to meditate—obviously, she hadn't done so for long. Now her unmistakable voice emerged from behind the face decoration, and in a concise manner—but in tones that noticeably quavered—she described our discovery in the Forest of Indistinct Murmurings, the journey to the Shrouded Mountains, the events in the Cavern of Immersion, and our long journey from there to New Yatsillat.

She sat down, rather heavily.

Reverie addressed the congregation. "Whatever you make of this, there are two certainties. The first is that, compared to our other Servants, these two are rather different in form. The second is that the dissonance brought to us by this one—" he gestured at Clarissa "—is far-reaching in its influence," he held his hands wide, "and has been accepted without question by all but a few."

One of the unclothed Magicians stood and said, "The parliamentarian Yarvis Thayne and I represent that minority."

"Father Yissil Froon," Reverie responded, "you are the oldest, longest serving, and wisest of us—but see how many oppose you, or at least disagree with you!"

"That does not make me wrong."

"But why do you object?"

"Because long ago, the Saviour looked upon the Yatsill and found us pleasing, though we lacked self-awareness, did not recognise the glory of Phenadoor, and were little more than animals. But it angered the Saviour to see us taken by—"

A ripple of disapproval ran through the congregation, interrupting him. Someone hissed, "Blasphemy!"

Father Mordant Reverie rapped on the lectern and snapped, "Be careful what you say! As the survivor of many, many cycles, you are held in very high regard, but that does not grant you licence to transgress."

"I understand," Yissil Froon replied, "but cannot explain my objection without some reference to that which may not be spoken of in the sight of the Saviour. I shall be as circumspect as possible."

"See that you are. Continue."

The Magician bowed and continued, "The Saviour created a division. At Immersion, some of the children were made Working Class, and thus could never be taken, while the others were endowed with intelligence, language, and self-knowledge. These latter, the

Aristocrats, were able to transmit their abilities to the Working Class and raise them from the animal state, but to do so, they sacrificed immunity—they could still be taken."

Reverie nodded, held his arms out, and said, "We, the Aristocracy, are both honoured and cursed. Honoured because we are vehicles for the Saviour's will and reveal to the Working Class that the bliss of Phenadoor awaits; cursed because we know the same bliss is denied to us. This is common knowledge, Yissil Froon, not an explanation. What is your point?"

"It is this: we Magicians have a special function. We extend the Saviour's protection over our fellow Aristocrats that they may live for as long as possible before being taken. With the aid of Dar'sayn, we have been extremely successful in this endeavour, so much so that at each Immersion the Saviour has been able to make ever more Yatsill Working Class while reducing the number of Aristocrats."

"Indeed," Reverie agreed. "Is this not a good thing? Is it not the case that more and more Yatsill are thus gaining entry to Phenadoor?"

"Yes, it is."

"Are you certain? For all your sweet words, rumours persist that you were the first ever to drink Dar'sayn, and that you subsequently opposed its use."

"Those rumours are entirely unfounded, Father Reverie."

"Do you follow the will of the Saviour?"

"Of course I do! I am offended that you doubt it!"

"Then I ask you one more time, Yissil Froon: why do you object to the dissonance?"

"Because in complicating the manner in which we live, the dissonance places greater demands on the Working Class. The Aristocrats must therefore channel greater intelligence to them. Are enough of us remaining to do this? And can we Magicians do it while also protecting our fellows when the Saviour's gaze is averted? I fear not."

Reverie's long fingers tapped on the lectern. "Hum! You feel the dissonance has tipped the balance?"

"I do," Yissil Froon said. "Father Mordant Reverie, Mr. Aiden Fleischer is of no consequence. I have no objection to him remaining in New Yatsillat as one of the Servants. Clarissa Stark, however, as the source of dissonance, should be banished from New Yatsillat and exiled to the Whimpering Ruins, at the heart of the Shelf Lands."

I clutched my companion's wrist.

"The Shelf Lands are a long way from here," Reverie said. "Past the Shrouded Mountains and beyond even the Zull eyries."

"Precisely," Yissil Froon replied. "We began to change the moment she joined the Aristocracy. We know, then, that her influence can reach us from the Shrouded Mountains. To escape it, we must send her farther away even than that."

"And if we do, what then will become of this?" asked Reverie, indicating the chamber around us and plainly meaning the entire city.

"It will become irrelevant," came the answer. "We will not require it."

After a long pause, Reverie said, "Thank you, Father Yissil Froon. Sit, please." Again, he became quiet, lowered his head, and appeared to be lost in thought. Then he looked up. "I shall *not* send Clarissa Stark to the Whimpering Ruins."

I felt myself slump with relief.

He went on, "I shall recommend to Lord Upright Brittleback that she and her companion be allowed to remain with us, for I have faith that the imbalance between we Aristocrats and the Working Class will be corrected. However, when the Eyes of the Saviour look upon us again, if Immersion fails to increase our numbers, then I will follow your guidance, Yissil Froon. As to the roles these newcomers shall play, Miss Stark will train as a Magician with Mademoiselle Clattersmash. We can better monitor the dissonance if she joins us."

Father Yissil Froon stood again. He turned to Clattersmash and asked, "What does Yazziz Yozkulu call himself now?"

"Colonel Momentous Spearjab," she answered.

He nodded and addressed Mordant Reverie. "I recommend that Miss Stark's Servant trains as one of the City Guard with Colonel Spearjab."

Reverie angled his head to one side, as if taken aback. "A Servant in the Guards, Father? That's unheard of, and it makes no sense. Are we to arm him against his own release?"

"It is highly unusual, I agree, but just as you, some little time before Miss Stark arrived in New Yatsillat, were told in a Dar'sayn vision that she'd require the item you now see strapped over her eyes, so it was revealed to me that Aiden Fleischer would wield a sword. Only the Guards carry the weapon, hence he must join them."

The entire gathering chorused, "The Saviour knows all!"

"What? I can't be a guard!" I objected. "I haven't the constitution for that sort of thing!"

The beak of every crow mask in the chamber turned to point in my direction.

"It is not your place to object," Reverie said. "And in future, I advise you to speak only when you're spoken to." He turned back to Yissil Froon. "Very well, it shall be as you advise."

My mouth worked but no further words emerged. I was shocked. No one had ever before addressed me in such a fashion.

Mademoiselle Crockery Clattersmash, responding to a gesture from Reverie, moved out of the pews and approached us. She'd taken only a few steps when she suddenly reeled to one side and collapsed against a pillar, which she clutched at for support. A low moan sounded from behind her mask.

"Mademoiselle?" said Reverie, moving down from the lectern. "Are you unwell?"

"Yes," came the weak response. "No. Just a little dizzy. I shall be fine." She straightened, shook her head slightly, and stepped over to us.

"Come," she said, and led us out of the room, from the temple, and into the street. It immediately became apparent that while we'd been inside, New Yatsillat had expanded even more.

o o

We were given a large empty house on the city's fourth level, situated at the edge of a quiet little square with a fountain at its centre.

Three steps led to our double front doors, which opened onto a very spacious vestibule that gave access to five big, rectangular ground-floor chambers. A steep ramp sloped up the right-hand wall to the upper floor, on which there were six more rooms. The property was plumbed, and most of the rooms had a fireplace.

Mademoiselle Clattersmash told us we'd have plenty of time to settle in and sleep before commencing our training. She left, but we'd only just closed the door behind her when there came a knock upon it and we found ourselves in the presence of three plain-masked Workers—a furniture maker, a tailor, and a grocer. Each asked what we required, and it quickly became apparent to us that the provisions would be free of charge, for the concept of money was totally lacking in the Yatsill.

Adopting the philosophy that we might as well make ourselves as comfortable as possible as quickly as we could, we ordered from the furniture maker tables and chairs, beds, desks, sofas, armchairs, sideboards, armoires, bureaus, and a great many other things, every one of which had to be described in meticulous detail.

The tailor measured us from head to toe. I asked him to make me a black three-piece suit, top hat, and button-up boots. The latter had him bemused until I showed him my feet and described how they should be shod. Once he'd understood the concept, he was confident he could deliver and enthused about adapting the idea for Yatsill feet—though they weren't really feet at all, being more the pointed ends of the four legs. With regard to the suit and topper, he shook his head and mumbled through his mask, "No, mate. This ain't for the likes of you."

"What do you mean?" I asked.

"You're a Servant. It ain't seemly for you to sport togs like this."

Clarissa pulled me to one side. "Just to keep the peace while they're judging us, you'll have to pose as my Servant."

"Have I plummeted so far in the social order?" I cried out. "It's absurd!"

"It's necessary," she insisted. "But it's for appearances only, nothing more."

I was too tired to argue, so I settled for underclothes, shirt, trousers, jacket, and a cloth cap. I mollified myself with the thought that I'd at least have the boots I wanted.

"I'll also bring you a uniform," the tailor said. "A Servant in the City Guard, fancy that!"

"I don't much," I muttered.

Clarissa decided to forego the voluminous skirts of the British female and settled for a brown two-piece suit. She dispensed with the obligatory hat, saying she'd always hated the things.

"Trousers again!" I chided. "My initial suspicions about you were correct—you're a confounded bloomerist!"

The tailor had no objection to her choice, but added, "You'll require the robes of a Magician, too, ma'am."

Next we spoke with the grocer and, not being certain what comestibles might be available, asked him to use his own judgement and bring us a selection.

Finally, at long last, we were alone.

The tailor had left two thick blankets with us, which we now placed on the floor in one of the upper rooms, side by side, negligent of propriety and drawn to this socially shocking arrangement by virtue of our extreme experiences.

We stretched out, both exhausted.

"I understand absolutely nothing of this," I said. "The creatures talk complete nonsense. I obviously lost my mind when we left Theaston Vale and am becoming progressively more insane with every hour that passes."

"Then I'm also a candidate for Bedlam," Clarissa answered, "which I refuse to believe. Better to regard our circumstances as similar to those of Alice, whom Mr. Lewis Carroll had fall into a rabbit hole." She reached up to her forehead and touched the little bumps over her goggles. "Wonderland."

"Almost horns, Clarissa. Have you any idea what they are?"

"No, but they have something to do with the way my mind has been opened to the Yatsill."

"Opened?"

"Made accessible. The Yatsill are mimics. Incredible mimics. They're somehow mining my memories and knowledge, and this city is their interpretation of my impressions of London. They wear clothes and speak English because of me. Even the masks they wear come from my recollections of the Hufferton Hall *bals masqués*. I'm not sure they can help themselves."

"Yarvis Thayne and Yissil Froon appear to be rather resistant to your influence."

"Perhaps not as much as they like to believe. They spoke English, after all, and the way of life whose passing they lament was no more authentic than this—it was quite clearly an imitation of the Koluwaian culture. Remember what Yissil Froon said? The Yatsill were akin to animals until the Saviour looked upon them. I suspect that this process of having my mind made accessible by Immersion must, once upon a time, have also happened to a Koluwaian."

"What! You mean their god, the Saviour, was an islander?"

"I do, which explains why they regard the sea—or Phenadoor—as some sort of heaven, just as the Koluwaians did. What I don't understand, though, is this business of being 'taken.' We need to find out what it means and why the Magicians need to protect themselves and the rest of the Aristocrats from it. To quote Father Mordant Reverie, we have until 'the Eyes of the Saviour look upon us again.'"

"What do you think that signifies?"

"Tomorrow."

I sat up. "Tomorrow?"

"The Eyes of the Saviour are the suns, Aiden. When they set, they won't look upon us again until sunrise. We have until tomorrow."

"Thank goodness! I feel that we've been here for weeks and weeks, but it's barely even noon yet! Tomorrow isn't due for ages."

Clarissa gave a grunt of agreement and murmured, "But the night, Aiden. What happens during the long, long night?"

o o

"Get out of here! Run! Run!"

"Mr. Skin-and-Bones."

"Please!"

"Mr. Books-and-Bible."

"I'll kill you!"

"Mr. Thoughts-and-Theories."

The blade tore into her, slitting her stomach wide open. Her entrails slopped onto the cobbles. They writhed like tentacles, as if possessed of a life of their own.

I pulled on the sword and watched its blade slide out of her flesh, red and wet and gleaming.

She collapsed. My face was reflected in the black lenses of her goggles.

"No!" I screamed. "Not you! Not you!"

My terrified eyes filled the two dark circles, imposed onto her face as if they were her own—as if she'd just recognised the evil in me and was paralysed by fear of it.

Her eyes. My eyes.

The blackness of her lenses.

The blackness of my soul.

Her corpse suddenly lurched up, hands clutching my shoulders, fingers digging into my flesh.

"Aiden! Wake up!"

"Who will forgive me?" I yelled. "If there's no God, who will forgive me?"

"Stop it! You're having a nightmare!"

I pulled away, rolled onto my side, and curled up, my whole body shaking.

"It's all right," Clarissa said soothingly. "It's all right."

"Nine levels," I croaked. "This place has nine levels, just as Dante described in the *Divine Comedy*."

"We're not in Hell."

"I am."

She put a hand on my shoulder and looked down at me. "I don't think you've ever properly known yourself, Aiden. Hell is for the evil, but I think evil is more properly recognised by those who witness it than by those who commit it. I do not see it it you. Not at all."

My racing heart and panting respiration slowed. I rolled over and got to my feet, ran my fingers through my hair, and wiped the beads of sweat from my face. "Perhaps you're right," I mumbled, but I was not convinced. A terrible self-loathing was upon me—intense, the pressure from it almost a physical sensation.

To change the subject, I asked, "For how long have we slept?"

"I haven't a clue. Let's look outside."

After performing our ablutions, we descended the ramp to the ground floor, opened the front door, and stepped out into the bright yellow light. The suns were at the noon mark. A light breeze was blowing, sharp with citrus.

Overhead, a group—or perhaps I should say "school"—of whale-sized inflated membranes were pulling themselves over the city by means of filament-like dangling limbs. They were almost transparent and were emitting an airy piping. Ribbony things, like I'd seen before, were coiling along beside them.

Small chirruping creatures, like colourful marbles with corkscrew tails, were projecting themselves back and forth between the eaves of the houses.

"Hey!" a voice called. It was the tailor, squatting on his four legs beside the fountain in the square. He straightened up and raised four very large cloth bags. "I've been waiting. I've got your togs."

Having been almost naked for so long, the satisfaction I experienced back in the house some minutes later, as I stood kitted out in a full suit, was enough to drive away the horrors of my nightmare. Admittedly, my new outfit wasn't that of a gentleman, but the material was smooth and comfortable.

"From what is it woven?" I enquired.

"From a substance extruded by the Ptall'kors."

"I wish I hadn't asked."

My boots were of Kaljoor skin and more comfortable than any I'd ever worn on Earth.

As Clarissa exited the room in which she'd dressed, I doffed my cloth cap, bowed, and said, "Good day to you, young sir!"

"Very funny," she said, smiling. "I don't care if I look like a gent. This suit is far more practical than skirts and corsets and all the ridiculous paraphernalia that goes with them."

"Believe me, Clarissa, you are unmistakably female!" I replied, then immediately felt myself blushing at my uncharacteristic boldness.

She fluttered her eyelashes in jest, but I sensed she was secretly pleased, too, by my clumsy compliment.

The tailor checked us over to make sure everything fitted properly, then touched his fingers to his cap and made for the door.

"Wait a moment, please!" Clarissa called after him.

"Is there something else, ma'am?"

"Just a question. We've heard that Aristocrats are 'taken.' Could you perhaps explain to us what that entails?"

"By the Suns!" the Yatsill cried out, throwing up his hands in horror. "No! No! Such things mustn't be spoken of by the Working Class and certainly shouldn't be mentioned in the sight of the Saviour! My goodness! My goodness!"

He turned, practically ran to the door, and left the house without looking back.

"That was helpful," I observed.

Moments later, the grocer arrived with three assistants and basket after basket of foodstuffs. He explained each item—the fruits, nuts, vegetables, and meats—then presented us with a case of cooking implements. Clarissa thanked him then asked him about being taken. He shrieked and raced away.

The furniture man knocked at our door. He'd brought a Ptall'kor into the square, piled high with furniture, which he and his seven helpers unloaded and carried into our new home.

Clarissa said to me, "I'll spare him," and let the Yatsill depart without interrogation. "Did you notice how they arrived one after the other, Aiden? I think it's obvious from what we've heard so far that the Aristocracy transmits intelligence to the Working Class through some sort of telepathic channel. It appears they also bestow upon them a remarkable ability to be organised and efficient."

"Perhaps being an Aristocrat has made you telepathic, too," I suggested. "You knew Colonel Spearjab's hunting party had caught one of those Quee-tan creatures before there was any evidence to suggest it."

Before she could respond, there came yet another knock at the door and a Yatsill poked his mask into the vestibule. "'Scuse me," he said. "I have a cab waiting outside for Guardsman Fleischer."

"Um. That's me," I said.

"You're to get into uniform, sir, and I'm to take you to Crooked Blue Tower Barracks for training. Colonel Spearjab's orders."

"Very well," I responded reluctantly. "Wait outside, would you? I'll be with you presently."

The messenger withdrew.

"I don't know how I'll cope without you beside me," I said to Clarissa.

"As best you can. And at least you have a home to come back to."

I pulled a package from the bag the tailor had given me and unwrapped my uniform. To my dismay, instead of pulling from it the good old British reds, I found myself clutching French greys of the Napoleonic era.

"Clarissa! What the dickens is in that head of yours!"

"Oops!" she said, sympathetically. "Sir Philip Hufferton taught me a lot of history, Aiden, so think yourself lucky. You might have ended up in armour!"

I took the uniform into one of the rooms and changed into it. The furniture maker had left us a dressing table, and while examining myself in its mirror, I couldn't help but utter a groan. I looked preposterous. My hair was too long, I was sporting a bushy beard, the jacket and trousers drooped off my skinny frame as if they were still on a clothes hanger, and my new boots didn't match the outfit at all.

Swallowing what pitiful remnants of my pride remained—a small meal indeed—I went back into the vestibule and gave Clarissa a rueful salute. I realised, as I did so, that my hands were shaking.

I released a shuddery breath and admitted, "I'm afraid to be alone."

"You'll have Colonel Spearjab with you," she reminded me. "He's a familiar face."

"A perfectly foul face, but masked, at least. I suppose I'd better be off. Will you be all right?"

"Yes. I daresay I'll be summoned by Mademoiselle Clattersmash in due course."

"Well," I said. "Here goes."

I stepped out of the house.

"In you get, chum!" the cab driver called from atop his conveyance.

I opened the cabin door, climbed in, and sat down. The vehicle jolted into motion. The Kaljoor pulled it out of the square and onto a wide thoroughfare along which Ptall'kors, various wagons, and other hansoms were travelling. To either side, Yatsill were beetling past, some in working men's suits and flat caps, some in skirts, bustles, and bonnets, with parasols held over their heads, and some in evening suits and toppers, swinging canes and touching their brims as they passed the "ladies."

During the first few moments of that cab ride, it occurred to me that, were it not for the fact the pedestrians were all four-legged and masked, it could almost be a summer's day in London, but the more I looked, the more I saw the falsity of this impression. A "sandwich-board man," for example, bore not an advertisement for "Pear's Soap" or "Lipton's Tea," but for "Touchmeddle's Quee'tan Steaks, Raw and Dripping with Goodness! Get them while you still can!" and when we passed—wonder of wonders!—a theatre, I saw that its billboard proclaimed "The Astonishing Leotard," together with an illustration of a quadrupedal tightrope-walker juggling coloured balls while balanced on two parallel lines.

That the signs and hoardings were written in English was in itself a marvel, but to see the letters and numbers of my native language rendered in an endless variety of strange lines, curves, and angles fair muddled the mind.

I was driven past a row of shops—Hearty Henry's Haberdashery,

Twitch's Bakery, Scoop the Grocer, Paddlecloud's Hardware Store, Disparage the Butcher, Dignity's Olde Tea Shoppe, Rebuttle's Tremendously Big Pottery Emporium—then we turned right onto one of the great tree-lined avenues that sloped steeply down, cutting through the nine terraces from the top of the city all the way to the fishing village at the bottom. This thoroughfare descended at such a sharp angle that the driver stopped the hansom, unharnessed the Kaljoor, and hitched it to the back of the cabin, so rather than towing the conveyance, the beast was now lowering it down the incline.

Traffic was much heavier and there were roadworks everywhere. We were surrounded by carts transporting goods and materials to and from the various levels of the city. Those going up were struggling against the escarpment; those going down were fighting against the pull of gravity, and I witnessed a number of them coming a cropper and spilling their loads, which went tumbling away toward the sea far below.

Hawkers stood at every corner, their sing-song sales pitches adding to the general cacophony:

"Hot P'tezznam roots! Hot P'tezznam roots! Freshly dug and boiled soft!"

"Who'll buy my Kelumin flowers? Lovely Kelumin flowers! Brighten your home! Who'll buy my Kelumin flowers?"

"Knives sharpened! Pots polished! Knives sharpened! Pots polished!"

We left the fourth terrace and traversed the fifth and the sixth, both of which were now almost entirely filled by the new residential districts. The seventh had been transformed into a beautiful park with lakes and bandstands, banks of exotic flowers, and thickets of curiously formed trees. I saw Yatsill strolling along the footpaths and others enjoying picnics on the bluish-green grass. There was also a small group of unclothed individuals marching along bearing placards that read: *Reverse the changes! Back to the old ways! Say no to the dissonance!*

At the seaward edge of the park, along the top of the almost sheer drop that fell to the next terrace, the Yatsill had built a high crenellated wall with bastions spaced evenly along its length. Initially, I took this to be a defence against seagoing marauders, but as we passed onto the eighth terrace through a tremendously tall gateway, I realised the battlements were facing inward, not outward. This made no sense. If the Yatsill feared a land attack, why was the wall here rather than at the top of the first level? And what, exactly, was the nature of the threat? I determined to find this out as soon as possible.

Beyond the wall, the eighth terrace contained forts, parade grounds, and barracks. There were also builders' yards, paper mills, printworks, and the premises of metalworkers, carpenters, and glassblowers.

The cabbie drove me to a military establishment and dropped me at the gate, above which a sign read "Crooked Blue Tower Barracks" despite there being no tower present, crooked, blue, or otherwise. Out of habit, I patted my pockets in search of loose change to pay for my ride. Of course, I had none, and regardless, the hansom clattered away before I could have handed over any coins.

A sentry—Working Class—stepped forward and said, "You must be Fleischer."

"Yes," I responded, then foolishly added, "How did you know?"

The Yatsill regarded me through the holes of his mask and said, "You're underequipped in the leg and elbow department, Guardsman. Go through, please. Colonel Spearjab is waiting for you."

He held the portal open and I passed through into a large courtyard. There were about thirty Workers in it, all dressed in Napoleonic grey. Five of them were wielding swords—chopping, slashing, and stabbing at ten-foot-tall tree stumps—while the others watched.

A figure strode over to me. When he spoke, I recognised the voice of Colonel Momentous Spearjab coming from behind the long-beaked crow mask.

"Ah-ha! There you are, old chap! We've been waiting for you! What! What! Here, take this."

He held out a scabbarded sword, hilt first.

I looked at it and felt the heat sucked out of my body.

"We've been practising but we're not bally sure of the technique," Spearjab said. "Show us, would you? Hey?"

I shook my head and took a step back. "I can't. I don't know how to use it."

"Come come, old fellow. Harrumph! Give it a try."

Again, I shook my head.

"I say," Spearjab grumbled. "I *am* a colonel, you know. A *colonel*, I say! Humph! Humph! You *do* realise you have to obey my jolly old orders, yes? The thing of it is, this *is* an order. What! Take the sword."

I drew an unsteady breath, reached out, and closed my fingers around the weapon's grip. Spearjab maintained his hold on the scabbard as I slowly pulled the weapon from it. It scraped free and I stumbled a little, surprised by its weight. It was much heavier than I had anticipated.

"Good show!" the colonel murmured.

I looked down at the hilt, at the ornately carved quillons and studded pommel.

"Please, no."

It was the sword the Valley of Reflections had shown to me—the weapon I would use to kill Mademoiselle Crockery Clattersmash.

o o

CHAPTER 6
GUARDSMAN
AND MAGICIAN

How much time had passed since I'd last awoken in a bed? I had no idea, but when I finally did so once again, it was not the pleasure it should have been, for my entire body ached abysmally. Every muscle felt bruised. My hands were blistered and I could hardly straighten my fingers. When I sat up and swung my legs to the floor, the pain was so excruciating I couldn't help but moan in distress.

I had no memory of my return to the house—though I could vaguely recall a cab driver helping me out of a hansom—nor did I know how much time had passed since then. By the angle of the light slanting in through the gap in my curtains, I guessed it to be no small period.

Curtains! There'd been none before! With another moan, I pushed myself upright, hobbled across the room, and pulled the draperies open. The square below was empty, the only movement being from the water of the tinkling fountain. I looked down at myself and found, to my surprise, that I was wearing blue-and-yellow-striped pyjamas. Then I turned and surveyed my bedchamber. The walls had been painted a very pale green. A dressing gown was hanging from a hook on the door. There was a wardrobe to my left, its doors open, showing it to be full of clothes. A pair of slippers poked out from beneath the end of my bed.

I squeezed my eyes shut and opened them again, bemused.

I could smell toast.

In a trice, I donned the gown, put on the slippers, shuffled out through the door, visited the bathroom—which I discovered had been fitted with a tub—then descended the ramp.

The house had been transformed. There were rugs on the floors, vases on shelves, incomprehensible artwork on the walls, cushions on the sofas, and all manner of homely knick-knacks around the place.

"Good gracious!" I exclaimed.

Clarissa came out of the kitchen. She was wrapped in the yellow robes of a Magician. "You're awake!"

"I don't think so. Surely I'm dreaming!"

"You were gone for ages, came home in a daze, and slept for what must have been twenty-four hours. As you can see, we've been busy."

"So I see! We?"

"Kata has been appointed as our housekeeper. Come through— there's tea and toast."

With my eyes wide and my jaw dangling, I followed her into what had become a very well-appointed kitchen. Kata, who was cleaning the work surfaces, turned and smiled. "Hello, Mr. Fleischer."

"Kata! I'm happy to see you again!"

I gingerly lowered myself into a chair at the table. Clarissa placed a cutting board before me on which sat a tub of butter, a pot of jam, and a plate piled high with toasted bread. She added to it a teapot, covered with a knitted cosy, cups and saucers, a jug of milk, and a bowl of sugar.

She laughed at the expression on my face. "These are the products of a Dar'sayn meditation, Aiden."

"How—how so?" I stammered.

"The Magicians use the fluid to enhance their connection to the other Yatsill. I drank the stuff during my first training session with Father Spreadflower Meadows at the Temple of Magicians."

"Who? I thought you were to be taught by Mademoiselle Clattersmash."

"I was, but her dizziness has developed into an illness of some sort, so Meadows, one of her acolytes, has taken over her duties. My session with him involved imbibing this Dar'sayn fluid. It put me into a peculiar state of mind. I became consciously *joined* to the Yatsill, and I learned a lot."

"Joined? Telepathically?"

"Yes. I was right about the Working Class. It's hard to believe, but they have only the most rudimentary intelligence. Everything we see them accomplishing—their efficiency, their craftsmanship, even their ability to communicate with language—is by virtue of the acumen transmitted to them by the Aristocrats."

I chuckled. "Am I to take it, then, that you, being one of the latter, used the same mental channel to plant a knowledge of tea and toast into the species?"

She smiled and nodded. "In a manner of speaking. As I suspected, the Yatsill have excavated, mimicked, and, in some respects, adapted my memories, but they work on a broad canvas. I was able to communicate greater detail to them, especially where things that'll make you and me more comfortable are concerned. Their natural enthusiasm did the rest. As a matter of fact, they'd already created a rough approximation of tea—our English obsession—but I was able to refine their recipe. Then they set out to replicate bread, reproducing its texture and flavour as closely as possible. And so forth."

"On which subject—" I said, and tried to pick up a knife. My fingers wouldn't cooperate. Clarissa took over, applied butter and jam to a piece of toast, and handed it to me. I took an eager bite and tasted something similar to strawberries but with a spicy edge.

"Of course, I didn't confine myself to trivialities," she continued.

I swallowed and exclaimed, "There's nothing trivial about this!"

"True. But I also refined what they'd already picked up from me concerning mechanical engineering. In future sessions, I shall try to give them more. With their fervour and astounding proficiency, they'll soon make Yatsillat a better approximation of London. We shall feel quite at home!"

"If we can get used to having four-legged neighbours."

"I tried to find out more about this 'being taken' business, too," Clarissa continued, "but in that was singularly unsuccessful. They block the entire subject from their own minds."

I watched our housekeeper as she took oddly shaped and strangely coloured vegetables from a bag and started to peel them.

"Kata," I said, "were you born on Ptallaya?"

"Yes, sir, and my father. But my mother was from a place called Futuna."

"It's an island some distance to the north and west of Koluwai," Clarissa put in.

"Why was she sent here, Kata?" I asked

"To serve and to have children."

"Are many of the Servants born here?"

"Most are, but newcomers appear in the Forest of Indistinct Murmurings each time the Eyes of the Saviour open. Like all of us, they serve until they are released."

"Released? I've heard that term used once or twice before. What does it mean?"

"It is when we are sent to your world as a reward for our service."

I looked at Clarissa and said, "Home!" then to Kata, "How do we get released?"

"The gods will decide," she answered, and her tone signalled an unwillingness to discuss the matter any further.

It took six rounds of toast and two cups of tea to stop my stomach from grumbling. When I'd eaten my fill, we left the kitchen, crossed the black-and-white-tiled floor of the big square vestibule, and settled in our lounge. It was a bright and cheerful room, with tall windows in two of the walls.

I was telling Clarissa about my training.

"It was brutal. Over and over, I was ordered to assault a tree stump with a heavy sword."

"You brought the weapon back with you," she said. "It's by the front door."

"I have to carry it whenever I'm on duty. I'm positive the dashed thing is heavier than I am. I could barely stand up by the time Spearjab released me. There's not a single part of me that doesn't hurt."

"Exercise has never been your forte, but I'm sure you'll adapt to it."

"I don't want to! I never want that accursed blade in my hands again. It's the one I saw in my vision, Clarissa. The one I shall use to murder Mademoiselle Clattersmash!"

"It is? How curious! But if you really saw the future, then you should regard the vision as an opportunity."

"An opportunity to do what?"

"To change it."

For the briefest of moments, my heart filled with hope. Why hadn't I realised that before? Of course! All I had to do was avoid ever being alone with Mademoiselle Clattersmash!

The image of the Yatsill's butchered corpse invaded my mind's eye. It blurred and became the ragged carcass of Polly Nichols.

"It won't work," I whispered. "I have no control over my Mr. Hyde."

For the first occasion in all the time I'd known her, I witnessed my friend lose her temper. Slapping her hands down onto the arms of her chair, she shouted, "Why the blazes do you persist with this absurd notion, Aiden? You are *not* Jack the Ripper! For crying out loud, don't you think we *all* have a darkness within us? Don't you think I've imagined wreaking a terrible revenge on Rupert Hufferton for what he did to me? He killed my father! Caused my mother to die of grief! He made a twisted ruin of me and threw me out of my home and into the streets. I was an outcast, and it was his fault. I haven't just imagined murdering him—I've spent hour after hour daydreaming how I might bring him down, deprive him of his riches, destroy his reputation, take away everything he holds dear. I've even thought how satisfactory it would be to hold him prisoner and torture him! Horrible things! Horrible!"

I stared, open-mouthed, at her.

"It's natural!" she insisted. "It's perfectly normal to harbour such thoughts about a person who's done you a terrible wrong!"

"But——" I began.

She halted me with a palm directed at my face. "No. Just listen. That Tanner girl and her father made of you a victim and gave you little choice but to leave Theaston Vale. Anyone would react with rage at that, but up until then your life had been a sheltered one, your character mild, your emotions unformed. You didn't know how to articulate your fury, so you locked it deep inside yourself and refused to acknowledge it. Then, in London, when you stumbled upon the corpse of Polly Nichols, you experienced primal fear. The horror of that experience was also suppressed and got mixed up with your imprisoned wrath. It left your memory impaired and is causing you to doubt the integrity of your own character. You imagined that Jack, to commit those dreadful murders, must possess the same intensity of anger as you, and since you find it inconceivable that anyone *but* you could possibly possess it, you've concluded that you must be the Ripper. Bad logic!" She leaned forward until her goggles were close to my face. "You are *not* a murderer!"

My heart rejected her assertion, but intellectually she made perfect sense. I said, "How, then, do I overcome this delusion?"

"You are akin to a dormant volcano. If you erupt, it might be destructive. If, however, you can find a way to relieve the pressure in a more measured fashion, that will do much to calm your inner turmoil."

I looked at my blistered hands. "Perhaps if I throw myself into this training?"

"Yes! Physical activity!"

"If I'm up to it. I'm already a wreck."

"I'm sure a hot bath will help. You relax here while I light the fire and put some buckets of water to heat."

While Clarissa fussed around me—and almost certainly to stop me dwelling on my fears—she talked about the estate she'd been given. It was comprised of the house we were in, a farm just outside the city, a manufacturing plant on the first level, and a block of dwellings on the second. The residents of the latter would be her workforce when she decided what her factory should produce.

"Some mechanical contrivance or other," she said. "I have no idea how long we're going to be here. It may be for the rest of our lives, so I might as well make myself useful."

"Contrivance?"

"Hmm. I've been thinking about those long avenues. They're ridiculously steep. It occurred to me that they might benefit from cable trams, like the ones they've been constructing in San Francisco."

"Judging by the number of spills I saw on them earlier, I'd agree."

My bath was soon ready. Among the new items in the bathroom, I found a cut-throat razor crafted at my companion's behest by one of the city's knife makers. After some work, I was finally able to liberate my chin from its outrageous beard. My hair, on the other hand, was almost down to my shoulders and I felt oddly disinclined to cut it. Having shaved, I thankfully gave myself up to the tub's steaming water, its heat penetrating my sore muscles all the way to the bone.

Maybe Clarissa was right. I wasn't the Whitechapel killer. But still I could feel that black something inside of me. I wanted to know it. I needed to be sure it hadn't committed the acts I attributed to it. Cautiously, with my eyes closed, I mentally probed inward.

I sank into shadows.

Nothing. For a long time, nothing.

Then, as if hands were reaching into me to dredge the images from the depths of my mind, I saw the sword, the blood, and Polly Nichols, torn, gutted, dead. Her eyes were looking up into mine. The two deep lacerations in her throat worked like mouths. They chorused: *"You think I might find happiness with a dusty old bookworm? A tall, thin dullard? A bundle of sticks bound together in last century's clothes? Why, I would rather be alone for the rest of my life than be bonded to a wretched scarecrow like you!"*

She spat. Her blood splashed onto my boots.

I opened my eyes. My jaw was clenched. My fingers were white, gripping the sides of the bathtub.

"Damn you!" I hissed. "Damn you, Aiden Fleischer!"

After remaining in the water until it had cooled to tepid, I dried myself, returned to my room, and dressed in a loose shirt and fairly shapeless trousers.

As I was descending the ramp, there came a knock at the front door. Clarissa stepped into the vestibule behind me just as I opened the portal to find a cabbie on our doorstep.

"Come to take you to the barracks, chum," he said.

I turned to my friend and slapped a hand to my forehead. "Already? Am I to get no respite, Clarissa?"

"Apparently not," she replied.

○ ○

While I was occupied with my second painfully long training session, the Yatsill built their first printing press and opened a newspaper office. I knew nothing of this, and even had I been told wouldn't have digested the information, for I didn't possess the capacity to train and think at the same time. Such was the strain on my body that my brain simply shut down in order to avoid the pain. I remember only the flashes of the sword, the thuds of metal on wood, the clashes of metal on metal, and Colonel Spearjab's voice insistently demanding that I do more, work harder, stop slacking, chop, guard, slice, riposte, dodge, thrust, fight fight *fight*!

Again, the cab ride home made no impression on me. So weary was I, the colonel could have launched me there by catapult and I wouldn't have known it. My awareness ceased entirely at some point before I left Crooked Blue Tower Barracks and didn't return until I was woken up by a loud voice below my window.

The absurdly titled *New Yatsillat Trumpet* had launched with a sensational headline.

"Read all about it! Read all about it! Parliamentarian murdered! Read all about it! First murder in New Yatsillat!"

I found Clarissa in the lounge with a newspaper in her hands.

"You were asleep when I left for the Temple of Magicians and still asleep when I got back," she said. "You must have been exhausted. Did the newsboy wake you?"

"Yes. Murder?"

"Yarvis Thayne. He was found outside his home. It appears that someone attacked him with a sword and shattered his shell. His internal organs were spread across the pavement. A ghastly business."

I staggered and caught at a chair to support myself. I croaked, "Were you here when I returned from training?"

"Yes. You were all done in and went straight to bed. You didn't even eat. You must be famished. I'll ring for Kata—she'll prepare you some breakfast."

She reached for a small handbell but hesitated when I cried out, "Wait! Stop! Tell me—tell me, was I—was I—?"

"Covered in blood? No, Aiden, you weren't. Neither was your sword. I know what you're thinking and you can get it out of your head immediately. You didn't kill Yarvis Thayne."

She rang the bell.

"But what if I left the house while you were out?" I said.

"Do you remember doing so?"

"No."

"Your sword was in exactly the same place by the door when I returned and Kata said you hadn't stirred. If you'd got up, dressed, taken your weapon, and left the house, don't you think she'd have noticed? Even if she failed to see or hear you depart, she'd have realised the blade was missing. No—you were asleep the entire time, there's no doubt about it."

I flopped into a chair, weak with relief.

"Murdered," I mumbled. "Murdered!"

"It puts us in an awkward position. He was a figurehead for those who oppose the changes our presence has brought about. No doubt he, like Father Yissil Froon, wanted me banished to the Shelf Lands."

I grunted a response.

"If the Yatsill knew how to investigate a murder," Clarissa went on, "which they probably don't, they'd have to place us on their list of suspects."

Kata entered and bobbed a curtsey. Clarissa asked her to brew a pot of tea and grill a couple of Kula'at—a species of fish that tasted remarkably similar to smoked mackerel. As our housekeeper headed for the kitchen, my companion said, "Yarvis Thayne's death isn't the only bad news. Mademoiselle Clattersmash's ailment appears to be spreading. According to the *Trumpet* there are four hundred and fifty-six reported cases so far. Like murder, sickness is a new phenomenon for the Yatsill." She rustled the newspaper. "This reports the two events as if they're nothing more than intriguing novelties. You and I should take them rather more seriously."

"If we are to investigate, where should we start?"

"I shall ask Yissil Froon whether he or his supporters have been in any way threatened. You, meanwhile, should try to educate Colonel Spearjab in matters of policing the city. Let's make the City Guard live up to its name, else what's it for? I've not even seen it using the watchtowers!"

"I know," I replied. "I've asked Spearjab and my fellow trainees again and again what the city is defending itself against but all I receive by way of response is evasiveness and the phrase 'the Saviour's Eyes are not always upon us.' The same as when I've asked about being 'taken.'"

"I've experienced the same evasiveness from the Magicians. Apparently these are taboo subjects during the light of day—perhaps we'll learn more when night finally arrives. Keep pressing the subject, Aiden. In the meantime, if you don't mind, I'm going to turn one of our rooms into a laboratory. I want to take blood samples and see if I can get to the bottom of this outbreak."

° °

Guardswoman Lily Wheelturner emitted a squeal of pain and staggered backward, hopping on three legs.

"By the Suns!" Colonel Momentous Spearjab shouted. "Good move, lad! *Good move*, I say! Ha ha! What!"

Time had passed. I'd lost count of how many training sessions I'd endured since the death of Yarvis Thayne—maybe twelve, perhaps fifteen. The two suns were now sinking toward the ocean.

I couldn't by any stretch be regarded as proficient with the sword, but during that long period, I had at least acquired skills enough to defend myself against Wheelturner's attack. She'd made a clumsy thrust at my stomach that I'd evaded by turning sideways, allowing her blade to skim across the tough padding around my torso while

I used my momentum to spin and swing my weapon against one of her upper thighs.

I lowered my sword and flexed my shoulders, trying to work the stiffness out of them.

"No slacking!" Spearjab bellowed.

Wheelturner lunged forward and slashed down at my head. I side-stepped and, with unrestrained viciousness, smashed the pommel of my weapon into her mask, which broke in half and fell from her face.

"Disengage!" the colonel ordered.

Stepping away, I glared at my opponent's four glittering eyes. I was angry. The rules of training stated that thrusts and cuts must be directed only at padding—thin but very robust material covering the torso, arms, and legs—but she'd repeatedly swiped at my unpro-tected head.

"Bravo, Fleischer!" Spearjab called, then, turning to the other guards, he added, "You see! Ha ha! That's how it's jolly well done! What!" He indicated that Wheelturner and I should get back in line, then waved another pair of trainees forward. They began to fight, their swords clanging.

The gruelling exercises, which had occupied almost all my waking hours, together with the heavier gravity and what proved to be a very nutritious diet, were having a visible effect on my phy-sique. My bones were already sheathed in expanding and hardening muscle and the constant pain—for every session pushed my body to its limits—had given my face a sort of flinty grimness, quite unlike its former guilelessness.

My proposition—made some time ago—that the City Guard should man the watchtowers and patrol the streets had initially been greeted by the colonel with a response of "utterly unnecessary when the Saviour is looking upon us." However, after I pointed out that Yarvis Thayne's murder had occurred in the sight of the Saviour, and that the killer was still on the loose and might strike again, and that the protesters against change were growing in number and becoming rather more disruptive and unruly, he took the sugges-tion to Lord Brittleback. The prime minister immediately passed a mandate giving the City Guard powers and duties commensurate to those of London's Metropolitan Police. The guardsmen now divided their time between patrols and training, with one exception—me. For some unfathomable reason, Colonel Spearjab was convinced that I was the resident expert in swordplay, and so kept me at Crooked Blue Tower Barracks to pass my so-called skills on to my fellows. His assumption was, of course, wholly erroneous. I knew no more of the sword than he did. The endless training had, though, bestowed upon me greater endurance and strength than I could have possibly imagined. I'd learned that the human body, when placed under terrible duress, possesses an astonishing capacity for adaptation.

The suns were by now at the five o'clock mark, with the thin crescent moons clustered close to them. It was impossible to calculate the length of time Clarissa and I had been on Ptallaya, though in Earthly terms, surely it must be measured in many months, perhaps even a year. The temperature had gradually increased and warm rains were now sweeping across the city at regular intervals.

I had not seen much of my companion. That she was very busy was obvious. In addition to her schooling with the Council of Magicians, she was also contributing many marvels to the Yatsills' burgeoning new culture. Her manufacturing plant was constructing three-wheeled, tiller-steered, steam-driven autocarriages, many of which were already navigating the roads; big power houses were being built at the top of each avenue to pull the subsurface chains the trams would use to travel up and down the steep inclines; a more sophisticated sewerage system than the original was half-installed; and New Yatsillat's factories and foundries were all being refitted with more efficient machinery. In addition, my friend had introduced a citywide postal system, which meant we now had an address: 3 Dissonance Square, Fourth Terrace, New Yatsillat.

Off to my right, Lily Wheelturner crumpled to the ground.

"Swords down!" Spearjab ordered.

We gathered around my erstwhile opponent who was sprawled motionless but for small tremors that shook her limbs.

Spearjab said, "I say! She looks to be in a bad way, what! Humph!"

I pushed one of my fellow guardsmen aside and crouched beside the stricken Yatsill.

"Lily, can you hear me?"

The fronds that fringed her mouth had turned a pale grey. They flopped loosely as her lips moved. "I can't get up."

"Does your head hurt? My apologies, I didn't mean to strike you so hard."

"You . . . didn't. Not . . . not my head. I feel . . . I feel weak. Can't . . . think straight. Perhaps . . . perhaps Phenadoor calls me."

One of the other guardsmen said, "Are you chilled?"

"Yes," she whispered. "Cold."

"I feel it, too," he said. He turned to the colonel. "In fact, sir, I feel jolly rotten."

"Aye, me as well," another agreed.

Spearjab's fingers waggled with agitation. "Anyone else?"

The rest of the Yatsill shook their heads and there were various murmurs of, "No," "Not me, sir," and "I feel fine."

"Righty-ho," the colonel said. "Wheelturner, Flapper, and Stretch—remain here. We'll call a carriage and get you to a bally Magician. Humph! The rest of you are dismissed."

With a last glance at the ailing guardswoman, I divested myself of the practice padding, saluted Colonel Spearjab, left the military compound, hailed a cab, and was driven home.

It was plain that Wheelturner and the other two had come down with the sickness that was now endemic across the city—thousands of Yatsill were suffering, Aristocrat and Working Class alike. Last time I'd seen Clarissa, she was close to a breakthrough in her analysis of blood samples. I hoped she'd now have something to report.

The cab dropped me at the corner of Dissonance Square.

My friend was outside Number Three, tinkering with the engine of our new autocarriage.

"Hello!" she said. "Have they let you out early?"

"Yes. Three more of the Yatsill have been taken ill. Has your laboratory borne fruit?"

"I'm afraid so."

I strode over to her, noticing as I did so that three top-hatted Aristocrats were loitering nearby. They were glancing repeatedly at us and muttering among themselves. My arrival appeared to have disconcerted them somewhat. Perhaps they wanted a private word with my friend. They could wait until I went indoors to bathe.

"Afraid, Clarissa? Why afraid?"

She used a rag to wipe oil from her hands. "I've been working with Mademoiselle Clattersmash—she's still weak but manages to get around—Father Spreadflower Meadows, and another Magician, Father Tendency Clutterfuss. They all specialise in medicine. They've examined the blood samples and have reached the same conclusion as I."

"Which is what?"

"That the infection was brought here by you."

"Me?"

"The illness is *kichyomachyoma*, Aiden. There is a microorganism in your blood, presumably injected by the spider that bit you on Koluwai. A counteragent of some sort—I've yet to identify it—has rendered you immune to its deleterious effects, but it's still active and has somehow been communicated from you to the Yatsill, and now from Yatsill to Yatsill."

I slumped against the autocarriage. "No!"

"The infection caused severe malarial symptoms in you, but in the Yatsill it manifests more like a mild flu but with one noticeable difference: the victims experience a debilitating 'loosening' of their telepathic connection to their fellows. This lessens the intelligence of the Workers and causes a sense of isolation in the Aristocrats, which, Clattersmash says, is by far the most disturbing aspect of the illness."

"Have you found a cure?"

"Not yet, but the microorganism cannot survive in the blood of the islanders, and as I say, though active in yours, is rendered harmless to its host by an active counteragent. Those two lines of inquiry will, I hope, lead me to the solution."

"I can't believe I've been the cause of this," I groaned.

"There's every chance you'll also provide the remedy."

"Should I be quarantined?"

"It would be pointless. The infection is already too widespread."
She looked me up and down. "And speaking of health, Aiden, my
goodness—what a transformation has been wrought in you! You've
filled out so much we'll have to ask the tailor to supply new clothes.
You look a different man."

"A man who can't remember the last time he didn't ache all over.
How I miss my quiet little vicarage and my books!"

"Do you really mean that? Are you not feeling a certain fulfilment
in the physical challenges you face every day?"

I snorted, as if she'd spoken an utter nonsense, but as a matter
of fact, she was right. Physically—despite the disease I apparently
carried—I'd never felt better in my life. I didn't even notice the drag
of Ptallaya's gravity any more and was experiencing an unexpected
exultation in our strange new existence. However, for whatever
reason, I couldn't quite bring myself to admit to this, so I replied,
"Constitutionally, I'm more suited to holding a Shakespeare than a
sword, but I've lost my position in life and am left with no options.
I have no social standing. I've become naught but a common soldier.
And now you tell me I'm a plague carrier!"

"Hardly that!" she objected.

"I'm going to take a bath," I grumbled, and marched into the
house, feeling inexplicably irritated that my friend should have identified that I, a scholar and clergyman, was starting to enjoy spending
my every waking hour in mock combat.

I was halfway up the ramp to the upper rooms when I heard
Clarissa give a loud cry of alarm. In an instant I was down again,
across the vestibule, and back out through the door. My companion
was standing against the autocarriage. Blood was streaming from her
left shoulder. She was swinging a large spanner back and forth, and
the three Aristocrats were crouched in front of her. They'd pulled
swords from beneath their jackets.

"What in the Saviour's name do you think you're doing?" I yelled,
striding toward them.

In answer, one of them threw himself at me, chopping downward
with his blade. My training took over. Without thinking, I pivoted,

and his weapon flashed past less than two inches from my face. In the same instant the tip of his sword clanged on the cobbles, I drew my own and, in doing so, slammed my forearm into his neck. His head snapped back, his top hat rolled away, and he stumbled from me, giving me the space to slash at him. His hand went flying, still clutching his weapon. With a scream of pain, he squatted and scuttled out of reach, clutching at his spurting stump.

A wave of revulsion hit me as I felt my inner demon squirm with sick delight, rejoicing at the damage I'd inflicted upon the attacker. I lowered my sword, stepped back, and stammered, "I'm—I'm sorry." I was torn, as if two personalities were grappling for dominance of me. One would not hesitate to take a life in order to protect Clarissa. The other could barely lift the blade, so afraid was it that if I started killing I'd not be able to stop.

I teetered backward as one of the other Yatsill came at me, but as I did so, I saw the third creature take a swipe at Clarissa, who barely managed to block his blade with her spanner. My sword came up automatically and I parried my new opponent's first swing, then—with my body rather than my mind in control—slashed at one of his legs, slicing it off beneath the first knee joint.

I leaped away from him to defend my companion.

The third Yatsill saw me coming and scurried backward into the square, giving himself more room to manoeuvre. I realised at once that this creature knew what he was doing. His stance spoke of someone well practised with the sword, though how he came by such skill was a mystery, for only the Working Class trained as guardsmen. Even before we engaged, this appreciation of his ability sent a thrill of fear through me. Crossing blades when you are well padded and your opponent is under strict instructions only to aim at that padding and not hit hard is one thing, but facing a foe who's under no such compulsion is quite another. I'd seen for myself how readily these Ptallayan swords could sink into the hard wood of tree stumps. Wielded with strength, they could easily slice straight through a limb, as I'd already found.

Had I been alone, perhaps I would have succumbed to the insistent part of me that wanted to drop my weapon and take to my heels. As it was, I couldn't possibly leave Clarissa, so my only option was to fight.

The Aristocrat stepped in and swung at me. Our blades met and, after a shimmering sizzle as they slid along each other's length, were immediately whirling so fast that an unpractised eye would see nothing but flashes as they again and again reflected the light of the twin suns. The square echoed with clangs and clashes. My enemy was terrifyingly fast and vigorous, setting me on the defensive from the outset. Somehow, somewhere, he'd worked long and hard to acquire such skill. It had given him confidence and a technique that, by Yatsill standards, couldn't be faulted. In addition, his only concern was to cause my demise, while I was distracted by the knowledge that his companions were nearby, nursing their wounds, and capable at any moment of attacking me from the rear or, worse, of plunging their swords into Clarissa. In addition, while he obviously held no compunction about murder, my fear of killing caused me to frequently miss opportunities to turn the attack on him.

That initial flurry of passes and parries ended with a clumsy lunge on my part. It was diverted with such ease that my opponent actually stepped back and made the clicking noise I knew to be a Yatsill laugh as I tottered sideways, only just regaining my footing.

The burst of rage this incited was immediately quelled by the realisation that he was trying to provoke me. I ducked and wheeled just as Clarissa shouted a warning and the three-legged Yatsill thrust from behind, aiming between my shoulder blades. I was lucky. As I sank down and twisted, he missed my face by a hair's breadth, and the edge of my blade caught the flat of his with all the force of my spinning body, breaking his weapon clean in half. The point clattered away across the cobbles. I completed my gyration and raised my blade just in time to block my principal adversary. Now I settled into defending myself and did so without a single riposte, hoping the Aristocrat would exhaust himself. Dimly, under the chimes and scrapes of battle, I heard the two creatures behind me run from the square, probably under threat from Clarissa's heavy spanner. That

was the last thing, beyond my opponent, to impinge on my awareness, for now a sudden focus descended upon me—a sharpness of
attention quite unlike anything I'd experienced before. It was as
if time itself changed, so that every alteration in the angle of my
adversary's shoulders, every adjustment of his stance, could be examined and analysed in meticulous detail. Indeed, my mind appeared
to encroach upon the immediate future so that my reflexes operated
slightly ahead of his, allowing me to dodge every thrust, parry every
sweep, evade every trick.

It felt as if many minutes were passing, although in truth they
were mere seconds, but they were enough to drain his energy. Then
I saw a slightly too careless thrust coming, deflected it with ease,
stepped in, and used my left hand to punch him in the head. He
staggered back in the direction I wanted—toward the fountain in
the centre of the square.

The tables turned. I changed my tactic from defence to an all-out
assault, putting into practice every technique I'd developed at Crooked
Blue Tower Barracks. To earthly connoisseurs of swordplay—the
Alfred Huttons, Egerton Castles, and Richard Burtons—no doubt I'd
have appeared woefully clumsy. However, while I was no d'Artagnan,
I began to feel myself a match for my opponent, and now forced him
into retreat with a flurry of slashes and jabs that, I'm sure, from his
perspective made my point seem everywhere at once. I struck the mask
from his face, cracked the shell of his upper left arm, and scored a
furrow across his trunk. "Stop!" he cried out, but I didn't. Instead, I
pressed my attack and demanded, "Who are you? Why did you try to
murder my friend?"

"I don't know!"

"Are you following orders?"

"Yes!"

"From whom?"

In an act of wild desperation, he exposed his entire torso to a
thrust—which I didn't take—and swung his weapon full force at my
head. I raised my own at an angle to meet it, causing his sword to
hiss along its length, showering sparks a good six inches above me,

then stepped in and kicked him savagely between the legs—a barbarous move that was just as effective on a Yatsill as it was on a man. He doubled over, moaned, and dropped his weapon. I delivered an uppercut to his face, my fist squelching into the boneless flesh. He rocked backward, spraying blood into the air, tripped over the lip of the fountain, and went plunging into the water.

After kicking his sword out of reach, I waited for him to emerge. He struggled to his feet and swayed, weighed down by wet clothes and exhaustion. Blood streamed from his wounded arm.

"Answer me!" I snapped, levelling my blade at his chest. "Who ordered this attack?"

With difficulty, he clambered up onto the fountain's low wall.

His four bead-like eyes met mine. Though they were expressionless, as was normal with the Yatsill, I detected a peculiar blankness in them, as though his mind wasn't his own. He shook his head, then whipped up a hand, grabbed the tip of my sword, and propelled himself forward onto it. The metal sank through the vertical seam of his body shell and emerged from the middle of his back. His corpse thudded against me, causing me to tumble to the ground with it on top. My head cracked against the cobbles and everything blurred.

When the world came back into focus, I realised that Clarissa was dragging the dead creature off me.

"Are you all right?" I groaned. "Your shoulder is bleeding."

"A small wound. Nothing I can't fix with a poultice. And you, Aiden? Your hand is spouting blood and your cheek has been laid open. Is that the worst of it?"

"It is." I pushed myself to my feet and looked at my right hand. At some point during the conflict I'd lost my little finger, though I hadn't felt it. Now the pain began to throb abysmally.

I looked at the fallen Yatsill. "I couldn't kill him."

"You didn't need to—he threw himself onto your blade."

"But Clarissa, I *had* to kill him in order to protect you, but something in me prevented it. I was battling myself as much as I was battling him."

"Good. You'll have no more Jack the Ripper delusions, then!"

I gave a grunted agreement, but I was puzzled. My inner conflict had been far deeper than I could put into words and had felt somehow unnatural, as if my hesitancy hadn't been wholly of my own volition.

I moaned as the pain in my hand grew worse, then shook my head to clear my muddled thoughts and asked, "Why, Clarissa? Why attack you?"

"I have no idea. Stay here—I'll fetch my medical pack."

My friend, as a Magician, had been trained to treat wounds using Ptallaya's various herbs, many of which possessed remarkable healing properties. She now brought some from the house and applied them to my hand and lacerated cheek, fastening them against my skin with an adhesive leaf. Immediately, the pain was numbed.

"Your first duelling scar," she murmured, "and your finger will quickly grow back."

"Grow back?" I echoed. "How is that possible?"

"The miracle of Ptallaya. Remain here and rest. I'm going to report this atrocity. Shall I fetch you something to drink?"

I nodded wearily.

After treating her own wound and supplying me with a bottle of water from our kitchen, she mounted the autocarriage and drove off. I sat down and leaned against the wall of the fountain. The dead creature was sprawled nearby, still transfixed by my sword. Its blood seeped between the hard cobble-like shells, exactly as Mademoiselle Clattersmash's had in my vision. All of a sudden, I was trembling violently, and, partly out of shock, partly at sheer relief at having survived, I began to giggle like a madman.

o o

I was still half-dazed and using the wall of the fountain for support when a convoy of steam-vehicles came panting into the square. Clarissa and Father Mordant Reverie disembarked from the first, Lord Upright Brittleback and Mr. Sepik from the second, and Colonel Momentous Spearjab and two guardsmen from the third.

I straightened and greeted them all as they gathered around the corpse.

"I'd just delivered our sick chaps to the Magicians when I heard," Spearjab said to me. "Harrumph! Are you injured?"

"Only slightly."

"Humph! Humph! I understand the three Aristocrats were after Miss Stark. What!"

"Yes."

Lord Brittleback exclaimed, "What a bloody mess!" He addressed Spearjab. "Are all your guardsmen accounted for, old fruit?"

"They are indeed, Prime Minister—harrumph!—and my troops are Working Class, not jolly old Aristocrats like the assailants!"

"Ah, yes, of course!" Brittleback responded. "I don't understand it. The Yatsill are not violent. And the fact that Miss Stark is of the Aristocracy makes it even more incredible. Attacking one of our own? It's bloody impossible!"

"Apparently not," I put in.

Clarissa said, "Perhaps they were supporters of Yarvis Thayne and blame me for his murder."

"They were acting on orders, I know that much," I offered. "And if they supported Yarvis Thayne, then they must also support Yissil Froon."

Father Mordant Reverie shook his head. "If you're proposing that Yissil Froon might be behind this, I have to disagree in the strongest possible terms. He's one of my most respected Magicians, and the eldest of us all. If anything, your suspicion suggests two hidden forces at work in the city, one supporting the dissonance and responsible for the murder of Thayne, the other against it and the source of the attack on Miss Stark."

"Or a single force whose motives are rather more complex than we can currently guess," Clarissa suggested.

"Is there any discontent among the Aristocrats?" I asked.

The prime minister gave an awkward shrug—a gesture that didn't come easily to a Yatsill. "The Workers are restless, but not the Aristocracy."

"There's a problem with the Working Class?" Clarissa asked. "How so?"

"They are becoming increasingly uppity. The glassmakers have ceased work completely and I've received reports of widespread carelessness and disobedience. It's bloody inconvenient and, to be perfectly frank, I'm not quite sure what to do about it. But that's all beside the point." He thought a moment, before addressing Spearjab again. "Colonel, I want you to instigate a search for the two surviving assassins."

Spearjab saluted and said, "Righty-ho! Perhaps the dissonance—" he gestured at Clarissa "—could provide a description? Hey?"

My friend glanced at me and shook her head. The Yatsill all looked similar to us.

"Their masks were the same," Clarissa said. "Plain and unadorned."

"One of them lost his right hand," I added, "and the other the lower part of one leg."

"Ah!" Brittleback said. "Well done! That'll teach 'em! Father Mordant, perhaps these individuals will visit a Magician for treatment."

"I shall make enquiries, Prime Minister."

Brittleback wriggled his fingers and flicked a hand toward the corpse. "Colonel, would you and your men dispose of this bloody thing, please? And I'd like a couple of your troops on permanent sentry duty outside Miss Stark's house."

Spearjab replied, "Humph! Yes! What! I say, Prime Minister, it occurs to me that Guardsman Fleischer has contributed enough to the training of the City Guard. In addition to placing two sentries in the square, I shall assign him permanently to Miss Stark. What! What!"

"Bloody good show!" Brittleback exclaimed.

Spearjab looked at me. "Never leave her side, is that understood, old thing?"

"Perfectly!" I replied, feeling as if a great weight had been lifted from me.

"Well then," Brittleback announced, "we each have our part to play, but you, Colonel, will coordinate the investigation. I'd particularly like to know whether this has any connection with the murder of Yarvis Thayne."

"Absolutely! Absolutely! I'll place guards with Yissil Froon, too. He might be in danger. *Danger*, I say!"

"Good thinking, Colonel! Do it at once, please!"

So saying, the prime minister mounted his vehicle, was followed aboard by his tall, silent aide, and they departed. Spearjab and his two subordinates loaded the dead Yatsill onto their autocarriage and went rattling away.

Father Reverie looked up at the sky. Its pale yellow had deepened, taking on an orange hue. The shadows were lengthening. Drops of rain were beginning to fall. "Rest for as long as you need, Miss Stark," he murmured without looking down, "then attend to your various projects. Whatever of them can be completed in short order, I recommend you get them done." He lowered his head and turned his crow mask to me, "And you, Guardsman Fleischer, keep your sword sharp. The Eyes will soon be closing."

He crossed to his vehicle, clambered into it, and without a backward glance, drove off.

"Oddly enough," I said, "I feel much happier."

Clarissa pushed me toward the house. "Because your training is finished?"

We stepped in and walked across the vestibule.

"Because we won't be separated any more."

As we entered the kitchen, I was overcome by an impulse. Grabbing my friend's elbow, I turned her to face me then pulled her into a tight embrace. "I nearly lost you!" I whispered, pressing my face into the crook of her neck. "Clarissa, I nearly lost you!"

She put her arms around me. "But thanks to your own bravery, you didn't."

I held her, perhaps longer than our close friendship warranted, but I couldn't let her go and didn't care about decorum. The thought of being without her was unbearable—and it struck me that it wasn't being alone on Ptallaya I feared, but the possibility I might be without Clarissa Stark *anywhere*.

I released her and stepped back, my hands still on her upper arms. She was beautiful.

"I've never asked you," I said, looking at the dark goggles. "What colour are your eyes?"

"Brown." To my surprise, she reddened slightly and quickly changed the subject. "You're shaking like a leaf, Aiden—sit down. Are you still hungry? I'll prepare us something to eat."

I laughed. "Do you remember when you first arrived at Theaston Vale? It feels like such a long time ago, but you said you couldn't enjoy my hospitality with the odour of the road upon you. In the same vein, I cannot sit here after a bloodthirsty battle while you cook for me, so, if you don't mind, I'll go and wash while you work your magic at the stove."

A little later, while splashing water over my face, I paused and, with my eyes closed, revisited again that horrible moment when the Yatsill had thrown itself upon my sword. I re-experienced the grating vibration running up my arm as the blade slid through its shell, the hot blood spurting across my fingers, the weight of the body impacting against me, and the final exhalation rattling in my ear.

What had I felt? Did an internal Jack the Ripper relish the kill? Had a monster risen from my shadows?

No, there was no monster.

I'd been aware only of overwhelming shock and repulsion, but, again, there was also the strange notion that an exterior force had drawn the reaction out of me. Now I felt entirely differently. Grimly satisfied. I was *glad* the beast had died. Glad because he'd tried to execute Clarissa and I'd been responsible for his failure. Furthermore, having just killed, I knew for certain that it was for the first time. Whatever the darkness in me was, it certainly *wasn't* the Ripper.

Clean, and somewhat calmer, I rejoined my friend.

"How's your hand?" she asked.

"It doesn't hurt at all."

We ate a large meal, during which I asked, "Why don't you manufacture a pistol? I'd feel happier if you were armed."

"The Yatsill have forbidden it. They see no use for such weapons.

Besides which, I'd hate to introduce firearms to this world. Our own has suffered enough because of them."

"Will you at least carry a sword?"

"I'd be too clumsy with it. A dagger. I'll carry a dagger."

After our meal, we moved to the lounge where we sat and chatted. Outside, the rain had quickly developed into a heavy downpour. Clarissa stood and wandered over to one of the windows. Looking out, she observed, "There are never any clouds, yet it rains."

"And it never rains but it pours—with ever greater frequency."

"It's late afternoon, Aiden. We have a very, very long night ahead of us. What a fool I've been!"

"Fool? Why?"

"Because it's only just occurred to me to manufacture street lamps. Had I thought of it earlier, the whole city could've been illuminated by dusk. As it is, by the time I have them designed and the machinery to make them constructed, it'll be too late."

"The Yatsill must have managed well enough before our arrival," I noted.

"Hmm. True. With burning brands in the Koluwaian fashion, I'd wager."

She turned and stretched. Much time had passed since her immersion and subsequent transformation but it was obvious that she still delighted in her healthy limbs and straight back.

"I think I'll turn in," she said.

I gave a sound of agreement. I was tired. We retired to our respective rooms.

○ ○

Time on Ptallaya is more subjective than on Earth and disconcerting in its effects. One might work and sleep, work and sleep, work and sleep again, look at the suns, and find they've apparently not moved at all—or embark on what feels like a short task only to discover, upon its completion, that the two orbs have visibly shifted and shadows have lengthened.

During the final stretch of the long Ptallayan day—I'd guess a month in Earthly terms but could be utterly wrong—the weather continued to worsen. A hot breeze started to blow from the land across the bay as if the Eyes of the Saviour, as they neared the horizon, were dragging all the air they'd heated after them. The quality of light around us gradually deepened to a rusty orange. The rains came more frequently, fell harder, and lasted longer.

New Yatsillat suffered. An alteration in the climate hadn't been taken into account when the city was built. Various of its materials rapidly deteriorated as they were first battered by the ferocious downpours, then swiftly dried by the torrid winds, then hit by rain again. Buildings leaked. Roofs collapsed. Walls cracked. The new sewerage pipes overflowed and burst. A section of the eighth terrace—as it happens, the district where Crooked Blue Tower Barracks had been located—collapsed and slid onto the ninth level, burying part of the fishing village.

To make matters worse, the Working Class approached the required repairs with a complete lack of diligence, performing their work in a very slapdash manner, taking far too long about it, or, increasingly, failing to do anything at all.

Amid this erosion, the flu-like sickness spread through the city like wildfire. Those of the Workers who came down with it reverted to a near animal state. They divested themselves of their garments, gathered at the seafront, and refused to leave. Kata told us, "They think they are dying and await the call of Phenadoor."

The Aristocracy fared a little better. They became weak and suffered spells of dizziness and amnesia, but were at least able to function.

Meanwhile, Colonel Spearjab made no progress with his investigation. The two surviving assailants hadn't been treated by any of the Magicians, or, it appeared, seen by anyone else.

Whatever had motivated the attempt on Clarissa's life remained a mystery.

"There've been no further moves made against you," I noted, "and none against Yissil Froon or anyone else. I wonder what our mysterious enemy is up to?"

We were walking home. Clarissa had taken a break from her

ongoing research to join me for lunch at our local restaurant—a meal marred by bad service and which ended prematurely due to the establishment's front window suddenly falling in, scattering shards of glass across the entire dining area.

Rather than responding to my musing, my friend, who'd been somewhat preoccupied throughout the meal, suddenly looked around as if only just realising where she was.

"The sky is red!" she murmured. "It's late! I didn't realise."

"The suns are setting," I said. "You've been holed away in that laboratory of yours for ages!"

A strong gust of wind whistled through the eaves of the buildings to either side of us. We'd opted to walk in the middle of the street in order to avoid falling roof tiles. There was little traffic—the city was becoming ever quieter and less active.

"Ages? Really? It doesn't feel like it."

"You've been busy, that's why. I, on the other hand, have had very little to do and the time has dragged awfully."

She didn't answer.

I looked at her. "Clarissa?"

"Hmm?"

"Did you hear me? What's wrong? You hardly said a word during lunch."

She sighed and frowned. "I'm sorry, Aiden. I'm finding it almost impossible to think straight. I appear to have affixed on a memory and it's replaying over and over, like an annoying tune that lodges itself in one's head."

"What memory?"

"Of the blueprints that Sir Philip Hufferton and I drew up when I was a youngster. I find myself dwelling on their every detail, their every line, and I can't stop myself. I have no idea why."

"Blueprints for what?"

"Extravagant war machines. Impractical, childish things. Why in Heaven's name are they playing on my mind so?"

I shrugged. "I remember you mentioning them once. What caused you to recall them in the first place?"

"That's the thing of it—nothing! They simply popped into my thoughts out of nowhere, and now they won't go away!"

We stepped over the rubble of a fallen chimney.

"You've been working too hard," I suggested.

"I'll keep going until I drop, if necessary. *Kichyomachyoma* may not be fatal to the Yatsill but it's debilitating enough to bring the city to a standstill." She put a hand to her head. "I just wish my brain would cooperate with me."

We arrived home and Clarissa resumed work in her laboratory with Mademoiselle Crockery Clattersmash, Father Spreadflower Meadows, and Father Tendency Clutterfuss. These three had been a constant presence in the house for no small amount of time now and I was beginning to feel a sense of camaraderie with them—even with Clattersmash, who'd so abruptly denied me my priesthood after the Ritual of Immersion. It was an affection I knew Clarissa felt more intensely—even to the point of real friendship—which, I suppose, was to be expected, as she was more or less constantly in their presence, working to the same end.

A little while after our return, there came knocking at our front door. I put aside the *New Yatsillat Trumpet*, left the lounge, and went to answer the summons. The wind had died and now yet another of the rainstorms was battering the city. The Koluwaian woman standing on our doorstep was drenched, with water streaming from her lank hair.

"I have a message from Father Mordant Reverie," she said. "He would like you and Miss Stark to attend him at the Temple of Magicians immediately. The matter is urgent."

Before I could invite her in to dry off, the Servant turned and disappeared into the monsoon-like downpour.

I closed the door and went to the laboratory. Clarissa and her three colleagues were bent over the paraphernalia of chemical research, each engrossed. I cleared my throat to attract her attention.

"What is it, Aiden?" she asked in an abstracted tone.

"Father Reverie wants to see us."

She straightened and clicked her tongue impatiently. "I need to finish this analysis. I'm finding it difficult enough to concentrate as it is—I really don't need to be interrupted. Confound it! Why is my mind obsessing so?" She thudded the base of her hand against her forehead. "It's getting worse!"

"He wants us at the temple right now, Clarissa. Perhaps the distraction will do you good."

She gave another inarticulate expression of exasperation and turned to Clattersmash. "Do you feel strong enough to continue for a little while, Mademoiselle? I notice you're trembling."

The Yatsill nodded. "I feel weak but I'll carry on, my dear. Do you mind if I sleep in one of your rooms should I require respite?"

"Not at all. I'll return as soon as I can."

We took our leave of the Magicians and exited the house. While I held an umbrella over Clarissa, she unfurled and clipped down our autocarriage's protective leather hood. We boarded the vehicle and set off with the torrent thundering so noisily on the skin roof we could barely converse. When we reached the main avenue, we found that it was practically a waterfall, so we abandoned the machine and jumped onto one of the new trams instead. It took us up to the third terrace with water sloshing noisily past its wheels. When the conveyance stopped we disembarked, and almost the instant we stepped into the flood, the rain ceased.

To our left—looking out over the rooftops—the choppy sea sparkled under the flushed, inexplicably cloud-free sky. The suns were already, for the most part, below the horizon, with just the molten smears of their apexes showing. Around us, the shadows were dense and purplish.

A short walk brought us to the temple. We mounted the steps and entered. My companion informed a Magician of our appointment. The Yatsill went away and returned a few moments later with Father Mordant Reverie, who said, "I must take you both to one of New Yatsillat's highest towers that the Saviour's Eyes may look upon you before they close."

He turned us around and steered us back out, guiding us to an autocarriage parked nearby. We boarded it, he took the tiller, and moments later we were chugging back toward the avenue.

"Oh!" Clarissa suddenly cried out. She massaged her temples. "It's stopped!"

"The blueprints?" I asked.

"At last!" she breathed. "I thought I was going insane! But—" She put her fingers to the bump above her right eyebrow.

Father Reverie turned his mask to her. "You feel your thoughts are being muffled, perhaps, Miss Stark?"

"Yes! As if my mind is being wrapped by a blanket."

I looked at her, shocked. "Please! You're not coming down with *kichyomachyoma?*"

"No, Aiden. This isn't the sickness. It's something else—a sort of suppression—and I sense it descending upon the whole city."

Reverie clicked the fingers of his free hand together and said, "The Magicians are sequestered in the temples and are now extending the Saviour's protection over the city. That is what you feel."

There was less water cascading down the avenue now, and the autocarriage navigated the slope with minimal difficulty. The Magician drove us to the top level and stopped at a watchtower next to a paper mill.

"Come," he said, and led us inside and up a long spiralling ramp. It eventually ended in a circular room with round widows set closely together in its walls. A huge lens stood before one of them, mounted on an ornate wheeled brass frame.

From this height, a tremendous vista was open to us: the flame-coloured ocean with the blazing smudges at its horizon; the monumental cliffs at the outer edges of the bay; the broad terraces encrusted with buildings; the mountain range to the north; and a vast expanse of hills and plains beneath a sky that, landward, had now turned the deepest of crimsons and in which two of the moons were set close together.

Reverie pulled the lens to one of the seaward-facing windows. We moved to stand beside him and watched in silent contemplation as the two yellow suns slowly slipped out of sight, leaving a band of orange light over the sea.

The long day had finally ended.

He adjusted the glass and said, "Look."

Peering through it, we saw that he'd focused the apparatus on the large crowd of *kichyomachyoma*-infected Working Class who stood at the seashore. One by one, they were slipping into the water, swimming out, and disappearing under the surface.

"Phenadoor embraces them," he said. "They go to a better world." He sighed. "As one of the Aristocrats, such rapture will never be mine. My fate lies elsewhere. I, and all the other Aristocrats, will eventually be taken."

"By what?" Clarissa asked.

I expected her question to be answered with the infuriating evasiveness we'd become accustomed to. Instead, Reverie wheeled the lens to the other side of the room and gestured for us to join him there.

Puzzled, we did so and looked out over the rolling landscape. Three of the mammoth Yarkeen creatures were floating in the far distance. For what I guessed to be five minutes, nothing happened and the Magician remained silent. Then he said, "That is what will dictate my future," and pointed.

On the horizon, the tip of a burning orb suddenly rose into view. I watched, dumbfounded.

It was a third sun, and it was gigantic—at least ten times larger than Earth's.

It was blood red.

∘ ∘

CHAPTER 7

RED

There was no night on Ptallaya!

The top edge of the gargantuan sun, a hellish inferno, erupted over the edge of the world. Inside the room, everything turned a vermilion hue. Outside, the landscape transformed.

I drew an unsteady breath. "What's happening?"

Father Mordant Reverie gestured toward the mounted lens and said, "Use that."

I reached for it and pulled the frame to the window. Magnified through the glass, I could see in better detail that the land beyond the city was undergoing a startling metamorphosis. The leaves of the various trees were turning black; thorny weed-like growths—also black—were coiling up from under the ground; and clawed, armoured, dangerous-looking creatures, some like spiny lobsters, others incomprehensible jumbles of jagged-edged limbs, were digging themselves out of burrows. The three Yarkeen changed in a matter of seconds from transparent to jet, and their long tentacles sprouted nasty-looking barbs.

"That which may not be spoken of in the sight of the Saviour is now upon us," Reverie said. His mask suddenly bulged outward. Reaching up, he removed it. The lumps over his eyes were lengthening and thickening. I watched as they rapidly grew into horns, curling upward until their pointed tips were almost directed backward. At the same time, his body colour divided into stripes, some deepening to black, the others brightening to yellow, until his carapace had taken on the appearance of a tiger.

I glanced at Clarissa and was thankful to see that her forehead bumps were unaltered, her skin the same.

Reverie jerked his head toward the curved band of red fire and continued, "The Heart of Blood is rising, and soon its gods will come to Ptallaya."

"Gods? Do they threaten us?" I asked, thinking of the City Guard and the defensive wall.

"They do. Now I am free to tell you the truth of this world. Once, long ago, Ptallaya was as you see it now and had been that way for all its existence: a place of savagery and conflict ruled over by the wicked creatures we call Blood Gods. Then the Saviour's Eyes opened and looked upon it and found there was nothing pleasing to see, until, eventually, the Yatsill wandered into sight and were judged to be good. So the Saviour cast the Blood Gods out and made the Yatsill the new rulers of Ptallaya. However, the Heart of Blood itself could not be supplanted, so a balance was established. When the Saviour's Eyes are open, the world is ours. We journey to the Forest of Indistinct Murmurings to recover the Servants who are delivered here from your world and to milk Dar'sayn from the fruit of the Ptoollan trees that our Magicians might be strong; and we take our children to the Cavern of Immersion to be made Aristocrats or Working Class. But when the Saviour's Eyes close, the jealous Blood Gods return to Ptallaya. They possess the Aristocrats and attack Phenadoor—for they want to destroy it."

"Why?" I asked.

"Because Phenadoor is good and the Blood Gods are evil." Reverie sighed and his eyes glittered. "Father Yissil Froon is fearful. He says there are now too many Workers and too few Aristocrats. The Magicians will take Dar'sayn to strengthen their protective powers but our supply isn't sufficient for the challenge we face. Besides which, many Magicians are stricken with illness."

"Father Reverie," I interrupted, "Miss Stark and I were with Colonel Momentous Spearjab's party during the journey to the Shrouded Mountains. He collected a great deal of Dar'sayn from the Forest of Indistinct Murmurings—surely it hasn't been used up already?"

"It has been mislaid."

"Mislaid? How?"

"I do not know."

"Might it have been stolen?"

"Yes, that is possible, though I do not understand who would do such a thing, or why."

My eyes met Clarissa's and I saw she was thinking the same as me—our enemy had made another move.

"It is a calamity," Father Reverie said. "When the Blood Gods come, it will be more difficult to resist them." He raised his hands and examined them. They were shaking. "I feel that even I will be taken this time."

Clarissa made to speak but Reverie stopped her with a curt gesture. "Yissil Froon is my most valued counsellor but he has already secluded himself in order to meditate. Even if I knew where he was, he'd be in too deep a contemplation to respond to my presence. I have no recourse, then, but to trust my own instincts. I'm of the opinion that your research into the affliction that has befallen us is of crucial importance. If you do not find a cure, the Aristocracy, stricken with the disease, will have little resistance to that—" He pointed again at the red sun. "Mademoiselle Clattersmash and her colleagues will continue to assist you. Work fast, please. The situation is dire." Reverie turned to me. "Aiden Fleischer, you are a Servant yet you have been placed with the City Guard. Be alert. Your life is in danger. Now leave me. I have many things to consider, not least being whether your dissonance, Miss Stark, is advantageous to us or a danger. If New Yatsillat survives the current cycle, it might still be better if you are banished to the Whimpering Ruins on the Shelf Lands."

"*Better* is hardly the word I'd choose," I murmured.

Having been summarily dismissed, my companion and I left the room. As we stepped onto the ramp, we heard the Magician murmur to himself, "What does the Saviour intend? If only I knew this, then I might bear these losses."

We descended through the corkscrew passage, now weirdly illuminated by the crimson radiance, and I was reminded of my terrible nightmares on Koluwai—those horrific visions in which I moved through my own arteries.

"I'm baffled," I said. "We've been here all this time, I've asked repeatedly why there's a City Guard and a defensive wall, but received nothing but prevarication—and now Reverie just outs and tells us that we're to be invaded!"

"As we discovered," Clarissa responded, "there are things that cannot be mentioned in the sight of the Saviour. Lips have been sealed by the power of religion—or, at the very least, by superstition."

"What manner of creatures are these Blood Gods, I wonder, and why am I in particular danger?"

"It appears that we shall soon find out."

We came to the door, passed through it, and went down the steps to the street. With the hellish light shining from the land-ward horizon, the whole of New Yatsillat had sunk into shadow and become a well of darkness beneath the ruby sky.

Clarissa stopped and peered around.

"Something else?" I asked.

She made a small noise and raised her hands to her eyewear. She hesitated for a beat, then suddenly took hold of her goggles, pulled them from her face, and left them dangling around her neck.

Her eyes were wide open.

"I can see, Aiden! This light—something about it allows me to see without protection! Without pain!"

"Your eyes," I gasped, stepping back in shock. "They're bright yellow!"

"Yellow?"

She looked at the sky, then across the city toward the sea. "It's visible to me—the Magicians' shield. It looks like an aurora borealis. I can see it radiating from various points around the third terrace. Except—" She furrowed her brow. "Except there's a particularly strong source down there—" She pointed to the northern edge of the bottom terrace.

"From the fishing village?"

She nodded and murmured, "It's different. Powerful. Pure."

"But I thought it was a purely telepathic phenomenon."

"It is—but I don't know how to describe it to you except in visual terms. Hum! What would a Magician be doing down there? Reverie said they'd confined themselves to their temples—but there are no temples on the ninth level."

"Perhaps it's Yissil Froon. Shall we go there?"

"We haven't time. The cure has to be the priority—I must get back to my laboratory."

We crossed to a Kaljoor-drawn hansom cab parked at the side of the road. Its driver, Working Class, was unchanged—we soon learned that only the Aristocrats had become "horned tigers" like Father Reverie. Clarissa called up to him to ask if he could drive us to the third terrace. He turned his mask to us and said, in the dullest of voices, "What was that?"

"I asked if you are available," she said. "We need to be taken to Dissonance Square."

The Yatsill flexed his fingers slowly. "Dissonance Square, you say? Where's that?"

"I just told you. Third terrace."

"Hmm?"

"By the Suns!" I exclaimed. "Aren't you listening? We want to be driven home."

The creature made no response, either lost in thought or just too stupid to comprehend.

"Come on," Clarissa said.

We moved away, soon reached the avenue, and decided it would be quicker to walk the rest of the way home, which was a fair distance but downhill all the way. The city had suddenly become almost completely silent, with its traffic at a standstill. A heavy mist was drifting in from the sea. Groups of Workers stood about, partially obscured by the gloom and condensing atmosphere.

"They look bewildered," I observed.

"Whatever intelligence was transmitted to them before," Clarissa remarked, "it wasn't enough to keep them properly engaged with the work they're expected to do. Now the Magicians' protective mantle is blocking what little intellect the rest of the Aristocrats can transmit. It's as if the Working Class has regressed to its natural animal state. This imbalance between Aristocrats and Workers is an unqualified disaster for the Yatsill."

I sent a breath whistling through my teeth. "If the extreme weather continues and the labourers remain immobilised, New Yatsillat will be in a terrible state of disrepair by the time the yellow suns rise again."

"Worse. The Yatsill lack foresight. It was the roots of the forest that held these steps of land together. When the trees were cleared, the whole bay became prone to mudslides. There's a perfectly enormous engineering job ahead of us. We'll have to shore up every level, and we need to do it as soon as possible or New Yatsillat could be swept into the sea."

"How can you do it if the Workers are incapacitated?"

"I may have to recruit the Servants."

I was suddenly struck by a thought so disturbing it stopped me in my tracks. "Clarissa, *kuhyomauhyoma* is aggravating the situation by weakening the mental connection between the Yatsill."

"It is, yes."

"And I'm the origin of the sickness. Yarvis Thayne opposed my presence here and he was murdered. You are trying to find a cure, and an attempt was made on your life. Doesn't it suggest that Iriputiz purposely infected me and sent me here to cause this problem?"

Clarissa's eyebrows went up, creasing the skin around the two bumps on her forehead.

"It does," she said.

"And also that he was working on behalf of the Blood Gods and has allies here in the city?"

"Yes."

"I was half-insane with pain during the witch doctor's ritual, but I distinctly remember him shouting, 'Not you!' when you threw yourself onto the altar. I don't think your being here and being made an Aristocrat were a part of his plan, which means all this—" I waved an arm at the city surrounding us "—was unanticipated by the enemy."

Clarissa stood and thought for a moment. "Hmm," she grunted. "And I wonder how much it complicates matters for them?"

She set off at a fast pace down the steep thoroughfare, calling back, "Hurry, Aiden! If that baleful sun makes the enemy more powerful, then my colleagues and I are in greater danger, for surely the Blood Gods or their agents will try to stop our research!"

We hurried home and, upon arriving in Dissonance Square, were surprised to find Kata standing in the gloom with three other Servants. All were wearing flowers in their hair and strung around their necks. They appeared excited.

"It is nearly the time of release," our housekeeper informed us as we hurried past her. "Will you wish it upon me?"

"Is it what you want?" Clarissa called back, mounting the steps between the two guardsmen who were supposedly standing sentry duty at our front door but looked more like they were lounging.

Kata shrugged. "This is my home. I know of Koluwai only through stories. If I could stay here, I would, but it is tradition to be released."

"Then I wish whatever you truly want for yourself," Clarissa responded.

We entered the vestibule and crossed to the laboratory. Fathers Clutterfuss and Meadows were both still at work, striped and horned, fussing over their test tubes, flasks, and Bunsen burners, but Mademoiselle Clattersmash, also transformed, stood a little apart, apparently in a daze, her limbs twitching strangely.

Clarissa announced, "I believe *kichyomachyoma* is being used as a weapon. The fact that we are seeking a cure puts us in danger. It's likely the Blood Gods have agents in the city who might be stronger now the Heart of Blood has risen."

A test tube shattered on the floor.

"I'm sorry," Father Meadows mumbled. "I'm all fingers and thumbs today."

"Are you all right?" Clarissa asked.

"I think I've succumbed to the disease, Miss Stark."

"You are trembling. Do you need to lie down?"

"I shall work for a little longer."

"Very well, but when you rest, please do so here. You shouldn't leave the house without a guard to accompany you."

Meadows grunted an acknowledgement.

Mademoiselle Clattersmash's head turned slowly to face us. "Come with me," she said, in an oddly hollow voice. "I have something to show you. It will clarify matters."

She pushed past us and left the room. We followed her to the front door, puzzled.

As we stepped back out of the house and into the square, I snapped at the sentries, "Stand to attention! Stop slouching like that! Draw your weapons and keep them in your hands. Be ready to defend the house."

One grumbled an unintelligible response, slid his sword from its scabbard, and reluctantly straightened up. The other didn't move.

Kata and her three companions were chatting happily, their mood a striking contrast to the sense of oppression caused by the carmine sky, the impenetrable shadows, and the swirling fog.

Clattersmash ignored the Servants, crossed the square, and entered one of the roads that led out of it. Clarissa and I trailed behind.

"Is this really necessary, Mademoiselle?" my friend asked. "Where are you taking us?"

"To a place where you'll find the answer," came the cryptic reply.

"The answer to what question?"

There was no response. She moved on.

We ran after her, turned a corner, and proceeded along a residential street, then, a few minutes later, entered a dingy passage. We rounded another corner, and another, until we were deep in the maze of narrow alleys that criss-crossed behind the city's main thoroughfares.

Finally, Clattersmash stopped beneath a leaning tenement building and turned until her crow mask was pointing straight at us. Its tip was shaking. Tremors were running up and down the Yatsill's body.

"You—" she began. "You must—must—must—"

Her head suddenly jerked backward. She screamed. Her hands flew up to the front of her jacket and the sharp fingers dug into the material and ripped it open. The jacket, and the waistcoat and blouse beneath, were torn asunder. She clutched at her mask and yanked it away. Her vertical mouth was spread wide, the inner beak gaping.

"My name is Mademoiselle Crockery Clattersmash!" she screeched. "And I am taken!"

Clarissa backed away, bumping into me. I pushed her aside and drew my sword.

The front seam of Clattersmash's body cracked open as if being pushed apart from within. A knot of red, suckered tentacles swelled out from the widening gap. Her face sank into the hood-like shell of her head.

"Clarissa! Run!" I shouted.

Clattersmash collapsed onto the cobbles and a repulsive tangle of thrashing limbs bulged out of her. The carapace of her arms and legs turned semi-transparent as the inner flesh withdrew, sliding out, wet and glistening. A sickening thing of squirming appendages and pulsating organs rose from the wrecked Yatsill.

"I must feed," it said, in guttural, bubbling Koluwaian. A dripping limb extended and pointed over my shoulder. "Then I must take that one to Phenadoor."

I risked a quick glance back and saw Clarissa pressed against the side of the alley, her hand covering her mouth.

"I told you to run!" I yelled. "Get out of here!"

The Blood God—for, undoubtedly, that's what the monster was—lunged forward, lashing out at me. Automatically, my blade went up and sliced through tentacles.

As it had before, my training guided my movements, but from the moment I engaged with the creature I knew that something was wrong. I had to kill it, that was plain, but I couldn't. As it hit out at me again and again, my sword met and removed its limbs, yet I was incapable of striking a fatal blow. Disgust welled up within me; a hatred of the violence I was forced to do; a surge of utter abhorrence, not at the monster that faced me but at the one I'd become if I killed it.

My feelings weren't real. I realised it immediately. As I ducked and dodged the thrashing appendages, carving at them with my blade, it was absolutely clear to me—for the first time—that my interior battle wasn't interior at all. Since my arrival in New Yatsillat, my emotions had been manipulated from without. Something was preventing my natural recovery from the lingering shock and fear I'd felt at discovering Polly Nichols' corpse and was, instead, accentuating and perverting the memory.

Of course I wasn't Jack the Ripper! The very notion was patently absurd!

Smacking across my face, a limb ripped the flesh of my cheek and a squirming length of muscle slapped down onto my shoulder, curling over my back and around my waist. It ripped my jacket and shirt away and suckers latched on to my skin. I felt spines pierce my flesh. Instantly, as venom was injected, the strength drained out of me and I dropped to my knees.

Dimly, I saw that the Blood God possessed a skeletal structure. The front of it was exposed. I raised my sword and pressed its point against the creature. All I had to do was thrust the blade home.

Do it! Do it!

My arm shook, my vision blurred, Polly Nichols rose up and looked down at me, her intestines looping to the ground, the gashes in her throat mouthing the words, *I don't even consider you a man!*

Shame and humiliation flooded through me.

The fatal blow was paralysed.

I raised my head and screamed my frustration and terror.

The tentacle suddenly loosened and slipped from me. I fell sideways. At the periphery of my vision, I saw Clarissa clinging to the back of the creature, plunging her dagger into it again and again. The thing flopped to the ground, flailed wildly for a moment, and lay still. My friend rolled off it and stood, swaying, her eyes glazed.

I struggled to my feet. "Clarissa!"

She staggered forward. I caught her as she buckled but hadn't the strength to hold her. We both went down in a heap.

A minute or so went by, and we lay breathing heavily before pushing ourselves upright to regard the fallen thing.

"It's all right," I said huskily. "You killed it."

She picked a strip of my shredded clothing from the ground and used it to wipe her dagger blade. Sheathing the weapon, she said, "Poor Mademoiselle Clattersmash."

I shivered. "I don't know what's happening here, Clarissa, but we're right in the middle of it. I've been used to weaken the Yatsill, and a powerful influence has kept me in a state of emotional confusion, accentuating my natural timidity and fears. Look—" I turned and pointed at the gutted corpse of the Yatsill.

In that instant, everything was as it had been in my Yarkeen vision.

"That is exactly what I saw in the Valley of Reflections." I gazed into my companion's yellow eyes. "How deeply have I been manipulated?"

She took a deep breath, released it slowly, and gave a slight shrug. "I don't know, Aiden. Let's get back to the house."

I sheathed my sword and looked down at myself. My clothes were hanging in tatters and I was covered from head to foot in gore, some of it my own. The Blood God had lacerated the right side of my chest, my back, and both my arms. Round sucker marks dotted my skin.

"I feel numb, but when the venom wears off, this is going to hurt."

We began to retrace our steps but hadn't got very far before my legs started to give way. Clarissa stepped in and lent me physical support.

The fog had become so impenetrable we could see only a few feet in front of us, and when we finally reached Dissonance Square, the figures standing in it were all but obscured. We approached and discovered them to be Father Clutterfuss, Kata, and two of the three Koluwaians we'd seen with her earlier. The third was on the ground at their feet. He was dead.

Clarissa left my side and squatted beside the body. After a brief examination, she said, "Drained of blood. There are sucker marks all over him."

Kata nodded. "He has been released."

"Father Spreadflower Meadows was taken," Clutterfuss said. He pointed at the corpse. "The Blood God fed."

I rounded on Kata. "Is this what it means to be released?"

She nodded. "It is how we are sent to Koluwai."

"This man hasn't been sent anywhere, Kata! He's been killed!"

"His body is gone, but his spirit will be reborn on your world."

I, who had once been a priest, snorted disdainfully. "Absurd!"

"Where are the sentries?" Clarissa asked.

Clutterfuss answered, "They chased after the Blood God. It will try to enter Phenadoor, as they always do after first releasing a Servant. Perhaps it will be stopped at the wall."

"Mademoiselle Clattersmash has also been taken," Clarissa said. "And you, Father? How do you feel?"

"I am quite well, thank you."

"Let me see your hands, please."

The Yatsill held out his arms. His long fingers were moving slowly but steadily, without the trembling and jerking that had been so noticeable in his colleagues.

"Good," Clarissa said. "Will you come inside and help me to dress Aiden's wounds?"

"Of course."

I ordered Kata to follow us.

"But I'm waiting to be released," she said.

"I'll not have you killed," I responded angrily. "Get inside, at once!"

Our housekeeper reluctantly followed us in. The shell of Father Meadows was lying on the vestibule floor.

Clarissa said, "Kata, clean up as best you can. We'll arrange to have the body removed as soon as possible." She steered me through into the laboratory. Clutterfuss entered and closed the door behind us. They sat me on a bench and started to clean my wounds. I looked at my hand. My missing little finger was already half-grown back.

"Father," I said, "Miss Stark and I have been on Ptallaya for some time now. Why did no one tell us that the Blood Gods invade through the Yatsills' bodies?"

"Only through the Aristocrats," he corrected. "We do not speak of the Blood Gods when the Saviour's Eyes are open."

"Why not?"

"To speak their name is to give them presence."

"As ever," Clarissa muttered, "superstitions and traditions bar the way to truth."

I winced as she dabbed lotion on my wounds. "Do you think there's another world orbiting the suns?" I asked her. "Is that where those horrible creatures come from?"

"Ptallaya doesn't orbit, Aiden. If it did, all three suns would periodically be visible at the same time, and I'm quite certain that never happens. Am I right, Father?"

Clutterfuss answered, "The Eyes of the Saviour and the Heart of Blood are eternally opposed."

"In which case, this planet must hang revolving between the twin suns on one side and the red on the other. As for whether there's another world out there, it's a possibility, I suppose." She looked over my shoulder. "What is it, Father?"

The Yatsill, while cleaning the cuts on my back, had given a small exclamation.

"This," he said. "It was beneath Mr. Fleischer's skin."

Clarissa reached past my head. When she pulled her hand back, I saw she was holding a very small object. She examined it. "It appears to be a seed of some sort."

"Iriputiz cut me all over and pushed seeds into the incisions," I told her. "They burned like the fires of Hell."

"And when we awoke on Ptallaya, your symptoms were gone. We might have the answer. This seed could contain the cure for *kichyomachyoma*."

"Then let us get back to work," Clutterfuss urged.

Having treated my injuries, my companions returned to their chemical apparatus. I told them I'd take care of the corpse in the vestibule, which I did by the simple expedient of dragging it outside and leaving it in a corner of the square. With the city in crisis, there seemed no other choice. Certainly, I was unlikely to find Workers possessed of enough wherewithal to take it away. Besides, I was unwilling to go off in search of any. I hadn't forgotten that the thing that burst out of Mademoiselle Clattersmash had pointed at Clarissa and said, "I must take that one to Phenadoor."

The Blood Gods wanted my companion.

Some little while later, my presentiment was proven correct. I'd closed and locked all the window shutters and had just locked Kata in her room—she'd been persistently attempting to sneak out of the house—when something thumped at the front door. I crossed to it and shouted, "Who's there?" The portal rattled as the thumping was repeated. I drew my sword, reached out, pulled the door open, and was confronted by a Blood God. "I have already fed," it gurgled in the language of the islanders. "I will not harm you. Do not attack. Let us be civilised."

"Very well. What do you want?"

"I sense the presence here of one I must take to Phenadoor for examination. Please, stand aside."

I levelled my weapon at the beast. "Who wants to examine her?"

The thing's eyes swivelled toward my blade. "I do not know."

"Then who told you to come for her?"

"I am newly emerged. Something communicates with me but I do not know what it is, only that I must obey it in order to secure good status in my society."

"I'll be civilised up to a point," I said, "but I'll kill you rather than allow you anywhere near her."

"That is unfortunate. It means we must fight."

The Blood God lunged at me. I stepped back and slammed the door in its face, quickly sliding the bolts home. For some time, the thing pounded and scraped at the portal, then at the windows, but it eventually gave up and departed.

Five more times the creatures came to the house and five more times I denied them entry. When the sixth visitor arrived, I didn't bother to leave my chair. The door rattled beneath the onslaught but held firm. Then a muffled shout reached me. "Why the blazes won't you let me in! I know you're in there! Indeed I do!"

Recognising the voice of Baron Hammer Thewflex, I strode to the door, and, with my sword drawn, opened it a crack. Thewflex was indeed on our front steps.

"Show me your hands," I demanded.

He did so. They were steady.

"How do you feel?"

"Absolutely fine, old chap," he replied. "I only wish I could say the same of my colleagues!"

"Come in."

"The confounded Blood Gods are everywhere," he said as he entered. "I was practically tripping over the blessed things all the way here."

I closed the door after him, called for Clarissa, then said, "It is a peculiarly tranquil invasion. Are your people putting up no resistance at all?"

"The City Guard are doing what they can, but the disease has knocked the population sideways. I've seen more Guards staring into space than swinging their swords. The situation is thoroughly catastrophic!"

Clarissa stepped from the laboratory with Father Clutterfuss, and Thewflex reported, "I came to tell you that Lord Brittleback and Father Reverie have just been taken. The House of Lords and Council of Magicians are in disarray. The Heart of Blood isn't yet a quarter risen, and already New Yatsillat's Aristocrats are dwindling so fast that we've lost all influence over the Working Class. Do you know where I might find Father Yissil Froon, Miss Stark?"

Clarissa handed a small flask of liquid to our visitor. "Drink this, Baron—it's the cure. We've just perfected it. No, I haven't seen Yissil Froon in a long while. Apparently he's sequestered himself somewhere in order to meditate. Why do you want to see him?"

Thewflex removed his mask, swallowed the formula, and replaced his face covering.

"The protection provided by the Magicians simply isn't working. I was hoping Yissil Froon could advise me. Indeed I was. Indeed! Indeed!"

"Father Clutterfuss has two bottles of this cure," my friend said. "You and he should go and ensure that every remaining Aristocrat receives a dose. Treat the Magicians first. The stuff isn't Dar'sayn, but it might, at very least, give them a little more strength."

"Righty-ho, but I fear it's come too late, Miss Stark. The outlook is bleak."

The two Yatsill went to the door. Thewflex turned back and said, "You are one of the very few Servants left, Mr. Fleischer. Do you hope for release?"

"Most certainly not," I answered.

"Then guard yourself well." He gave a nod of farewell and, with Father Clutterfuss, departed.

I addressed my companion. "I'm more concerned with guarding you. The Blood Gods appear intent on taking you into the sea."

"Then you'd better sharpen your sword," she responded, "because we have to leave the house."

"It's too dangerous! Those infernal creatures are everywhere!"

"Maybe so, but Baron Thewflex was right—we have to find Yissil Froon. As Father Mordant Reverie suggested—and Clutterfuss has since confirmed—he's survived a great many cycles of Ptallaya's yellow and red days, and if there's any way we can help the Yatsill to survive this invasion, he's the one to tell us how. We must go to where the shield emanates from the fishing village. I feel positive that Froon is its source."

I hesitated. More than anything else, I wanted to keep my friend safe, but she was right—we couldn't stay in the house forever. There were already deep cracks appearing in its walls. Like every building in the city, it was falling apart.

"Very well—but keep your dagger drawn and don't leave my side."

We donned our coats and stepped out into the pea-souper. The vapour glowed redly around us. Driving would have been perilous in the extreme, especially with the roads being littered with abandoned vehicles and rubble, so we walked to the avenue and made our way down it. I kept my hand on my sword's hilt, expecting at any moment to see a Blood God come writhing out of the roiling murk. What few of the Working Class we passed were unclothed and docile. There was no sound other than the occasional rumble and clatter as buildings collapsed.

"This place was built on my memories," Clarissa muttered, "and has crumpled into nothing. Is my past so flimsy?"

I touched her hand. "Your remarkable mind may have given form to New Yatsillat, but do not judge yourself by what's happened to it. It's become what it is through the actions of beings entirely alien to us."

"Exactly as my life on Earth was ruined by a being utterly alien to my working-class background—an aristocrat. I sometimes think I'll forever be denied a place where I feel I belong."

"I hardly think the Aristocrats here are responsible for this chaos. They've been invaded by an evil predator."

"Evil, Aiden? We shall see."

We continued on down the steep and wide thoroughfare, stepping carefully over networks of cracks and deep fissures, passing from the fourth level to the fifth, on to the sixth, then across the muddy seventh. Through the fog, we saw that parts of the defensive wall had subsided, and when we came to the gate, its six guards didn't even challenge us—they were staring into space, oblivious to all.

The eighth terrace was devastated, having for the most part slipped onto the ninth. Two Blood Gods were squirming through the mud and debris, vague forms in the haze, heading toward the sea. I stopped Clarissa and we stood motionless until the things had passed.

A crash echoed from far off—yet another building tumbling to the ground.

"By heavens!" I exclaimed. "The magnitude of destruction is incredible! The city is deteriorating as fast as it was built!"

Clarissa pointed to our right. "The emanation is coming from over there."

We reached the lowest part of New Yatsillat and found it half-buried by rubble from above. Abandoned boats floated aimlessly in the bay. Thousands of Yatsill had taken to the water and were feeding much as seals do, diving from view and bobbing up a few minutes later with fish in their mouths. It was hard to believe these creatures possessed a language, let alone that they'd been capable of creating a civilisation.

"Look!" my companion cried out. "What is that?"

I followed her pointing finger and saw an orange light sliding along beneath the surface of the water. We watched until the fog swallowed the illumination.

"Some sort of machine?" I speculated. "How many more mysteries can we deal with?"

We moved on.

Clarissa led me northward, steering past some heaps of fallen masonry and clambering over others. She put her fingers to her temples. "This telepathic transmission is strong, but it does at least drown out my obsessing over those blessed blueprints."

"I thought you'd stopped thinking about them."

"Maybe. I can't tell. I suspect they're still knocking around inside my skull, but their racket has been thoroughly muffled." She pointed ahead to where the terrace abutted the high cliff face. "If Yissil Froon is the source of the psychic protection, we're very close to him."

We continued on until, finally, we came to a row of warehouses—mostly still standing—that had been erected against the cliff. Clarissa entered a narrow gap between two of them.

"I'm blind as a bat," I grumbled a few moments later as we were engulfed by pitch darkness.

Clarissa took my arm. "I can see clearly. There's a cave just ahead."

Beneath my feet, I felt the cobbles give way to bare rock.

"It's a natural tunnel," my companion murmured. "Put a hand on the wall to your left. Let it guide you."

The passage wound from side to side, gradually sloping upward.

After many minutes had passed, Clarissa said, "It looks like it opens onto a large space. Not far to go now."

I squinted into the blackness but saw nothing.

A few paces later I heard trickling water and jumped as a

quavering voice, speaking Koluwaian, called to us from somewhere ahead. "Welcome. I'm glad to meet you at last. Come sit with me."

"Who is it?" I hissed.

"An elderly woman," Clarissa answered softly.

"Please," the voice said. "Come! Come!"

Clarissa tugged my arm and whispered, "She's sitting in the centre of a cave. There are mushrooms and some sort of lichen growing all around the place. The water you can hear is a stream falling from a niche in one of the walls. My goodness! The woman is very old! She's emaciated, and—and she has yellow eyes!"

We moved a little further forward then stopped and Clarissa pulled me down to the floor. I sat cross-legged and waited patiently.

Just in front of us, the thin reedy voice said, "I greet you, Clarissa Stark, Aiden Fleischer. Heh! Heh! My name is Pretty Wahine. The Yatsill call me the Saviour."

CHAPTER 8
GODS

I uttered a cry of astonishment. The Yatsills' god was alive!

"You've been made an Aristocrat," Clarissa observed, then said to me, "She has the little bumps over her eyes."

I squinted and strained to see but couldn't make out a single thing. The lack of light was total.

"Yes, my child. As have you. Life on Ptallaya is strange! Heh! Heh!"

My friend asked, "You came here from Koluwai?"

Pretty Wahine didn't respond immediately. She wheezed in the darkness—the respiration of an ailing, ancient body.

She said, "There is a hole over the island. We know that to be true—don't we?—for we fell through it!"

"We did," Clarissa agreed.

"I was a young woman when it took me—walking in the hills with my husband, Yaku—dear Yaku! How I loved him all that time ago! How he changed!"

"He was transported with you?"

"He was. We were sucked into the sky and awoke in a forest. Oh! We were afraid to move—we didn't understand where we were—but I became thirsty, and saw fruit around us, so I cut into one and drank its juice. Yaku warned me not to. He said it might be poisonous. But I did it anyway."

"Dar'sayn," Clarissa murmured.

The old woman cackled—an uncanny dry rustling that sent prickles up my spine. "Heh! Heh! And you know what it does, yes?"

"It alters the mind."

"That's right! Heh! Heh! We slept, and when I awoke I could feel that, far away, there were people. Yaku was frightened to look for them, but I told him I would go. He could come with me, or stay alone. He came!"

She laughed again but it developed into a fit of coughing. We waited patiently while she recovered, then Clarissa asked, "They were the Yatsill?"

"Yes! Yes! Not people at all! We walked and walked until we found them—and when we did, Yaku tried to run away, but I knew they wouldn't harm us, so I made him stay, and we travelled with the Yatsill on a Ptall'kor to a valley, where we ate the meat of Yarkeen. I had a vision. I saw people of Koluwai being consumed by demons. Yaku also dreamed things, but he would not tell me what, and afterwards he became quiet and different."

I felt anchored to reality only by the touch of Clarissa's hand where it rested on my arm, and suddenly realised that I was succumbing to a mesmeric power that radiated from the old woman. I spoke, hoping that by engaging with the conversation I'd overcome the effect. "In what way different, Pretty Wahine?"

"He was keeping secrets, my boy."

Again she paused and struggled for breath. As Theaston Vale's vicar, I'd sat at the bedsides of the elderly on many occasions. I recognised the sound of impending death when I heard it, and——Pretty Wahine's psychic power notwithstanding——I was hearing it now.

Perhaps two minutes passed before her voice pierced the darkness again.

"At the end of the valley, we entered a cavern where I fell into a pool, and it gave me these bumps over my eyes. After that, all the Yatsill could speak my language. The same happened to you, yes? Heh!"

Clarissa made a sound of acknowledgement.

"Funny creatures!" the old woman exclaimed. "Like children! Copy, copy, copy! They brought us to this bay, drove the animals from the trees, and built villages in the branches, just like the ones I'd grown up in. Home! Home! Heh! Heh!"

"Animals?" my companion asked. "Do you mean Quee'tan?"

"Quee'tan, yes. Shoo! Shoo! Shoo! Away with them all!"

"How long ago was this, Pretty Wahine?"

"Oh, very much time has passed, my child. Very much time! Dar'sayn makes me live forever! Heh! Heh!" She stopped, wheezed, and went on, "Things then were not as they are now. All the Yatsill were Wise Ones. There were no Shunned."

"Now they call themselves Aristocrats and Working Class," I interjected.

"Heh! They pluck the words from Clarissa Stark. Right out of her head! Copy, copy, copy!"

"And they call the Koluwaians and their descendants Servants."

"Pah! There were none before. None of my people. Just me. Just Yaku. We lived with the Yatsill until—Oh!—the red sun rose and the demons came. Blood Gods! They entered the Yatsill and killed them all. Yaku and I hid in this cave while the horrible things tried to escape into the sea. Heh! Before they reached the water, they died. No more Blood Gods. No more Yatsill."

A rumble penetrated the darkness—a building collapsing somewhere close to the mouth of the tunnel—reminding me that outside, under the onslaught of the fiery red orb, New Yatsillat was rapidly disintegrating.

Clarissa's fingers, still wrapped around my forearm, tightened slightly.

"The big sun set," Pretty Wahine said, "and the little suns rose. No night on Ptallaya! And the Yatsill children came out of the nurseries and went away. We lived by ourselves, and—Oh!—I was scared. Yaku was not Yaku. I feared him. He knew things but would not tell me. Heh! Heh! I knew things, too! Yes I did! Yes! Yes! The Dar'sayn had changed me. I felt the children returning! I knew they weren't the same! They went away with no more brains than Quee'tan—driven to the Pools of Immersion by instinct, just like animals—but came back Wise Ones! Heh! Heh! And the tree houses were filled, and life was as it was before."

"Until the Heart of Blood rose again," Clarissa murmured.

Another cackle. Another coughing fit. Painful gasping. Then: "My child! My child! You know what Dar'sayn can do! You know!

You know! Before the yellow suns set, I sent a Yatsill to the forest to fetch more of the juice! Yes! More! More! It made me strong! With it, I could use my mind to stop the demons."

Pretty Wahine suddenly lowered her voice to a barely audible whisper. "But don't tell Yaku! Oh no! Secret! Where is he? Where? Where? He mustn't have the power. He will misuse it. Only Yissil Froon knows!"

"Yissil Froon?" Clarissa and I exclaimed.

"It was he I sent to the forest. He drank Dar'sayn and helped me protect the Yatsill. Only a few fell. And, again, the Blood Gods that came died before reaching the sea. Heh! Heh! Dead! Dead!"

She drew a long, shuddery breath and emitted a long, eerie moan. I flinched away from the sound. There was madness in it.

"Another cycle. Heh! Now there were adults to take the children to Immersion, and Ptall'kors to hasten the journey. Yes! And Yissil Froon went for more Dar'sayn. But—Oh! Oh!—he found Koluwaians! They had fallen through the hole. My Yarkeen dream! Food for the Blood Gods, to replace the Quee'tan! Oh! Poor people! Poor people! And I was very afraid because Yaku was happy. Happy! Why? Why? When he left the cave to meet the islanders, I drank more Dar'sayn and used my mind to hide away from the Yatsill— and even from my husband! I couldn't trust him any more. I didn't understand him. He had become very strange and secretive! Now only Yissil Froon knew how to find me. The rest forgot this cave. They forgot me!"

"Not entirely," I noted. "They consider you a god. They call you the Saviour."

"They remember only that someone once changed them!" she answered. She fell silent for a moment before going on, "The demons came again. I stopped many, but still some possessed the Yatsill. Some, yes. Oh! Oh! It was as I'd foreseen—the Blood Gods fed on the people and escaped into the sea. Every cycle now, the same! For a long, long time! More Koluwaians came to Ptallaya!"

She sucked at the air, her lungs creaking, and said, "Always, at the rising of the two suns, Yissil Froon brought me more Dar'sayn.

Heh! I think he wanted it. Him! Ha! I controlled his mind. I would not let him keep it all for himself! I made him share it with a small number of Wise Ones and I sent my power through them to protect the Yatsill. The Blood Gods always took a few but not many. Not enough to eat all the Koluwaians, and so children were born, and families lived in the tree houses. But I hid! I hid! Heh! Heh!"

By heavens, how old was Pretty Wahine? For how many generations had she survived like a hermit, hidden away in this cave? Was Clarissa, who'd also taken Dar'sayn, now endowed with such an extended lifespan?

"Heh! Heh!" the woman crowed. "Change! Change! Always change! Now, at Immersion, some of the Yatsill children were Shunned."

Clarissa interrupted. "Do you know why?"

"No, my child. No! Maybe Yissil Froon knows—Dar'sayn has made him a clever one, oh yes!—but I have not spoken with him. He started to conceal Yaku from my senses. It is not good! So I hid myself from Yissil Froon, too. Oh! Oh! Where is Yaku? Where? Where? Dead by now, surely! Dead and turned to dust. But not me! I have been in darkness for so long—Alone! Alone!—eating the mushrooms and the moss. Growing older and older."

"And always fighting the Blood Gods," Clarissa said.

"Yes! The Dar'sayn made my mind very strong! I drank so much that I stopped needing it. Heh! Heh!"

"But why, Pretty Wahine? Why continue to defend the Yatsill?"

"Immersion! I went into the pool! You know, my child! You know! The same happened to you! It joins you to the Wise Ones, yes?"

"It's true," my companion replied. "I have never felt such a sense of belonging."

"Heh! They shape themselves from your thoughts and memories. Of course you belong! As do I, for there is still much of me in them!"

I heard Clarissa sigh. She said, "I've already experienced the loss of one home. Now I feel I'm losing another. I don't want to. How can we fight the Blood Gods?"

"I am dying," Pretty Wahine answered. "Finally! Finally! So, my child, you must learn to do what I have done. I will show you how to use your mind to stop the demons taking the Yatsill. But we need Dar'sayn."

"There is none." Clarissa responded. "The Magicians have run out of it."

"Find Yissil Froon! Always, he wanted to be the only Yatsill to drink it, and he hoards it jealously. I had to force him to release it to his fellows. He didn't like that! No! Find him, my child, and make him give you whatever of it he has, then return to me. But don't let him follow! No! No! And Aiden Fleischer, you must hasten to the forest to fetch more of the stuff. More Dar'sayn!"

"I won't be parted from Clarissa!" I objected.

"She will be safe, my boy. I will protect her."

My sword was sheathed at my side. I wrapped my fingers around its hilt. I'd developed a confidence in my aptitude with the weapon despite my inability to kill and wasn't afraid of what was sure to be a perilous journey, but leaving my friend behind in the city was another matter entirely.

"Aiden," Clarissa said, "this might be the only way to save New Yatsillat. If we don't try, what will become of us? Where shall we live?"

Reluctantly, I stood. "Very well. I'll get Dar'sayn."

I drove an autocarriage along the base of the Mountains That Gaze Upon Phenadoor toward the Forest of Indistinct Murmurings—toward the spot where I'd arrived on Ptallaya. The Heart of Blood had by now completely cleared the horizon. Its crimson light glared down and caused everything beneath to writhe in agony—or at least that's how it appeared, for the trees and plants had contorted into awful shapes and sprouted spines and thorns as if to defend themselves from the dreadful illumination.

Ptallaya looked exactly as I imagined Hell.

The terrain sloped up into the mountains on my left but its

undulations were smooth and, so far, had presented no challenge to my vehicle apart from occasional boulders that required steering around. Wildlife had been kept at bay by the autocarriage's loud chugging, for which I was thankful. The various beasts I'd spotted had been nasty-looking things, all claws, horns, and teeth.

At one point in the journey—now a long way behind me—I'd been disconcerted by a long stretch of hillside upon which purple pumpkin-like plants grew in abundance. They were so prevalent that it was impossible to steer around them, but to my horror, whenever I drove over one, crushing it beneath my vehicle's wheels, the whole slope emitted a horrible shriek of agony. The vegetables, it appeared, were merely the exterior protrusions of a huge living organism that dwelled beneath the soil. For some considerable distance I was assailed by these awful screams, and the strain on my nerves, together with my attempts to avoid as many of the pumpkins as I could, exhausted me. Nevertheless, once past that horrible hillside I pushed on, and had now been travelling for such a long time without rest that I simply couldn't stay awake any longer.

I drew the autocarriage to a halt, unfolded and clipped down its leather cover to afford me some protection from the ghastly sunshine, then made myself as comfortable as possible in the seat. I slept.

After a period of insensibility, a distant screeching brought me back to consciousness. I wiped the sleep from my eyes, looked around to see where the noise was coming from, and saw, streaming over the brow of a hill about half a mile away, a pack of ten or twelve unmistakably carnivorous animals. They were glossy black, with hard spiky exoskeletons, bulbous heads, clacking mandibles, and eight limbs apiece ending in talony digits. I recognised them instantly as Tiskeen, the species I'd once seen while approaching New Yatsillat, but transformed and no longer the harmless creatures they'd been under the yellow suns.

I hastily jumped out of the autocarriage, stepped back to its engine, and fired up the boiler. I'd left it burning gently while I slept and the mechanism was still hot, so it started immediately—which was just as well, for the Tiskeen were fast and obviously fixated upon me as their next meal. I scrambled back into the seat, pressed down on the footplate, and accelerated away with the pack in eager pursuit.

At a medium velocity, the autocarriage had navigated the terrain with little trouble, but now, as I forced it to its limits, it began to rattle and jolt with such severity that I feared it might shake itself apart, and a glance back revealed that, even at such great a speed, I wasn't going to outrun the pack. Nor could I defend myself against so many with just a sword.

I had little choice.

For the first time in my life, I hissed a string of expletives—shocking language for a vicar!—before veering the machine around a boulder, reversing course, and speeding straight back at the oncoming beasts. They were upon me in seconds, at the very last moment splitting into two groups, with the greater number of animals attempting to dodge to the right. I yelled incoherently and yanked the tiller around. The world cartwheeled as the vehicle smashed into the bigger group, propelling me into the air. I thudded onto the ground, rolled, tottered to my feet, and pulled my sword free, turning to face the carnage.

"Not dead!" I bellowed—a defiant shout that was, I admit, tinged with surprise.

The surviving Tiskeen turned toward me and extended their mandibles, displaying irregular holes in the front of their heads—holes lined with multiple rows of long, sharp teeth.

"Oh," I said. "Damn."

Just as I resigned myself to being eaten alive, there came a tremendous detonation. The autocarriage's boiler erupted, spurting flame, smoke, and boiling steam. The shock wave slapped into me and sent me back down to the ground. Pieces of metal went skittering past. I curled into a ball until the clattering of falling shrapnel stopped, then quickly pushed myself up and stood with my weapon at the ready. Blood dribbled into my eyes. My ears were assailed by high-pitched squeals.

Through an expanding cloud of hot steam, I saw the vehicle lying on its side, split wide open. The broken carcasses of Tiskeen were scattered about, either hit by the machine or blasted by the subsequent explosion. Some were writhing in their death throes. Others twitched spasmodically as the last vestiges of life left them. Four had survived, though two of them were obviously mortally wounded.

I dragged a sleeve across my eyes—the blood was flowing freely down my face. I had no idea how badly hurt I was and there was no time to find out—the remaining Tiskeen were leaping at me.

"No!" I snarled. "Clarissa needs me! I'll not fail her, you ugly brutes!"

The first beast came pouncing through the dispersing mist, its jaws and talons extended. I swung my sword into the side of its head. With a loud crunch, hot blood sprayed and the thing tumbled away, kicked, and lay still. The second was on me before I'd recovered my stance. I fell beneath it and gave a shriek of agony as its teeth sank into my right shoulder. Unable to turn my blade, I repeatedly hammered the pommel into one of the creature's eyes.

"Get off! Get off!"

Its hold on me eased slightly. I pushed my legs up under its body and heaved it away, my clothes and skin ripping as its grip came loose. The Tiskeen was back in an instant, but not before I had time to raise the point of my sword, which caught it in the chest. Claws slashed, the creature squirmed, slowed, and became still.

I heaved the dead weight to one side, stood, pulled my weapon free, staggered, and almost fell. The remaining two Tiskeen were dragging their bleeding bodies toward me. I righted myself and met them each with a swing to the head, putting as much strength behind the blade as I could muster. It was enough. They died.

Bizarrely, I giggled.

Dropping my weapon, I sank to my knees and knelt with my head bowed, blood oozing from my hair, and my breath coming in rapid and painful gasps. For a few moments, I could do nothing except cling on to consciousness. As my respiration slowed, I began to feel the pain of my wounds. A deep laceration in my scalp was bleeding profusely. Deep puncture wounds marked my shoulder and chest. There was also a chunk of flesh missing from my left thigh. A deadly lassitude was creeping over me. I knew if I gave in to it, I'd probably bleed to death while I slept. I pulled a packet of dried and salted fish—Kula'at—from my pocket, took a strip, and chewed on it to keep my mind focused, while from another pocket I retrieved a pack of medicinal herbs given to me by Clarissa. I treated my injuries.

I had killed. Unintelligent monsters, it's true. But I had killed.

The bleeding abated. I rested and, in a semi-dazed fashion, examined the little finger of my right hand, which had by now been completely restored. Mimics they may have been, but the Yatsill obviously knew how to apply the intelligence Clarissa gave them to the resources of their own world, for no Earth medicine could match such a feat.

The temperature was increasing and a vaguely sulphurous aroma now marred Ptallaya's lemony air. At my back, the mountains held the sea fogs at bay. In front of me, the wrecked autocarriage steamed, popped, and creaked as its split boiler settled. Behind it, the terrain rippled to the distant horizon, which shimmered in the heat.

I used the sword to lever myself upright, crossed to the vehicle, and recovered my knapsack. After slaking my thirst from a water bottle, I slung the bag over my uninjured shoulder, turned away, and started walking. What remained of the journey would be tough—I was sorely weakened and limping badly—but that didn't concern me as much as the return trek. I was confident I could cope with the exertion and physical dangers, but in the time it would take, what would become of New Yatsillat? What would become of Clarissa?

The Forest of Indistinct Murmurings occupied either side of a shallow river—little more than a stream—that ran out of the savannah and cut through a broad valley at the northernmost end of the mountain range. To the west, the Ptoollan trees followed the watercourse until they abutted the ocean. To the east, beyond the valley, they fanned out for about seven or eight miles then rapidly thinned and gave way to open land.

Clarissa and I had arrived on Ptallaya just within the southern edge of the forest, close to where the land dipped into the valley. Despite the funk I'd been in back then, now, when I surmounted a rise and looked down at the spot, I recognised the topography and the place where we'd emerged from the trees to climb aboard the Ptall'kor.

The demolished autocarriage was many miles behind me. I was footsore and exhausted, weak from my wounds, and very hungry. There'd been little by way of fruit or berries on the barren foothills I'd chosen for my route, and the supply I'd brought with me had run out.

Twice more, animals had attacked me. They'd fallen to my blade. I'd sustained no further injuries.

Descending the incline, I reached the outermost Ptoollan trees. Since I'd last seen them, their trunks had turned black and sprouted thorns and the raised roots were now bristling with spines. Nevertheless, I was able to push my way through the barbs into the hollow space beneath one of the trees, and there curled up and instantly fell into a deep and dreamless sleep.

When I next opened my eyes, I found the side of my face encrusted with blood. My head wound had reopened at some point, bleeding profusely before clotting. I sat up, crawled into the open, and stood. A wave of dizziness sent me reeling. I was in bad shape and desperately needed something to eat.

I moved deeper into the forest. The fruits had changed considerably since I was last there. Some were huge empty shells, broken wide open as if animals had removed the inner flesh, leaving just the skin to dry and calcify. Others were shrivelled and shrunken, obviously dead and rotting. The possibility that I'd travelled all this way for nothing—that there was no Dar'sayn to be milked—was too grim even to consider.

The odd murmuring that gave the forest its name was absent but I could hear, from a little way ahead, a faint sound that resembled weeping. Hoping it was being emitted by a mature fruit, I continued forward and quickly realised I was approaching the very clearing where I'd taken my first terrified steps on Ptallaya. A few moments later, I peered through a tangle of roots and saw the little glade. A creature, blue-black in colour, was squatting in the middle of it, and I knew at once it was a Zull, though this was the first living example I'd seen in close proximity. Where the Yatsill were four-legged and two-armed, the Zull was four-armed and two-legged, with what appeared to be a loose cloak of skin falling from its shoulders and attached to the back of the upper limbs. The head resembled that of an earthly ant, but four-eyed and with a complex multi-jointed set of mandibles. A white patch marked the left side of its face.

The thing was sobbing like a child.

I stepped into the open and said, in Koluwaian, "Are you hurt?"

The creature started and scrabbled backward, raising its arms as if to ward me off.

I held my hands out to show they were empty. "It's all right. I mean no harm."

"Wha-what? You speak, Thing?"

"I speak, and I'm not a thing, I'm a human being. Why are you weeping?"

"Because—because I have been cast out of Phenadoor, and because others of my kind have died. Look." The Zull pointed to one of the dried fruits and I suddenly realised that it and the other shrivelled ones were the same that Colonel Momentous Spearjab's party had taken Dar'sayn from. The larger and now empty shells, by contrast, had, as far as I knew, escaped the Yatsills' attentions.

"Others of your kind?" Even as I asked it, the truth flashed into my mind—a terrible revelation. Reaching up to one of the gourd-like objects, I touched it and said, "Your people come out of these?"

"Yes, after we are banished from Phenadoor."

They weren't fruits. They were cocoons. Dar'sayn was some sort of placental fluid.

Stunned by this realisation, I stood speechlessly gazing at the Zull. Its four silvery eyes glittered as it regarded me.

"You are a curiosity," it said.

My mouth worked silently before I was able to utter, "My—my name is Aiden Fleischer."

"I am Gallokomas."

I looked around me at the broken and shrunken cocoons, then back at the creature. "Why do you say you've been cast out of Phenadoor?"

"Because I feel it."

"You remember being there?"

"No. I am newborn. I have no recollection of the blissful life that went before. I know only that I lived it, and now cannot, for it is forbidden to return. I must have done something very wicked to have been punished this way."

I moved closer to the Zull and knelt beside it. I felt light-headed. My clothes were hanging in ribbons, red-stained, and my skin was smeared with dried blood.

I said, "Do not judge yourself harshly. I have learned that one should not presume evil in oneself without irrefutable evidence of it."

"I am no longer in Phenadoor. Is that not evidence enough?"

"It is no evidence at all. Perhaps when you join with the rest of your kind, you'll find out more about where you have come from and why you are here."

"The rest of my kind," Gallokomas echoed. "Yes." He pointed to the East. "I am drawn in that direction. I think they are there."

I nodded. "I've heard they live in eyries between the Shrouded Mountains and the Shelf Lands."

"I do not know those places. And you, Thing—where are your people?"

I didn't have the strength to explain Earth and space and the planets, so nodded toward the South and said simply, "There. Some distance away. A place called New Yatsillat."

"I feel that you are anxious to return. Why did you leave it?"

Not wanting to confess that I'd come to the forest to extract Dar'sayn and unwittingly kill the Zull's fellows, I answered with a question: "Is my anxiety so apparent?"

"I am aware of those things that are absent within you."

"How?"

"It is obvious to me. You are joined to another of your kind and are currently lacking that one's presence. You think of this New Yatsillat place almost as a home but lack confidence that it can offer you safety. You are uncertain and are searching for something to believe in."

"Can you hear my thoughts, Gallokomas?"

"No. Your mind is closed but your emotions play over its surface. I understand your need and must help as best I can. I will take you to New Yatsillat."

"You would assist a stranger?"

"Of course. Why would I not?"

"I am grateful, but it is a vast distance to walk."

By way of reply, Gallokomas stood, the cloak of skin on his back suddenly inflated like a balloon, and he rose five feet or so above the ground.

"You propose carrying me?" I asked.

"Yes, but first we must eat. Remain here. I will return."

He shot upward and disappeared over the treetops.

I sat and rested my head in my hands. I hadn't yet seen a single source of Dar'sayn, and even if I had, I wouldn't extract the liquid now I knew that, in doing so, I'd kill an intelligent being. So what would become of New Yatsillat? Without a fresh supply of Dar'sayn, could the Magicians muster strength enough to preserve themselves for the duration of the red sun's day?

Gallokomas wasn't gone for long, and when he returned he was carrying a large bunch of black banana-shaped fruits.

"Much of what I found on trees and bushes was poisonous," he said, "but these will not harm us. Eat, Thing."

We filled ourselves with the bland-tasting stuff, then the Zull hooked a pair of hands beneath my arms and lifted me into the air. Propelling himself forward by means of a rippling fringe that ran along the top and sides of his buoyancy sac, he transported me to the river in the bottom of the valley and there settled that we might drink from the clear, fresh water.

I washed my wounds and began to feel some strength returning to me.

We didn't linger for long, and for that I was glad. The sooner I was reunited with Clarissa, the better.

Gallokomas picked me up, shot with breathtaking speed up to such an altitude that the entire forest became visible, like a dark wedge in the landscape beneath us, then we sped southward.

We flew at a tremendous velocity. My hair streamed backward, the air forcing tears from my eyes, and we had to yell to converse. To our left, the red sun glowered. To our right, the serrated peaks of the mountain range piled upward, and between them the sea shone unpleasantly like freshly spilled blood.

"Phenadoor," Gallokomas shouted. "Perhaps I will return there once I have atoned for my sins."

"What is it like to live in Phenadoor, Gallokomas?"

"I have no memory of it, but I feel I was rewarded there for my every action, so that existence was fulfilling and I wanted for nothing."

"Many of the Yatsill enter it to die, believing they'll be reborn into a better life."

"What are Yatsill, Thing?"

"They are sentient creatures, like yourself. Did you not encounter them in Phenadoor?"

"Perhaps, but if I did, I have forgotten it."

We flew on and on. A hot wind gusted from the East. The land slipped by far below us. Finally, the mountain range began to lose its height.

I pointed ahead to where the side of a slope was scarred with quarries. "New Yatsillat is near."

Gallokomas altered his course slightly. We gradually lost altitude and I saw the strip of jungle and the Yatsill farms laid out beyond it. Further ahead, where before I had seen columns of smoke and steam rising, there was nothing. The factories were obviously idle.

The Zull dropped closer to the ground, cleared the edge of the bay, and flew out over the city.

It wasn't there any more.

I gave a cry of dismay.

New Yatsillat, which had risen at such a phenomenal speed, had fallen into the sea with equal precipitateness. The huge terraces had collapsed and massive trails of rubble streaked the muddy slopes. The fishing village was entirely buried. There was barely a single building standing. In the awful red light, the whole bay looked like a hideous open wound.

Campfires flickered at one side of what remained of the fifth level. I pointed at them and cried out, "Take me down there, Gallokomas!"

The Zull veered away. "I cannot. I will set you down at the top of the bay."

"But I need to go to that fire. My companion may be there."

"I must ask forgiveness, Thing, for I find that I possess an inexplicable aversion to the creatures you call Yatsill."

"I assure you, they are harmless."

"I am not afraid, but I cannot approach them."

Though I was beside myself with frustration, when Gallokomas landed I turned to him and said, "You have greatly assisted me, my friend. I thank you."

"I will circle above," he replied. "When you have established that all is well, wave to me. I will see you. But if you require further assistance, return to this spot and I will come."

"Are you not eager to join the rest of your kind?"

"Later. I cannot leave one who is in need."

"I am humbled by your compassion."

Much to his astonishment, I took one of his hands and gave it a hearty shake.

"What was that?" he asked.

"A bond of friendship."

"I like it."

I smiled, turned away, and set off down the cracked and crumpled remains of one of the large avenues. To either side of it, the destruction was tremendous. New Yatsillat had fallen as if built from sand. What remained of its buildings stood like the ragged stumps of broken teeth, their upper sections gone, the roofs that covered them disintegrated and swept away. I clambered over fractured girders and piled debris, broken glass and almost unrecognisable fragments of furniture and vehicles. Off to my left, three Ptall'kors were drifting, apparently without purpose. I saw the body of a Kaljoor, still harnessed to a hansom cab, crushed beneath the remains of a fallen tower. I stepped on a sandwich board that bore the legend *The Petticoat Parlour, First for Female Attire!* and felt a hollowing grief for a shattered dream. New Yatsillat might have become my home. Instead—*this*.

And Clarissa. Where was Clarissa?

With no little difficulty I descended to the fifth level and made my way toward the fires, where I found approximately two hundred individuals gathered. As I drew closer, I waved and shouted, "Hi, there!"

Human and Yatsill faces turned and someone waved back and called my name.

"Kata!" I exclaimed. "Is that you?"

"Yes, Mr. Fleischer," my housekeeper replied as I joined the group. "I still have not been released. I think I shall never see Koluwai."

"You certainly won't if you're devoured by a Blood God. Where is Miss Stark?"

A Yatsill—one of the Aristocracy—stepped forward and said, "I'm afraid she has been taken, Mr. Fleischer."

I recognised the voice. "Baron Thewflex! You don't mean—you don't—she wasn't—?"

"Possessed? No. I apologise. That was a poor choice of words. Indeed, it was! I mean to say she was carried into Phenadoor by a Blood God."

"Carried into the sea?"

"Yes."

I sat down heavily, my jaw slack, my brain unable to cope with this news.

"The Magicians couldn't protect us," Thewflex said. "The Blood Gods have taken all the Aristocrats but those you see here." He flicked his fingers toward the other Yatsill, then pointed at the sea-shore and continued, "And the Working Class are now lazing about down there. They are little better than animals. Indeed! Indeed! There aren't enough of us remaining to share intelligence with them." He sighed and shook his head.

"Then she is drowned," I whispered, and my vision narrowed to a pinprick.

"The rest of us might still be taken at any time," Thewflex said. "Though we've all had Miss Stark's medicine and the pace of the invasion appears to have slowed. In any case, we shall have to wait until the Saviour looks upon us again and the new children mature before we can rebuild the city—yes, indeed!—and, of course, only then if plenty of the young are made Aristocrats at Immersion."

I couldn't engage with his words. They flowed past me without meaning. Nothing mattered any more. Clarissa was gone.

Picking a burning brand from the fire, I turned away and left the group, unable even to bid them farewell. I walked back through the debris to the avenue and there, bracing myself against the remains of a wall, bent over and pulled desperately at the air, feeling that I might pass out from lack of oxygen. My legs could hardly hold me. The ruins slewed past vertiginously. My ears were assaulted by an animalistic whine, which, in a moment of horror, I realised was coming from my own mouth.

"Please," I croaked. "Please, no."

Maybe I stood there for hours, maybe for mere minutes. I have no conception of how much time passed before I pushed myself upright and stumbled on, descending the steep slope all the way to the lowest level. Then it must have taken me at least two hours to climb across the rubble to Pretty Wahine's cave. Certainly, I remember replacing the brand on at least three occasions, putting its flame to other pieces of wood and taking them up in its stead.

I stepped into the cave's entrance and followed the tunnel—the way illuminated by my fire—to the chamber at its end. Pretty Wahine lay within, dead, her glazed yellow eyes staring at the ceiling. I bent over her and saw that her skin was dotted with sucker marks. Obviously, a Blood God had found her. Perhaps her powers had failed as her great age finally took its toll. She was unable to hide Clarissa or even her own refuge any longer.

Poor woman. She had asked for none of this. A simple islander, and little more than a child when she'd been transported to Ptallaya—fear, and perhaps a degree of madness, had made of her a hermit. And a god!

Leaving the Saviour's final resting place, I retraced my steps and made the long climb back to the top of the bay.

Eventually, I reached the place where I'd parted from Gallokomas. The Zull floated down from the sky and stood before me.

"She's gone," I said. "The Blood Gods took her to Phenadoor, where she surely drowned."

"Why?"

"I cannot guess. The creatures are a mystery to me."

"No, Thing. I mean, why would she drown?"

"My species cannot survive in the sea, Gallokomas."

"Nor can mine. But Phenadoor is not the sea."

"What?"

"Phenadoor is not the sea."

I frowned, feeling confused. "Then what is it?"

"It is a great mountain beyond the horizon that rises from the waters and touches the sky."

"A—a mountain?"

"Yes. I do not know where my knowledge comes from. Perhaps I have remnant memories."

"But Phenadoor is land? An island?"

"I am certain."

"Then Clarissa could still be alive!"

"That is true. What are these Blood Gods?"

I gestured toward the red sun. "They come when the Heart of Blood rises. They invade the bodies of the Yatsill and attack Phenadoor."

The Zull shook its head. "No. It is a place of peace."

"Whatever it is, Gallokomas, if the Blood Gods have Clarissa with them, and if they go to Phenadoor, whether to attack it or not, then I have to go there, too. Will you take me?"

"I cannot approach Phenadoor any more than I can approach the Yatsill. It is forbidden."

"Can you get me close?"

"I would have to drop you into the sea."

"Within sight of it?"

"Yes, I could do that."

"Then I'll swim the rest of the way."

Gallokomas looked to the East, where the gigantic sun blazed, and said, "My kind await." He turned back to me and his complex multi-jointed jaw flexed slowly. His expressionless eyes shone with an internal light, silvery and penetrating. The membrane on his back began to reinflate. "I feel the strength of your need," he said, "and so cannot refuse. But once I deposit you in the water, I will have to leave you to fend for yourself. It will be too difficult for me to remain so close to Phenadoor. It pushes me away. Like all the Zull, I am forsaken."

"If all the Zull are as generous as you, my friend, then you should not regret your current status, for you are to be admired and cherished."

He rose a couple of feet into the air, flitted around me until he was at my back, then took hold of me as before and shot upward. We swooped over the bay and headed out to sea.

Once we'd travelled beyond sight of land, I lost all sense of time and distance. Ptallaya was reduced to three elements: a bright red sky overhead, a dark red sea below, and a blood-red orb above and to the rear of us. None of the moons was visible.

I was still weak from my wounds, and even in the best of health had never been a strong swimmer, but if there was any possibility that Clarissa still lived, then I had no option. I had to find her, even if it meant losing my own life in the attempt.

After an immeasurable period, Gallokomas shouted, "Look down to the left, Thing."

I did so and saw, about a mile away, a ball of orange light

slipping along underwater—the same phenomenon Clarissa and I had observed off the shore of New Yatsillat.

"Fly over it!" I yelled.

The Zull altered course and moments later we were above the illumination. I could now see that it shone from the centre of a long ovoid object travelling at great speed just beneath the surface. I felt certain it was some sort of machine.

"There's another ahead of us," Gallokomas observed.

We flew on, seeing more and more of the lights, and soon realised they were coming and going from a point directly ahead of us. Then a bright twinkling light, like a rising star, burst over the horizon.

"Phenadoor," Gallokomas exclaimed. "I will take you as near to it as I dare, but already I feel it pushing me away."

As we drew closer to the dazzling radiance and my eyes adjusted, it was revealed to be a vast cone-shaped mountain of pink crystal—probably white under the yellow suns—which reared up from the ocean and towered into the sky.

"I'm struggling," my escort groaned. We began to lose altitude.

"What is it, Gallokomas? What prevents you from approaching? Is there a physical resistance?"

"No, Thing. I feel a sense of . . . of transgression in coming here. I will have to drop you very soon."

"Please, get as close as you can manage. I can't swim this distance."

Plunging downward, the Zull sped along just a few feet above the surface of the water. At such proximity, our velocity felt tremendous, but still Phenadoor grew only slowly before us, gradually rising over the horizon and expanding until it appeared impossibly massive and completely blocked the western skyline from view.

Gallokomas reduced speed, came to a stop, and gasped, "It hurts! I cannot take you any farther!"

I tried to gauge the distance to the shore of the mountain. It was too far for me, I was positive, but I had no option other than to make the attempt.

"Drop me here, Gallokomas, and go to your people, taking with you my sincere gratitude and friendship."

"I hope you find your companion, Thing. Phenadoor will offer you peace and fulfilment, but if you ever suffer the misfortune of being expelled from it, as I was, seek out the Zull. I will ensure that you are well received."

I thanked him and, without further ceremony, he loosed his grip on me and I plunged into the ocean. The moment I splashed into the surprisingly warm water, the weight of my sword dragged me under. Fool that I was, I'd forgotten I was wearing it! Panicking, I wasted precious moments grappling with the leather harness to which the scabbard was attached, until, realising my idiocy, I gave up on the buckle, pulled the blade free, and discarded it. I kicked for the surface and reached it just as my lungs were about to burst.

I trod water for a few moments. Gallokomas was already a distant dot in the sky. I was alone.

After pulling away the harness and what remained of my shirt, I started to swim, adopting a slow and relaxed stroke I hoped I'd be able to maintain for some considerable distance. I very much doubted I'd reach the crystal mountain without having to rest but, fortunately, the sea was extremely salty, which made me buoyant, and a gentle current was assisting me. When I grew weary, I'd be able to float and recoup my strength while still drifting in the right direction.

No thoughts passed through my head during that long test of endurance. I concentrated only on my rhythmic respiration and the movement of my limbs.

If I reached my destination, what would I find there? The Yatsill had been unaware it was an island. To them, the whole sea was Phenadoor, a heavenly realm they aspired to. And for the Zull, it was a lost Paradise. But what of the Blood Gods? Were they really attacking it, or did Phenadoor extend to them the same state of beatitude the other races claimed?

I stopped. Perhaps an hour had passed and I was noticeably closer to the island, but something had just flashed beneath me. I trod water, turned, searching for the source of the fleeting light. Suddenly the current switched direction and hit my side with considerable force, carrying me spinning along. I tried to swim against it but it became more powerful by the second and sent me helplessly reeling in a wide arc. To my horror, I realised I was caught in a whirlpool. Bright orange light flared at its centre. Before I could fill my lungs, I was dragged under. My pulse thundered in my ears. I struggled, became disoriented, and lost track of up and down. Darkness closed in.

☼

I opened my eyes and looked up into the appalling features of a Blood God.

"I am Koozan-Phay," it said, speaking Koluwaian. "You are not damaged."

I sat up. I was in a medium-sized chamber. Its walls were of metal upon which hung frames containing intricate shapes carved from crystal.

"Where am I?"

"In *Underconveyance Two-Zero-Two*."

"And what is that?"

"A merchant vessel. It travels under the water. We were collecting food from the farms on the seabed when we detected you and took you from the surface. We are entering Phenadoor. Your injuries have been attended to. Are you hungry?"

"Yes."

The creature shuffled to one of the frames and raised a tentacle, the end of which split into a myriad of thin fingerlike appendages. They brushed over a pattern of crystals.

"He is ready for sustenance."

It turned back to me. "You are Aiden Fleischer. There is no other on Ptallaya with your exact physical structure and colouring. The Quintessence instructed us to keep watch for you."

"What is the Quintessence?"

"It is the One whose design the Mi'aata follow."

In response to my puzzled expression, the Blood God tapped itself with a tentacle. "We are the Mi'aata."

Movement drew my attention to one of the walls. A floor-to-ceiling panel of a shimmering pearl-like substance had suddenly dissolved into the air. A Blood God—or Mi'aata—entered through the revealed doorway. It was carrying a platter of fruit and vegetables, which it handed to me.

"Eat," the newcomer directed, before addressing Koozan-Phay. "We have arrived and the underconveyance is secured."

Koozan-Phay replied, "Order the cargo unloaded, Zantar-Pteen. The crew may then go to their prayers."

Zantar-Pteen made a gesture—perhaps the equivalent of a bow—and departed. The door rematerialised. I laid into my meal, too famished to consider anything else. Koozan-Phay watched me patiently and said nothing until I'd finished.

"I will now take you to a holding cell where you'll remain until you are summoned. Do not be concerned, Aiden Fleischer—you are not a prisoner and will not have to wait for long."

"And then?"

"Then the Quintessence will decide whether your knowledge and skills can benefit Phenadoor."

"And if I'm found lacking, will I be eaten?"

"I do not understand your question."

I couldn't help but growl my response. "Your people decimated the Yatsill and drained blood from the Koluwaians."

"Yatsill? Koluwaians? I do not know these things. The Mi'aata are peaceful. We have little contact with the other species of Ptallaya. Certainly, we do not attack or consume them."

"I witnessed it with my own eyes, Koozan-Phay."

The Mi'aata stood silently for a moment, then said, "This is very disturbing. As a simple merchant I cannot perceive where the truth of the matter might be situated. It must be placed before the Quintessence. Come."

I stood and followed him to the pearl panel, watched it dissolve before my eyes, then stepped after him through the portal and into an arched passageway. We moved along it, passing other Mi'aata, all intent on their various tasks, until we came to a junction. Here we turned left and exited the vessel through a round door. As we descended a ramp, I looked back at *Underconveyance 202*, then at the chamber in which it had docked.

The ship, settled on the surface of an inlet, was smooth, silvery, and shaped somewhat like a long, narrow fish. On top of its midsection, a crystal dome bulged outward, and from it a bright orange light glowed.

I realised that I was going to have to completely revise my impression of the Blood Gods, for the vessel was obviously far more advanced than anything my own race had created.

The inlet lapped at the edges of a spectacular grotto, an irregularly formed cavern of bluish rock veined with white crystals that flashed and glinted, illuminating everything within. When Koozan-Phay heard my exclamation of wonder, he said, "Our scholars tell us that when Ptallaya was young, Phenadoor fell to it from Tremakaat Yul."

We crossed the dock and entered a jewel-encrusted tunnel.

"What is Tremakaat Yul?"

"The purple eye that circles this world."

The moon with the dark blotch. There was no astronomical terminology in the Koluwaian lingo, but the concept that something could "fall" from Tremakaat Yul suggested to me that the Mi'aata might possess some knowledge of celestial matters. Perhaps, then, they would better understand the explanation of my and Clarissa's origins than the Yatsill had done.

The tunnel sloped upward. We frequently passed openings to the right and left, and encountered many other Mi'aata, to whose fearsome appearance I was now becoming more accustomed. They weren't the octopus-like cephalopods I'd initially taken them for. Upon closer inspection, I saw the same hints of a skeletal structure I'd spotted in the creature that burst out of Mademoiselle Crockery Clattersmash, and their six tentacles—which appeared to be interchangeable as arms or legs—were multi-jointed rather than boneless.

Their "faces" were similar to those of the Yatsill in that they were four-eyed with a vertical mouth. The eyes, though, were far more expressive, each being possessed of an iris and sideways-blinking lids. The mouth was merely a slit, which made a horrible trembling motion when the things spoke.

That the Mi'aata were more intelligent than the Yatsill was suggested by the various instruments and contraptions—all constructed from crystal—which lined the tunnel and various chambers we passed through. Where the Yatsill were mimics, the Mi'aata were obviously innovators, and had created a mechanical science based—I later learned—on "resonating frequencies." It was certainly more sophisticated, quieter, and less odorous than the engineering of my own world. Whether it was any more reliable, though, remained open to question, for I saw that many of the devices were under repair—either being dismantled by Mi'aata or put back together. This was true of the rooms and corridors we passed through, too—their walls, floors, and ceilings appeared to be in a constant state of renovation, so much so that I was prompted to ask Koozan-Phay whether Phenadoor was suffering some sort of structural decay.

"Not at all," he replied. "We renew because the Quintessence says it is necessary."

He led me into a small room. A pearl panel materialised in the doorway behind us, then, moments later, vanished again to reveal a different corridor beyond. Presumably the room was a passenger lift, like the ones used in New York, but I'd felt no sensation of movement and had no idea whether we'd gone up or down.

We traversed more corridors and chambers until we entered a long and narrow space with many doors set in its sides. A Mi'aata stepped forward and greeted us. "Is this Aiden Fleischer?"

"It is," Koozan-Phay confirmed.

"He will wait in Cell Nineteen."

"Very well."

I was escorted into a square compartment.

"I will come for you when the Quintessence wills it," Koozan-Phay said. "Eat if you become hungry, bathe, and sleep." He backed out of the doorway and a panel faded into view between us. I placed a hand on it. It was solid. I was confined.

The chamber contained items of food and a folded blanket on a shelf; what looked like a stone bath filled with a clear, steaming jelly-like substance; a block that would serve as a chair; and a hole in the floor that I guessed was a commode. Spherical objects, about the size of tennis balls, extended from stalks at each corner of the ceiling. They resembled eyes, and, indeed, swivelled to follow my every movement.

I stood quietly, then shrugged, slipped off the pitiful remnants of my trousers and boots, and climbed into the bath. The glutinous slime closed over my limbs, tingled against my skin, and sucked the soreness and exhaustion out of me. I put my head back and my eyelids began to droop.

A mellow voice sounded, projected into the room by a means I was unable to identify. "Phenadoor is just. Your status and rewards will always be commensurate with the value of your contribution, whether the latter be material or intellectual. This is an equitable society. Serve it well and you will be well served. Status One can be achieved by all. Opportunities are unlimited. Be unflagging in your efforts. Be diligent in your work. Be conscientious in your actions."

There was a brief silence before the voice spoke again.

"Phenadoor is efficient. Phenadoor is self-sustaining. Phenadoor is perfect. As a component of Phenadoor, you will be fulfilled, for what you do contributes to the continued welfare of all, and what all others do contributes to your own well-being."

My respiration slowed and deepened. I slipped into a doze but was jerked out of it by another pronouncement.

"Work hard. Do your duty. Put Phenadoor first. You are important. You are essential. Phenadoor needs you. You need Phenadoor."

"What I bloody well need," I muttered, "is sleep."

"Do not be indolent. Do not be distracted. Do not waste your time. There is no need for recreation. There is no need for imagination. There is no need for art. There is no need for philosophy. There is no need for resistance. The Quintessence knows what is best for you and what is best for Phenadoor. Trust in the Quintessence."

I made a noise of exasperation. For how long must I endure this nonsense?

"Revolution is a crime. Dissent is wrong. Those who oppose the will of the Quintessence threaten the natural balance of Phenadoor. The Divergent are destructive. The Divergent must abandon their erroneous thinking. The Divergent must submit to the will of the Quintessence."

A respite, then: "Attempts to reclaim Manufacturing Bays Six, Seven, Eight, and Nine have failed. Two hundred and thirteen Mi'aata were injured by the Divergent occupiers and will join the Discontinued this cycle. The Quintessence thanks them for their service to Phenadoor. Access to Zones Twenty-two and Twenty-three is restricted. The Divergent are ordered to abandon their occupation of those areas."

I climbed out of the bath. The moment I did so, a warm wind blew through the room, drying me in moments. It stopped and I looked for its source but found nothing.

After putting the blanket onto the floor, I lay on it and rested my head in the crook of my arm. Sleep came in fitful stops and starts. I was repeatedly jolted awake at the beginning of each proclamation then drifted back into oblivion with the voice still ringing in my ears.

For hour after hour, the pronouncements went on, extolling the virtues of Phenadoorian society, promising high rewards for hard work, insisting that only practical pursuits were of any value, and demanding that the "Divergent" give up what was obviously an attempt at revolution.

Phenadoor, far from being a paradise, was apparently a society in upheaval.

Eventually, the door faded and Koozan-Phay stepped in. I sat up.

"I trust you are well rested, Aiden Fleischer."

"Hardly."

"No? That is regrettable. Did the proclamations familiarise you with the wonder that is Phenadoor?"

I got to my feet. "You could say that, yes."

"Excellent. I have good news."

I raised my eyebrows questioningly.

"I am to take you to the Quintessence immediately."

He gestured for me to follow and led me out of the cell and back to the silent lift. This time, the doors opened onto a different floor, and after we'd passed along a succession of corridors, we came to a large semicircular portal guarded by four Mi'aata, each holding a pikestaff topped with a blade of crystal. One of the sentries stepped forward and addressed my escort. "You are Merchant Koozan-Phay and this is Aiden Fleischer. Enter and stand before the Quintessence—all-seeing, all-knowing—and may you both be favoured."

Koozan-Phay acknowledged the guard, the door faded, and we stepped through the portal into a circular chamber. I stumbled and gasped, astonished at what I saw, for the entire space was an enormous geode filled with refracting, scattering, fragmenting light, almost blinding in its brilliance, and in the centre of it there was a . . . what? A natural outcrop? A machine? An obelisk? I couldn't tell. But however it might be classified, the object was simply breathtaking; a glinting array of facets, angles, planes, and edges; a towering monolith about thirty feet high and fifteen wide; a black crystal of incredible proportions, and faintly visible, motionless inside it like flies suspended in amber, three Mi'aata.

"They are the One, the Quintessence!" Koozan-Phay whispered to me.

Lights flickered through the translucent formation and the voice I'd endured in my cell boomed so loudly that I flinched and moved to cover my ears.

"Merchant Koozan-Phay, you have retrieved Aiden Fleischer and have thus contributed to the furtherance of the Mi'aata. We move you from Status Twenty to Status Eighteen. You may transfer your household to Zone Eighteen. We give you a gift of three additional trade routes. You will be lauded in the proclamations. You have done well. We are pleased. You are dismissed."

"My gratitude," Koozan-Phay replied. "My allegiance. My service always to the Mi'aata." He touched my arm, turned, and left.

The sparks played slowly through the internal angles of the monument.

"Aiden Fleischer," the voice thundered, "we are the Quintessence. The Absolute. The Eternal. Your companion, Clarissa Stark, was rescued from the Divergent. We have looked into her mind and have seen that you are from another world. Your species is strange to us."

I winced. "Not so loud! You'll split my skull!"

"Your companion is unable to describe the means by which you travelled to Ptallaya. We require that knowledge."

"I have no more idea of it than she does. Is she all right? Let me see her."

"Your wish will be granted or denied according to how well you serve the Mi'aata. We will look into you."

I felt invisible fingers push through the bones of my skull. They tore it apart. Someone screamed. I had no conception that it was Aiden Fleischer making the noise or Aiden Fleischer hearing it. The agony exploded—an instant—an eternity—and was gone.

The probes partially retracted and I reassembled.

I was lying on the floor, breathing heavily.

"Curious! Clarissa Stark's thoughts are accessible but her emotions are veiled. The reverse is true of you."

I sat up, but that's as far as I got. My legs were shaking too much to support me.

"*This* predominates," the Quintessence continued. "What is it?"

My chest tightened. I struggled to draw breath. I saw the corpse in Buck's Row, but it wasn't Polly Nichols—it was Alice Tanner. Light reflected dimly from puddles of blood. The stuff oozed along the razor-edge of my blade and dripped onto the cobble-like shells. Fury blazed through me.

The Quintessence took hold of the illusion, examined it, untangled it, straightened it, gave it lucidity, and forced me to recognise the truth of it.

I wasn't feeling anger at all. It was something entirely different, something that had been first twisted and contorted by my experiences, then infiltrated by an exterior power and made dark and impossible to face.

It was fear.

Fear!—now imbued with a sharp clarity like that of a clear winter's day, so severe and uncompromising it was inconceivable to me that I'd ever mistaken it for anything else.

My heart throbbed wildly.

The Quintessence's senses burrowed like termites beneath my skin. Then they withdrew and left me slumped on my side, waiting for the strength to seep back into my trembling limbs.

"One who means you harm has exploited you, Aiden Fleischer. I have undone its interference. You are corrected. However, I cannot repair the damage you do to yourself. Why have you perpetuated this other emotion?"

"What other emotion?" I whispered.

A scene unfolded from memory—my father, standing at the door of the little church in Theaston Vale, a smile on his amiable face, his eyes twinkling with intelligence and good humour.

I moaned with pain as my stomach constricted.

"Explain!" the Quintessence demanded.

"I can't."

"You can."

Again, the horrible infiltration of my emotions, that squeezing and adjusting, and all of a sudden I couldn't help but talk and blurted, "I followed my father's path and imitated his faith."

"We understand the peculiar concept of *father*, but not your response to it. Clarify. What is *faith*?"

"Faith is—is—" I stopped and wrestled with my thoughts. This interview was already proving torturous, but it was also ripping away the knots that had ensnarled my feelings for so long. What I wanted now, above all else, was to be liberated from my inner conflicts, that I might be able to act decisively. If, to achieve such a freedom, I must submit to the Quintessence's invasive interrogation, then so be it.

My pulse slowed. I gathered a reply and delivered it word by word, straining to keep my voice steady and my meaning clear.

"Faith is to have conviction in, and gain comfort from, a hypothesis, despite there being no empirical evidence to support it. In my father's case, the premise was that all existence is created by a single supreme being, and that its meaning cannot truly be understood until a life has been lived and the actions taken during it have been judged by the creator."

A long silence followed my statement. I managed to clamber to my feet and stood weakly, watching the motionless trinity.

Finally, it spoke again. "The notion presupposes a different manner of existence that can only be properly perceived after, and possibly before, the current one."

"Yes, it does."

"We are intrigued. Why do you not share your father's faith?"

I shrugged. "Proponents of the hypothesis claim the creator is perfect and good. If that's true, why is existence so flawed? Why does the opposite of good exist—conflict and suffering and injustice—the things we term 'evil'? Are they to test us, so we might be judged? Are we, then, nothing but an experiment? Why has a faultless creator fabricated something so unsound that it requires evaluation? It makes no sense. There is no logic to it. I cannot believe in it."

"Yet you mimicked acceptance of it."

"I desired the equanimity and happiness that I saw in my father."

"You were unable to achieve those things independently?"

"I was afraid to try. I was a coward."

"But you hoped imitation would develop into authenticity."

"Yes."

"And the result?"

I swallowed and took a few trembling breaths before answering.

"Guilt! The emotion you've identified is guilt. I wasted time. Lived a lie." I gritted my teeth, fisted my hands, and snarled, "And when I finally found the courage to come out of hiding—*this*! Here! Ptallaya! Where I have control over *nothing* and am pushed from one predicament to another. Whatever I do, it makes no damned difference and no damned sense!"

There was another long pause, then the Quintessence responded, "Aiden Fleischer, by rejecting your father's hypothesis you also rejected a context through which your experiences and actions might have meaning. Also, you made central to your repudiation the notion that your creator is responsible for the defects that you perceive in existence. What if that is untrue? Might there not be a second agency at work? If there is a creator, why not also a destroyer?"

I instantly recalled Clarissa's insistence that evil did not spring from specific circumstances but existed independently of them, as a causeless force. She'd once asked, "Do you not think it time you gave the Devil his due?" But no, I couldn't bring myself to do that. The Bible says of Lucifer: *Thou wast perfect in thy ways from the day that thou wast created, till iniquity was found in thee.* In other words, the Devil was a faulty product of a supposedly flawless progenitor. What, though, if Clarissa had been wrong in attribution only? What if evil came not from one of God's own creations but, as the Quintessence had just suggested, from a source equal to and separate from the deity?

"Yes," I murmured. "It's a more plausible proposition."

"Might it not then also be true," the Quintessence said, "that these conflicting forces echo through every level of existence, from the macroscopic to the microscopic; in every animal, vegetable, and mineral; in every social structure; in every individual?"

"I don't oppose the concept."

"Then in order to gain another context, and thus achieve the meaning, equanimity, and happiness you desire, you must better understand the opposition we have identified."

A peal of bitter laughter escaped me. I quoted myself: "To do the greatest good, I must know its opposite." They were the exact words I'd said to Clarissa Stark so long ago, and now they were being reiterated by a bizarre intelligence on another world!

"I can help you," the Quintessence boomed.

"How?"

"The evil you must confront—it is here."

"It's—what?"

"If our conjecture has validity, Aiden Fleischer, then Phenadoor exemplifies the perfection of the creator. Under my guidance, it has been a perfectly balanced society. However, it is now at the brink of crisis."

I gave a slight grunt of recognition and said, "The proclamations mentioned something called the Divergent."

"Yes. For many cycles, the ocean has delivered to us fewer and fewer newborn, and those we have received have been perverted in thought and spirit. They are filled with deviant ideas and violent intentions. Their minds are closed to me. They are Divergent."

"The ocean delivers the newborn?"

"The Mi'aata are formed in its waters."

"And the Yatsill?"

"To what do you refer?"

I opened my mouth to reply but hesitated. The Quintessence wasn't aware of the Yatsill? What, then, had become of all the Working Class who'd slipped into the ocean as the Heart of Blood rose? If they didn't swim to Phenadoor, where did they go?

"They're a species I've encountered on Ptallaya," I said.

"The Mi'aata have little contact with the lesser life forms. They are immaterial."

"Very well. So what has caused these Mi'aata to become Divergent?"

"It is a mystery—one that has continued without change for a number of cycles. But during this last, there have been further oddities. The number of newborn has unexpectedly risen almost to normal, but they are marred by an even greater degree of mental corruption. Also, they have become organised, and have isolated ten manufacturing plants, where they now construct we know not what. In attempting to find out, we sensed a controlling presence among them, and further investigation led us to discover Clarissa Stark. Wresting her from the Divergent cost many Mi'aata lives and did not have the result we expected, for it was quickly apparent that she was not the presence we had sensed."

"So this thing that controls them—it is the evil you referred to?"

"It is. We cannot locate it but we know it is here. We can feel its poison, its instability. Whatever else it is, it is most certainly insane. And this creature—"

"Creature? Do you mean to suggest that it's not a Mi'aata?"

"We do. And this creature, Aiden Fleischer, is the same creature that manipulated your emotions and partitioned your companion's mind. Obviously, whatever its scheme, you both have a role to play, albeit unwittingly."

I tensed, and my hand automatically shifted to rest on my sword hilt. I felt disconcerted to find that it wasn't there.

Hoarsely, I barked, "Explain *partitioned*!"

"Some areas of Clarissa Stark's mind have been blocked from us. Other parts have been filled with unusual mathematical formulae. We have tried to decipher them but they loop back on themselves and we become ensnared. Recently, it occurred to us that perhaps this is their very purpose. Clarissa Stark is a decoy. The formulae were planted in her to keep us occupied."

I felt a pure hard anger ignite inside me.

The Quintessence continued, "This insidious enemy must be located and defeated. That is the task I now assign to you. Fulfil it and you will do a great service to the Mi'aata—and resolve your own difficulties."

I felt a sudden sourness and resentment. My father's God had expected me to spread the Word. I'd failed. The Yatsill's god had expected me to fetch Dar'sayn. I'd failed. Now the Mi'aata's god wanted me to confront its enemy. It would be nice, I thought, if, just for once, I could set my own agenda.

"Let me see Clarissa first."

"Your companion is in the care of my Status Four scientists. You will not be permitted to enter Zone Four until I raise you to the appropriate level. I will not award you Status Four until you have served to my satisfaction."

I considered the three entombed Mi'aata, looked around at the glittering chamber, then sighed and gave a curt nod.

The Quintessence said, "Good. Then, Aiden Fleischer, I hereby declare you Non Status and condemn you to servitude in the mines."

"Wait! Servitude? The mines? What are you talking about?"

"You will labour alongside the captured Divergent. Befriend them. Interrogate them. Do whatever is necessary to identify the one who is influencing them."

"But you said they're insane!"

"Your mission will not be easy. Succeed, and a high position in Phenadoorian society shall be yours. Fail, and you will remain in the mines."

"I can't accept those terms! There must be another way!"

"There is none. You have no choice."

The door behind me vanished and the four guards entered.

"Take him."

CHAPTER 9

ESCAPE

The equivalent of two Earth months, at least, must have passed, and my body, though muscular and toughened by all my trials and tribulations—and, of course, by Ptallaya's gravity—was at the limit of its endurance.

I'd learned that Phenadoor was honeycombed with tunnels, which varied in size from tall and wide corridors to little more than crawl spaces. One particular passage burrowed at a sheer angle into the mountain's base then out beneath the seabed where it split into multiple branches. From these, veins of a deep blue crystal had been chipped away at, initially by generation after generation of low-status Mi'aata, and latterly by captured Divergent. The much-prized crystals were a primary component in Phenadoorian technology.

I'd been placed in Unit 22, a work party of nine Divergent, all baffled by my presence, and each responding to it with vagueness, hostility, eccentricity, or incomprehensible madness. Mostly, they avoided me as much as possible. The exception was an individual named Tharneek-Ptun, who appeared inexplicably drawn to me and persistently engaged me in conversations that made little sense and that he carried on whether I acknowledged him or not.

When Unit 22 wasn't employed on one of the long back-breaking shifts, it occupied quarters carved out of the side of the main passage. The Mi'aata slept in gelatine-filled troughs. This was not the same healing stuff I'd bathed in upon my arrival in Phenadoor and I found its slimy texture unpleasant, so I'd drained my trough and put a rough blanket in the bottom. My bed was hard and uncomfortable, but every time I lay in it I was too exhausted to notice and immediately fell into a deep and dreamless slumber, unconscious even of the continual pronouncements that echoed through the tunnels.

"Wealth and comfort can be yours if you make the well-being

of Phenadoor your primary purpose. Those who work the hardest are the most rewarded. Do not doubt. Do not question. Do not lose focus. Remember that, in striving for the betterment of Phenadoor, you are striving for yourself."

As usual, it was a siren that woke me, and a Mi'aata warden who forced me to my feet. Like all his fellows, the brute was armed with a crystal-topped pikestaff, the tip of which delivered an agonising bolt of energy to anyone it touched. He employed it freely and viciously, jabbing the weapon repeatedly into my ribs. My muscles spasmed, my limbs jerked, and I let out a cry of pain.

"Get in line outside!" he ordered. "And the rest of you filth! All of you! Outside. Now!"

We stood and shuffled from the small room, lined up in the roughly hewn tunnel, and with the wardens harassing our every step began to walk along it, following its sloping floor downward.

Tharneek-Ptun, at my side, mumbled, "We descend once again, and in doing so fold inward, do we not?"

I gave what had become my standard response to his irrational statements. "Indeed so."

"And in folding inward we mine our own resources."

The atmosphere was dense and hot. All the tunnels were lit by glowing crystals and fitted with pipes that sprayed a fine mist of seawater over the Mi'aata to cool them and keep their skins moist. Noisy pumps then removed the water to prevent flooding. While this was beneficial to my fellows, it caused me great discomfort and my skin was covered with sores that couldn't heal beneath the onslaught of corrosive salt water.

Following a zigzagging sequence of slopes, we were mercilessly prodded along, descending deeper and deeper until, eventually, we reached one of the mine faces.

"Take up your tools and get to it!" a warden snapped.

"Digging ever inward!" Tharneek-Ptun muttered. "How far into your own mind have you gone, Mr. Fleischer?"

"Too far," I answered. "And you?"

"Right up to the barrier."

My interest was piqued. So far, my unit had offered little by way of useful information, though the more coherent of them had railed against the social order of Phenadoor, calling it stagnant and self-absorbed. The rest of Ptallaya, they claimed, was primitive and undeveloped, so why not expand into it? But if such sentiment came from a unifying source—as the Quintessence suspected—my fellows appeared to know nothing of it.

"Barrier?" I asked.

Tharneek-Ptun remained silent and hammered at the vein of crystal while a warden passed by, then responded, "That which blocks true revelation. The insurmountable. The impenetrable."

"And if you could pass this barrier, what would be revealed?"

"My origin. Have you never wondered what you were before you were born?"

"I'm not sure I was anything. Besides, I'm rather more concerned with what I might be now, while I live. What's the first thing you remember, Tharneek-Ptun?"

"I recall the sea, and being taken aboard an underconveyance. That is all."

"And New Yatsillat?"

"What is that?"

A warden approached and bellowed, "You two! Less talk, more work!" He thrust his pikestaff into the small of my back. I jerked and cried out, fell and lay twitching, then recovered, struggled back up, and returned to my labours. As my assailant moved away, I snarled in English, "I swear, if that lout comes near me again, I'll kill him!"

Tharneek-Ptun uttered a cry of surprise and dropped his tools. The warden turned back at the noise. My companion quickly snatched up his implements and attacked the rock face with overt enthusiasm. It was enough to satisfy the guard, who grunted and wandered away. I waited until he was out of hearing range then asked, "Are you all right, Tharneek-Ptun? You're trembling."

No reply was forthcoming and the Divergent Mi'aata remained uncharacteristically silent for the remainder of the shift.

I worked on, the muscles of my arms, shoulders, and back

becoming increasingly fatigued until they first burned then became totally numb. It was impossible to judge how long we were at the mine face, but by the time the shift ended I was dazed with exhaustion, half-starved, and barely able to stand.

A siren blared.

"Back to your quarters!" a warden shouted.

We formed a line and began the interminable trek back along the tunnel. Barely aware of what I was doing—focused only on putting one foot in front of the other—I knew nothing more until I found myself standing beside my bed.

Behind me, Tharneek-Ptun stretched his limbs, almost doubling in height, and said, "Gaaaah!"

I spun and looked at him in astonishment.

He touched my shoulder with the tip of a tentacle and said, very quietly, "Get some sleep, old thing. But I shall wake you later. We need a little confab."

"Great heavens!" I cried out. "You're speaking English!"

He nodded, then moved to his trough and climbed in.

I stood a moment, my mind reeling, then, unable to remain conscious any longer, collapsed onto my blanket and passed out.

Immediately—or that's the way it felt—I was jogged back to my senses, opened my eyes, and saw him looking down at me.

"Come with me," he whispered.

I heaved myself out of bed and looked around. The other Mi'aata were dormant. Tharneek-Ptun took me by the wrist, pulled me to the door, peeked out, saw that no patrols were in sight, and dragged me into the corridor. We moved rapidly down the slope, unchallenged—for, logically, it was the upper parts of the tunnel that were guarded, not the lower—until we came alongside a small opening in the base of the right-hand wall. My companion pushed me down onto all fours and propelled me through before squeezing himself in after me.

"Crawl forward," he ordered.

With my lassitude quickly dissipating, I moved through the tight, irregular tunnel.

"Not much farther, old chap."

The passage soon widened into a small asymmetrical chamber—a space of softly illuminated crystal surfaces with three other openings in it. Here we stopped.

"Is it really you?" I asked.

"It most certainly is! New Yatsillat. The City Guard. Old Brittleback. It's all returned to me! What! What! I remembered it the moment I heard you speak English! Harrumph!"

"Colonel Spearjab!"

"Exactly so! Colonel Momentous Spearjab, formerly Yazziz Yozkulu, latterly Tharneek-Ptun, at your service, old boy! Ha ha! I say, what a rum do! What! What! Look at me! I'm a confounded Blood God! Humph! Humph! Humph!"

"But—but—how?"

As soon as I asked the question, the answer came to me. There could be only one explanation! The Blood Gods—the Mi'aata—didn't invade the Yatsill at all. Rather, it was a case of metamorphosis. The one transformed into the other. The first didn't understand the true nature of the second, while the second had no memory of the first.

"How? I have absolutely no idea!" Spearjab responded. "I'm as baffled as can be! Harrumph! But you, old chap—how came you to Phenadoor? Hey? What?"

"Your fellow Mi'aata took Clarissa Stark from New Yatsillat and brought her here. I came to find her."

"She's here? Why?"

"To distract the Quintessence, apparently. Frankly, I'm surprised your fellows had wits enough to do it. The Divergent—as the more recent generations of Mi'aata are called—aren't very rational."

Spearjab raised a couple of tentacles to his head. His four eyes rolled and squinted. He muttered, "Yes. It *is* jolly difficult to think."

"The Quintessence says you are deviants."

"Pah! Phenadoor's ruler lacks imagination. He resists progress. He demands that everything be rebuilt over and over and develops nothing new. Here, everything is always the same, the same, the same! That is not Mi'aata destiny! We need to create and explore and advance. We must dominate and—"

He stopped and groaned and whispered, "My goodness!"

I placed a hand on his side. "What is it, Colonel? For a moment there you sounded quite different. Are you in pain?"

"Harrumph! There is something crawling around inside the old noggin. Makes it awfully hard to order one's thoughts, what! It is a—a—a *waiting*. A *gathering*. A *preparing*."

"Is it sentient? An individual? Here in Phenadoor?"

"Yes, old thing. *There*." He pointed up to the left. "It emanates from that direction. What! What! Humph!"

"Colonel, the Quintessence suspects that a hidden presence in the mountain is controlling the Divergent. Is that what you sense? Could you lead me to it?"

"I rather think I could, yes. Humph! That's if I can keep my bloomin' wits about me and stay on the straight and narrow. It wouldn't do to be subverted! Not at all! What! What! Just not cricket! Not cricket, I say! Give me a moment, would you?"

I waited while Spearjab sat hunched over, his four eyes closed, his mouth quivering with effort. When he finally spoke again, his voice was slurred.

"Difficult. I feel—divided. *Divided*, I say! But we can proceed. I should warn you, though—it'll be jolly dangerous."

"We have no choice, Colonel. We are caught up in some sort of vast plot. My and Clarissa's transportation to Ptallaya, the dwindling of the Aristocrats, the murder of Yarvis Thayne and the attempt on Clarissa's life, the increasing numbers of Divergent Mi'aata—all these things are connected, I'm certain. But to what end, and who is responsible?"

"Quite! Quite! But our absence will be noticed. The bally fiends will search for us."

"Then we must move fast."

Spearjab looked at me. His speech became less strained. "I say, in New Yatsillat, I was thoroughly miffed to see so many Aristocrats taken by the Blood Gods. But what ho! What ho! Now I know they weren't taken at all! They are all here——*here*, I say!——but the poor blighters aren't aware of themselves. They can't recall their past existence. I've been fortunate, what! In remembering your language, I've remembered myself, and I'm thoroughly grateful, old thing. Thoroughly! Now the great revelation——the secret of our origin—— must be shared with all the Mi'aata, hey? First, though, I want to know what infernal rotter is meddling with my mind! Harrumph! Follow me. Tally-ho!"

He crawled to one of the other openings and stepped through into the narrow tunnel beyond. I followed him up its steep incline, heading toward the heart of the mountain.

"A question, Mr. Fleischer," he said, after a few moments had passed.

"Yes?"

"That word I used. What in the name of the Saviour is cricket?"

☼

We climbed for what felt like hours. The tunnel twisted and turned, sometimes angling upward so sharply that it was almost vertical. Occasionally, other passageways branched away from it, and, eventually, we entered one of these and continued on. Being too narrow for regular use, these channels through the rock and crystal were uninhabited and we encountered no other Mi'aata, though on a number of occasions we caught glimpses, through crevices, of populated corridors.

Undetected, we pushed on, drawing upon reservoirs of strength we hadn't even suspected in ourselves, through gleaming gem-encrusted burrows and along lengthy passages of bare rock, completely unlit, groping our way forward until something twinkled in the darkness ahead and we emerged into another stretch of glowing crystals.

Despite being dressed only in the ragged remnants of my trousers, now little more than a loincloth, I perspired freely——and bled, too, for sharp edges sliced at my skin and I suffered many knocks and scrapes. Most of all, I was afflicted with thirst, and by the time

Spearjab announced, "What! What! We are close, old chap! Very close! We've just passed into Zone Four. Humph!" I felt I might lose my mind if I didn't find water soon.

We came to a narrow opening on our left and my companion directed me to look through it. I did so, and the sight that met my eyes was overwhelming. The cleft overlooked a vast illuminated cavern, so large that the far distance was somewhat obscured by the intervening atmosphere. Hundreds of buildings, tall and pointed, rose into the air, many storeys high but still not so tall as to come near the roof that arched overhead. Ramps spanned the distances between the structures, and wheeled vehicles—they were too far away for me to make out their design—traversed them. Other vessels flew between and around these elevated thoroughfares, making the whole settlement a hive of activity as thousands upon thousands of Mi'aata went about their business, whatever that might be.

"The Quintessence told me Clarissa was on this level," I muttered. "I suppose she's in one of those buildings."

"I should say so," Colonel Spearjab replied.

"Damnation!" I cursed, realising that I would never find her unassisted. I had no choice but to complete my mission and report back to the trinity. "Let's move on, Colonel."

The tunnel was horizontal now, running around the edge of Zone Four. We progressed through it until we came to a fairly large empty and dimly lit cavern, which, to my sheer delight, had a clear stream bubbling out of its floor, forming a deep pool to one side. Without hesitation, I threw myself down and gulped at the cold, revitalising water. Then, after my companion had also drunk his fill, I immersed myself fully and rubbed the sweat, dirt, and blood from my skin. Spearjab slid in after me and we faced each other, relishing the soothing chill.

"Oh dear! They have discovered our absence, Mr. Fleischer. I can feel it. Humph! Your mind is impervious to them—they'll not detect you unless you are seen—but Mi'aata minds are all connected. What! What! Eventually they'll trace my whereabouts."

"How soon?"

"I think we'll be safe for a little while longer, and we're very close to our quarry now. Ha! It is a strong, extremely well-shielded mind. Yes, indeed! *Extremely well shielded*, I say!"

"But you can detect it?"

"Quite so! Quite so! Because I'm Divergent, you see, and it's extended its influence over all of my kind. Harrumph! The confounded brute is keeping us befuddled and half-bonkers until it needs us. But——ha ha!——I can trace the influence back to its source, what!"

"You're remarkably coherent, under the circumstances."

"I have you to thank for that, old thing. You've jogged me out of my bewilderment, so to speak——kicked life into the slumbering Yatsill in me! Incidentally, whoever our mysterious plotter is, I feel that I am acquainted with them."

"From where?"

"I haven't the foggiest. *Not the foggiest*, I say! Harrumph! Harrumph! Shall we push on?"

I nodded, and in short order we were once again squeezing ourselves through a narrow passageway.

The tunnel eventually split into two. Spearjab led me into the left-hand branch, which began to slope downward. Not long after we'd entered it, I became aware that voices were echoing faintly from somewhere ahead.

"We're there! Don't make a sound! Lips sealed, what!" the colonel warned.

Inch by inch, we crept forward.

There were two voices. As we approached them, their conversation became more distinct, and both participants sounded familiar to me.

"——are far more advanced than the Koluwaians I have sent to you and outnumber your kind by thousands to one."

"Do not concern yourself. The manufacturing plants are working at full capacity. It was fortunate that my attempt to kill the woman failed, for what I subsequently found in her mind has proven most

useful. Her machines are almost finished, and the moment I demonstrate them, your world will buckle, of that you can be sure."

"The Quintessence has not detected this activity?"

"The trinity knows the plants have been commandeered, of course,
but what little access I allowed the Quintessence to the woman kept
it so distracted that it has no conception of how far our plans have
advanced."

Colonel Spearjab flattened himself against one side of the tunnel
and indicated that I should pass him. I pulled myself forward.

"What of my return to Koluwai?" the second voice asked. "It will
be the last, yes? I have been through the rupture too many times
already. I'm being disfigured by the scar tissue."

"Your frequent crossings have caused your body to permanently
resonate with the path—that is why you can now traverse it even
when it is quiescent—but what healed you before is now damaging
you. Do not be anxious. Do exactly as you are instructed and it will,
indeed, be your final crossing. The detrimental effects won't kill
you."

"Very well. I shall endure it one more time."

"*Underconveyance Ninety-eight* will be departing very soon with the
first group of Discontinued. The crew has been coerced. They will
take you as close to the shore as you need. You understand how the
crystal functions?"

"Yes. It is attuned to the far end of the rupture."

"That is correct. Be careful with it, for I have found no other
like it. How confident are you in travelling to the destination we've
selected as our first target?"

"I can do it, though it will cost me much."

"You will have riches beyond imagining—and power, too—if you
succeed."

I came to a letterbox-sized chink in the rock and peered through
into a bright crystalline room. There were two individuals in it. One
was a Yatsill, the other a robe-wrapped and masked human. I recognised them immediately and quietly hissed, "Yissil Froon and Sepik!
How in blazes did they get here?"

"By the time you have relocated the other end of the path," Yissil Froon said, "I will have no further need for Phenadoor's resources and will use the machines to transport the Divergent to the Forest of Indistinct Murmurings. My army will be there by the time the Heart of Blood fully sets—arriving as the rupture properly opens. You must travel back through it immediately. I will detect your arrival and direct the Divergent to your position. The rupture will take them."

"I shall depart at once."

"No. First the woman must be dealt with. She has served her purpose. I have learned all I need from her. The obstacles I placed in her mind will not confound the Quintessence for much longer. If he learns the truth of Mi'aata origins, he will seek to restore the balance and there will be no further generations of Divergent. Unacceptable! My army must continue to grow."

"Shall I bring her to you?"

"There is no need. I have much to do and many to influence. I must immediately enter into a deep meditation in order to maintain my grip. I trust you to act independently until I can contact you again. Go to the girl at once and eliminate her. I shall divert her guards. Then make your way to *Underconveyance Ninety-eight* and play your part as arranged. Soon, Mr. Sepik—soon we shall gain the resources of an advanced world and use them to return and conquer this one. An entire world each, my friend! An entire world each!"

Sepik bowed, crossed the chamber, and disappeared through a narrow doorway.

I turned to Colonel Spearjab, leaned close, and whispered urgently, "Can you locate Sepik's mind and follow him?"

"Yes. He is very distinct, what!"

"Then lead on, as fast as you can!"

Heaving himself past me, Spearjab moved through the twisting tunnel. I followed, my heart hammering, my mind repeating over and over those dreadful words: *Eliminate her.*

To my great relief, we'd gone only a short distance when the crawl space suddenly expanded, giving us room to stand. The colonel shot forward around a bend, then raced along a straight, gloomy passage. I ran behind, disregarding my battered body's complaints, forcing it by sheer willpower to overcome its extreme fatigue. When had I last eaten? How long since I'd enjoyed a full night's sleep? I didn't know and it didn't matter. Sepik was on his way to murder Clarissa Stark. I had to stop him.

We clambered through an irregularly shaped hole into a bright corridor, turned left, and came to a pearl-panelled door.

"The beastly thing is behind this," Spearjab whispered.

"Open it."

The Mi'aata made a gesture and the panel silently dissolved, revealing a three-walled room with an oddly formed vehicle standing in its centre. The contraption faced the open side of the chamber, through which the towers of Zone Four were visible. Sepik was standing with his back to us, bending over the rearmost part of the machine and making adjustments to a number of crystalline controls.

I leaped forward, grabbed the Koluwaian around the waist, lifted him high, and slammed him onto the floor. His cry of alarm was cut off as I kicked him onto his back, fell knees-first onto his stomach, and ground my forearm into his throat. I used my free hand to rip the mask from his face, flinging it aside.

The witch doctor Iriputiz looked up at me.

"By God!" I cried, rearing backward. "You!"

The man's mouth worked but only a faint croak emerged.

Bunching my fingers in his robes, I hauled him to his feet and, unable to stop myself, sent my fist smashing into his mouth, once, twice, a third time. He sagged and would have fallen but I held him upright and shook him until his head snapped back and forth and his broken teeth rattled. Blood dribbled from his split lips.

"I'll kill you!" I screamed. "I'll bloody kill you!"

I drew back my arm to strike him again but a tentacle wrapped around it and Colonel Spearjab's voice penetrated the red fog of hatred and vengeance that had enveloped me.

"Mr. Fleischer! You need him alive!"

I hesitated. My wits swam back into focus. I took deep breaths. Spearjab released my arm and I let it fall, but maintained my grip on the islander and glared into his eyes.

"If you want to live, Iriputiz, you'd better damned well talk. Where is Clarissa Stark?"

"She—she is being held in—in Tower Forty-six" he stammered, pointing weakly toward Zone Four. "I was—I was just going there."

"Yes, and I know why, you murdering hound!" I shook him again and slapped his face. "Take me to her or, I swear, you'll die so slowly that the torture you put me through on Koluwai will seem nothing but child's play!"

I spun him around and twisted his arm up behind his back until he shrieked, then pushed him against the vehicle. After quickly examining the machine, I muttered an imprecation and turned to Spearjab. "There's not room for all of us, Colonel."

"Oh well, not to worry, hey!" he said. "It isn't a good means of escape, anyway—the fliers operate well inside Phenadoor but outside they can't stray far from the jolly old mountain. Their frequencies are highly localised. What! What!"

I thought for a moment, then levered the witch doctor's arm again until he moaned with pain. "Where is *Underconveyance Ninety-eight*?"

"Dock Twelve!"

"Can you find it, Colonel?"

Spearjab waggled a limb. "If they don't capture me first, old chap. Ha ha! What! Harrumph!"

"Then go. When you get there, remain concealed and watch out for me. I'll join you as soon as I can. If I reach it before you, I'll wait for as long as possible."

The Mi'aata gave a tentacular salute and withdrew, heading back the way we'd come. I didn't envy him the tunnels.

I returned my attention to Iriputiz. "Your choice is simple; cooperate or die."

"I want to live."

"Get into the machine."

The vehicle was gondola-shaped with two large outcroppings of blue crystal at the front and two at the back. I could see neither an engine nor any means of locomotion.

I climbed in, sat behind my prisoner, and gripped him by the neck. "Any trickery and I'll snap your spine."

He mumbled his understanding and began to manipulate controls on a panel in front of him. The vehicle hummed and waves of light rippled down the crystals. It rose smoothly from the floor, eased forward, then flew from the room and sped out into the immense cavern.

We only travelled a short distance—our destination was on the near side of Zone Four—but the flight was long enough that I was able, by careful observation, to understand the machine's surprisingly simple controls. By the time we spiralled down onto a platform that projected from one of the upper storeys of a tower, I was confident that I'd be able to fly it myself.

I looked around. We were at a dizzying height and most of the busy traffic was below us. The platform was not easily visible from the neighbouring buildings. I was already aware that Yissil Froon was employing his mental powers to keep the guards distracted, so had little fear of discovery. I was more concerned that Iriputiz would attempt to betray me, so after we landed I kept a tight hold of him as I clambered out of the flier. Hauling him after me, I dragged him over to the building's wall and rammed him into it, slapping his face again and feeling a satisfying sting in my palm. He was an old man and I was acting like a vicious thug but didn't care. There was nothing I could do to him that would match the agony he'd inflicted upon me, no amount of pain I could subject him to that he didn't deserve.

"Lead me to her."

He indicated a door. I pushed him over to it, he made a gesture, the panel faded, and we passed through onto a ramp that angled upward to our left and downward to our right. We followed it down.

"Reverend Fleischer, I can—"

"Don't call me that!" I snapped.

"I'm sorry. Please listen. I can give you power—"

"I don't need it."

"Not here! Not on Ptallaya! On Earth! I'm to travel back to Koluwai, and from there to your country—to London. The crystal will cause the far end of the path to follow me."

I pushed him on down the walkway. "Path?"

"The rupture. The thing that spans our world and this."

"Why move it over London?"

"Yissil Froon intends to send his Divergent Mi'aata through. That's why he's been breeding the creatures. When they emerge from the Yatsill and consume human blood, it poisons them, affects their brains, makes them susceptible to his influence. They are to be an army of conquest, using war machines designed by Clarissa Stark. Your country, as the most powerful nation, will be the first to be invaded. Once it's brought to its knees and its resources are seized, the rest of our world will buckle. Work with us, Rev—Mr. Fleischer. I am to become Yissil Froon's representative on Earth. I will make you my General. You can have your choice of riches!"

I was so astounded by his audacity that I almost stumbled.

Digging my fingers into him, I gave the witch doctor a shake and hissed, "*Why*, Iriputiz? Why did you send me to Ptallaya?"

"Because my wife was preventing the Yatsill from developing into Mi'aata. I couldn't locate and stop her. So, instead, I infected you with the *kichyomachyoma* disease, which my own people cannot carry, and sent you here to spread it among the creatures. It weakened their ability to receive her help, made them more liable to transform."

Wife?

A veil of secrecy and deceit lifted.

"Yaku! You are Yaku!"

Suddenly, I understood almost everything.

"Move faster!" I commanded.

I forced the witch doctor ahead until, having descended three levels without encountering a single Mi'aata, we came to a door that was guarded by two. Neither responded to our approach, and when we reached them, I saw that their eyes were glazed over. Yissil Froon held them in his thrall.

I reached out, took hold of one of their pikestaffs, and plucked it from a loose grip.

"She's in here," Iriputiz said. He made a gesture and the door faded. We stepped through.

The room was square, unadorned, and unfurnished but for a long table at its centre. Clarissa Stark was stretched out on it, held down by straps around her wrists and ankles. She turned her head as we entered, her yellow eyes met mine, and she croaked, "Aiden!"

Then she saw Iriputiz and uttered a cry of amazement.

I pushed the man forward. "Untie her!"

Iriputiz obeyed.

"They've been battling inside my mind," Clarissa said, her voice hoarse with emotion. "The Quintessence and Yissil Froon. Froon has examined everything I know about Earth. He filled me with mathematical formulae to keep the Quintessence occupied."

"Clarissa, I'm going to get you off this island," I responded.

I pushed Iriputiz aside and helped my friend to sit up. I nodded toward the islander. "As you can see, Iriputiz is no stranger to Ptallaya. He comes and goes as he pleases. He is Yaku, Pretty Wahine's husband, and also Mr. Sepik of New Yatsillat."

Clarissa rubbed her wrists and looked at the Koluwaian. "Your wife is dead. Her ability to hide away failed her and she was killed by a Blood God."

The old man shrugged and said, "She means nothing to me."

I prodded him with the pikestaff. He jerked and gave a screech as the weapon's tip sent a shock through him.

"Take off your robes," I ordered, and turned back to my companion. "There are no Blood Gods, Clarissa. Those bumps on your head—I think some sort of paired parasitical creature has burrowed into your scalp. The things endow the Yatsill with increased intelligence and telepathic abilities, while also causing them to slowly metamorphose into the creatures that inhabit this mountain, the Mi'aata."

Seeing the look of horror on her face, I added, "Judging from Pretty Wahine's long life, they're somewhat incompatible with human physiology. They can't transform you, other than to correct the malformations you suffered as a child. They also extend your lifespan and connect your mind to the other hosts."

Iriputiz was now standing in nothing but a loincloth, though the crystal he wore was still hanging against his narrow chest. I passed the pikestaff to Clarissa, gestured for the islander to hand me his robes, and started to put them on.

I said, "I've been piecing it all together. I was wondering why, after Pretty Wahine arrived on Ptallaya, the Mi'aata used to die before reaching the sea. I think it's because, when they break out of their Yatsill shell, they must immediately feed. It gives them the strength required to make their way here to Phenadoor. Quee'tan were their natural prey, but the Yatsill, who fashioned their society on Pretty Wahine's memories of Koluwai, drove the Quee'tan out of the forest when they built tree houses."

I glared at Iriputiz, finished dressing, and pointed at his crystal. "I want that, too."

Reluctantly, he removed it and handed it over. It tingled against my skin as if charged with electricity. I looped its string around my neck and continued, "The Mi'aata were then further hampered by Pretty Wahine. She interpreted their emergence as a demonic invasion. The mental powers she'd gained through the consumption of Dar'sayn allowed her to counter it by suppressing the Yatsills' metamorphosis. The natural evolution of the species was almost completely halted."

With a jerk of my hand, I ordered the witch doctor to the door. Clarissa followed him, limping slightly, and I fell in behind. We exited the room. The guards were still in a stupor. We passed them without incident and started up the ramp.

"Yissil Froon was the first Yatsill to drink Dar'sayn," I said. "He took it in large amounts. It gave him greater mesmeric control— and insight. He saw the true nature of the relationship between the Yatsill and the Mi'aata. That's when he approached you, isn't it, Iriputiz? After he realised."

The Koluwaian swallowed nervously and nodded.

"And what did he do?" Clarissa asked.

"Answer her!" I barked.

Iriputiz moaned and said, "Some of my people fell through the rupture. They were brought to Yatsillat. When the Heart of Blood rose, what few Mi'aata hatched fed off their blood and fled to the sea. Yissil Froon could listen to their thoughts. He could influence their actions. With his mind, he followed them and discovered Phenadoor."

We came to the door that led to the platform where the flier was parked. I pushed Iriputiz through it, whirled him around to face me, and kept shoving until he was standing with his heels at the very edge of the precipitous drop. I repeated Clarissa's question. "And what did he do?"

Glancing fearfully down at the streets far, far below, the old man stammered, "He—he—he sent me back through the rupture to fetch more people."

"For the new Mi'aata. To make them insane. To make them susceptible to his influence."

"Y-yes. Pretty Wahine had disappeared. We could not find her. But she was still interfering. Even so, some Mi'aata were born at every rising of the Heart of Blood. They required food."

I placed my right forefinger in the middle of the witch doctor's chest and held it there while addressing Clarissa.

"Yissil Froon knew of Earth from this hound. And he knew from the sick Mi'aata that Phenadoor was scientifically advanced. He realised that, with its manufacturing power and the growing number of Divergent, he could create an invasion force."

"Surely you don't mean that he intends to attack our world, Aiden!"

"I mean exactly that. Get into the vehicle, please."

I applied a slight pressure to the Koluwaian's chest. He swayed backward, his arms windmilling as he fought for balance.

"Please!" he yelled.

"Clarissa," I said. "Can justice be evil?"

So softly that I could barely hear her, she replied, "If it's true justice, I don't see how it can be, Aiden."

I gave a grunt of agreement and pushed.

The witch doctor's eyes went wide, his mouth opened, and he toppled backward and vanished from sight. A long receding wail rose from below and quickly trailed away to nothing.

I turned, paced over to the flier, climbed in, and began to manipulate the controls.

Clarissa remained silent.

"There are certain matters," I said, quietly, "that I am beginning to see in black and white."

The vehicle moaned quietly and rose into the air. I steered it high over Zone Four.

"Is there a way out of here?" I asked.

"To the left. A shaft of red light is shining in—there must be an opening."

I spotted the beam and directed the craft toward it. The light was streaming into the cavern at an angle that suggested the red sun had made considerable progress across the sky since I'd last seen it.

"I was Yissil Froon's plague carrier," I called back to my friend. "His means to overcome Pretty Wahine's influence. He needed me in New Yatsillat. So when Yarvis Thayne tried to raise opposition to our presence, Froon had him murdered."

"By whom?"

"The same Yatsill that attacked you, I expect. My guess is he dominated them mentally and made them train to fight. I doubt they really understood what they were doing. Froon made a show of supporting those who wanted us banished from the city, but in reality, the only one he wanted gone was you."

"Because I was trying to find a cure?"

"And also because the Yatsill were mimicking your inventiveness. You weren't meant to be transported to Ptallaya—and you certainly weren't meant to be a host for the parasite. He was afraid your level of intelligence, transmitted to the Yatsill, might lead them to realise what he was up to. That's why he tried to have you banished to the Whimpering Ruins, and why, having failed, he then orchestrated the attempt on your life. Later, in surreptitiously investigating your mind, probably in search of a weakness, he encountered the plans that you and Lord Hufferton had drawn up for war machines. That's when you suddenly became useful to him."

"So that's why the blueprints were going around and around in my head!" she exclaimed. "But, Aiden, I was immature when I dreamed up those machines. It was done as an exercise, nothing more. The designs are impossibly extravagant. I doubt they would even function."

"Perhaps not if constructed by men on Earth, but here on Ptallaya, with Mi'aata science, who knows what's possible?"

A long moment went by, silent but for the air whistling past, then Clarissa said, "There's something I still don't understand. Why are the parasites entering fewer and fewer Yatsill? Why is the Ritual of Immersion failing?"

"I have a theory, but if you don't mind, I'll wait until I have evidence to support it before I share."

"I don't mind, but why keep it to yourself?"

"Because," I answered, "if it's true, I will have to completely revise my understanding of what it means to be evil."

I saw that the sunlight was streaming through a large orifice in the side of the cavern. I steered our vehicle into it, sped through a short tunnel, and shot out into the open, veering around and down to fly low along the base of the mountain.

Dock Twelve was easier to find than I'd anticipated. There were a great many caves around the base of Phenadoor, nearly all of them with docks visible just inside, mostly empty, the fleet of underconveyances obviously out at sea. However, after completely circling the vast mountain, we passed a solid vertical cliff along which vast doors were lined—all closed.

"The manufacturing plants," Clarissa declared.

"How do you know?"

"The Quintessence was obsessing over them. I picked up its thoughts when it was digging around in my head."

The twelfth cave to the right of the plants was occupied by one of the underwater vessels—*Underconveyance 98*.

I brought our vehicle to a halt and allowed it to sink down until it was just five feet or so above the gently rolling water.

"That's the ship we're looking for," I said. "The one that'll transport us back to the mainland. Shall we try it?"

"I don't see that we have much choice."

"Hopefully, Colonel Spearjab will be somewhere nearby."

"The colonel? Here in Phenadoor?"

"He's Mi'aata now, but hearing me speak English restored his memories. I wouldn't have found you without him."

"Then I owe my life to both of you."

I turned to face my one-time sexton. She was almost naked. Like my own trousers, hers had been reduced to little more than tatters. Her shirt was lacking sleeves and buttons and did little to cover her. The goggles still hung about her neck. Her skin was smudged with dirt and bruises and scored with scratches, her hair lank and matted, and her weird yellow eyes slightly wild with urgency, fear, and excitement.

She looked spectacular.

"I love you, Clarissa Stark."

She smiled, and her face, already stained red by the crimson light, blushed a deeper hue. I didn't need any other response.

We stood. I took the pikestaff from my friend, we climbed over the side of the flier, and jumped into the sea.

It wasn't far to swim but, even so, I'd underestimated the severity of my exhaustion and found myself struggling, especially with the heavy weapon—its shaft was made of buoyant wood but it was difficult to drag through the water—and Iriputiz's robes tangling around my limbs. By the time we climbed up onto a shelf of rock beside the cave entrance, I could do nothing but lie on my back panting. Clarissa put her hands under my shoulders and dragged me a few feet to one side to ensure we couldn't be spotted from the dock. She sat beside me and said, "Rest a moment. Get your strength back."

We were silent for a while, before Clarissa asked, "When did you realise the truth?"

"When the Quintessence showed no knowledge of the Yatsill. I remembered all those Workers entering the sea, thinking they were going to Phenadoor. Suddenly I recognised that they were the Yatsill in their most natural form, just animals sporting in their natural environment, free from telepathic influence."

"And free of the parasites," my friend said. She touched the two lumps on her forehead and grimaced.

"Yes." I thought for a moment, then asked, "What does Phenadoor normally make in those manufacturing plants?"

"From what I could gather, underconveyances and large dome-like structures that the Mi'aata affix to the seabed to house farming communities. Also, Phenadoor's infrastructure is constantly being replaced, so parts are always required."

"I noticed as much."

"Very little actually *needs* replacing. The work is demanded of the Mi'aata simply to keep them occupied and enslaved. The Quintessence is a dictator, Aiden. Phenadoor is all the trinity wants it to be and nothing more. Inevitably, in reaction to such despotism, extremes are born, giving us monsters like Yissil Froon, whose desire to escape his fate as a component of this languishing autocracy has led him to seek power elsewhere. It's sending him along a path of destruction that threatens to annihilate millions of innocents."

I sat up, removed my robes, and wrung the water from them. "You think that's his motivation? Well, one way or another, we'll defeat him, and when we do, his hold over the Divergent will be gone. Perhaps when they reveal the truth of their origins to the rest of the Mi'aata, it will stimulate questions, and discontent at the suppression of imagination and creativity will cause an uprising. The Quintessence's days might well be numbered."

"What chaos Froon generates!"

We rested for a few moments longer. I looked at the sun. It was very low—its nadir almost on the horizon—and I realised my journey to the Forest of Indistinct Murmurings and subsequent time in Phenadoor had occupied a far, far greater period than I'd initially estimated. A deep longing overcame me—I wanted that infernal globe gone! I yearned for two little yellow eyes to look down upon Ptallaya again!

"We'd better move," Clarissa said. "I can feel the Quintessence searching for me. I've learned from bitter experience that I can only resist its mental intrusions for short periods."

I stood, put the robes back on, and, after wrapping the hood around my head to conceal my face, took up the pikestaff and led my companion around the ledge, into the cave, and onto the dock. A few Mi'aata were working at its far end and three were standing by the underconveyance's gangplank, but otherwise Dock Twelve was sparsely populated. We slipped behind a stack of crates and, remaining concealed, moved around the periphery of the cave until we came to an arched opening. I took a tight hold of Clarissa's arm, as if she was my prisoner, and strode into the open, giving the impression that we'd just entered through the doorway. One of the Mi'aata moved away from the gangplank and met us halfway to it.

"Mr. Sepik, we've been waiting." I saw that his four eyes had a peculiarly distracted quality about them. Yissil Froon's doing, for certain.

Imitating the witch doctor's whispery voice, I replied, "Can we depart at once?"

"Yes. One of the Discontinued came aboard moments ago and our hold is now full. If more want to make the trip, they'll have to try another vessel."

I had no idea what he was referring to, but, acting on intuition, I asked, "What was this latecomer's name?"

"Tharneek-Ptun."

I gave a nod of satisfaction. Good! Colonel Spearjab had found his way aboard!

We followed the Mi'aata up the gangplank and entered the ship. Its corridors were narrow and its rooms small. We were escorted to a chamber and I was told, "These are your quarters. What shall I do with this one?" The Mi'aata looked at Clarissa.

"She will remain in my custody," I answered. "I have to interrogate her."

The floor suddenly vibrated.

"Ah," the other exclaimed. "We are leaving Phenadoor. There will be time to sleep if you wish it. You can place your prisoner with the Discontinued in the hold at the end of this corridor."

He departed.

Safely ensconced in the small room, I drained its trough and put my robes in the bottom of it. "This will be your bed, Clarissa. I'm afraid it won't be very comfortable, but it's better than nothing. I'll sleep on the floor."

We settled down, both too worn out to worry any more about our security.

"What happened to you in New Yatsillat?" I asked.

"Poor Pretty Wahine," my companion replied. "She pushed herself beyond all endurance trying to protect the Yatsill and her abilities eventually failed her. I'd just returned to the cave after a fruitless search for Yissil Froon when three Mi'aata burst in. Two grabbed me while the third killed the old woman. I was then dragged into the sea. I lost consciousness, woke up in one of these vessels, and was taken to Phenadoor."

"I should never have left you," I said. "My trek to the Forest of Indistinct Murmurings was a complete waste of time. Well, almost."

"Almost?"

"I met a Zull. I'll tell you about it after we've slept."

I was conscious of nothing more until I was awoken by the touch of a tentacle against my leg. A Mi'aata had entered the room. I sat up and immediately became aware that my face was exposed. The creature didn't react—probably, I realised, because it was unfamiliar with Iriputiz's appearance.

"We have arrived," it said.

"Already?"

"Yes."

As Clarissa stirred, I thanked the Mi'aata and told it we'd be on deck presently. It handed me a tray, on which there was a skin of water and an assortment of fruits and vegetables, then left us alone.

Clarissa groaned. "My muscles are as stiff as wood."

"Mine, too. Good gracious, Clarissa, we must have slept for hours and hours. Phenadoor is a long way from the mainland, yet the voyage is already over!"

"I'd hoped for an opportunity to study the vessel. How do Phenadoorian machines function? I can hear no engine, have seen no fumes, can smell no oil—I'm intrigued!"

"Crystals and frequencies, that's all I know," I replied. "Perhaps we'll one day have an opportunity to learn more."

"Unless we find our way back to Earth."

I looked at her. She returned my gaze. There was no need to say it—we both saw an odd reluctance on the other's face. Despite the wounds and exertions and losses, the dangers and our merciless opponents, we were both more engaged with the business of living than we'd ever felt on our own world.

We ate, quenched our thirst, left our quarters—taking our captured pikestaff with us—and followed the corridor to a ramp that led to the ship's deck. A group of a dozen or so Mi'aata had gathered outside. A great many of them were of an unhealthy hue, their skin pale and blotchy, their limbs quivering uncontrollably.

The creature who'd ushered us aboard at Dock Twelve—the "captain," though the Mi'aata don't use such terminology—met us and indicated the group. "The Discontinued. The strongest of them will help you to shore."

I looked landward and immediately recognised the northern-most limits of the Mountains That Gaze Upon Phenadoor. We were floating about a mile offshore, directly opposite the narrow mouth of a river that emerged from a densely forested valley.

"It's the Forest of Indistinct Murmurings," I told Clarissa.

The Discontinued started to flop over the side of the ship. One of them approached us and said, "Follow me in." Though he spoke Koluwaian, I recognised—from small markings above his left eyes—Colonel Momentous Spearjab.

I turned to bid the captain farewell but he'd already wandered away, obviously uninterested now his duty was discharged.

Spearjab jumped into the water and Clarissa and I dived in after him. He gripped us under the armpits and began to swim. We were all on our backs and thus able to converse.

"I say, Miss Stark!" he exclaimed. "How perfectly splendid to see you! And looking as fit as a fiddle, too! At least, I assume so, not knowing what a confounded fiddle actually is. Ha ha! What! What!"

"Well, I'm a lot better for meeting you again, that's for certain," she said.

I asked our friend whether he'd encountered any problems getting to the ship.

"None at all! I went straight through the tunnels, avoided the populated thoroughfares, and when I reached the dock, declared myself Discontinued. Harrumph! What! I was hustled aboard with nary a 'by your leave!' Humph! Humph!"

I glanced to my right and saw the other Mi'aata swimming nearby.

"Discontinued? What does it mean?"

"They are the aged and diseased ones, old thing. They've lived their lives and are now on their way to jolly well die."

"On their way to where?" Clarissa asked.

"I'm faking it, dear lady, so can't possibly know. They probably don't even know themselves—what!—they're driven by instinct. Shall we follow and find out?"

"Yes," I answered, though I already had an idea of what we were going to see.

Looking past the colonel's face at my companion, I asked, "Clarissa, are we far enough away from Phenadoor? Can Yissil Froon or the Quintessence still infiltrate your mind?"

"I think we're safe, Aiden. Are we returning to New Yatsillat?"

"No. The destruction you witnessed continued after you were taken and the city is no more. Perhaps, when the yellow suns rise and the Yatsill children visit the Pool of Immersion, they'll return and rebuild it, but I think our destiny lies elsewhere."

"You have somewhere in mind?"

"I do, but first we must deal with the threat to Earth."

Upon reaching the shore, we crossed a wide expanse of sand until we came to the treeline, then stood with the rays of the sun shining on our backs and watched the Discontinued file into the forest. Once a little distance had been established, we trailed behind them, pushing our way into the shadows and past the spiny roots. Moisture dripped onto us and I passed my robes to Clarissa that she might be better protected. The atmosphere was thick and humid, the late afternoon of the Heart of Blood stifling and oppressive. There was a heavy scent in the air, spicy and not altogether pleasant.

We hiked beside the river until, finally, the Discontinued moved away from its bank and headed for a clearing, which was perhaps a couple of miles to the west of the one in which Clarissa and I had arrived and where, later, I'd met Gallokomas. We stopped at its perimeter and, concealed by foliage, observed the group.

"I say, I feel I'm committing a terrible act of desecration," Colonel Spearjab whispered.

The Discontinued climbed into trees on the opposite side of the clearing, dragged themselves out onto branches, then lowered themselves until they were each dangling by a single tentacle.

"What are they doing?" Clarissa murmured.

"Exactly what I expected," I replied. "Watch."

Slowly, beads of viscous liquid swelled from the creatures' skin. The droplets ran together until the Mi'aata were completely coated in a thick clear slime. They became utterly still. Gradually, they darkened.

"The fruits!" Clarissa exclaimed. "They were—are—they are pupae!"

I nodded. "The Yatsill metamorphose into Mi'aata, which, in turn, transform into Zull."

"Zull!" my two friends cried out.

"What! What!" Spearjab added.

"Each phase of life loses its memory of the one that went before," I continued, "and each is conducted entirely separately from the others."

"This is incredible!" Clarissa whispered.

"But all going terribly wrong," I observed. "You asked why the ritual of Immersion is failing. Because Pretty Wahine's arrival was calamitous! She cut into a chrysalis thinking it was a fruit and drank the placental fluid, which later came to be known as Dar'sayn. When she encouraged its collection by the Yatsill, they were unaware that in milking the fruits they were actually killing the descendants of their own kind—and the consequences extended even farther than that, for when we were at the Shrouded Mountains, Kata told me the Zull go there to die. I think, when they do, a part of them enters the water in the form of parasites."

Clarissa's eyes widened. "Great heavens! The parasites hijack the Yatsill, the Yatsill change into Mi'aata, the Mi'aata become Zull, and, in their death throes, the Zull deposit the parasites. Full circle!"

"Precisely. An astonishingly complex life cycle, and one that has been thrown into chaos not by Yissil Froon, but by an innocent and well-intentioned woman from Earth."

"Hallo? Hallo? What?" Spearjab said. "Who is this individual you keep referring to?"

"She was known to you as the Saviour, Colonel."

The irony of that title escaped none of us.

CHAPTER 10
†HOOMRA

A s we left the clearing, the new pupae began to emit the soft and incomprehensible sounds that gave the forest its name.

"Perhaps they're dreaming of what they'll become," Clarissa suggested.

We returned to the bank of the river where we collected a number of bamboo-like reeds. Following Colonel Spearjab's directions, we pounded some of them with stones until they split, then extracted long fibrous strands, which we used to bind large thorns—broken from the roots of the Ptoollan trees—to the ends of the others. Thus, in addition to the pikestaff, we were now armed with makeshift spears.

We pushed on eastward, following the watercourse upstream. I told my companions about Gallokomas and his generosity. "If he's at all typical of his race, then perhaps we can persuade the Zull to help us."

"You intend us to trek all the way to their eyries?" Clarissa asked.

"I think they'll be watching out for us. I hope so." I looked back at the Heart of Blood. "It'll take too long to get there on foot."

After much walking, we climbed out of the valley and traipsed onward, eventually traversing an area of thinning forest until we finally emerged onto rolling savannah.

I swatted away a cloud of tiny globe-shaped creatures that had decided to swarm around my face and said, "If we keep the sun at our backs, we'll be going in the right direction."

"I say! The river flows from the Shrouded Mountains," Colonel Spearjab put in. "I'd prefer to stay close to it, if you don't mind. Humph! I have to moisten my skin from time to time. *Moisten*, I say! Ha ha!"

The colonel's welfare was important to me, so I acceded to his request.

I noticed that Clarissa was gazing back the way we'd come, her eyes levelled at the sky above the forest. She looked perplexed.

"What is it?" I asked.

"Something in the air over the trees. Do you see it?"

"I see steam rising from them. Is that what you mean?"

"No. There's a sort of—a sort of a kink in the atmosphere. A fold. It reaches up as far as I can see—disappears into the heavens. It's drifting slowly back and forth. I think it's Yissil Froon's rupture, Aiden, though it appears inactive at the moment."

Try as I might, I couldn't detect anything unusual, and neither could the colonel.

We pressed on with our journey. It was interminable. We stopped and slept at least eight times—I lost count—and successfully defended ourselves against attacking predators on numerous occasions. We ate what non-poisonous fruits and berries we could find, and we drank from the river.

Finally, Clarissa uttered a cry and pointed to a distant cloud, dark against the red sky. Peering at it, I saw it was comprised of little dots that were wheeling and darting around a Yarkeen.

"How shall we attract their attention?" Clarissa asked. "With a fire?"

"I don't think it'll be necessary. Some of them are coming this way."

We stood and watched as eight dots detached from the flock and flew toward us.

"They must have eyes like eagles," my companion noted.

"Four each!" I added.

The Zull drew closer, circled us, swooped down, and landed a few yards away. In form, they were identical to Gallokomas, but unlike my friend, whose inky-blue skin had been unmarked except for a white patch on the face, these were covered from head to foot with tattoos, all bright yellow, linear, and somewhat maze-like in design.

One of the Zull walked forward and addressed me in Koluwaian. "You are the Thing, Aiden Fleischer?"

"Yes. I'm pleased to meet you. My companions are Clarissa Stark and Colonel Momentous Spearjab. He is a Mi'aata. Did you learn of me from Gallokomas?"

"We did. All the Zull have been watching for you. My name is Artellokas. I presume you have been cast out of Phenadoor?"

"In a manner of speaking."

"You are welcome to make your home in Thoomra."

"That is the name of your eyries?"

He nodded. "We will carry you there, if you choose."

"That would suit us very well, thank you, Artellokas."

The Zull looked from me, to Clarissa, to the colonel, then back at me. Its mandibles opened slowly then clicked shut.

Clarissa said, "Yes, Colonel Spearjab and I have these——" she touched the bumps on her forehead "——but our friend does not."

Puzzled, I turned to her. "What?"

"It's the obvious explanation, Aiden."

"For——?"

Clarissa looked confused. "For why Artellokas can't discern what you are——are——Oh!" She put a hand to her head and addressed the Zull. "Did you——did you——?"

There was a moment of silence, then she gasped and took a step back. Colonel Spearjab announced, "Clear as a bell! As a *bell*, I say! We had them in New Yatsillat, don't you know. Bells, that is. Harrumph!"

Artellokas looked at him and asked, "That noise you are making is a language?"

"Humph!" the colonel responded.

"Yes," I said. "It's called English." I looked from one to the other of my companions. "What's happening?"

"He can speak to us!" Clarissa said. "Without making a sound!"

Artellokas clicked his mandibles again and said, "The Zull often converse nonverbally. I am curious, Aiden Fleischer, that I can neither hear your thoughts nor communicate my own to you."

"But you can feel my emotions, yes? It was the same with the Yatsill and the Mi'aata."

"We will limit conversation to the audible. What are Yatsill? From whence is this thing called English?"

"There is much to discuss, Artellokas."

"Then let us go to Thoomra at once."

The Zull stepped over to us, but those that approached Colonel Spearjab hesitated and fidgeted skittishly. The colonel backed away from them.

"You're nervous of contact," I noted. "The Zull, Mi'aata, and Yatsill all possess an instinct to avoid one another. Can you overcome it? Colonel Spearjab isn't at all dangerous."

"Harmless!" Spearjab agreed.

One of the Zull nodded and said, "We shall try."

He moved cautiously over to the Mi'aata, followed by two others. They were visibly trembling. The one who'd spoken reached out, gingerly touched Spearjab with a fingertip, then turned to the others and said, "I am uninjured."

Reluctantly, they gathered around the colonel and took a hold of him. Others lifted Clarissa and me, and we were all swept up into the air and away toward the far-off mountain range.

The huge sun had just touched the horizon and was rippling and wavering like a paper lantern impacting the sea and crumpling in on itself.

☼

The eyries were magnificent.

Thoomra consisted of thin columns of rock—hundreds upon hundreds of them—all about a mile high, which flared out into broad flat surfaces at their tops, their edges almost touching. On these, the Zull had created farms and small clusters of exquisitely fashioned buildings, decorated with delicate curves and flourishes, almost like works of art.

Zull society was based on an extremely simple but effective principle, it being generosity of spirit. Each individual cultivated an awareness of what his fellows required and did whatever he could to provide for them, while, in turn, making no secret of his own wants and accepting whatever help was offered. Pride, selfishness, and avarice were non-existent. Thus goods, materials, and services quickly found their way to wherever they were needed. Every Zull willingly contributed whatever he could to society and automatically strove to do the best work possible without expectation of reward. There was no central government, no unions or committees, no king or prime minister, president or chieftain.

I was reminded of how the flocks of Zull flew in a similar manner to Earth's starlings, a great mass of them manoeuvring through the air, somehow avoiding collisions. Such cognisance of one another appeared miraculous in flight, but even more magical in the settled community, for I knew of no human population that could match it. My species is too fearful to focus on giving and too haughty to admit to any deficiency, believing that to do either would, one way or another, lead to a loss of all one's resources.

Upon our arrival at the eyries, we were given a house to live in, food to eat, water and a wine-like beverage to drink, and told to rest and recover our strength. I asked to see Gallokomas and, in short order, he floated down onto the terrace where I was relaxing with my companions. His skin now bore the same markings as the rest of his race.

After making introductions, I gripped his hand and said, "It is very, very good to see you again, my friend!"

"Thing! I am happy you are here," he replied, "though saddened that you, too, have been banished from Phenadoor."

"Phenadoor is not the blissful place you imagine, Gallokomas. You lost your memory of it when you left, but mine is not impaired, and I must tell you that there's much danger associated with the crystal mountain, and the threat extends even to Thoomra."

His jaw mandibles twitched and he cocked his head slightly to one side. "In what manner?"

"Am I correct in thinking that the population of Zull is falling?"

"You are. I have learned this since my arrival. Our numbers are chronically reduced and the situation will soon have serious consequences if it continues. Do you have an explanation?"

I gestured toward Colonel Spearjab. "How do you feel about this Mi'aata, Gallokomas?"

He contemplated my companion for a moment, before answering, "Peculiar. There is a vague sense of familiarity, yet also an awareness that such a reaction is somehow a transgression." The Zull suddenly switched from Koluwaian to English. "I'm sorry, Colonel Thing, I mean no offence, but I find you repugnant, though I can't explain why."

"Harrumph! Harrumph! Harrumph! No offence taken!" Spearjab responded. "The sentiment is mutual—and regrettable. What! What! *Regrettable*, I say!"

"Gallokomas, how do you know English?" I asked.

"It is in the colonel's mind. In Miss Stark Thing's, too."

"And in mine."

"But yours is inaccessible."

I made a sound of understanding and gestured toward Spearjab. "The colonel speaks English because he was once a Yatsill, and the Yatsill learned the language from Miss Stark. As do all his kind, he transformed into a Mi'aata and went to Phenadoor, which they inhabit. When the Mi'aata's lifespan is ending, they journey to the Forest of Indistinct Murmurings and there transform into Zull."

Gallokomas remained silent. His silvery eyes sparkled as he contemplated this revelation.

I continued, "And when the Zull go to the Shrouded Mountains to die, they deposit tiny creatures into the waters. These attach to the Yatsill, which are a separate species, bestow intelligence upon them, and cause their slow metamorphosis into Mi'aata. You are all parts of a long life cycle. You are an intertwined species."

Still there was no response.

I told him how Pretty Wahine had unintentionally interfered, resulting in fewer Yatsill transforming, and had caused the death of many Zull before they were able to hatch from their cocoons. I then explained how her actions had also given rise to Yissil Froon, who'd subsequently cast his destructive spell over generations of Mi'aata.

"Now he intends to use them to conquer my world. My people will, of course, resist the invasion. Thousands of Mi'aata will die, which means a further and much more dramatic drop in the Zull population. Soon, this remarkable species of yours, which goes through so many distinct phases of life, will not be able to sustain itself. Extinction beckons, Gallokomas. We must stop Yissil Froon."

The Zull raised his four hands to his head and held it. "Thing! You are putting many strange and disturbing thoughts into me!"

"I am telling you the truth."

"I believe you, but I do not like it."

Colonel Spearjab said softly, "My goodness! The unutterable has been well and truly uttered. What!"

"You told me you are from a place called New Yatsillat, Thing," Gallokomas said. "Now you say you are from another world."

"We lived in New Yatsillat after we were transported to Ptallaya."

"Transported? By what means?"

"There is a rupture in space, one end of which opens over the Forest of Indistinct Murmurings, the other over a small island on my world. It becomes active on Ptallaya at each sunset, compressing an unimaginable distance and making travel between the worlds possible. Yissil Froon's ally—who traversed the path so many times he gained the ability to do so even when it was dormant—planned to reposition the far end over a populated area of my world by means of this crystal." I lifted the stone that hung around my neck. "I stopped him."

"So the plan is defeated, Thing?"

"No, Gallokomas. Yissil Froon is inconvenienced, but I think it very likely that he'll still send his war machines to Earth. He'll have to start his invasion from the island, that is all. He's lost the advantage of surprise. It's not enough to stop him."

The Zull floated a few inches into the air.

"He'll begin when the suns change?"

"Yes."

"I will share this news with the rest of my kind. We must commence our preparations at once."

"Will you send a patrol to watch over the forest?"

He nodded. "Give me the crystal. You have already met Artellokas—he is one of our scientists. Perhaps he and his fellows can discover a way to use it against Yissil Froon."

I hesitated, then slipped the cord over my head and handed the gem to the Zull. He took it, inflated his flight bladder, rose into the air, and zipped away.

It might appear paradoxical to claim that a sense of urgency overtook the eyrie before then observing that the equivalent of a week or so passed during which my companions and I rested, healed, and familiarised ourselves with the Zulls' remarkable culture, but, though the red orb was setting, it was sinking at such a snail's pace that we had plenty of time to spare while our hosts mobilised.

Thankfully, Clarissa and I were given new garments, though these were a far cry from anything that Earthly standards of decency demanded. In my case, they consisted of nothing more than a kilt and sandals that laced up to my knees, and in Clarissa's, a short, light dress, a wide girdle, and footwear similar to my own. She wore her goggles pushed up high over her forehead to hold back her thick mane of hair.

The colonel remained unclothed and spent most of the period lazing in a bath—"Meditating! *Meditating*, I say! It's the old noggin. Still somewhat befuddled, what! There's a lot to take in! Yatsill! Mi'aata! Zull! I hardly know where or what I am any more! Harrumph!"

My companion and I left him to it, enjoyed each other's company, and puzzled over the Zulls' various machines, which were so mystifying they might have operated on principles of magic rather than science. Many were hidden within the walls of the buildings, and upon closer inspection—achieved through the removal of panels—were revealed to have no moving parts at all, nor any elements I could recognise or understand. One of these baffling contraptions functioned to disseminate information, which was displayed on a large surface of concentric circles affixed to a wall in the community room of each dwelling. Like the mechanism itself, the display was so arcane as to be impossible to grasp, consisting in the main of overlapping shapes, clustered points of light of various hues and intensity, and sequences of symbols that were, Gallokomas explained, numerical in meaning.

"The apparatus is called the Life of Thoomra," he said. "It supplements our instinctive awareness of who requires what by monitoring the production and availability of resources."

The Life of Thoomra also transmitted the spoken word across distances, like the newly invented telephone device I'd read so much about prior to my departure from Theaston Vale—the Zull could only communicate telepathically when in close proximity.

Shortly after I'd assured Gallokomas that Clarissa, the colonel, and I were all in a fit state of health, the device was employed in this manner to relay to the rest of the community a meeting between us and a small group of Zull. The gathering was somewhat akin to a council of war. Clarissa had already been questioned about the machines she and Lord Hufferton had designed, and had redrawn many of her blueprints from memory. The contraptions all required coal to power their engines, but as this was an unknown resource on Ptallaya, Artellokas speculated that Yissil Froon would find a way to use Phenadoor's own technology. He held up Iriputiz's crystal and said, "In theory, the frequencies that characterise stones like this could be amplified and adjusted to cause water to boil. The engines would thus be rather less cumbersome than those you have devised, Miss Stark."

"Making the machines lighter and more manoeuvrable," my friend muttered.

"Oh yes, very much so. They could even travel underwater and in the air. However, while the crystals are a great advantage, they are also the machines' most serious weakness."

"Why so?"

"Because by interfering with their transmissions, we can cripple the engines."

"You have a method?"

"We think so. We are creating weapons that will project a narrow beam of sound. The frequency will automatically adjust until it resonates with whatever crystal it's aimed at. When that resonance is achieved, the sound will intensify until the gem cracks. This will render it useless."

"Like an opera singer breaking a glass," I mused. "It's going to be a noisy battle."

"I don't know what you are referring to, but no, the sound will be well beyond the range of hearing."

Artellokas informed us that Thoomra's manufacturers—who were more artisans than industrialists—were already producing prototypes.

After the scientist had finished his report, a Zull who'd been keeping watch over the forest joined us and revealed that underconveyances had been landing a large number of Mi'aata at the mouth of the river. "But they are unarmed and appear sick. They go into the trees and become still among the branches."

"The Discontinued," I said. "They are not a threat. In fact, they will become Zull."

The meeting finished after it was decided to send a party to New Yatsillat to recover any surviving Koluwaians. Due to the likelihood that, like Gallokomas, the Zull would find it difficult to enter the remains of the city, the responsibility fell to Clarissa and me. We'd be landed at the lip of the bay and would then make a foray into the ruins while our escorts circled overhead.

Before we set off, my two companions and I were carried to a particularly broad-topped eyrie, crowded with workshops, and were ushered into the presence of a Zull who proved to be a medic, scientist, and tattooist. Without causing me the slightest pain, he etched onto my inner right wrist a small spiralled design. He then did the same to Clarissa before adding the odd little symbol to one of Colonel Spearjab's limbs. When the procedure was finished, Artellokas, who'd accompanied us, said, "Apply pressure to the centre of the symbol and speak Miss Stark's name into it."

Mystified, I raised my hand, pressed the middle of the spiral with my thumb, and said, "Clarissa Stark."

Clarissa gave a squeal and jumped about a foot in the air. My voice had sounded from her wrist!

"It will enable you to speak across a distance with anyone you know who also carries the device," Artellokas said. "Just press the symbol and say their name to contact them. There is no limit in range, but the tattoo will wear off in time. Most of us have them renewed each cycle."

Her eyes wide, Clarissa put her wrist to her mouth, pressed the tattoo, and said, "Aiden Fleischer. Can you hear me?"

Despite myself, I gave a yelp and jerked sideways as her words issued from my arm. "Unbelievable!" I cried out. "This is simply astonishing! How can it possibly work?"

"It is a difficult process to explain," Artellokas answered.

Clarissa asked, "Will you teach us the principles of Zull science once we've dealt with Yissil Froon?"

"I will. Come. We have more to give you."

We were next taken to a studio, on the same eyrie, where Artellokas presented us with beautifully crafted and ornate pistol-like contrivances fashioned from wood and a brass-coloured metal. Their barrels flared out like that of a blunderbuss. "They discharge a burst of sound that will render any opponent unconscious," he explained. "The Zull do not kill."

I slipped my "sound gun" into its holster and belted it around my waist. Clarissa and Colonel Spearjab followed suit.

Artellokas crossed to a bench, picked up a long, heavy object wound with material, then returned and handed it to me. I unwrapped it to reveal a beautifully crafted scabbard in which a perfectly balanced sword was sheathed.

"This Zull awareness of the needs of others, and willingness to provide for them, will never cease to amaze me," I exclaimed, for I'd been feeling strangely naked without a blade at my hip.

Next, Artellokas produced three objects consisting of tangled belts and skins. He led us outside and asked me to extend my "forelimbs." I held my arms out sideways. Artellokas slipped the belts around me and affixed them until I was tightly harnessed. The skin drooped down my back like a cape. He directed my attention to a large metal disc at the point where the straps crossed my chest.

"Slide a digit upward across it."

I did so. The skin instantly inflated and, with a yell of surprise, I began to float into the air.

Clarissa laughed as I kicked wildly, struggling to regain my balance.

"What ho! What ho!" Colonel Spearjab bellowed. "Hup-hup!"

Artellokas floated up to me. "Slowly slide a digit down the control."

I did so and gradually lost altitude.

"Cover it with your hand," he said.

The action brought me to a halt about six feet from the ground.

"Slide up to go higher. Slide down to sink lower. Tap to go fast. Press to slow down. Cover to stop. Touch the top edge to go forward, the bottom edge to go backward, the right edge to go right, the left edge to go left."

I experimented as directed and was soon shooting about, unable to resist the temptation to holler in delight. In no time at all, I felt I'd mastered the contraption, though when I tried to land, I found myself stumbling to my knees and skidding to an undignified halt in front of Clarissa.

"Splendid!" I cried as she assisted me to my feet. "Simply marvellous, Artellokas!"

"You feel the need to engage with the enemy," he said. "This will allow you to fight alongside us."

Clarissa and the colonel eagerly donned their harnesses and were soon flitting about overhead with many an exhilarated scream and bawled, "What! What!"

We practised until we considered ourselves proficient, then

left Artellokas and raced each other home, where we were met by Gallokomas and a large flock of Zull. Without further ado, we all set out for New Yatsillat.

It was now that I—like my companions—discovered how clumsy a flier I was, for the Zull appeared incapable of maintaining a straight line, instead swooping and darting around and about one another in such a dizzying fashion that I began to lose track of up and down. Whatever instinct allowed them to avoid collisions was sadly lacking in me, and my attempts to emulate it caused nothing but trouble. Had I maintained a steady course, all would have been well, but every time a Zull swept close to me, I couldn't help but try to steer clear, and in doing so inevitably bumped into another, losing my balance and becoming thoroughly upended. For the initial part of the flight, I tumbled and spun through the air like a leaf in a tempest. Had I been stable enough to look for Clarissa and Colonel Spearjab, I'd have seen them in similar straits.

I was becoming thoroughly queasy when a couple of Zull came to my assistance and, by grasping my legs and holding me steady— refusing to let me dodge this way and that as was my wont—soon had me convinced that no one was going to collide with me. Finally, I was able to fly smoothly and unaided, and saw that my friends had benefitted from similar attention.

The flock proceeded in a westerly direction, and the sun, now swollen to even more gigantic dimensions, glared directly into our eyes. We first passed over the hilly and forested land that stretched between the eyries and the Shrouded Mountains. The shadowed valleys below were cut through with streams and rivers, which, reflecting the crimson sky, reminded me of the rivulets of blood I'd seen trickling between the cobbles of Buck's Row, causing me to wonder whether Jack the Ripper was still at his grisly work in London.

The climate had by now settled. There were no more rains or strong winds. Instead, a stifling humidity closed around us, which, in collusion with the sun's awful illumination, seemed to compact the wide-open spaces, as if the sky was pressing down.

Even when we reached the mountains and soared high over them, there was no sense of increasing distance between the ground and the heavens.

"A lid has been placed over Ptallaya," I shouted across to Clarissa, who was at that point flying alongside me, "and we are cooking beneath it!"

We swooped through the clouds of steam that bubbled up from the peaks, emerged from them, and saw the Valley of Reflections below us. I recalled my horrible vision and thought again of the Whitechapel killer. The notion that I was Jack the Ripper appeared totally absurd now, but had been such a potent impression at the time that Yissil Froon had been able to take it, exaggerate it out of all proportion, and use it to cripple my ability to properly assert myself.

I gritted my teeth. I had a score to settle!

The rocky terrain flattened into broad savannah. Herds of animals moved far below us—most, it appeared, fleeing from predators. Off to our left, I saw eight Yarkeen drifting slowly over a patch of forest, their tendril-like appendages ripping at the foliage.

We flew at a terrific speed. The air, which now held the odour of burned toast, whistled past my ears. As far as I was able to estimate—though I must admit that by now my sense of time was almost entirely lost—it took us less than two Earth days to cover the same distance that the Ptall'kor had required perhaps months to traverse.

We landed just once. Clarissa, the colonel, and I stretched and worked the kinks out of our shoulders, ate a light meal, then rested for a short period before Gallokomas ordered the flock back into the air.

More savannah, then the Mountains That Gaze Upon Phenadoor rose over the horizon, silhouetted black against the harsh purple sunset. The terrain became increasingly familiar to me. The Yatsill farms slid into view.

"Let's set down in the fields," I shouted to Gallokomas. "We should take a look at the nurseries."

While the rest of the flock circled overhead, my companions and I spiralled down and came to rest beside one of the papery structures. The Zull and Mi'aata both hastily backed away from it.

"I shouldn't be here," Gallokomas moaned.

"Dashed uncomfortable, what!" Spearjab agreed. "Familiar, though, I must say. Harrumph!"

"You're repulsed by the nursery," I noted. "Excellent!"

Gallokomas twitched his mandibles. "Excellent, Thing? Why excellent?"

"Because if you're made uneasy, then the nursery must be occupied."

"Ah, I see. It is very queer, this aversion."

I gripped a fold that served as the structure's door and eased it open. Moist heat was expelled from within. Squinting into the darkness, I saw a crowd of Yatsill squatting motionlessly, apparently asleep, though their fingers were moving incessantly.

"The children are safe," I told the others. "This is very good news. When the yellow suns rise, they'll make their migration to the Cavern of Immersion. Some will be made Aristocrats. They'll transmit a degree of intelligence to the rest, and in generations to come, as the Mi'aata and Zull populations are slowly restored, so too there'll be more seed parasites, until, at some point in the future, all the Yatsill young will play host to them, and the life cycle will be healthy again."

"Which means we must never again return to this area," Clarissa commented. "When this lot are made Aristocrats, I don't want them delving into my mind and overreaching themselves like their forebears did. This new generation will be free of Pretty Wahine and must also be free of me."

After we'd checked on two more nurseries and found them similarly well stocked, Gallokomas and Colonel Spearjab rejoined the circling flock while Clarissa and I flew out over the devastated city.

The campfires were still burning on the fifth level. We made our way down to them, gliding above the awful rubble and mud until we reached the flat space where the Koluwaians and surviving Yatsill had gathered. They greeted us as we landed, and Baron Hammer Thewflex—*sans* mask—and Kata pushed their way to the front of the crowd.

"Hallo! Hallo!" the baron exclaimed. "You're back, hey! Indeed you are!"

"Hello, Baron," I said. "I'm glad to see you." I addressed the Koluwaian. "Kata, we've come to take you and your fellow Servants away. We can't allow you to remain here as food for the Blood Gods."

She nodded wordlessly.

"Good show!" the baron exclaimed. "I think the bally invasion is over, old chap, but of course the fiends will return after the Saviour's Eyes have looked upon us once more. Take the Servants, by all means. The poor things have been very unhappy since the city was destroyed."

"And you, sir? What will you and your fellows do?"

Thewflex removed his top hat—careful not to catch it on his curling horns—and brushed dust from it. He waved it at the ruins. "We cannot rebuild here. No indeed! Even if we cleared away the debris, the land itself has slipped. I have it in mind to settle at the edge of the jungle on the other side of the farms. It's not too far from the sea, and there are still a few Quee'tan in the trees. Perhaps we could capture the jolly old things and breed them. What do you think about that, hey?"

Clarissa said, "It sounds like a very good idea, Baron."

Thewflex looked down toward the sea, where many of the Working Class were still frolicking in the water near the shore. "Perhaps if enough of the children are made Aristocrats, we'll be able to restore some wits to that confounded rabble."

We talked for a little longer, then bade the Yatsill farewell and led the Koluwaians up and out of the bay. Gallokomas and the colonel floated down to greet us. I drew Kata aside and said, "Each of you must decide whether to remain on Ptallaya or go through the hole in the sky to Koluwai. Those who choose to stay will be taken to the land near the Zull eyries. It is fertile and wooded and the Zull are very kind. They'll help you to build a village and you'll be able to live in peace."

She nodded slowly and put her hands up to cover her heart. "And for those who'd rather go to the other world, sir?"

"We'll try to send them, but I can't guarantee anyone's safety. I should warn you, too, that the Blood Gods pose a danger to Koluwai. If we fail to stop them, the population of the islands will become their prey."

"I will talk to my people."

The islanders gathered together. It didn't take them long to reach a decision. Kata returned to us and reported that the entire group had elected to remain on Ptallaya.

"None who arrived here from Koluwai remains, Mr. Fleischer. We were all born on Ptallaya. It is our true home, despite the traditions."

I placed a hand on her shoulder. "I think you've made the right choice. Gather food from the farms. Eat, then rest a while. We have a long journey ahead."

We didn't linger for long. The Heart of Blood was almost two-thirds sunk and time was running out. Shortly after the Koluwaians had filled their stomachs, the Zull flock descended and picked them up. We raced back to Thoomra.

The islanders were deposited a little to the west of the eyries, among the rolling hills and verdant forest. A large number of Zull remained with them and immediately set to work building houses in the trees and clearing land for vegetable farms. The rest of us continued on and found the eyries buzzing with activity. Thousands of Zull had gathered and weapons were being distributed among them. These "frequency cannons" had two parts. The first resembled a long straight tube. From the rear end of this, coiled cables stretched to the second, a box—ornate, in typical Zull fashion—with dials on its top and a plunger-like handle projecting from its side. To operate the device, one Zull balanced the tube on his shoulder and aimed it, while another, wearing the box strapped against his stomach, took readings and pressed the plunger to fix the sound output at the appropriate frequency.

Pistols, the same as those given to Clarissa and me, were also much in evidence.

I estimated that we had the equivalent of at least twenty-four hours to spare, so we returned to our house, where Colonel Spearjab immediately plunged into his bath and began to snore.

"He has the right idea," I said. "We should sleep."

Clarissa looked at me strangely.

"What is it?" I asked.

She stepped closer and rested her hands on my chest.

"You'll really join the fighting?"

"Yes, of course. Our world is threatened."

"Our world? Is it? I feel we belong here now. I don't want to go back."

My heart began to race.

"No. No, Clarissa. You're right. I don't want to return to Earth either. Nevertheless, we can't allow it to be invaded."

"But when the conflict is done, we can settle here, with the Zull?"

I thought about the man I'd been when she'd arrived on my doorstep, and recalled my parochial little vicarage in Theaston Vale with its dusty library and stultifying dullness. It filled me with disdain. It felt far more alien to me now than this world of three suns and bizarre creatures.

I put my hands over hers. "Yes, we can make our home here."

"Together."

I swallowed. "Yes."

She sighed. "What you said."

"Said?"

"When we were escaping from Phenadoor."

I tried to respond but found myself unable to speak.

Clarissa smiled.

"I love you, too, Aiden Fleischer." She leaned forward and put her lips to mine, then took me by the hand and led me into her room.

☼

Clarissa was already awake, nestled against my shoulder, when I opened my eyes.

"You are most definitely not the man who answered the door to me all that time ago," she whispered.

"You're a fine one to talk," I said drowsily. "Look at you!"

She giggled, and, after stretching a shapely leg into the air, sat up. "My metamorphosis is cosmetic, Aiden. As is yours—" Turning, she ran her fingers across the muscles of my stomach. "But with you there's something more. A far deeper change."

The last vestiges of sleep cleared. I propped myself up onto my elbows and looked into her startling eyes.

After a moment of thought, I said, "Cain and Abel."

One of her eyebrows arched at this unanticipated turn in the conversation, creasing the skin around the little bump above it.

I went on, "It's said that evil begets evil. I've always believed that, but it caused a crisis of faith in me, for, as you once pointed out, if you trace evil back to its source, you can't stop at Cain but must continue on to God."

"And how can we worship a God who's capable of evil?" Clarissa responded.

"We can't. And as the creation of one who begets evil, would we not all be Jekylls, liable to transform into Hydes at any moment?"

She suddenly blinked rapidly, gave a small exclamation, and said, "Gallokomas has just arrived on our terrace."

The Zull's voice sounded from my wrist: "Fleischer Thing!"

I pressed the tattoo and said, "Yes, Gallokomas?"

"The flock is gathering. Will you and your companions prepare yourselves, please?"

"Very well. We'll be with you in a moment."

Clarissa and I got up. She entered the washroom while I went to alert the colonel. When I rejoined her, I continued our conversation. "The Quintessence offered a solution to the dilemma. It suggested that, rather than being a product of God, evil is an entirely equal and opposite power."

She wiped her face with a towel and gave a disdainful snort. "That doesn't surprise me at all, Aiden. The Quintessence considers itself perfect. It makes the Mi'aata slaves to a moribund society in which all construction is nothing but pointless repetition. True creativity is suppressed. The trinity is blind to the iniquity of such a system. For the Quintessence, wrongdoing always comes from an exterior source, never from itself."

"Which is why I can't give credence to the notion of opposing deities," I replied. "It makes of us a battleground and allows us to disavow all responsibility for what happens."

We finished washing and re-entered the bedroom where we began to dress.

"Nor does it answer the essential question," I continued. "Which is, if God didn't create evil, what did? Something else? Do we now have to deny that God is the creator of all things? No, it won't do."

I buckled on my flight harness, feeling the comfortable weight of the pistol on my right hip and the sword on my left.

"What then, Aiden?"

"A chain of logic. If God is the epitome of good, there can be no evil in Him. If all things spring from Him, then they, too, must be comprised wholly of good. Therefore, evil is not a thing."

"Have you forgotten London? Jack the Ripper was unquestionably evil!"

"We have to make a semantic transmutation. We must say, instead, that Jack the Ripper was catastrophically lacking in goodness."

My companion scrutinised me thoughtfully. "Yes," she said, slowly. "Yes. I see the implication. Altering the perspective suggests a richer purpose to the business of living."

"Precisely. If you consider goodness as a spectrum, then at one end we have the unadulterated rectitude of God's creation, and it is toward this that we must travel in our thoughts and actions. But if we become selfish, if we indulge in our lusts, our gluttony, our greed, or any of the other deadly sins, then we turn away and move in the direction of diminishing virtue. Thus life challenges us to resist temptation and do the right thing. Every correct moral decision moves us closer to God. Every moment of weakness takes us farther away."

"Have you found faith at last, Aiden?"

"I can't have faith in God any more than I can have faith in the sky. He may be goodness manifest, but I've seen nothing to suggest that He's an interventionist. You were right to suggest that I've changed. I have. I've realised that, whatever world we happen to be on, we cannot afford any degree of dependence on a divine plan. It's up to *us* to address iniquity and injustice, and to succeed, we must indeed have faith—not in God," I placed a hand on the hilt of my sword, "but in ourselves."

Clarissa smiled and murmured, "The voyage is complete."

☼

CHAPTER II

BATTLE

"**W**e have never fought before," Gallokomas said. "You must guide the flock."

I looked up at the dense cloud of Zull circling overhead and said, "Yissil Froon is directing the Divergent, so the primary objective must be to locate him and break his mental domination of them. I reserve that particular mission for myself. Like all of your species, whether they are at the Yatsill, Mi'aata, or Zull stage, he can sense my emotions but not my thoughts. I hope that'll give me an advantage."

"Humph!" Colonel Spearjab interjected. "I owe the blighter a thrashing. A *thrashing*, I say! You'll allow me to accompany you. Remember, I can help you to locate him. What! What!"

By way of illustration, the colonel lifted the pikestaff we'd brought from Phenadoor and jabbed at the air with it.

"And if he applies his powers to you?" I asked.

"Harrumph! Harrumph! Granted, he controls the Divergent, old chap, but shocks and revelations have placed me in a unique position. I know what I was, what I am, and what I shall be! I rather think that gives me a better sense of myself than the bounder can handle. Ha ha!"

I smiled, but shook my head. "No, Colonel. When I confront him, I hope Yissil Froon will become sufficiently distracted that his hold over the Divergent loosens. I'd like you to move among them and help them reorientate themselves—have them abandon their weapons."

"Ah! Humph! I see. Well, orders are orders! What! What!"

"And me, Aiden?" Clarissa asked.

"We'll put you on one of the foothills overlooking the forest. You'll be out of harm's way, but with those remarkable eyes and your telepathic ability, you'll be able to follow the movement of the rupture and warn the Zull away from it. I don't want any of them sucked in and flung to Koluwai."

"Out of harm's way?" she protested. "After all we've been through, you consider me too delicate to engage with the enemy?"

"Of course not. I simply intend to make the best use of your specific talents, Clarissa."

She folded her arms angrily, glared at me, then, a moment later, relaxed and nodded. "Very well. I'll do it."

I turned to Gallokomas. "What of closing it? Have your scientists developed a method?"

"Regrettably, they have not, Fleischer Thing." He took Iriputiz's crystal from his bag and handed it to me. "This resonates only with the part of it that opens onto your world. We cannot use it here."

I felt myself go cold. "Then I have no choice. The only option is to do as Iriputiz intended, but rather than drawing the opening to a populated area, I must relocate it somewhere remote—even more remote than Koluwai—where no one will wander into it."

Clarissa murmured, "We'll go together, Aiden. I'll not be separated from you."

I smiled at her. "We can return to Ptallaya the moment the path becomes active again."

I hung the crystal around my neck.

Gallokomas looked toward the East. I followed his gaze and saw a wide band of orange light brightening the horizon. The Eyes of the Saviour would soon reappear. How I longed to see them!

"It is time," the Zull said.

☼

The Heart of Blood had almost completely set by the time we reached the Forest of Indistinct Murmurings. Only its tip showed, and directly overhead the sky had deepened to a band of such an intense purple that stars were visible in it—the first I'd seen from Ptallaya. The four moons, clustered closely together, shone brightly in the East, where the heavens were afire.

The flock soared over the dripping forest. The atmosphere was thick with steam. Thousands of tiny creatures bobbed lazily over the canopy, tethered to it by silken threads. Many of the trees were burdened with what appeared to be giant fruits.

"Do you see all the pupae, Colonel?" I shouted, pointing down through the mist.

"I do! I do! What! What! I hope they'll not be damaged! Harrumph!"

Led by Artellokas, the flock continued on, passed over the beach, and headed out to sea. Meanwhile, Clarissa, Colonel Spearjab, Gallokomas, and I, having veered to the left, landed on one of the foothills at the northernmost tip of the Mountains That Gaze Upon Phenadoor. It gave an unrestricted view over the entire forest.

Clarissa pointed to the north-east. "I see the rupture. It looks different. Unstable—like a quivering tube extending into the heavens." She pulled her goggles down over her eyes, then pushed them back up again. "We may have a problem. The light of dawn is becoming too bright for me. I shall have to wear my protection soon, and I can't see the rupture through the glass."

"Hold out for as long as you can," I said, "but not so long that you damage your eyes." I raised my arm to show the tattoo on my wrist. "And give me frequent reports."

She dipped her head in acknowledgement before turning to Gallokomas. They looked at each other and communicated silently. The Zull then said to me, "Miss Stark Thing will also speak to me through her tattoo, and I shall use my mind to pass her directions on to the flock. We—" He stopped as a jagged line of energy suddenly sizzled over the forest. "We will avoid *that*!"

"Or, to be more accurate," Clarissa said, "the mouth of the rupture. The storm might spread across the whole valley, but the mouth itself appears to be a fairly small phenomenon that moves about within the disturbance."

I watched the atmosphere flicker and flash for a few moments, then said, "Let's join our fellows."

Clarissa stepped over to me. "Be careful, Aiden." She leaned forward and kissed my lips.

Gallokomas made a sound of surprise. "Miss Stark Thing! What was that you did?"

"Something a possessor of mandibles shouldn't try," she responded.

"Humph!" Colonel Spearjab added.

The Zull, Mi'aata, and I floated into the air and raced seaward, shooting over the wide beach and across the water until the land had receded so far behind us that only the jagged peaks of the mountains were visible. Ahead, the flock, spread thinly, was wheeling back and forth over a wide expanse of ocean, every Zull's eyes looking down. We joined the patrol.

Hours passed before anything happened. The sky continued to darken on one side and brighten on the other. The calm surface of the water sparkled purple, red, and orange.

I considered the threat that faced us—a mad creature capable of controlling minds and armed with war machines, hungry for power and intent on invading the Earth. The odds were not in our favour. How could the peaceable Zull possibly oppose Yissil Froon?

Gallokomas suddenly pointed to one side and cried out, "Over there, Thing! A Zull has noticed something moving beneath the water!" He looked behind us. "And there!"

A large squarish object, submerged and only vaguely visible, passed below me. I saw more of them to the right and the left, obscured shapes sliding rapidly over the seabed, speeding toward the shore.

A quarter of a mile to our rear, a sudden explosion sent water bulging upward. Oval lights shimmered under the slowly rolling swells—flashes, indistinct activity, a second detonation.

"What is happening?" Gallokomas called.

Colonel Spearjab swooped in close to us. "Underconveyances! The Quintessence must be pursuing Yissil Froon's army! *Pursuing*, I say!"

A loud sequence of discharges shattered the surface, sending water so high that it splashed over us.

"Back!" I yelled. "To the shoreline! We'll strike as the machines leave the water!"

Zull engulfed me as, like a single entity, the cloud folded in upon itself, condensed, and streamed eastward. After a moment of confusion, I regained my bearings and rescued the colonel, who was spinning wildly in mid-air, his tentacles flailing. We joined the race, slapping at our gears' control units until we'd caught up with Gallokomas, hurtling along near the front of the throng. I reached his side and called, "Order the flock to keep moving back and forth along the beach. Let's not make easy targets of ourselves!"

Lightning flickered on the horizon ahead of us. I pressed the tattoo on my wrist. "Clarissa Stark. We're on our way back with the invasion force hot on our heels. I can see the storm."

"It's expanding rapidly, Aiden—spreading over the central expanse of the forest, about a mile inland. The rupture is at its western edge, moving northward."

In short order, we came to the shore, spread out over the wide ribbon of sand, and began to fly in a loop from one end of the beach to the other, with our faces to the sea. Behind us, the atmosphere was rent by electrical discharges while, approaching from the west, explosions continued to tear through the water, though they rapidly decreased in number and soon ceased altogether. The Quintessence's underconveyances had either retreated or been totally destroyed.

There followed a few minutes of tense silence, then, about a quarter of a mile from my position, something rose from the water. Before I could properly get the measure of it, a blinding bolt of energy arced out of it, lashed across the beach, and impacted against the edge of the forest. Wood and foliage erupted into the air with a deafening *crack*.

More things humped up onto the sand. They were metal machines, each a boxy rhomboid mounted on two very large rimless wheels—comprised of eight spokes ending in curved and studded "feet"—while a third, smaller wheel was affixed to the end of a shaft extending from the back. Twin funnels thrust upward from the rear of the vehicles. These were the first part of the contraptions to break the surface, and as they did so, valves popped open at their ends and thick plumes of steam came screeching out at high pressure, assaulting my ears and casting a veil over the scene for the entire length of the beach. This almost instantaneous pall glowed weirdly, illuminated from within by glowing crystals positioned at the end of short shafts, each protruding from the front of the machines. It was from these gemstones that the bolts of energy were released to terrible effect—the seaward edge of the forest was decimated before the flock could fire a single retaliatory shot.

The scene was deafening and chaotic, the air filled with pounding detonations and blinding flares. Splinters and branches whirled past. For a moment, I was paralysed from the shock of it, then a hand grabbed my arm, bringing me to my senses, and I saw that Gallokomas was at my side.

"They are concentrating their fire on the trees to either side of the river!" he shouted.

I squinted through the roiling vapour and saw that this was indeed the case. "They must be attempting to widen its path through the forest, Gallokomas! It'll give them a route in. Order our cannoneers to focus on the machines closest to the river's mouth. Disable them and they'll block the rest!"

He sent out a mental command and a large number of Zull rapidly gathered directly above the leading Divergent machines. Hovering in pairs, they aimed their cannons. For a few seconds nothing happened, as frequencies were adjusted. Then my ears popped and some of the war vehicles spluttered, jerked, and shuddered to a standstill.

The response was immediate and devastating. The other machines turned their weapons on the Zull, sending bolt after bolt crackling up into the flock—and where we'd restricted ourselves to disabling the enemy, the Divergent showed no such constraint. To my horror, I saw hundreds of Zull killed in the blink of an eye, their charred bodies raining down.

Gallokomas slapped his hands to his head and screamed as the slaughter sent telepathic shock waves through him. I held him by the shoulders, steadied him, and hollered, "For pity's sake, order them to keep moving!"

He recovered and nodded. Moments later, all the Zull were flying again, dodging through the haze-filled air, and far fewer of them were being hit.

"But we cannot aim our cannons properly!" Gallokomas observed.

"We shall have to do the best we can."

A final line of war machines exited the water. The Divergent forces were four vehicles deep and crowding toward the river.

I noticed hatches opening in the sides of the disabled contraptions. Mi'aata clambered from them and made for the trees.

Hitting my harness's control, I sped forward, swooped down, drew my pistol, and fired at the creatures. A mass of Zull pistoleers followed me. The Mi'aata, armed with pikestaffs, turned them upon us and sent shafts of lightning into our midst. More Zull fell.

I hovered for a second and wiped sawdust, sand, and sweat from my eyes. The war machines had started to batter the forest again, and foliage and powdered wood flew around us as they pushed forward. The vehicles were completely careless of the Divergent who were "on foot" and crushed many of them beneath their massive wheels. It occurred to me that Yissil Froon, wherever he was, possessed only small control over his forces—sufficient, perhaps, to drive them forward, but not enough to keep them properly organised.

I picked my next target, plummeted, slowed, touched the ground with my toes, aimed my pistol, fired an invisible beam of focused sound at a Mi'aata, and saw it slump and drop its weapon. Springing upward, I narrowly avoided an energy discharge, which sputtered past so close that it scorched the calf of my right leg.

A war machine rattled and died just beneath me, hit by a sound cannon, its crystal power source disabled. The hatch in its side swung downward. Tentacles emerged and gripped the sides of the opening. I dropped, landed, crouched, aimed, and sent the three crew toppling backward into the cabin.

The smouldering carcass of a Zull thudded into the sand a few feet from me, twitched, and lay still. I paced away from it and was swallowed by the swirling and ever-thickening cloud. Nebulous forms shadowed through it. Light flared and guttered. Booms reverberated, shook the ground, rattled my teeth.

Dimly, I became aware that someone was bellowing my name.

"Mr. Fleischer! Mr. Fleischer! I say, old thing! Harrumph!"

Colonel Spearjab and Artellokas descended.

"What is it, Colonel?"

"The pistols are having the desired effect, what! The Divergent hit by 'em are dropping their weapons and becoming thoroughly addled. *Addled*, I say! Old Yissil Froon can't control the blighters at all."

"They are filled with need," Artellokas shouted over the din of battle. "They want only to enter the forest to pupate."

"That's the last place they should go!" I exclaimed. "They'll be shot to pieces by their own forces!"

"Quite so!" Spearjab agreed. "But they are of my own kind— What! What!—and I retain a little of the old mental attachment to 'em. Mr. Artellokas here thinks he can—can—humph!—what did you call it, old chap?"

The Zull scientist raised a hand and tapped his own head with his forefinger. His accompanying words were lost in a cacophonous sequence of blasts.

I shouted, "What?"

"I said can amplify Colonel Spearjab's thoughts, Mr. Fleischer. Together, we might attract the Discontinued away from the conflict and toward the southern edge of the forest. It is safer there."

I ducked as a thick branch bounced past and splinters rained onto us. Pressing my inner wrist, I called, "Clarissa Stark!"

"Aiden! What's happening? It's pandemonium!"

"No time to explain. Where's the mouth of the rupture?"

"It's drifting in a north-eastwardly direction about a mile and a half inland—moving quite slowly at the moment."

"And the forest nearest your position—is it quiet?"

"Yes. The chaos is farther north along the beach."

I turned back to my two friends. "Do it. Artellokas, issue an order to the flock. Tell the pistoleers not to shoot at any unarmed Mi'aata."

Whatever acknowledgement I received was lost in a terrific

explosion and another shower of fragmented wood. By the time my eyes had recovered from the flash, my friends had departed.

Clarissa's voice pierced the ringing in my ears.

"Aiden! Aiden!"

"Yes, Clarissa?"

"Listen! Yissil Froon is still expecting Iriputiz to return through the rupture. That's not going to happen, which means our enemy will have difficulty pinpointing its position. When he realises his plan has gone awry, what will he do?"

I cursed under my breath. "He'll probably spread his army out among the trees until one of them is sucked into the thing, then the rest will make a rush to that position."

"Yes, that's what I thought, too. And the wider the war machines spread, the more Zull pupae will be destroyed."

"All right. Thank you."

I peered through the eddying murk. I wanted to speak with Gallokomas. Where had he got to?

As if by magic, having sensed my need, he dropped to my side. "You have orders, Fleischer Thing?"

"Yes! Follow me!"

We flew straight up until we were above the dirty and expanding cloud, then hovered and surveyed the battlefield.

I pointed at the indistinct war machines. "All the Divergent vehicles are on the beach now. It means we can get behind them. Their weapons are at the front, and unless the whole machine turns around, they can't shoot backward. Order the cannoneers to the waterline. From there, they must work hard to disable every vehicle. We have to prevent further destruction of the forest and protect the pupae. The armed Mi'aata will try to escape among the trees. Have our pistoleers follow and stop every one of them!"

Gallokomas gave a satisfied nod. "Yes! Good! But what of that——?" He pointed inland to where the atmospheric disturbance was fast filling the valley.

"Clarissa will tell you exactly where in the storm the mouth of the rupture is located. You must avoid it but, at the same time, prevent any Divergent Mi'aata from reaching it."

"I understand."

We parted. I joined the pistoleers as they first congregated, then swept forward en masse over the machines that clogged the river. Beams of electrical energy sliced into us. Zull fell before we passed the greatest danger and plunged into the forest. There, on foot, we engaged with the advancing Divergent.

A sort of guerrilla warfare now ensued and the combat took on a phantasmagorical quality. We were ahead of the blast zone but debris continually drifted from it to mingle with the steam and dust, making the atmosphere, in the hellish twilight, a sickly rust colour, and the nearby explosions and thunder, muffled by the dense air, were reduced to an almost unvarying rumble which, along with the shaking ground, gave the impression of a never-ending earthquake. Intermittently, a branch or clod of earth would come ricocheting through the tree trunks, while stuff constantly rained down on us from the canopy overhead. Through this maelstrom, from bole to bole, we stalked our prey.

The Zull could sense their enemy, but I possessed no such ability and was again and again taken by surprise as Mi'aata suddenly lurched out of the pall, raised their pikestaffs, and sent a jagged line of light whipping in my direction. Repeatedly, I dodged, ducked, dived, rolled, and raised my pistol only to have it seemingly fail in my hand. There was no report from the thing, no recoil, no sensation that it had discharged, nothing to tell me the confounded device had worked at all until I saw my target limply drop its weapon.

Always, the Divergent I hit shuffled off southward, while the Zull pistoleers and I, by contrast, gradually retreated toward the East, deeper into the trees, as the war machines continued to tear into the forest.

And now a further hazard endangered us:

"Aiden Fleischer!"

"Yes, Clarissa?"

"The storm has enveloped the whole valley now."

I looked up. With the ongoing barrage, I'd failed to notice there was fierce lightning overhead, too.

"The rupture is sliding toward the centre of the forest," she said. "If it continues on its present course, it will reach your position. Damnation! Just when you need me most, I'm going to lose track of it. I can hardly see, my eyes are watering so."

A Mi'aata rounded a tree trunk, pointed its pikestaff at me, and fired. I twisted but was knocked off my feet as the discharge ripped through the skin of my flight sac. Crashing down amid the roots of a Ptoollan tree, I fumbled for my pistol, threw myself to one side as the creature took another shot, then raised my weapon and pulled the trigger. My assailant rocked backward, the pikestaff slipped from its tentacles, and moments later the creature began to dazedly move away.

"Are you all right, Aiden?" came Clarissa's urgent voice.

"Yes. Hold out for as long as you can, but don't risk your eyes."

"All right. Stay safe."

I climbed from among the roots, pulled the shredded membrane away from my harness, cursed my ill-luck, and suddenly became conscious of a strange keening coming from behind me. This, in turn, made me aware that the reverberating thunder from the direction of the beach had lessened in intensity—the cannoneers must be winning out against the war machines. Turning, I stepped around the tree and discovered the source of the mournful noise—a large cocoon. Could the thing inside the leathery shell sense the bedlam occurring around it? Apparently so.

Feathery leaves cascaded from above, and, among them, Gallokomas. A nasty-looking burn furrowed his chest.

"You're injured!"

"Zull have died, Thing," he said. "I am merely hurt. We are fighting for the survival of our species, and through our sacrifices, we are beginning to overcome the Divergent. Many of their vehicles have been disabled."

"Can you carry me, Gallokomas? I want to assess our progress, but my flight apparatus has been destroyed."

He stepped forward, gripped me beneath the arms, and hauled me up through the canopy and into the sky over the forest. We flew low beneath the storm, skimming the treetops.

"It is dangerous here," Gallokomas said. "If we are not killed by the storm we might be shot by the remaining war machines. We must hurry past them to the sea, then we can ascend."

That we were in the line of fire was illustrated an instant later when a coruscating beam seared through the air to the right of us and came sizzling in our direction. Gallokomas pitched downward then swooped up, arced around the deadly beam, and sped out over the sand.

I looked to the right and the left. What of the Zull flock I could see through the haze appeared thinner, with half of it now hidden among the trees and the rest distributed along the beach. I was dismayed by the many bodies littering the ground. Our casualties were high.

By equal measure, the war machines, which had threatened so much, were more than two-thirds disabled, and the progress of those that still functioned was blocked by those that didn't. The mouth of the river—the easiest route into the forest—was completely jammed by incapacitated hulks.

"We should order the—" I began, but was cut off by one deafening report after another as spears of light pulsed past us and smashed into the forest, instantly reducing hundreds of trees to dust. Gallokomas rocketed upward, turned, and let out a cry of shock at what we saw floating motionless about two hundred feet over the sea.

It was a flying ship; a thing comprised of two immense cigar-shaped structures, set parallel to one another, both reminiscent of dirigible balloons—such as that flown by Henri Giffard in 1852—with a flat glass-covered platform spanning the distance between them. A big propeller was spinning at the front of the platform and another at its stern. Steam spouted from pipes set along the outer sides of the dirigibles and cannons poked from bulging domes, one atop each structure and one below. It was from the bottom pair that the hugely destructive light rays were shooting, cutting a broad channel through the trees and into the centre of the forest.

"Get above it, Gallokomas!" I yelled. "I want to see through the glass. I'll wager Yissil Froon is inside that behemoth!"

My friend plummeted down until we were just a few feet above the water then sped out to sea, angling away from the monstrous aero-ship. We went unnoticed as we circled around it and began to gain height.

"Aiden Fleischer!"

"Clarissa! Do you see it?"

"I never thought to! I designed the thing when I was barely sixteen years old. Yissil Froon is aboard—I can sense his presence!"

"What's its weakness? How do we bring it down?"

"It's unstable. If the Zull concentrate their attack on just one of the dirigibles, they might succeed in unbalancing the whole thing. Have Gallokomas order them to use the pikestaffs dropped by the Divergent."

Gallokomas heard this and telepathically issued the command. My friend and I had by now risen above the warship. We eased forward, approaching it cautiously from the back.

"What of the rupture, Clarissa?" I asked.

"I can't see it. I had to put my goggles on. I'm sorry, Aiden."

"Don't be. Stay undercover. We'll come for you when it's safe."

Gallokomas and I circled high over the glass-topped platform. I could see six Mi'aata inside, and, standing at the pointed prow, the unmistakable form of Yissil Froon, still a Yatsill.

An inky cloud of Zull came swirling through the sky toward us—a tiny attack force on its way to assault the gigantic aero-ship. Below us, the turret on top of the leftmost balloon swivelled until its cannon was directed at them.

"Warn them!" I shouted.

Energy suddenly snapped not from the weapon we were looking at but from its opposite number, which, unobserved by us, had turned and pointed in our direction. Blistering heat screamed past, scorching the side of my upper right arm. Gallokomas cried out, and before I could properly grasp what was happening, I was falling. The sky and sea and ship whirled around me. I caught a brief glimpse of my friend tumbling away, whether wounded or dead it was impossible to tell.

I hit glass, crashed through, and thumped onto a hard deck. Sharp fragments clattered and shattered around me. I struggled to retain consciousness, to draw in a clarifying breath, to comprehend what had just happened. I felt my eyes slipping up into my head. No! I couldn't allow it! Don't escape from the pain! Cling on to it! Use it to stay alert!

Rolling onto my side, I tried to lever myself up on an arm and failed. Glass crunched beneath me. Blood trickled across my skin. The four click-clacking feet of a Yatsill approached. I tried to speak but could only moan.

A familiar voice: "Aiden Fleischer!"

Long sharp fingers clamped around my neck and my thigh. I was heaved into the air and flung with great force against a flat bulkhead, bouncing off it to smack once again onto the metal floor. I tried to drag myself away from the oncoming footsteps but they caught up with me, chitinous digits dug into my hair, and I was yanked by it up onto my knees. Yissil Froon twisted my head around until I was looking into his ghastly face. His horns curled like those of a ram. His vertical lips gaped and the inner beak clicked in the rat-a-tat manner of Yatsill laughter.

Speaking English, he snarled, "Pitiful creature! You think to oppose me? Impossible!" He dragged me to my feet.

His hard right hand slapped my face, the serrated inner fingers ripping the flesh from my cheek, sending me reeling away and leaving him holding a clump of hair. I collided with a Mi'aata. Its tentacular limbs wound about me and hoisted me around to face Yissil Froon.

The Yatsill froze, then raised an arm and pointed at my chest.

"The crystal! You have the crystal! Where is Sepik?"

I managed a grin, and blood bubbled from my mouth. "He's splattered at the bottom of Zone Four, you damned maniac, and good riddance to the wretch!"

The Yatsill Magician hissed venomously. "No matter. I can do without him!"

I laughed. "You poor demented fool. You're delusional. Your

machines are constructed from the imaginings of a child! The Zull have already incapacitated most of them. Your army is a barely controlled rabble! Do you really think Earth will fall to such a pathetic mob? Millions inhabit my world! *Millions!* We'll design and construct superior machines. You won't stand a chance!"

Yissil Froon gazed at me. His fingers moved slowly. "I can manipulate minds," he said.

Three loud blasts rocked the aero-ship. The deck lurched and listed to the left. We all scrambled to regain balance, but my captor's hold didn't loosen.

"The Zull are attacking!" one of the Mi'aata crew reported.

"Retaliate! Kill them!"

The crew member had spoken in Koluwaian and the reply was barked in the same language, but Yissil Froon switched back to English when he addressed me again, and I noticed that when he did so, one of the other Mi'aata, standing a little way behind him, gazed at the Yatsill's back fixedly and moved its mouth as if silently repeating every word.

"Fleischer, you think you have the better of me, but you forget your own vulnerability. What I can do to you, I can do to all your kind."

The pain of my fall suddenly blossomed, an abysmal flower, its razor-sharp petals slicing through me, its fiery stigma blazing up my spine. Horror, cowardice, and shame throbbed through my veins.

"No!" I moaned, and clamping my teeth shut, I summoned the will to resist. It rose up inside me, a dark and bestial thing, a sickening ferocity—a monster.

I faced it, accepted it, embraced it, and in an instant, there was nothing abominable about it at all.

Letting out the breath I hadn't realised I'd been holding, I said, "You cannot coerce fear out of me. I no longer doubt myself. There's nothing for your vile mind to latch on to."

The vehicle pitched and weaved as the Zull fired more energy bolts into its side.

My captor's hold momentarily loosened.

I snatched the stock of my pistol, pulled the weapon out of its holster, curled my wrist, and fired backward into the creature. Its tentacles fell away from me.

"No!" Yissil Froon shouted. "Succumb!"

Two Mi'aata came flopping across the sloping deck, their limbs outstretched. I shot them. They sagged.

I heard an exclamation, "We're losing altitude!" and glanced back. It had come from one of two Mi'aata hunched over consoles at the prow of the platform. I swung my arm around, aimed, and fired. The creature staggered back, its four eyes blinking, its mouth opening slackly.

Yissil Froon pounced forward and knocked the pistol from my hand. He grabbed me by the harness and flung me sternward. I hit the deck and went skidding through broken glass until I bumped against the Mi'aata who'd been watching the Yatsill.

"I say! Steady on!" it exclaimed.

"Hold him!" the Magician ordered.

"I don't bloody well think so, old fruit!"

I looked up in wonderment. "Lord Brittleback?"

The Divergent returned my gaze. "That's it! *That's* what I was trying to remember! Lord Upright Brittleback! Of course!" It raised its tentacles and examined them. "By the Saviour! What in the name of Phenadoor has bloody well happened to me?"

Yissil Froon addressed the only Mi'aata remaining under his control. "Get the ship moving! Fly into the storm. Fast!"

Painfully, I pushed myself upright. "Lord Brittleback, would you stop that Mi'aata, please, while I take care of Yissil Froon?"

"Mi'aata?"

"The Blood God, Prime Minister."

"Ah, quite so! Jolly good!"

I drew my sword and faced my enemy. The deck was listing about twenty-five degrees to port. It jerked beneath my feet as the aeroship began to accelerate. Whatever advantage my blade offered was nullified by the Yatsill's four legs, which gave Yissil Froon much more purchase on such an unstable surface, as was immediately demonstrated when, with my first step toward him, my foot landed on a shard of glass and slid out from beneath me. I fell sideways onto my thigh, and before I could recover myself, Froon swooped forward, snatched the sword from my hand, snapped the blade in half over one of his thighs, and cast it aside.

"Pathetic creature!" he snarled. His fingers caught my neck in a vice-like grip and he hauled me into the air. "Without machines! Without an army! Even then, I can take your world!"

From the corner of my eye, I saw Lord Brittleback struggling with the Mi'aata at the controls.

"So the rupture still opens onto Koluwai, does it? Very well, the islanders will be the first to fall under my spell." The Yatsill slammed me down and crouched over me, his sharp fingers constricting my throat. "And from that island I shall spread my influence until it infiltrates your so-called civilisation." He leaned close until I could feel his breath upon my face. "I have seen inside Clarissa Stark's mind, Aiden Fleischer. I understand the nature of your Earth. I know your species is divided—that most are less developed than the Yatsill, while the rest are in the grip of powers every bit as stultifying as the Quintessence. What resentments and fears must seethe in the masses! What longings and frustrations! What angers and hatreds! *Those* shall be my weapons!"

I thought of overcrowded Whitechapel and its inhumane poverty, of the teeming masses of discarded, disenfranchised, and wretched poor, and of the monster born out of that Inferno, of Jack the Ripper. By God, if Yissil Froon loosed his mesmeric powers upon such misery, could he not produce from it a vast army of demonic murderers? How easy for him to take those whose path to goodness was already fraught with such terrible obstacles—deprivation, disease, corruption, drudgery, violence, humiliation—and cause them to turn away from it, to face in the direction of lessening good, to become evil!

"Ah, yes!" he hissed. "I see that you understand!"

I clutched at his wrists, tried to pull his hands away, but couldn't match his strength. With agonising slowness, he was throttling me to death.

The aero-ship began to shudder. Its propellers howled. At the periphery of my fast-clouding vision, I saw Lord Brittleback dragging the other Mi'aata away from the console.

"We're descending too fast!" it screamed. "We'll hit the trees!"

The port side of the vessel suddenly dipped. Yissil Froon and I, the stunned Mi'aata, and Lord Brittleback and his opponent all careened across the deck. The Magician let go of me as he fought for balance. He toppled over and collided with a bulkhead. I skidded into him, kicked at his face, and felt it squelch beneath the heels of my sandals. He knocked my legs away. The foot-long tip of my broken sword came skating by. I slapped my hand onto it and swung the metal up, around, and down, ramming it point-first into Yissil Froon's upper right arm, careless of the fact that in doing so I cut my fingers to the bone. The blade cracked through the carapace and into the soft flesh beneath. Blood spurted. The Magician screeched. One of his knees came up and impacted against the side of my jaw. I rolled away, my senses reeling, saw the shattered glass roof spinning past my eyes, caught a glimpse of Zull flying close, trees looming, and the zeniths of twin suns flaring over the horizon. I bounced off a metal wall and was thrown against the remains of the roof. The aero-ship corkscrewed downward.

"Brace yourself, Mr. Fleischer!" Lord Brittleback yelled. "We're going to hit the bloody ground!"

Yissil Froon seized my left ankle as I fell past him and pulled me into a crushing embrace. We were tossed around the cabin, rebounding from one side to the other. Lord Brittleback bumped against us, went whirling away, struck glass, smashed through it, and was sent flying out into the open air.

With a deafening roar, the machine ploughed into the Forest of Indistinct Murmurings.

"Aiden! Aiden! Answer me!"

Clarissa's voice penetrated my jumbled senses, cutting through the discordant shrieks, groans, and clangs of tortured metal. The deck was jumping and convulsing beneath my back. I opened my eyes and saw branches and foliage dragging past the jagged sides of the roof. The ship was still crashing through the canopy of the forest.

There was a girder across my body, pinning me down, excruciatingly heavy against my chest, but as far as I could ascertain, I hadn't sustained any grievous injury—miraculously!—though I was so battered that even raising my wrist to my mouth sent spikes of pain through me.

"Aiden! Please! Please!"

"Clarissa," I gasped.

It made no sense. Why wasn't the vessel slowing? Its propellers couldn't be rotating—the impact would have torn them apart—yet the aero-ship was grinding through the treetops, the boles so massive and densely packed that it couldn't fall through them.

"Oh, thank Heaven! Get out of there, Aiden! Quickly!"

I reached down, took hold of the girder, and pushed. It shifted, but not enough.

"I'm trapped!"

My ears were assaulted by cacophonous thunder and the crashes and squeals of the disintegrating flying machine. The deck bucked and shrieked. It banged against the back of my head. A gust of wind whistled through the ripped metal, bringing with it the scent of lemons.

"I can't get to you in time, Aiden! You're being pulled into the rupture."

"Don't try!" I responded. I heaved at the girder and managed to push myself a little way out from under it. "Report!"

"What?"

"Report! What has happened?"

I shoved the beam again, my lacerated fingers sending a spike of pain through me, and gained a few more inches of freedom. Then the deck suddenly angled upward, the girder came loose, and I heaved myself out from beneath it. I grabbed a fold of twisted metal to secure myself. The frenzied whistle of escaping steam sounded from the rear of the machine, drowning Clarissa's reply. I pressed my wrist to the side of my head and shouted, "Repeat! I can barely hear you!"

"The war machines are disabled! Colonel Spearjab and Artellokas are drawing the defeated Divergent to the forest below me. They're taking to the trees and pupating. The rest are being hunted. We've won, Aiden! But you have to get off that ship! It's almost at the mouth!"

To my left, a jumble of debris flew into the air and clattered upward out of the cabin. The storm was raging outside and everything was being drawn into it as if magnetised.

A buckled panel clanged aside and Yissil Froon burst into view. His body was dented and bloody, the shell ruined, his limbs broken. Still, he had strength enough to throw himself onto me with an inarticulate cry of rage, slicing his left hand down, its serrated digits gashing my chest. Then he was suddenly twirling into the air as the aero-ship jolted upward, and I saw him catapulted out of it and yanked into the sky.

I felt myself grabbed by a powerful force, as if gravity itself had reversed direction. The twisted deck plate was wrenched from my grasp and I was sucked out of the wreck.

The world pirouetted around me—trees, a band of purple, the moons, a streak of orange, Yissil Froon, the sea, the ship, lightning.

"Aiden! No!"

Clarissa's scream followed me into a vertical tube of iridescent energy. I was enveloped by numbing cold and felt a sensation of immeasurable speed.

The last thing I saw, as my senses fled, was the aero-ship, below me, flowering into a ball of flame as some part of its engine—probably the boiler—detonated.

o

My eyes were brimming with pale blue sky—a memory returned but oddly detached, as if belonging to someone else—and a syrupy scent clogged my nostrils. I felt dewy grass between my fingers. A bee flew lazily past my face.

Earth.

And I knew exactly *where* on Earth, too. The intoxicating perfume was unmistakable. It belonged to a small blossom-filled glade on one of Koluwai's hills, a clearing strewn with the corpses of Zull.

Dawn had just broken, the quality of the light told me that much, and the trees should've been alive with squawking birds and chattering monkeys. They weren't.

I slowly turned my head, cautious of pain. The foliage around me was littered with fragments of metal and ragged strips of material— pieces of the aero-ship and its two dirigibles. The destroyed machine had been coughed through the rupture.

A shadow slid over me. I tried to push myself upright but a heavy weight thudded down onto my chest, knocking me back, pinning me to the ground.

Yissil Froon glared down at me, his head trembling from side to side as if in the grip of a seizure. Drool oozed from his mouth and sprayed my face as he gave a clacking laugh and exclaimed, "It's better than I ever hoped! This world of yours is filled with so many minds! So many! And all consumed by panic and antipathy! It's positively . . . *delicious*!"

He looked up to the heavens and flung his arms out.

"I will have it!"

The fringed outer lips of his mouth stretched so wide they tore at the corners. His face receded into the shell of his head. The front seam of his ruined body split open and red tentacles writhed out of it.

He screamed, "I am Yissil Froon! I am Yissil Froon."

A network of cracks snaked across his exoskeleton. Wet flesh bulged through them.

"And I . . ."

I felt something solid on the ground beside my hand and curled my blood-wet fingers around it.

"Am . . ."

Yissil Froon's carapace fractured and fell away as a horribly malformed Mi'aata burst from within it.

"God!"

Instead of four eyes, it had seven, varying in size but all burning with madness; its limbs were of differing thicknesses, the suckers and spines distributed irregularly along their twisted length; its torso was contorted and stretched over with patchy, discoloured skin; it was monstrous; it was pathetic; it was still Yissil Froon.

The devil looked down at me and whispered, "Worship me."

"In all honesty," I replied, "I'd rather not."

I swept the object in my hand up and into the side of its head. The crunching impact sent the creature reeling sideways. I pushed myself away from it, jumped to my feet, and put my full weight behind a second blow. Tentacles wrapped around me but their grip was loose, the strength already draining from them.

I clubbed Yissil Froon again and again—and there was no wrath, no lust for vengeance, and no red mist before my eyes. I knew exactly what I was doing, and I did it without hesitation or regret. I smashed his head to a pulp, destroyed his sick brain, and wiped him from existence. Then I teetered, fell to my knees, and looked at the thing I was holding.

It was crusted with dried mud and smeared with gore, but it was recognisably the Webley-Pryse revolver given to me by the London Missionary Society so long ago.

They'd told me the life of a missionary is sometimes perilous.

CHAPTER 12
WAR

Even now, it seems absurd to me that a structure which spans the vast distances between planets is yet so sensitive that one end of it will follow a crystal no bigger in size than a cigar. Inevitably, my incredulity draws my consideration from the macroscopic to the microscopic, and I think of that which my own species has achieved, and stand aghast at the unprecedented destruction wrought two years ago by the splitting of an atom.

If something so inconceivably small can destroy Hiroshima, why not a crystal shift the end of a fold in space?

My account is almost done.

Five years have passed since my return to Earth.

With my bare hands, I buried the corpse of Yissil Froon in the Koluwaian jungle. His Mi'aata body had been as horribly distorted as his mind, due, no doubt, to his excessive drinking of Dar'sayn. In effect, he'd been consuming his own kind, so I suppose it only fitting that his remains are now rotting on an island where cannibalism was practised.

When I descended the hill and emerged from the undergrowth, I found Koluwai transformed. The tree houses were gone and the town of Kutumakau, though vastly expanded, was almost completely destroyed. What remained of its inhabitants were diseased, half-starved, and many of them badly wounded. I recognised no one, and none showed any interest in me.

After two days, during which I subsisted on fruit, nuts, and berries, I learned from an elderly man that a vicious war between Australia and Japan was raging throughout Melanesia. Koluwai had been, for the space of one catastrophic week, a battleground.

It took a further three days before I was able to persuade a fisherman to sail me to Futuna. From there I made my way with painstaking slowness north-westward past Vanuatu, through the

Solomon Islands, and on to Papua New Guinea. The scars of conflict were obvious throughout the region—the smoking hulks of battleships, burning towns, ravaged farms, and, everywhere, the dead.

While approaching Port Moresby, I encountered actual combat for the first time. By now, I knew the war was global, and understood what Yissil Froon had meant when he said the world was filled with panic and antipathy. I also realised that my Germanic surname might cause me trouble, so when I chanced upon a corpse—among the many fallen—that bore some physical resemblance to me, I rather shamefacedly appropriated the young man's uniform and identity papers and became Private Peter Edwards of the Australian Army.

If there's such a thing as divine retribution—or *karma*—I felt the full force of it later that day when I found myself in the middle of an artillery strike. A Japanese shell burst beside me and I knew no more until I regained consciousness two days later in a mobile hospital. My first act was to check that the crystal was still hanging around my neck—which is when I discovered that my left hand was missing. Strangely, I was thankful. Had it been the right, I might have lost the little spirally tattoo on my inner wrist. The thing doesn't function, of course, but it gives me comfort to speak into it each night before I sleep.

As soon as the rupture opens, I'll come back. I'll return to you. I promise.

The crystal was safe.

During the weeks of convalescence, I dwelled upon a fact that Private Edwards' papers had revealed to me. The Earth I'd returned to wasn't the one I'd left. There was a time discrepancy. Fifty-three years had passed since I was transported to Ptallaya. Certainly, I hadn't been away for so long a period. I still have no theory to explain it.

Whether the human race has advanced during those years is a moot point. Civilisation is crumbling. Creativity is employed solely to produce ever more fearsome engines of destruction. Earth's battle machines demonstrate that those built by Yissil Froon were, indeed, nothing but child's play. His army wouldn't have stood a chance.

Perhaps the shock of my injury lingered. All I know is that after I was invalided out of the Army, the next ten months passed in a blur.

I used my meagre pay to travel to Bermuda—a hazardous undertaking due to the many German U-boats that patrolled the Atlantic, and one made almost impossible by emergency restrictions. But by hook and crook I got there, and soon after my arrival, I found employment as clerk to a shipping agent. At the first opportunity, I abused my employer's trust by offering the less than respectable skipper of a small cargo vessel certain advantages in return for him taking me a thousand miles to the east of the island. We navigated toward an area of the Atlantic that careful research on my part had revealed to be particularly deep and very seldom travelled. It was here I intended to deposit the crystal, out of harm's way, planning to return to the spot when the rupture became active again.

Two days into the voyage, a torpedo narrowly missed us—our presence in remote waters had attracted the attention of an enemy submarine. We reversed direction and tried to steam back to Bermuda. The German vessel pursued and forced us far to the south and west of the island, until—perhaps two hundred miles north of the Bahamas—it launched another torpedo and hit us broadside. The ship went down.

I—and two crewmembers—survived. We clung to flotsam and gradually succumbed to exposure, hunger, and thirst as the hours turned into days. My companions slipped under the surface. I refused to die.

A British merchantman found me. Its crew lifted me aboard. I put my hand to my chest. The crystal was gone—on the seabed, as I'd intended, but not *where* I'd intended.

A few weeks later, the ship docked at Southampton. I was back in the land of my birth. Once again, I found work as a shipping clerk.

Time crawled by. The war and a lack of money prevented me from returning to Bermuda, but my job at least allowed me to monitor, to some extent, the region where I estimated the crystal lay, and fifteen months after my return to Earth, accounts of a freak storm came through. Ship captains reported that their compasses had become misaligned or spun wildly while crossing that particular expanse of ocean.

I'd missed my first opportunity to go home, to return to Clarissa.

o

The war ended.

By dint of determination and a frugal lifestyle, I'd saved enough to book passage back to Bermuda on a little independent trading vessel, *The Hermes*, under Captain Franklin Powell.

We are en route.

Two days ago, we heard by radio chatter that Flight 19 had inexplicably vanished. Fourteen men lost.

I know where they are.

Another fifteen months have passed.

The rupture is active again.

I have nothing more to tell.

We'll reach Hamilton in a matter of hours.

I can't help but consider it a figment of my imagination—all the turmoil, misery, and destruction. If I accepted it as fact, I'd lose my mind. I'd have to admit that Hell exists and I am in it. So I disengage. It's just a nightmare. A terrible fantasy.

Clarissa is waiting.

Only Ptallaya is real.

Only Ptallaya.

"Faith is to believe what we do not see; and the reward of this faith is to see what we believe."
—Saint Augustine

MARK HODDER
Q&A

1. You have a very interesting career path, from working at the BBC to becoming an award-winning novelist. Can you tell us about what influenced your decision to change professions?

I knew I wanted to be a novelist from the age of 11, when I first read Edgar Rice Burroughs' *A Princess of Mars*. Initially I was held back by a lack of faith. To me, novelists were akin to gods, and I was a mere mortal. By the time I graduated, I'd come to the conclusion that it might be possible for me to join their ranks, but it would require a key skill: the ability to write! Thus I steered myself into one copywriting job after another, working in practically every medium and on a very diverse variety of projects. So, though it may seem like I had a radical change of profession, the fact is that my earlier career was a sequence of steps, taking me to where I'd always wanted to be.

2. Your first novel, *The Strange Case of Spring Heeled Jack*, won the Philip K. Dick Award for Best Novel. What was your first reaction to that, and what did it mean to you as a writer?

When the novel was nominated for the award, my jaw hit the ground. When it won, I was speechless. It was a dream start to my dream career! From a purely practical perspective, the award had a huge impact by placing me in a spotlight and attracting the attention of agents and publishers worldwide. At a personal level, it was a fantastic affirmation that I could do the thing I most wanted to be doing.

3. **The Burton & Swinburne novels are wonderful alternate-reality 19ᵗʰ Century adventures, and your new book, *A Red Sun Also Rises,* is a Victorian adventure. What first got you interested in the period, and who most influenced your own work?**

My great-grandfather counted Sir Arthur Conan Doyle among his friends. They went to medical school together and were both Freemasons. When I was a kid, Sherlock Holmes felt like a part of my family. I revisit those stories every seven years or so and cannot overstate their influence. Through them, I became fascinated with Victorian history. Other influences include H.G. Wells, Wilkie Collins, the great pulp authors, and the classic trinity of horror—*Dracula*, *Frankenstein*, and *Jekyll and Hyde*.

4. **Steampunk and fantastical Victoriana seem to be enjoying a period of growth and renewed interest, both in print and as a pop culture phenomenon. What do you think is the driving force behind this?**

The question I always ask of a cultural phenomenon is: why now? The thing we call steampunk was around long before we knew what to call it, so why is it suddenly relevant? I pin it on two things. Firstly, steampunk references a time when the British Empire was at its most powerful. We currently live among its ruins—along with those of other empires—and are laying the imperialistic impulse to rest, which is an agonising process that requires much self-reflection and reassessment. Secondly, every culture depends for its stability upon powerful symbols and a sort of sub-language of manners and propriety. Those things change when the culture does, and I think they are changing now, which is why we reference the old and out-moded. To create something new, you must first fully recognise and acknowledge the old.

5. *A Red Sun Also Rises* is a stand-alone novel, unconnected to your earlier works. What were the reasons you wanted to tell this tale next?

Primarily, I wanted to pay homage to the planetary romances I enjoyed so much as a kid. But that genre has been dormant for a long, long time, primarily because its plots were extremely simplistic. So the challenge I set myself was to employ all the trappings of planetary romance but to hang them on a more sophisticated story.

6. The new book is a wonderful combination of themes, from the gothic to bizarre aliens. What made you want to incorporate so many different elements into one book?

In cookery, there are no more new ingredients. Everything is already out there. So a chef can either create a traditional dish or experiment by combining ingredients that haven't been combined before. An author has the same choice, to be generic or to be experimental. I don't like to feel in any way limited, and I like to have fun, so I don't hesitate to mix things up in order to tell an entertaining tale.

7. The tone of the book is very interesting, from the bleak realities of Jack the Ripper, to the almost childlike exuberance of the Yatsill. Was this a deliberate combination of light and dark, innocence versus the amoral, or did it just happen naturally?

I knew from the start that I wanted those contrasts. Some of them went in consciously, others grew organically as I told the tale.

8. The evolutionary aspect of the aliens in the book is very interesting. How did the idea come to you?

One of my current obsessions is with Darwin's theory of evolution and how profoundly it is misunderstood, misquoted, abused and scorned by those who have no proper conception of its elegance and beauty. Because my primary protagonist is a priest struggling with his faith, I wanted to place him in an environment where, initially, he doesn't recognise that he's surrounded by this intricate and carefully balanced cycle of life. Only gradually does it dawn on him that on Ptallaya, just as on Earth, nature is a self-sustaining system with a mechanism so refined, yet so delicate, that it is easily misunderstood. When you don't properly understand something, you can interfere with it without realising the damage you're doing. He comes to realise that this is what's been happening.

9. There's a small element of time slippage in the book, as well as hints about the Bermuda Triangle as we're introduced to Aiden in the 1940s. Are you interested in unexplained phenomena?

I'm a sceptic and a pragmatist. I don't believe in the Bermuda Triangle or UFOs but I do believe the Yeti exists and I'm convinced the universe is teeming with life. I also have a very peculiar conception of time, which I explore more fully in my Burton & Swinburne novels.

10. In all your books there is an element of social commentary, from Burton and Swinburne talking about the cultural and political movements of the day, to Aiden listening as Clarissa recounts her life story. As a novelist, how important do you feel this is?

I consider it essential because it adds authenticity to even the wildest of tales, because it allows me to explore my own stance (or lack thereof) with regard to culture and politics, and because it offers the reader an option to consider those matters, possibly in a new light.

11. *A Red Sun Also Rises* is wonderfully self-contained, but do you think we might see Aiden and Clarissa again one day?

The story occurs within a specific geographical area of Ptallaya. There are hints of what lies beyond it, but those places named aren't visited. So a lot more to discover! Also, I feel Aiden has further room for psychological growth. I know where I'd start with the sequel, so there's every chance I may one day write it.

12. Your next project is the second trilogy in The Burton & Swinburne Adventures – can you tell us a little about that?

The first trilogy ended with Burton in a fix and most of the supporting cast dead or transformed. The second trilogy begins with everything re-set, though with some characters in oddly different roles. How has this come about? As Burton becomes aware of the truth, he's led to a confrontation unlike anything I've written before. I'm having a lot of fun with this one!

Read on for an excerpt from *The Secret of Abdu El Yezdi*, the first book of the new Burton and Swinburne series.

A
BURTON & SWINBURNE
ADVENTURE

THE
SECRET of
ABDU EL YEZDI

also by Mark Hodder
available from Del Rey

DEL REY

CHAPTER 1

THE SUMMONING

> "When one creates phantoms for oneself, one puts vampires into the world, and one must nourish these children of a voluntary nightmare with one's blood, one's life, one's intelligence, and one's reason, without ever satisfying them."
>
> —ELIPHAS LÉVI, *Axiom XI of La Clef des Grands Mystères*

aptain Richard Francis Burton leaned on the basin, looked into the mirror, and saw Captain Richard Francis Burton glowering back. He scowled into the black, smouldering eyes and snarled, "I'm sick of your meddling! I'll live by my own choices, not by yours, confound you!"

His tormentor's glare locked aggressively with his own.

At the periphery of Burton's vision, behind the devil that faced him, the cabin door opened and a slim young man stepped in. He was prematurely bald but sported a very long and bushy beard.

"You're awake!" the newcomer exclaimed, leaning his silver-topped walking cane against the wall.

Burton turned, but when he stopped the room didn't—it continued to spin—and the other jumped forward and took him by the elbows. "Steady on, old chap."

There was something rather repellent about the man's touch, but Burton was too weak to shake him off, so submitted meekly as he was guided to his bunk.

The visitor shook his head disapprovingly. "I don't know what you think you're doing. Sister Raghavendra will have your guts for garters. Back into bed with you, sir. You need rest and plenty of it. You're not out of the woods yet. Not by a long shot."

Burton managed to shrug free from the other's grip and slurred, "Did you see him? Why won't he leave me be?"

"To whom do you refer?"

"Him!" Burton shouted, flinging a hand toward the mirror and almost overbalancing. "Dogging my every step, the old fool! Interfering! Always interfering!"

The younger man chuckled—a sound that inexplicably sent cold prickles up Burton's spine. "It's merely your reflection, and you're hardly old; just worn out, that's all. The fevers have taken their toll, but I'm sure you'll regain your looks once you've shaken off the malaria. Now come, lie down, I'll read to you awhile."

Burton shook his head, his knees buckled, and he sat heavily. "Reflection, be damned. If I ever meet the dog, I'll kick him all the way to Hades!"

The visitor gave a snort of amusement, and the odious nature of his presence finally registered in full. Burton looked up at him, his jumbled senses converging, bringing the man's penetrating blue eyes into focus, noting the wide and rather cruel-looking mouth and the polished, overdeveloped cranium.

Dangerous. The fellow is dangerous.

A tremor ignited in Burton's stomach and raced outward through his body, causing his question—"Who are you, anyway?"—to come out more as a teeth-rattling moan.

"Four times I've visited your room, Captain," the man replied, "and four times you've made that very same enquiry. The answer is as ever. I am Laurence Oliphant, Lord Elgin's private secretary. He and I joined the ship at Aden for passage to London."

Burton frowned and struggled to clarify his thoughts. Memories eluded him. "Aden? We're not at Zanzibar?"

"No, we're not. The *Orpheus* departed Zanzibar two weeks ago. It spent five days at Aden, has just departed Cairo, and is currently en route to London via Vienna, where it will pick up the foreign secretary, Lord Stanley."

"What day is it?"

"Night, actually. Wednesday, the thirty-first of August. Tomorrow, your long expedition will finally be over. You'll be glad to get home, I expect. I understand you have a fiancée waiting for you."

Burton lifted his legs onto the bed, waited for Oliphant to arrange the pillows behind him, and lay back. His limbs jerked and his hands began to shake uncontrollably. He felt himself burning, sinking, disconnecting.

He could sense the eyes of the Other Burton upon him.

Go away. Go away. Leave me alone. I haven't time for you now. I have to watch this fellow. There's something about him. Something wrong.

Oliphant went to the basin, wetted a flannel, returned, placed it on Burton's forehead, and sat beside him. "You've been out of commission for nearly a month, but Sister Raghavendra says you're through the worst of it. She thinks the fever will break within the next few hours." He tapped his finger on Burton's shoulder. "Why do you do it, Captain? Why push yourself so hard? First in India, then your mission to Mecca, and now Africa—what drives you to such endeavours?"

Burton whispered, "The Devil. He's inflicted upon me a mania for exploration."

"Ha! Well, this time Old Nick took you to the brink of death. You were lucky you had one of the Sisterhood of Noble Benevolence with you."

Sister Sadhvi Raghavendra. Her beautiful face blurred into Burton's memory then swam away.

"It wasn't luck," he murmured. "Is she aboard? I want to see her."

"She was here but half an hour ago. I'll call her back if you wish it."

Fragments. Broken recollections. Cascading water falling from the great lake—almost an inland sea—to begin its long journey to the Mediterranean. Standing on a hill overlooking it, his companion at his side.

Burton sucked in a deep, shuddering breath, feeling his eyes widen.

"John! My God! How is John?"

Oliphant looked puzzled. "John?"

"Lieutenant Speke."

"I'm afraid I don't know him. Half a mo! Do you mean the chap who was with you at Berbera back in 'fifty-five? The one who died?"

"Died?"

"I was in the Far East at the time, but if I remember the reports rightly, he took a spear meant for Lieutenant Stroyan. It pierced his heart and killed him outright. That was four years ago."

"Four years?" Burton whispered. "But Speke and I discovered the source of the Nile."

"The fever has you befuddled. As I say, Speke copped it during your initial foray into Africa. It was you, William Stroyan, George Herne, and Sister Raghavendra who solved the puzzle of the Nile. You'll be remembered among the greatest of explorers. You've made history, sir."

The information fell between Burton and the Other Burton and they fought over it. The Burton here, now—the *real* Burton, blast it!—knew the fact to be true. Lieutenant John Hanning Speke had been killed in 1855. The Other Burton disagreed.

That is not when he died.

It is. I was there. I saw it happen.

He died later.

No! He died defending Stroyan.

He sacrificed himself for you.

Get away from me! Leave me alone!

You need me, you dolt.

The argument melted into Burton's overheated blood and raged through his body. He felt his limbs thrashing and heard a wail forced out of him. "I've made history, you say? I've made history?" He started to laugh and couldn't stop. He didn't know why it was funny, but it was.

Funny and agonising and terrifying.

I've made history.

Dimly, he felt Oliphant rise from the bed and—through tear-blurred eyes—watched him cross to the speaking tube beside the bureau. The young man pulled the device free, blew into it, and put it to his ear. After a brief wait, he placed the tube back against his mouth. "This is Oliphant. Can you have Sister Raghavendra sent to Captain Burton's cabin? I think he's having a seizure." He clipped the tube back into its bracket, turned to face Burton, then raised his right hand and made an odd and complex gesture, as if writing a sigil in the air.

"You say you have a mania for exploration, Captain Burton, but to me, you appear to possess all the qualities of a fugitive."

Burton tried to respond but his vocalisation emerged as an incomprehensible bark. Flecks of foam sprayed from his mouth. His muscles spasmed.

"Perhaps," Oliphant continued, "you should consider the possibility that, when a man struggles to escape his fate, he is more likely to flee along the path that leads directly to it."

Burton's teeth chattered. The cabin skewed sideways, righted itself, and suddenly he could smell jasmine and Sister Raghavendra was there—tall and slim, with big brown eyes, lustrous black hair, and dusky skin burned almost black by the African sun. Eschewing—while she still could—the corsets, heavy dresses, and multiple petticoats of the civilised woman, she was wearing a simple, loose-fitting Indian smock.

She said, "Has he been at all lucid?"

Burton closed his eyes.

She's here. You're safe. You can sleep.

Oliphant's voice: "Barely. He was in the midst of one of his delusions. It's just as you told me. He appears to believe himself a divided identity—two persons, thwarting and opposing each other. Will he be all right?"

"Yes, Mr. Oliphant, he'll be fine. It's a normal reaction to the medicine I gave him. The stuff brings the malarial fever to a final crisis and burns it off with great rapidity. This will be his last attack. In an hour or two, he'll fall into a deep sleep. By the time we arrive in London, he'll be weak but fully recovered. Would you leave us, please? I'll sit with him for an hour or so."

"Certainly."

The creak of the cabin door opening.

The bunk shifting as Sadhvi sat on the edge of it.

Her hand removing the flannel from his forehead.

Oliphant whispering, "As the crow flies, Captain Burton. As the crow flies."

Oblivion.

Burton opened his eyes. He was alone. Thirst scratched at his throat but something else had yanked him from his sleep. He lay still and listened. The *Orpheus* thrummed beneath him, the noise of the airship's eight engines so familiar he now equated their background rumble with silence.

There was nothing else.

He pushed the sheet back, struggled out of bed—*Bismillah! So weak!*—and tottered over to the basin where he gulped water from a jug.

The mirror had been waiting. Hesitantly, he scrutinised the fever-ravaged countenance he saw in it: the sun-scorched but yellow-tinged skin, still marked with insect bites; the broad brow, beaded with sweat; the angular cheeks, the left furrowed by a long, deep scar; and the wildly overgrown forked beard that ill-concealed a forward-thrusting, aggressive jaw. He peered into the intense eyes.

My own. Just my own reflected.

He sighed, poured water into the basin, splashed it over his face, then closed his eyes and tried to concentrate. Employing a Sufi technique, he withdrew awareness from his trembling legs, from the ague that gnawed at his bones, from every sense but the auditory.

A few minutes passed before it impinged upon his consciousness again, but—yes, there it was, extremely faint, a distant voice, chanting.

Chanting? Aboard the *Orpheus*?

He gave the mirror a second glance, muttered an imprecation, then crossed to a Saratoga trunk, opened its lid, lifted out the top tray, and retrieved a small bottle from one of the inner compartments.

The label read: *Saltzmann's Tincture*.

Five years ago, when an inexplicable impulse had led him to first purchase the cure-all from a pharmacist named Mr. Shudders, his good friend and personal physician, John Steinhaueser, had warned him off the stuff. Its ingredients were a mystery, but the doctor was certain cocaine was principal among them. Burton wasn't so sure. He knew well the effects of cocaine. Saltzmann's offered something entirely different. It imparted the exhilarating sense that one's life was ripe with endless options, as if all the possible consequences of actions taken were unveiled.

"Richard," Steinhaueser had said, "it's as insidious as opium and almost as addictive. You don't know what it might be costing you. What if it permanently damages your senses? Avoid. Avoid at all cost."

But Saltzmann's Tincture had cured Burton of the various ailments he'd brought back from India, saved him from blindness during his pilgrimage to Mecca, kept malaria at bay throughout his ill-fated penetration of Berbera, and had—despite Sister Raghavendra's seconding of Steinhaueser's opinion—sustained him while he led the search for the source of the Nile. For sure, in the final days of the expedition, he'd succumbed to the fever that was currently burning through his veins, but it wasn't half as bad as those experienced by the members of the Royal Geographical Society who scorned Saltzmann's and relied, instead, upon quinine. Livingstone, for example, was very vocal in his opposition to it and suffered as a consequence. In his most recent dispatch, sent from a village near the headwaters of the Congo and received at Zanzibar four years ago, Livingstone had reported himself "terribly knocked up" and predicted that he'd never see civilisation again. *If only I had my faith to sustain me*, he'd written, *but the terrible things I have witnessed in these wicked lands have stripped it from me. I am no better than a beast*. He hadn't been heard from since, and was now presumed dead.

Saltzmann's. If Livingstone had taken Saltzmann's, he'd have maintained his health and seen a way out of whatever predicament he was in.

Burton broke the bottle's seal, popped out the cork, hesitated a moment, then drank half of the clear, syrupy contents. Moments later, a delicious warmth chased the ache from his joints.

He turned and lurched across the room to the door, lifted his *jubbah*—the loose robe he'd worn during his pilgrimage—down from a hook, wrapped it around himself, then pushed his feet into Arabian slippers.

A walking cane caught his eye. It was leaning against the wall. Its silver grip had been fashioned into the shape of a panther's head. He picked it up and realised it concealed a blade, which he drew and examined: an extremely well-balanced rapier.

Sheathing the weapon and using it for support, the explorer opened the door and stepped out into the passageway beyond, finding it warmly illuminated by bracket-mounted oil lamps. His cabin was on the lower of the *Orpheus*'s two decks, in the middle of the mostly unoccupied rear passenger section. William Stroyan's was a little farther along, closer to the stern observation room. He hobbled toward it. The corridor wavered around him like a mirage, and for a moment, he thought himself trekking across African savannah. He shook off the delusion and whispered, "Fool. You can barely stay upright. Why can't you just leave it be?"

He came to Stroyan's cabin and found its door standing partially open.

"Bill?"

No reply.

He rapped his knuckles against it.

"I say! Stroyan?"

Nothing.

He pushed the door open and entered. The lieutenant's bed was unmade, the room empty and lit only by starlight glimmering through the porthole.

Burton noticed his friend's pocket watch on the bedside table. He picked it up and angled its face to the light from the passage. Eight minutes to midnight.

Perhaps Stroyan was having trouble sleeping and had left this quiet area of the vessel to join the crew on the upper deck.

No. The bedsheets. The lieutenant is as neat as they come. Army training. He'd never leave his bedding twisted and trailing off the bunk like that.

And—

Burton grunted, took a box of lucifers from the table, lit one, and applied the spitting, sulphurous flame to a lamp, which he then lowered over the thing he'd noticed on the floor.

A pillow, darkly stained.

Blood.

He straightened, looked around again, saw the speaking tube, crossed to it, whistled into the mouthpiece, then put it to his ear and waited for a response.

A tinny voice said, "Yes, Lieutenant? What can I do for you?"

It was Doctor Quaint, the ship's steward and surgeon.

"It's not Stroyan, Doctor. It's Burton."

"Good Lord! I thought you were incapacitated."

"Not quite. Do you know where Stroyan is?"

"I haven't seen him since dinner, sir."

"I think someone struck him on the head and dragged him from his bed. Would you have the captain come down here, please?"

"Struck? Bed? Are you——?"

"I'm not delirious, I can assure you. Will you——"

"The captain. I'll tell him at once, sir."

"Thank you."

As he returned the speaking tube to its housing, the muted chanting touched his senses again. He cocked his head and listened. It was louder now, a single voice, generally low and rhythmic but occasionally increasing in volume, as if impassioned and unable to fully contain itself.

Curiosity got the better of him, turned him around, and drew him back out into the passage. His balance was off and he stumbled along as if drunk, but pushed himself onward, spurred by a growing impatience with his own weakness and an almost vicious determination to conquer it and discover the origin of the mysterious sounds.

As he passed the passenger cabin doors, each summoned a splintered recollection, as if they opened onto memories rather than empty chambers.

Number 35: Lieutenant George Herne. Like Burton, down with fever. He'd been left at Zanzibar, where, when he recovered, he'd be taking over as the island's new consul. Burton would miss him. Herne was a good sort. A little stolid and unimaginative, perhaps, but loyal. Unflappable.

Number 36: Gordon Champion. The airship's chief rigger. Dead. He'd crawled out along one of the engine pylons to investigate the inexplicable power failure that had immobilised the vessel just north of Africa's Central Lakes. He'd lost his footing. The slightest of misjudgments and——snap!——gone. That's how quickly, easily, and apparently randomly a life could be extinguished.

Number 37: John Hanning Speke. A beetle had crawled into his ear and he'd permanently deafened himself while trying to extract it with hot wax and a penknife.

What?

No.

There was no door 37.

That last never happened.

Burton reeled as a wave of dizziness hit him. He slapped a hand against the wall and rested for a moment. Why did he keep thinking about Speke? He'd hardly known the man.

This was a mistake. He should get back to bed. He was beginning to hallucinate again. He could see Speke's face as clear as day, the lieutenant's pale blue right eye contrasting starkly with the dark lens of his mechanical left.

Except Speke never had a mechanical left eye.

What is happening to me?

A voice pulled him back into reality. He looked up. The double doors to the observation deck were just ahead. The chanting was coming from behind them. It had just risen in pitch.

He wiped sweat from his eyes, closed them, and concentrated on the sweet tingle of the Saltzmann's Tincture as it oozed honey-like through his arteries. He felt it climbing his neck and easing into the back of his skull.

I've made history.

He would be accepted; offered an official position; hopefully, like Herne, a consulship. Damascus. He could marry Isabel and settle there; start his translation of *A Thousand Nights and a Night*. No one would again accuse him of being "un-English." No one would dare to call him "Blackguard Burton" or "Ruffian Dick." His years of exclusion and exile were over.

He tottered forward, holding tightly to the swordstick.

The chanting had greater clarity now. A man, repeating the same phrase over and over. Burton was an accomplished linguist, fluent in nearly thirty languages, but the incantation was utterly unfamiliar; a pulsating jumble of outlandish sounds and syllables, unfathomable, even to him.

He placed his left hand on one of the doorknobs, became aware of a pungent odour, paused, then twisted and pushed.

The door swung open. The explorer took two steps forward and stopped.

Laurence Oliphant halted in mid-recitation. His eyes met Burton's. He was standing in the middle of a pentagram painted on the floor. Clouds of foul-smelling smoke billowed from small brass censers positioned at its points. William Stroyan, obviously dazed and with blood dripping from a wound on his forehead, was kneeling at Oliphant's feet, facing away from him and toward Burton. Oliphant was gripping the lieutenant's hair and holding a large curved knife to his throat.

He sneered and slid the blade sideways.

Burton gave a cry of horror as blood spurted and his friend collapsed to the deck.

Oliphant raised his arms into the air. His eyes blazed triumphantly. "It is done! The way is open! I await thy coming, Master! I await thy coming! Thou shalt endure until the end!"

Barely aware of his own actions, Burton lifted the swordstick and drew the blade.

"That's my cane," Oliphant said.

The statement, so mundane amid such extraordinary circumstances, strengthened Burton's growing conviction that he was caught up in a fever-fuelled fantasy. He levelled the weapon at Oliphant—its tip shook wildly—and quickly glanced around, hardly comprehending what he saw. The walls of the observation room—three of glass; the fourth, at his back, of wood panels—were painted all over with squares, subdivided, each division containing a sequence of numbers. Beyond the glass, in the clear night sky, curtains of mul-ticoloured light were materialising, shifting and folding, blocking the stars, and fast making the night as bright as day.

"Your cane?" Burton mumbled.

A horrible bubbling diverted his attention back to Stroyan. He saw the lieutenant's life gutter and depart.

Burton's eyes snapped up to Oliphant, who held out a hand and said, "I'll have it, if you please. It is bespoke. The only one of its kind. I had it fashioned in memory of a white panther I once kept as a pet. Marvellous creature. Don't you admire the single-mindedness of the predator, Captain?"

Uttering an inarticulate yell, Burton hurled himself forward, but his left knee gave way and his charge instantly became an uncoordinated floundering. He stabbed at Oliphant's shoulder, intending a disabling wound, but his opponent slashed his knife upward and deflected the rapier, sending Burton even more off-kilter. The two men collided and crashed to the floor. They grappled, Oliphant's weapon tangling in the explorer's *jubbah*, Burton drop-ping the sword and seeking a stranglehold.

Oliphant cried out, "Get off me! It's too late! It's him you should worry about now. He knows who you are, Burton. He'll come for you! He'll come for you!"

Burton punched him hard on the left ear, then, as the knife came free of the cloth, caught the man's wrist and strained to prevent the weapon from being thrust into his chest.

Who does he mean? Who's coming for me?

Without loosening his grip, Burton jerked his arms to the side and gouged his elbow into the other's eye.

Too fragile for this. Too damned fragile.

Oliphant twisted. The knife sliced through cloth and scraped across Burton's ribs. The explorer yelped, rolled over until he was on top of his foe, then slammed his forehead into the man's face, hearing the back of the other's skull clunk loudly on the deck. Lord Elgin's secretary went limp. Burton pushed himself up, sat on Oliphant's stomach, and with all the strength remaining to him, sent his fist crashing across the man's jaw. His opponent became still.

There. That'll keep you quiet, you bastard.

Falling to the side, he flopped onto his back and blacked out.

The distant coughing of lions.

The soothing songs of his bearers as the safari settled for the night.

The jungle, as red as blood.

Red?

The Other Burton's voice: *Parallel all things are; yet many of these are askew; you are certainly I; but certainly I am not you.*

"Burton! Captain Burton! Captain Burton!"

He opened his eyes and saw Nathaniel Lawless looking down at him. The airship captain's eyes were of the palest grey, his teeth remarkably straight and white, his snowy beard tightly clipped. Second Officer Wordsworth Pryce and Doctor Quaint were standing to either side of their commander.

Burton moistened his lips with his tongue. He said, "The sky."

"I know," Lawless responded. "It's the aurora borealis. But this bright and this far south? In all my days, I've never seen the like. Are you all right?" He stretched down a hand and helped the explorer to his feet.

"Comparatively speaking, yes."

"You're covered in blood."

"Most of it is William's. I have a scratch across the ribs, nothing more."

Doctor Quaint interjected, "Let me see it."

"Later, Doctor."

Burton turned and saw that rigger Alexander Priestly and engineer James Bolling—both big, beefy men—were holding the unconscious Laurence Oliphant upright.

Lawless asked, "He killed Stroyan?"

"He did."

"Why? And what are all these scribbles on the floor and walls?"

"It was some sort of ritual. A summoning, I think. William was the sacrifice."

"Summoning? Summoning of what? From where?"

"I haven't a notion."

Burton picked up the rapier and its sheath, slid the one into the other, then supported himself on the cane and waited for his head to clear. The Saltzmann's was causing a ringing in his ears and had put a strange glow around everything he saw. Or was that caused by the rippling illumination outside?

He took a deep breath, blinked, and addressed the second officer. "Pryce, would you mind fetching my notebook from the bureau in my quarters? I'd like to make a record of these diagrams and numbers."

Pryce gave a nod and departed.

Lawless jerked a thumb toward Oliphant. "I suppose I should lock this lunatic in one of the cabins."

Burton slipped his hand into his *jubbah* and gingerly touched the laceration running down his left side. His fingertips slid through warm wetness. He winced, and nodded. "Strap him down onto the bed. Make sure he can't move. We'll give him to the police when we reach London. I'll have a word with Lord Elgin."

"I can do that," Lawless objected. "You should go back to bed. You look sick as a dog—your skin is jaundiced."

"I'm over the worst of it, Captain. The excitement appears to have jolted me back to my senses. I'd rather see Elgin myself, if you don't mind."

"As you wish."

A couple of minutes later, Pryce returned and handed over Burton's notebook. Oliphant was hustled away. Quaint bandaged the explorer's wound then summoned a couple of crewmembers and helped them carry William Stroyan's corpse off to the ship's surgery.

Burton pushed to the back of his mind the misery he felt at his friend's death. He sketched. Each wall, he noted, had been divided into a seven-by-seven grid, the outer squares of which were densely filled with numbers. The next squares in—five by five—contained fewer numerals. They surrounded three by three, in each of which only four-figure numbers were painted.

Burton couldn't work it out, but he felt sure some sort of mathematical formula was in operation, which led to what he guessed was the "sum" in the central square of each wall. Behind him, on the wood panelling, this final number was ten; on the wall to his left, eight; on the wall in front, one thousand; and on the right-hand wall, nine hundred.

He was aware of Lawless looking over his shoulder until the diagrams were copied, then the captain crossed the deck to one of the glass walls and stood beside it, gazing out at the sky. "You surely don't expect me to believe he magicked up the aurora?"

Burton shook his head. "He referred to someone he called his 'master.' As for the lights, perhaps Oliphant somehow knew they were coming and timed his ritual to coincide with them."

Lawless ran his fingernails through his beard. Over the course of the past year, he and Burton had become firm friends, but the airship captain still observed the proprieties and nearly always called the explorer by his rank. Now, though, he let that formality slip.

"Damnation, Richard! After all we've been through, I wanted to get us home quick sharp! Instead, we had to lay over in Zanzibar until Herne's position was confirmed, wait in Aden for Elgin, and now bloody Oliphant goes batty just as we're about to land in Vienna. I swear, if our new passengers demand yet another delay because of this, I'll get off the confounded ship and walk home."

"Passengers?" Burton asked. "Who's with Lord Stanley?"

"Only His Royal bloody Highness Prince Albert."

Burton's eyebrows went up.

"I know," Lawless said. "Quite a surprise, eh? I was informed less than an hour ago. Disraeli obviously considers the *Orpheus*—as the flagship of the fleet—the most suitable vessel to escort the prince home, no matter that we've been in Africa for over a year and are all sick and exhausted." He pulled out his chronometer and clicked open its lid. "We'll be landing in fifty minutes but our precious cargo won't come aboard until daylight, so I suggest you get some more sleep. You look done in."

Burton nodded. "I am. But when Elgin shows his face in the morning, send someone to wake me."

"Righto." Lawless glanced around at the floor and walls then out at the rainbow colours that shimmered from horizon to horizon. "Hell and damnation!"

Also by Mark Hodder:

THE SECRET of ABDU EL YEZDI

The Beast has been summoned, history will be unmade

Freshly knighted by King George V for discovering the source
of the Nile, Sir Richard Francis Burton has been made an agent
of the Crown.

His mission is twofold: solve a series of high profile disappearances and, even more astonishing, locate the spirit of a dead
mystic, Abdu el Yezdi, who has served the Crown as an advisor
since Queen Victoria was so monstrously assassinated.

Burton and Swinburne are back – pitted against a cabal
of dangerous men, facing seemingly supernatural entities
while fighting for their very existence...

available from Del Rey

DEL REY